STRANGENESS

BOOKS BY THOMAS M. DISCH

FICTION

The Genocides (1965)
Echo Round His Bones (1966)
Black Alice (1968)
(IN COLLABORATION WITH JOHN SLADEK)
Camp Concentration (1969)
Fun with Your New Head (Short stories) (1970)
334 (1972)
Getting into Death (Short stories) (1976)

POETRY

The Right Way to Figure Plumbing (1972)

ANTHOLOGIES

The Ruins of Earth (1971)
Bad Moon Rising (1973)
The New Improved Sun (1975)
New Constellations (1976)
(CO-EDITED WITH CHARLES NAYLOR)

STRANGENESS

A Collection of Curious Tales

❧✦❧

EDITED BY

THOMAS M. DISCH

AND

CHARLES NAYLOR

❧✦❧

CHARLES SCRIBNER'S SONS · NEW YORK

Copyright © 1977 Thomas M. Disch and Charles Naylor

Library of Congress Cataloging in Publication Data
Main entry under title:
Strangeness.
    CONTENTS: Disch, T. M. Luncheon in the sepulcher:
Poe and the gothic tradition.—Jackson, S. The
beautiful stranger.—Woolf, V. Solid objects. [etc.]
    1. Science fiction. I. Disch, Thomas M.
II. Naylor, Charles.
PZ1.S8987 [PN6071.S33]   823'.0876   77-23239
ISBN 0-684-14899-4

1 3 5 7 9 11 13 15 17 19 V/C 20 18 16 14 12 10 8 6 4 2

PRINTED IN THE UNITED STATES OF AMERICA

ACKNOWLEDGMENTS

Joan Aiken, "Elephant's Ear," copyright © 1960 by Joan Aiken. Reprinted by permission of the author's agent, Brandt & Brandt.
Brian Aldiss, "Where the Lines Converge," copyright © 1977 by Southmoor Serendipity. Reprinted by permission of the author.
Italo Calvino, "All at One Point," from *Cosmicomics* by Italo Calvino, translated by William Weaver, copyright © 1965 by Giulio Einaudi editore s.p.a., Torino; copyright © 1968 by Harcourt Brace Jovanovich, Inc., and Jonathan Cape, Limited. Reprinted by permission of Harcourt Brace Jovanovich, Inc., and (in Canada) by Jonathan Cape, Limited.

For Gracie, Mother, and Cardamum

CONTENTS

Introduction: Luncheon in the Sepulcher   THOMAS M. DISCH   1

The Beautiful Stranger   SHIRLEY JACKSON   9

Solid Objects   VIRGINIA WOOLF   17

Where the Lines Converge   BRIAN ALDISS   23

All at One Point   ITALO CALVINO   60

The Waiting Place   SARAH ORNE JEWETT   64

Sketches Among the Ruins of My Mind   PHILIP JOSÉ FARMER   74

Elephant's Ear   JOAN AIKEN   115

Bodies   JOYCE CAROL OATES   124

Running Down   M. JOHN HARRISON   145

The Roaches   THOMAS M. DISCH   175

The Last Supper   RUSSELL FITZGERALD   185

Among the Dahlias   WILLIAM SANSOM   198

Under the Garden   GRAHAM GREENE   205

The Holland of the Mind   PAMELA ZOLINE   253

Elephant with Wooden Leg   JOHN SLADEK   286

The Wardrobe   THOMAS MANN   303

STRANGENESS

INTRODUCTION

Luncheon in the Sepulcher:
Poe and the Gothic Tradition

ᄃ·ᄀᄃᄋ

THOMAS M. DISCH

" 'There is no exquisite beauty,' says Bacon, Lord Verulan, speaking truly of all the forms and *genera* of beauty, 'without some *strangeness* in the proportion.' "

It is easy enough to assent to this proposition, which comes upon us at the beginning of Poe's "Ligeia." The exquisite beauty of that tale certainly has more than a little strangeness in its proportion, as do the stories collected in this volume. So, if your preference is all for the practice of storytelling, and if its theory has no lure for you, let us make an amicable parting here. You have my assurance that your taste for strangeness will be gratified abundantly, diversely, and perhaps, in one or two instances, to excess. What can an introduction do, finally, but offer that assurance?

Now, for the rest of us left in the study, a rhetorical question: Is it true, as Poe insists, that *all* the forms and *genera* of beauty are endowed with strangeness? Is it not rather the specific virtue of classic art that it smooths away all traces of the "grotesque and arabesque" to reveal some irreducible wholeness, to offer us the no less exquisite (if not always so immediately arresting) beauty of the Ideal? I don't mean only the classic art of Homer and Praxiteles, or of Raphael and Palladio. In this normative sense, the cool architecture of a Cubist still life, or a movie such as *The African Queen*, in which admirable people perform noble deeds in Hollywood's most stately style, can be said to be classical.

With Poe, the Ideal is experienced as oppressive (as in "The Domain

of Arnheim"), the normative as ridiculous ("The Devil in the Belfry").
Indeed, without too great distortion to his aesthetic, one could reverse
Bacon's formula and say that there is, in Poe, no strangeness without
some beauty in the proportion; no horror that lacks an underlying loveli-
ness.

Bear with me, readers. There *is* a reason why, though there is not a
single story by Poe in this volume, he is the subject of this introduction.
It is not so straightforward a reason as cause-and-effect: I don't maintain
that all the writers represented here are in a direct line of descent from
Poe (though I'd be surprised if there were any who were not on familiar
terms with his best work). In fact, such fantasists as Bierce, Lovecraft, and
Bradbury, who are too visibly his inheritors, have been deliberately ex-
cluded from the contents page. Likewise, there are no stories by writers of
the "Southern Gothic" school, since their kinship with Poe is at least of
the degree of cousinship. And again, on the grounds that few readers
need to be pointed the way to such golden oldies, none of the celebrated
progeny of C. Auguste Dupin, Poe's primordial detective, will be met
with here. These have been the acknowledged heirs. I believe that Poe's
real accomplishment and influence have been greater than this list of
legatees would suggest—and his significance greater still.

His significance is as a touchstone, as the first perfected form of a dis-
tinctively modern kind of sensibility. This is not the Poe known to his
own countrymen, but the Poe celebrated by Baudelaire: Poe considered
as a contemporary of Kierkegaard. Americans have always had difficulty
viewing Poe in this light, for we are likely to encounter him first at too
tender an age and to continue to think of him, in our later years, as a
writer for children. That used to be my own case, certainly. I loved to
terrify my younger brothers, and myself, reading aloud "The Tell-Tale
Heart" by the light of a flashlight. My brothers have since assured me
that these were vivid renderings, and I know they were sincere, so it can't
be said that I was entirely missing the point—or that Americans do, in
general. And part of the point (which Baudelaire misses, as surely as we
miss his) is that Poe is as much a charlatan and barnstormer as he is a
mystic and modernist. Since an adequate account of his entire artistry is
beyond the scope of anything less than a book, and since that book already exists, I will limit myself to recommending it (*Poe, Poe, Poe, Poe,*
Poe, Poe, Poe by Daniel Hoffman) and to continue trying to make my
single, if elusive, point about him—which is that his work embodies everything in the gothic tradition that can command serious, adult atten-

tion; and further, that this tradition is much broader than it has usually been reckoned.

Before setting forth a general theory of either Poe or the gothic sensibility, I'd like to consider some of the specific ingredients to be found in his stories. Not the obsessive themes, such as incest or inhumation, for these, besides having received ample attention elsewhere, are idiosyncratic and limiting; nor yet the ornamental, fustian style, of which the same can be said. I mean such specifics as the landscapes he evokes, which are at once so nebulous and so minutely observed, or the peculiar humor of his "grotesque" tales, or the maniacal voices of so many of his narrators. The voice, for instance, of the murderous lunatic who tells "The Tell-Tale Heart": "Now this is the point. You fancy me mad. Madmen know nothing. But you should have seen *me*." This is at once a dry burlesque of high paranoid style and a lyric to delight the soul of R. D. Laing. For, of course, besides being absurd, it is true: madmen do possess a knowledge that is denied to others. As the same narrator observes: "The disease had sharpened my senses—not destroyed—not dulled them. Above all was the sense of hearing acute. I heard all things in the heaven and in the earth. I heard many things in hell. How, then, am I mad?"

Since those words were written the possibility that madness may be—at least for fictional purposes—a higher form of wisdom has become a staple of generations of writers, some of whom one would not readily class with Poe. The stories in this volume by Joyce Carol Oates and by Virginia Woolf are both prime examples of this vein of psychological horror, or Naturalized Gothic. Oates's affinities with the gothic have occasionally been noted, but . . . Virginia Woolf? Yet her tale "Solid Objects" cannot be considered a fluke, for the same theme of madness as a form of visionary experience is even more intensely rendered in what I believe to be her most representative novel, *Mrs. Dalloway*. Other stories in *Strangeness* inhabit this same intriguing, penumbral zone between dementia and poetry, but to say which ones would be to spoil the unfolding of more than one ingenious plot. Another entire volume might be filled with tales in this vein that have acquired the status of classics: for example, "The Turn of the Screw," "The Yellow Wallpaper," "Silent Snow, Secret Snow," as well as novels like *The Sound and the Fury* or *Some of Your Blood*. It is very nearly a genre in its own right.

Poe's humorous tales are not as widely read as his exercises in the macabre, but they have not been without their influence. Poe's is a humor of utter alienation. The workaday world involved in its business and domestic affairs becomes a kind of clockwork nightmare, in which ridiculous catastrophes overtake grotesque human automatons, like the unfortunate Psyche Zenobia, who is beheaded by the minute hand of a giant clock and describes the entire process in the first person: "I was not sorry to see the head which had occasioned me so much embarrassment at length make a final separation from my body. It first rolled down the side of the steeple, then lodged, for a few seconds, in the gutter, and then made its way, with a plunge, into the middle of the street."

What underlies this kind of humor is the realization that stories, being no more than words on paper, do not have to follow the rules that govern the day-to-day workings of the universe. The writer is free to fabricate . . . anything at all! The freedom is a dangerous one, but like all other freedoms, once it has been set loose upon the world, it becomes impossible to suppress. In this anthology the stories by John Sladek and Joan Aiken are of this type, and Samuel Beckett, Harry Mathews, and Michael Moorcock have each written a *trilogy* of masterful and magnificently funny novels that may be said to spring from the same tradition.

The relevance of landscape to the craft of fiction is a harder matter to expound, yet in Poe's case it is crucial. Often it is all there is. His two longest fictions, "The Narrative of A. Gordon Pym" and "The Unparalleled Adventures of One Hans Pfaal," are little more than extended travelogues, in which the only significant interactions are between the isolated protagonists and their environments. These landscapes, whether on the monumental scale of the whirlpool in "The Descent into the Maelstrom" or reduced to the claustrophobic dimensions of a coffin in "The Premature Burial," are always inimical in a manner identifiably Poe's. The single most succinct rendering of his typical milieu occurs in "The Fall of the House of Usher," when the narrator describes one of the "pure abstractions" painted by Roderick Usher: "A small picture presented the interior of an immensely long and rectangular vault or tunnel, with low walls, smooth, white, and without interruption or device. Certain accessory points of the design served well to convey the idea that this excavation lay at an exceeding depth below the surface of the earth. No outlet was observed in any portion of its vast extent, and no torch or other artificial source of light was discernible; yet a flood of intense rays rolled throughout, and bathed the whole in a ghastly and inappropriate splendor." It would be a century before surrealists like de Chirico, Dali, and Tanguy would create canvases in the stripped-bare style of Roderick Usher, and they were followed by a generation of French writers who pursued a very similar aesthetic. In practice I find the English practitioners of the *roman nouveau*—particularly J. G. Ballard and Brian Aldiss—more compellingly readable than Robbe-Grillet and others like him. Readers unfamiliar with this genre could not do better than to turn to Aldiss's novella "Where the Lines Converge," which is an epitome of this kind of infernal geometrizing.

A landscape need not be reduced to diagrammatic plainness for a family resemblance to this kind of avant-garde gothicism to be observable. Much of the fascination of "hard-core" science fiction lies in its creation of environments as spare and enigmatic, as full of strangeness, as any *roman nouveau*. Arthur Clarke's *Rendezvous with Rama* is the very apotheosis of this kind of science fiction, being an account of the systematic (and not very dramatic) exploration of an alien artifact, which its explorers never really come to understand. The novel ends, like Poe's "Pym," with a question mark the size of an iceberg. It's altogether maddening, as of course it's meant to be.

In "The Black Cat," another of Poe's mad narrators declares: "My immediate purpose is to place before the world, plainly, succinctly, and without comment, a series of mere household events." That statement might well stand as an epigraph before many of the tales that follow. Poe was one of the first gothic artists to have understood that terror likes to warm its feet at the domestic hearth, that it has no need for exotic paraphernalia. Shirley Jackson's "The Beautiful Stranger" is an excellent example of such curdled coziness, as is her classic story "The Lottery." (For a further consideration of why this should be, may I recommend Freud's brief "Essay on the Uncanny"? Beginning with the simple observation that the German word for "uncanny," *unheimlich*, is often used interchangeably with its opposite, *heimlich*, or "homelike," Freud deduces a series of consequences as baroque as any of the ratiocinations of C. Auguste Dupin.)

Readers of Poe soon come to the conclusion that the ultimate source of strangeness lies even closer to home than the hearth; it is to be found in the blood-dark depths of the heart, or even deeper, in the soul. All Poe's landscapes, from the arctic desolations at the end of "Pym" to the tatty eclecticism of the "Venice" described in "The Assignation," and most notably the House of Usher and its environs, are externalizations of what is forever unwitnessable within. Poe is no dramatist; he speaks in a single voice to which even Echo does not reply. His secondary characters, when they exist, are mere wraiths, names without substance. Invariably they are on hand to serve as victims: Fortunato in "The Cask of Amontillado,"

Madeline in "Usher," the wife in "The Black Cat," the nameless old man in "The Tell-Tale Heart." But the isolation of Poe's protagonists is greater still, for even when their contest is between themselves and their environment, that environment is really but the flimsiest of tissues, a screen on which the protagonist (who is Poe) projects his inner conflicts; he inhabits, so to speak, his own dreams.

This may sound like a criticism, and indeed I don't think it is a method that would serve a novelist very well, but for short stories it has proven a highly effective formula. Stories as diverse as Greene's "Under the Garden," Zoline's "The Holland of the Mind," and Mann's "The Wardrobe" all employ this same procedure.

I stated earlier, in passing, that Poe can profitably be considered a contemporary of Kierkegaard. What they may be said to have in common is an expertise in the etiology of the hidden disorders of the soul, specifically that condition known as "alienation." However, for both writers the traditional term, "damnation," is more to the point.

Poe secularized the idea of damnation. For all his gothic paraphernalia, he seldom has recourse to supernatural explanations. In this he is following the Devil's own advice, as it has been presented through such able interpreters as Goethe and Baudelaire, who observes in one of his prose poems that "the Devil's cleverest wile is to convince us that he does not exist."

Whether or not the Devil exists is a matter of opinion, Baudelaire notwithstanding. The existence of the damned, however, is a matter of observable fact, and Poe was one of that fact's best observers. All the specific qualities of his art referred to earlier become, when viewed in this light, facets of a single torment. The heightened awareness of his madmen is not different from the unholy knowledge ascribed to such earlier gothic protagonists as Faust, Manfred, or Melmoth. To the damned soul, sealed within its selfhood, the world can appear only as ridiculous or threatening. From this fact proceeds the peculiar, skewed character of Poe's humor, the insubstantiality of his *dramatis personae*, and of his landscapes as well. The damned are all, all alone: the Other is invisible to them in all its forms—in nature, in social institutions, in personal relations—except insofar as these forms have also been corrupted by evil, and then the vision of the damned is most acute.

I say this not in disparagement of Poe, but by way of homage. Damnation—or, if you prefer, alienation—is the central theme of Romantic literature. It ties together such diverse works as Wordsworth's "Immortality

Ode," Blake's "Songs of Experience," Coleridge's "Ancient Mariner," and de Quincey's *Confessions*. And these represent simply the first sounding of the theme, which swelled, by the latter part of the century, into pandemonium. Within the chorus Poe's voice remains, even today, one of the most distinct.

Put it another way. Say that the problem is how we are to understand our human destiny, in all its complexity and ambiguity, without the support provided by the theoretical apparatus of religion; especially, how we are to face the problems of evil, of death, of despair, in a world deserted by the friendly gods of its springtime. Simply to look the other way, denying the problem's existence, is (as Kierkegaard argues in *The Concept of Dread*) to consign oneself to damnation in its darkest (if also its most common) form. But to face the problem is a treacherous business as well, and the *safest* way to do so is vicariously, through the agency of art.

An interest in diseases is necessarily a morbid interest, and this is—let us admit it—the nature of our interest in Poe, and in the gothic tradition in general. That does not make it an unhealthy interest. Dualities must be studied in pairs. Health and disease are phases of a single process. The road to heaven, as mapped by Dante and many other expert cartographers, proceeds through the central avenues of hell.

And what has all this to do with the business at hand? I hope a great deal, though I must leave some of the inferences for readers to draw themselves, as they ponder the stories that follow. Finally, I think, the reason for establishing influences, noting resemblances, and sorting stories into categories and genres is to be in a position to say, "If you thought *that* was good, then you should try *this*." Often, though, standard categorization schemes are not of much practical use. I would like to think that to speak of a gothic tradition in the larger sense implied by the diversity of stories in this collection, a diversity that has in common a sensibility deriving from Poe's, may be of use to readers dissatisfied with the usual fare of anthologies of this genre.

The Beautiful Stranger

SHIRLEY JACKSON

What might be called the first intimation of strangeness occurred at the railroad station. She had come with her children, Smalljohn and her baby girl, to meet her husband when he returned from a business trip to Boston. Because she had been oddly afraid of being late, and perhaps even seeming uneager to encounter her husband after a week's separation, she dressed the children and put them into the car at home a long half hour before the train was due. As a result, of course, they had to wait interminably at the station, and what was to have been a charmingly staged reunion, family embracing husband and father, became at last an ill-timed and awkward performance. Smalljohn's hair was mussed, and he was sticky. The baby was cross, pulling at her pink bonnet and her dainty lace-edged dress, whining. The final arrival of the train caught them in mid-movement, as it were; Margaret was tying the ribbons on the baby's bonnet, Smalljohn was half over the back of the car seat. They scrambled out of the car, cringing from the sound of the train, hopelessly out of sorts.

John Senior waved from the high steps of the train. Unlike his wife and children, he looked utterly prepared for his return, as though he had taken some pains to secure a meeting at least painless, and had, in fact, stood just so, waving cordially from the steps of the train, for perhaps as long as half an hour, ensuring that he should not be caught half-ready, his hand not lifted so far as to overemphasize the extent of his delight in seeing them again.

His wife had an odd sense of lost time. Standing now on the platform with the baby in her arms and Smalljohn beside her, she could not for a minute remember clearly whether he was coming home, or whether they were yet standing here to say good-by to him. They had been quarreling when he left, and she had spent the week of his absence determining to forget that in his presence she had been frightened and hurt. This will be a good time to get things straight, she had been telling herself; while John is gone I can try to get hold of myself again. Now, unsure at last whether this was an arrival or a departure, she felt afraid again, straining to meet an unendurable tension. This will not do, she thought, believing that she was being honest with herself, and as he came down the train steps and walked toward them she smiled, holding the baby tightly against her so that the touch of its small warmth might bring some genuine tenderness into her smile.

This will not do, she thought, and smiled more cordially and told him "hello" as he came to her. Wondering, she kissed him and then when he held his arm around her and the baby for a minute the baby pulled back and struggled, screaming. Everyone moved in anger, and the baby kicked and screamed, "No, no, no."

"What a way to say hello to Daddy," Margaret said, and she shook the baby, half-amused, and yet grateful for the baby's sympathetic support. John turned to Smalljohn and lifted him, Smalljohn kicking and laughing helplessly. "Daddy, Daddy," Smalljohn shouted, and the baby screamed, "No, no."

Helplessly, because no one could talk with the baby screaming so, they turned and went to the car. When the baby was back in her pink basket in the car, and Smalljohn was settled with another lollipop beside her, there was an appalling quiet which would have to be filled as quickly as possible with meaningful words. John had taken the driver's seat in the car while Margaret was quieting the baby, and when Margaret got in beside him she felt a little chill of animosity at the sight of his hands on the wheel; I can't bear to relinquish even this much, she thought; for a week no one has driven the car except me. Because she could see so clearly that this was unreasonable—John owned half the car, after all—she said to him with bright interest, "And how was your trip? The weather?"

"Wonderful," he said, and again she was angered at the warmth in his tone; if she was unreasonable about the car, he was surely unreasonable to have enjoyed himself quite so much. "Everything went very well. I'm pretty sure I got the contract, everyone was very pleasant about it, and I go back in two weeks to settle everything."

The stinger is in the tail, she thought. He wouldn't tell it all so hastily if he didn't want me to miss half of it; I am supposed to be pleased that he got the contract and that everyone was so pleasant, and the part about going back is supposed to slip past me painlessly.

"Maybe I can go with you, then," she said. "Your mother will take the children."

"Fine," he said, but it was much too late; he had hesitated noticeably before he spoke.

"I want to go too," said Smalljohn. "Can I go with Daddy?"

They came into their house, Margaret carrying the baby, and John carrying his suitcase and arguing delightedly with Smalljohn over which of them was carrying the heavier weight of it. The house was ready for them; Margaret had made sure that it was cleaned and emptied of the qualities which attached so surely to her position of wife alone with small children; the toys which Smalljohn had thrown around with unusual freedom were picked up, the baby's clothes (no one, after all, came to call when John was gone) were taken from the kitchen radiator where they had been drying. Aside from the fact that the house gave no impression of waiting for any particular people, but only for anyone well-bred and clean enough to fit within its small trim walls, it could have passed for a home, Margaret thought, even for a home where a happy family lived in domestic peace. She set the baby down in the playpen and turned with the baby's bonnet and jacket in her hand and saw her husband, head bent gravely as he listened to Smalljohn. Who? she wondered suddenly; is he taller? That is not my husband.

She laughed, and they turned to her, Smalljohn curious, and her husband with a quick bright recognition; she thought, why, it is *not* my husband, and he knows that I have seen it. There was no astonishment in her; she would have thought perhaps thirty seconds before that such a thing was impossible, but since it was now clearly possible, surprise would have been meaningless. Some other emotion was necessary, but she found at first only peripheral manifestations of one. Her heart was beating violently, her hands were shaking, and her fingers were cold. Her legs felt weak and she took hold of the back of a chair to steady herself. She found that she was still laughing, and then her emotion caught up with her and she knew what it was: it was relief.

"I'm glad you came," she said. She went over and put her head against his shoulder. "It was hard to say hello in the station," she said.

Smalljohn looked on for a minute and then wandered off to his toybox. Margaret was thinking, this is not the man who enjoyed seeing me cry; I need not be afraid. She caught her breath and was quiet; there was nothing that needed saying.

For the rest of the day she was happy. There was a constant delight in the relief from her weight of fear and unhappiness, it was pure joy to know that there was no longer any residue of suspicion and hatred; when she called him "John" she did so demurely, knowing that he participated in her secret amusement; when he answered her civilly there was, she thought, an edge of laughter behind his words. They seemed to have agreed soberly that mention of the subject would be in bad taste, might even, in fact, endanger their pleasure.

They were hilarious at dinner. John would not have made her a cocktail, but when she came downstairs from putting the children to bed the stranger met her at the foot of the stairs, smiling up at her, and took her arm to lead her into the living room where the cocktail shaker and glasses stood on the low table before the fire.

"How nice," she said, happy that she had taken a moment to brush her hair and put on fresh lipstick, happy that the coffee table which she had chosen with John and the fireplace which had seen many fires built by John and the low sofa where John had slept sometimes, had all seen fit to welcome the stranger with grace. She sat on the sofa and smiled at him when he handed her a glass; there was an odd illicit excitement in all of it; she was "entertaining" a man. The scene was a little marred by the fact that he had given her a martini with neither olive nor onion; it was the way she preferred her martini, and yet he should not have, strictly, known this, but she reassured herself with the thought that naturally he would have taken some pains to inform himself before coming.

He lifted his glass to her with a smile; he is here only because I am here, she thought.

"It's nice to be here," he said. He had, then, made one attempt to sound like John, in the car coming home. After he knew that she had recognized him for a stranger, he had never made any attempt to say words like "coming home" or "getting back," and of course she could not, not without pointing her lie. She put her hand in his and lay back against the sofa, looking into the fire.

"Being lonely is worse than anything in the world," she said.

"You're not lonely now?"

"Are you going away?"

"Not unless you come too." They laughed at his parody of John.

They sat next to each other at dinner; she and John had always sat at formal opposite ends of the table, asking one another politely to pass the salt and the butter.

"I'm going to put in a little set of shelves over there," he said, nodding toward the corner of the dining room. "It looks empty here, and it needs things. Symbols."

"Like?" She liked to look at him; his hair, she thought, was a little darker than John's, and his hands were stronger; this man would build whatever he decided he wanted built.

"We need things together. Things we like, both of us. Small delicate pretty things. Ivory."

With John she would have felt it necessary to remark at once that they could not afford such delicate pretty things, and put a cold finish to the idea, but with the stranger she said, "We'd have to look for them; not everything would be right."

"I saw a little creature once," he said. "Like a tiny little man, only colored all purple and blue and gold."

She remembered this conversation; it contained the truth like a jewel set in the evening. Much later, she was to tell herself that it was true; John could not have said these things.

She was happy, she was radiant, she had no conscience. He went obediently to his office the next morning, saying good-by at the door with a rueful smile that seemed to mock the present necessity for doing the things that John always did, and as she watched him go down the walk she reflected that this was surely not going to be permanent; she could not endure having him gone for so long every day, although she had felt little about parting from John; moreover, if he kept doing John's things he might grow imperceptibly more like John. We will simply have to go away, she thought. She was pleased, seeing him get into the car; she would gladly share with him—indeed, give him outright—all that had been John's, so long as he stayed her stranger.

She laughed while she did her house work and dressed the baby. She took satisfaction in unpacking his suitcase, which he had abandoned and forgotten in a corner of the bedroom, as though prepared to take it up and leave again if she had not been as he thought her, had not wanted him to stay. She put away his clothes, so disarmingly like John's, and wondered for a minute at the closet; would there be a kind of delicacy in him about John's things? Then she told herself no, not so long as he began with John's wife, and laughed again.

The baby was cross all day, but when Smalljohn came home from nursery school his first question was—looking up eagerly—"Where is Daddy?"

"Daddy has gone to the office," and again she laughed, at the moment's quick sly picture of the insult to John.

Half a dozen times during the day she went upstairs, to look at his suitcase and touch the leather softly. She glanced constantly as she passed through the dining room into the corner where the small shelves would be someday, and told herself that they would find a tiny little man, all purple and blue and gold, to stand on the shelves and guard them from intrusion.

When the children awakened from their naps she took them for a walk and then, away from the house and returned violently to her former lonely pattern (walk with the children, talk meaninglessly of Daddy, long for someone to talk to in the evening ahead, restrain herself from hurrying home: he might have telephoned), she began to feel frightened again; suppose she had been wrong? It could not be possible that she was mistaken; it would be unutterably cruel for John to come tonight.

Then, she heard the car stop and when she opened the door and looked up she thought, no, it is not my husband, with a return of gladness. She was aware from his smile that he had perceived her doubts, and yet he was so clearly a stranger that, seeing him, she had no need of speaking.

She asked him, instead, almost meaningless questions during that evening, and his answers were important only because she was storing them away to reassure herself while he was away. She asked him what was the name of their Shakespeare professor in college, and who was that girl he liked so before he met Margaret. When he smiled and said that he had no idea, that he would not recognize the name if she told him, she was in delight. He had not bothered to master all of the past, then; he had learned enough (the names of the children, the location of the house, how she liked her cocktails) to get to her, and after that, it was not important, because either she would want him to stay, or she would, calling upon John, send him away again.

"What is your favorite food?" she asked him. "Are you fond of fishing? Did you ever have a dog?"

"Someone told me today," he said once, "that he had heard I was back from Boston, and I distinctly thought he said that he heard I was dead in Boston."

He was lonely, too, she thought with sadness, and that is why he came, bringing a destiny with him: now I will see him come every evening through the door and think, this is not my husband, and wait for him remembering that I am waiting for a stranger.

"At any rate," she said, "*you* were not dead in Boston, and nothing else matters."

She saw him leave in the morning with a warm pride, and she did her housework and dressed the baby; when Smalljohn came home from nursery school he did not ask, but looked with quick searching eyes and then sighed. While the children were taking their naps she thought that she might take them to the park this afternoon, and then the thought of another such afternoon, another long afternoon with no one but the children, another afternoon of widowhood, was more than she could submit to; I have done this too much, she thought, I must see something today beyond the faces of my children. No one should be so much alone.

Moving quickly, she dressed and set the house to rights. She called a high-school girl and asked if she would take the children to the park; without guilt, she neglected the thousand small orders regarding the proper jacket for the baby, whether Smalljohn might have popcorn, when to bring them home. She fled, thinking, I must be with people.

She took a taxi into town, because it seemed to her that the only possible thing to do was to seek out a gift for him, her first gift to him, and she thought she would find him, perhaps, a little creature all blue and purple and gold.

She wandered through the strange shops in the town, choosing small lovely things to stand on the new shelves, looking long and critically at ivories, at small statues, at brightly colored meaningless expensive toys, suitable for giving to a stranger.

It was almost dark when she started home, carrying her packages. She looked from the window of the taxi into the dark streets, and thought with pleasure that the stranger would be home before her, and look from the window to see her hurrying to him; he would think, this is a stranger, I am waiting for a stranger, as he saw her coming. "Here," she said, tapping on the glass, "right here, driver." She got out of the taxi and paid the driver, and smiled as he drove away. I must look well, she thought, the driver smiled back at me.

She turned and started for the house, and then hesitated; surely she had come too far? This is not possible, she thought, this cannot be; surely our house was white?

The evening was very dark, and she could see only the houses going in rows, with more rows beyond them and more rows beyond that, and somewhere a house which was hers, with the beautiful stranger inside, and she lost out here.

Solid Objects

ᘓᘐᘓᘐᘓ

VIRGINIA WOOLF

The only thing that moved upon the vast semicircle of the beach was one small black spot. As it came nearer to the ribs and spine of the stranded pilchard boat, it became apparent from a certain tenuity in its blackness that this spot possessed four legs; and moment by moment it became more unmistakable that it was composed of the persons of two young men. Even thus in outline against the sand there was an unmistakable vitality in them; an indescribable vigour in the approach and withdrawal of the bodies, slight though it was, which proclaimed some violent argument issuing from the tiny mouths of the little round heads. This was corroborated on closer view by the repeated lunging of a walking-stick on the right-hand side. "You mean to tell me . . . You actually believe . . ." thus the walking-stick on the right-hand side next the waves seemed to be asserting as it cut long straight stripes upon the sand.

"Politics be damned!" issued clearly from the body on the left-hand side, and, as these words were uttered, the mouths, noses, chins, little moustaches, tweed caps, rough boots, shooting coats, and check stockings of the two speakers became clearer and clearer; the smoke of their pipes went up into the air; nothing was so solid, so living, so hard, red, hirsute and virile as these two bodies for miles and miles of sea and sandhill.

They flung themselves down by the six ribs and spine of the black pilchard boat. You know how the body seems to shake itself free from an argument, and to apologize for a mood of exaltation; flinging itself down and expressing in the looseness of its attitude a readiness to take up with something new—whatever it may be that comes next to hand. So

17

Charles, whose stick had been slashing the beach for half a mile or so, began skimming flat pieces of slate over the water; and John, who had exclaimed "Politics be damned!" began burrowing his fingers down, down, into the sand. As his hand went further and further beyond the wrist, so that he had to hitch his sleeve a little higher, his eyes lost their intensity, or rather the background of thought and experience which gives an inscrutable depth to the eyes of grown people disappeared, leaving only the clear transparent surface, expressing nothing but wonder, which the eyes of young children display. No doubt the act of burrowing in the sand had something to do with it. He remembered that, after digging for a little, the water oozes round your finger-tips; the hole then becomes a moat; a well; a spring; a secret channel to the sea. As he was choosing which of these things to make it, still working his fingers in the water, they curled round something hard—a full drop of solid matter—and gradually dislodged a large irregular lump, and brought it to the surface. When the sand coating was wiped off, a green tint appeared. It was a lump of glass, so thick as to be almost opaque; the smoothing of the sea had completely worn off any edge or shape, so that it was impossible to say whether it had been bottle, tumbler, or window-pane; it was nothing but glass; it was almost a precious stone. You had only to enclose it in a rim of gold, or pierce it with a wire, and it became a jewel; part of a necklace, or a dull, green light upon a finger. Perhaps after all it was really a gem; something worn by a dark Princess trailing her finger in the water as she sat in the stern of the boat and listened to the slaves singing as they rowed her across the Bay. Or the oak sides of a sunk Elizabethan treasure-chest had split apart, and, rolled over and over, over and over, its emeralds had come at last to shore. John turned it in his hands; he held it to the light; he held it so that its irregular mass blotted out the body and extended right arm of his friend. The green thinned and thickened slightly as it was held against the sky or against the body. It pleased him; it puzzled him; it was so hard, so concentrated, so definite an object compared with the vague sea and the hazy shore.

Now a sigh disturbed him—profound, final, making him aware that his friend Charles had thrown all the flat stones within reach, or had come to the conclusion that it was not worth while to throw them. They ate their sandwiches side by side. When they had done, and were shaking themselves and rising to their feet, John took the lump of glass and looked at it in silence. Charles looked at it too. But he saw immediately that it was not flat, and filling his pipe he said with the energy that dismisses a foolish strain of thought:

"To return to what I was saying—"

He did not see, or if he had seen would hardly have noticed, that John, after looking at the lump for a moment, as if in hesitation, slipped it inside his pocket. That impulse, too, may have been the impulse which leads a child to pick up one pebble on a path strewn with them, promising it a life of warmth and security upon the nursery mantelpiece, delighting in the sense of power and benignity which such an action confers, and believing that the heart of the stone leaps with joy when it sees itself chosen from a million like it, to enjoy this bliss instead of a life of cold and wet upon the high road. "It might so easily have been any other of the millions of stones, but it was I, I, I!"

Whether this thought or not was in John's mind, the lump of glass had its place upon the mantelpiece, where it stood heavy upon a little pile of bills and letters, and served not only as an excellent paper-weight, but also as a natural stopping place for the young man's eyes when they wandered from his book. Looked at again and again half consciously by a mind thinking of something else, any object mixes itself so profoundly with the stuff of thought that it loses its actual form and recomposes itself a little differently in an ideal shape which haunts the brain when we least expect it. So John found himself attracted to the windows of curiosity shops when he was out walking, merely because he saw something which reminded him of the lump of glass. Anything, so long as it was an object of some kind, more or less round, perhaps with a dying flame deep sunk in its mass, anything—china, glass, amber, rock, marble—even the smooth oval egg of a prehistoric bird would do. He took, also, to keeping his eyes upon the ground, especially in the neighbourhood of waste land where the household refuse is thrown away. Such objects often occurred there—thrown away, of no use to anybody, shapeless, discarded. In a few months he had collected four or five specimens that took their place upon the mantelpiece. They were useful, too, for a man who is standing for Parliament upon the brink of a brilliant career has any number of papers to keep in order—addresses to constituents, declarations of policy, appeals for subscriptions, invitations to dinner, and so on.

One day, starting from his rooms in the Temple to catch a train in order to address his constituents, his eyes rested upon a remarkable object lying half-hidden in one of those little borders of grass which edge the bases of vast legal buildings. He could only touch it with the point of his stick through the railings; but he could see that it was a piece of china of the most remarkable shape, as nearly resembling a starfish as anything—shaped, or broken accidentally, into five irregular but unmistakable points. The colouring was mainly blue, but green stripes or spots of some kind overlaid the blue, and lines of crimson gave it a richness and lustre of the most attractive kind. John was determined to possess it; but the more he pushed, the further it receded. At length he was forced to go back to his rooms and improvise a wire ring attached to the end of a stick, with which, by dint of great care and skill, he finally drew the piece of china within reach of his hands. As he seized hold of it he exclaimed in triumph. At that moment the clock struck. It was out of the question that he should keep his appointment. The meeting was held without him. But how had the piece of china been broken into this remarkable shape? A careful examination put it beyond doubt that the star shape was accidental, which made it all the more strange, and it seemed unlikely that there should be another such in existence. Set at the opposite end of the mantelpiece from the lump of glass that had been dug from the sand, it looked like a creature from another world—freakish and fantastic as a harlequin. It seemed to be pirouetting through space, winking light like a fitful star. The contrast between the china so vivid and alert, and the glass so mute and contemplative, fascinated him, and wondering and amazed he asked himself how the two came to exist in the same world, let alone to stand upon the same narrow strip of marble in the same room. The question remained unanswered.

He now began to haunt the places which are most prolific of broken china, such as pieces of waste land between railway lines, sites of demolished houses, and commons in the neighbourhood of London. But china is seldom thrown from a great height; it is one of the rarest of human actions. You have to find in conjunction a very high house, and a woman of such reckless impulse and passionate prejudice that she flings her jar or pot straight from the window without thought of who is below. Broken china was to be found in plenty, but broken in some trifling domestic accident, without purpose or character. Nevertheless, he was often astonished, as he came to go into the question more deeply, by the immense variety of shapes to be found in London alone, and there was still more cause for wonder and speculation in the differences of qualities and designs. The finest specimens he would bring home and place upon his mantelpiece, where, however, their duty was more and more of an ornamental nature, since papers needing a weight to keep them down became scarcer and scarcer.

He neglected his duties, perhaps, or discharged them absent-mindedly, or his constituents when they visited him were unfavourably impressed by the appearance of his mantelpiece. At any rate he was not elected to represent them in Parliament, and his friend Charles, taking it much to heart and hurrying to condole with him, found him so little cast down by the disaster that he could only suppose that it was too serious a matter for him to realize all at once.

In truth, John had been that day to Barnes Common, and there under a furze bush had found a very remarkable piece of iron. It was almost identical with the glass in shape, massy and globular, but so cold and heavy, so black and metallic, that it was evidently alien to the earth and had its origin in one of the dead stars or was itself the cinder of a moon. It weighed his pocket down; it weighed the mantelpiece down; it radiated cold. And yet the meteorite stood upon the same ledge with the lump of glass and the star-shaped china.

As his eyes passed from one to another, the determination to possess objects that even surpassed these tormented the young man. He devoted himself more and more resolutely to the search. If he had not been consumed by ambition and convinced that one day some newly-discovered rubbish heap would reward him, the disappointments he had suffered, let alone the fatigue and derision, would have made him give up the pursuit. Provided with a bag and a long stick fitted with an adaptable hook, he ransacked all deposits of earth; raked beneath matted tangles of scrub; searched all alleys and spaces between walls where he had learned to expect to find objects of this kind thrown away. As his standard became higher and his taste more severe the disappointments were innumerable, but always some gleam of hope, some piece of china or glass curiously marked or broken, lured him on. Day after day passed. He was no longer young. His career—that is his political career—was a thing of the past. People gave up visiting him. He was too silent to be worth asking to dinner. He never talked to anyone about his serious ambitions; their lack of understanding was apparent in their behaviour.

He leaned back in his chair now and watched Charles lift the stones on the mantelpiece a dozen times and put them down emphatically to mark what he was saying about the conduct of the Government, without once noticing their existence.

"What was the truth of it, John?" asked Charles suddenly, turning and facing him. "What made you give it up like that all in a second?"

"I've not given it up," John replied.

"But you've not the ghost of a chance now," said Charles roughly.

"I don't agree with you there," said John with conviction. Charles looked at him and was profoundly uneasy; the most extraordinary doubts possessed him; he had a queer sense that they were talking about different things. He looked round to find some relief for his horrible depression, but the disorderly appearance of the room depressed him still further. What was that stick, and the old carpet bag hanging against the wall? And then those stones? Looking at John, something fixed and distant in his expression alarmed him. He knew only too well that his mere appearance upon a platform was out of the question.

"Pretty stones," he said as cheerfully as he could; and saying that he had an appointment to keep, he left John—for ever.

Where the Lines Converge

༺⌒༒⌒༻

BRIAN ALDISS

Anna Macguire drove to see her father whenever she could. The opportunities grew fewer and fewer, although she knew he needed help. She said to herself, "I go as often as I can because I love him as much as I am capable of doing, given the limitations of my nature. Since those limitations were to large extent fixed by the dreadful way he and my mother brought me up, then he has only himself to blame if I do not turn up as often as he would like."

She had another excuse ready to explain why she went to Crackmore less often than formerly. Since the new airport had been built, Crackmore had become extremely difficult to reach. The old main road, the A394, had been severed. It ended at Ashmansford now, and a lengthy detour was needed, meandering through all the lesser roads skirting the west side of the airport. True, a new spur had been added between Packton and Bucklers Wick, but that was only useful for traffic approaching from the west. Then again, the fast new airport road ran really in the wrong direction. Anna had used it once, driving right into the airport and out again at the north side; but she had lost her direction and was forced to make a detour through Plough and North Baldick.

She had said to her boy-friend, as she called him, in one of her small flat jokes, "It's all sort-of-symbolic of the way old people are cut off. Every time you improve a means of transport—i.e., build a new airport—you lose a generation. I'm sure Pop sees it that way."

She actually said "i.e.," as Trevor reported to his buddies in the office the next day. That was a Friday. By then, Anna, having scrounged a day off from the lab, was turning off just north of Ashmansworth, watching anxiously for the sign to Watermere.

Felix Macguire was due to retire from King Aviation Systems when the plan for the new airport was passed officially. Judy had been alive then.
"We'll be able to flog this property for twice what it's worth," he said. "How'd you like to go and live in the Algarve, my love?"
"I'm getting too old for change," she said.
"We could swim nine months of the year."
"I'm too old to get into a swim-suit," she said.
He smiled at her then, as part of the plan he had carried out tenaciously for over thirty years to keep her as happy as possible, for his own sake, and said gallantly, "I'd rather see you swimming in the nude."
Eventually, the representative of a firm of land-developers came and made an offer for Macguire's house and gardens. The offer was disappointingly small.
Felix and Judy hung on for a bigger offer. "We'll force them to improve their bid," he said. "We can wait as well as they can."
They waited. They were only on the margins of the new development. A new offer never came. Felix wrote and accepted the old offer. The firm wrote back five weeks later (addressing the letter to P. McGuine) to say there was no longer any necessity to purchase the property referred to. Judy died before the first runway was completed.
The barriers of the airport came swinging along, mile after mile of green-plastic-clad chain-link unrolling, munched off the road that passed Macguire's drive, and strode over the ditch that drained his pathetic little piece of orchard. There was one house still occupied next to Macguire's, owned by a pleasant retired art-auctioneer called Standish who kept three Airedales. He had mis-played his hand much as Felix had, and was stuck with deteriorating property. On the evening of the day that the fence went by his land, secured by an enormous roaring machine that spat ten-foot concrete fence posts into the ground at five-meter intervals, Standish shot his dogs, poured petrol all over the ground floor of his house, lit it, ran upstairs to his bedroom, sat himself down at a desk before a faded portrait of himself as a little boy, and blew his brains out. Felix heard the shots, even above the roar of an SST coming in.
From then on, he let weeds grow in his garden and the beeches become shaggier in the drive. He stayed indoors, concentrating on developing an advanced system of vision screens he called the Omniviewer, and thinking about the growing inhumanity of man.

"Oh, piss!" said Anna. She steered the Triumph into the side of the road and pulled the map over to her. She had gone wrong somewhere. She didn't recognize this stretch of road at all. She should have been through Wainsley by now. The map remained inscrutable.

She climbed out and stood in the road. There was no traffic. Anonymous countryside all round. Being a townswoman, she could not tell whether or not the fields were properly tended. The only landmark was an old railway station down a lane, its ruined roof showing across the nearest field. No rails served this monument to an obsolete transport system. Huge elms choked by ivy stood everywhere; she watched a transport plane appear to blunder between them like a huge moth.

A man stood in front of her. He might have materialised out of the ground. She thought immediately, "It's true, I wouldn't mind being raped, if we could go somewhere comfortable, but he might have all sorts of horrible diseases. And he might strangle me when he'd finished."

But the man simply said, "You aren't going to Casterham, are you?"

"No, I don't think so. I want to get to Crackmore. Do you know if I'm going the right way?"

He'd never heard of Crackmore. But he set her right for Wainsley, and she drove on again. At the last moment, she offered him a lift, but he refused; he wasn't going to be led on.

"I'm so isolated," she said aloud, "so isolated," as she drove.

But she had to admit to herself that it was a half-hearted protest; after all, she could always have *asked* the man if she wanted it that badly. People did, these days.

The self-focusing cameras were his especial contribution. Light-and-motion-sensitive cells ensured that lenses focused on him whenever he entered a room. Working slowly, spending a generous part of every day out in the workshop-laboratory next to the disused garage, Felix built himself a spy-system, which would record any movements within the house.

When he had a few thoughts to express, Felix uttered them aloud and the house swallowed them as a whale swallows plankton—and would regurgitate them later on request.

"The Omniviewer is designed purely for self-observation; it is introspective. All other spy-systems have been extravert, designed to watch other people. Their purposes have generally been malign. The parallel with the human senses is striking. Human beings are generally motivated throughout life to watch others and not themselves, right from the early days in which they begin to learn by imitation and example . . . I must remind the grocer when he calls that that last lot of tinned meat gave me diarrhea . . ."

Leaving the workshop, he went through the garage into the hall, which he crossed, and entered the living room. This he had bisected with partitioning some while ago, when he had been feeling his way towards a correct method of procedure for his experiments. It was in the far corner of the living room, the south-pointing corner of the house, that he had built his main control console. The workshop contained an auxiliary console.

From the main console, he could direct the movements of the nine cameras situated about the house, mainly on the ground floor. On monitor screens before him, he could keep a zealous eye on most corners of the house—and above all on himself. Several times, he had detected movements that roused—indeed, confirmed—his suspicions, and of these he kept careful note, recording place, time, and appearance and gesture of the alien pseudo-appearance. "Alien pseudo-appearance" was his first, half-joking, label for his early discoveries.

As usual, when he began work in the morning, he ran through a thorough check of all electronic equipment and sightings. That took him till noon. It was more than a check. It was a metaphysical exploration. It was a confirmation both of the existence of his world and of its threatened disintegration.

He switched the cameras on in turn, according to the numbered sequence he had given them, beginning with Number One. In this way, organisation was held at maximum. Not until much later in the morning would he get round to testing Camera Nine, perched outside on the chimney-stack of the house—none of the other cameras, except Five and Three, were situated for looking beyond the confining walls; that was not their province.

As Camera One briefly warmed, a scatter of geometrical patterns flashed like blueprints across the small monitor, grew, grew, burst, and were instantly gone. An unwavering picture snapped into being on the tiny screen.

This camera was located on its pivot in the wall behind Felix and some two feet above his head. As it was at present directed, beamed downwards and ahead (he carefully read off its three-dimensional positioning on a calibrated control globe), it showed the control console itself, with its switches and monitors, and Felix's right hand resting on the desk; the back of Felix's head was visible in one corner; so was the lower half of the partition, on which a giant viewing-screen had been erected. Also visible were the edge of the carpet, part of the wall, and a section of the window sill. The pattern on the monitor was a restful one of converging angles, relieved by the greater complexity covering about a third of the screen of the console.

Felix scrutinized the view in a leisurely and expert manner. In many ways, One always provided the most absorbing view, if not the most interesting perspectives.

After a thorough scrutiny, he switched on the large viewing-screen. Before viewing it direct, he watched it light in the monitor-screen, via One.

The scatter of particles cleared and the tiny screen showed him the lower strip of the large screen, on which part of the console with the monitors was visible. On Number One of these tiny monitors, he could see the image of the lower strip of the large screen, with its line-up of monitors on the console. On the first of those monitors was a blur of light which the definition, however good, would not resolve into a clear image. Better lenses were probably the answer there, and he was working on that.

Satisfied at last with optical details, he set the camera controls to Slow Scan.

Camera One had a scan of two hundred and ten degrees laterally and a little less in the vertical axis. Among the many pleasures of its field of vision—to be taken in due turn—was the view at 101.40 N, 72.50 W, which gave the corner of the room, where the south-east and south-west walls of the house met at the ceiling, as well as an oblique of the right-hand of the two windows in the front (south-east) wall. The merging and diverging lines were particularly significant, and there was the added pleasure of the paradox that although almost all the window could be seen, the view was so oblique that little could be observed beyond the window, except an insignificant stretch of weedy gravel; this seemed to reduce the window to a properly insignificant stature.

Also desirable, and considerably more complex, was the view at 10.00 N, 47.56 E. It gave one insignificant corner of the console, looking over it toward one of the two doors in the L-shaped room which led into the hall-passage. Through this door, the camera took in a dark section of the passage, the doorway of the dining room beyond, and a segment of the dining room including a bit of the table with a chair pushed in to it (the dining room was never used), the carpet, a shadowy piece of ceiling, something of one of the two windows, and Camera Six, which stood on a bracket set in the wall at a height slightly less than that of

One. 10.00 N, 47.56 E became even more engrossing when Six was functioning, since it then showed One in action; and, when One was in motion, its slight and delicate action was the only observable movement.

There were automatic as well as manual controls for each camera, so that "favourite" or "dangerous" or "tranquil" views could be flicked over to at a moment's notice. There were also programmed automatics, by means of which the eight indoor cameras ran through a whole inter-related series of sightings of high complexity and enfiladed the entire volume of the house—for Felix had his moments of panic, when the idea that he had caught an unsuspecting movement, a figure all too like his own, would send his adrenalin-count rocketing and his heart pounding, and he would snap into a survey of the whole territory. His recording system allowed him to play-back and study any particular view at leisure.

Frequently, he saw shots which filled him with grave doubt, as he played them back and allowed his heart-rate to ease. Although no figures were revealed—his opponents were very clever—their presence was often implied by shadows, dark smudges, mingled fans of light and shade on carpet. They were there, right enough, meddling deliberately; and although no doubt some of the discrepancies in the visual record could be ascribed to aircraft passing low overhead, they were unwise to think he would always use that excuse as a pretext for believing in their non-existence.

When he had thoroughly tested out Camera One through its entire sphere of scan, Felix left it running—and it would run now until he closed down after midnight—and switched on Camera Two.

Camera Number Two was on the far wall of the workshop. It had been the first of the series of cameras to be installed. It overlooked the length of the narrow workshop, including the screens of the auxiliary console, and the door at the far end, which always stood open (not only for security reasons but because the coaxial cable running to the rest of the house prevented its closure) to give a view into the garage, piled high with its old grocer's cartons and crates of tapex.

Although none of the cameras offered a very colourful scene, Two gave the greyest one. As, under Felix's control, it commenced its slow scan, it had nothing bright to show, although rolling towards the roof like an upturning eye, it picked up a patch of blue sky through the reinforced glass skylight.

When it lit obliquely on the three blown-up photographs on the inner wall, Felix slowed the motor until the view was held almost steady and stared with satisfaction at the images of the photographs thrown on the big screen before him. There he saw three gigantic sea-going creatures, each remarkably similar to the next in its functional streamlined form. Something of his original thrill of horror and discovery came back to him as he looked.

He said aloud: "My evolutionary discovery is greater than Charles Darwin's, or his grandfather's . . . greater and far more world-shaking. Darwin revealed only part of the truth, and that revelation has ever since concealed a far greater and more awesome truth. Do you hear me out there? I have the patience and courage of Charles Darwin . . . I too will wait for years if necessary, until I have incontrovertible proof of my theories . . ."

Still staring at the images of the photographs, he switched to playback. He sat listening to his own voice, filtering softly through the house.

"-man being are generally motivated throughout life to watch others and not themselves, right from the early days in which they begin to learn by imitation and example . . . I must remind the grocer when he calls that that last lot of tinned meat gave me diarrhea . . . My evolutionary discovery is greater than Charles Darwin's . . ."

He heard himself out and and then added, "The proof is mounting slowly."

He smiled at the pictures. They were more than a statement of faith; they were a defiance of the enemy. In truth, he inwardly cared little for his own bombast broadcast through the silent and possibly unoccupied rooms; yet it gave him a certain courage—and courage was needed at all times by all who moved towards the unknown—and of course it had a propaganda value. So he sat quietly, breathing regularly under his tattered sweater, as he watched the viewpoint of Two crawl lethargically past the marine shapes and up the formless areas of wall.

When Anna reached what was left of Crackmore, the morning was well advanced. She stopped the car at the filling station and got petrol. She had a headache and a sniffy nose. The pollen count was high, the midsummer heat closed about her temples.

"Oh God, don't say I'm going to get one of my streaming colds! What a bore!"

With a feeling of oppression, she saw as she left the untidy station that the village had entered a phase of new and ugly growth. A big filling station was under construction not a hundred meters away from the one at which she had stopped. Next to it, a pokey estate of semi-detacheds was going up. A new road to the connecting road to the airport was being built, cutting through what was left of the old village. Although, admittedly, the old village was nothing to get excited about, at least it had preserved a sense of proportion, had been agreeably humble in scale. Now a gaunt supermarket was rising behind the old square, dwarfing the church. Everywhere was cluttered and uncomfortable. She was amazed—as so often before—at how many people showed a preference for an inhuman environment. As she drove by the road-making machines, a jet roared overhead, reminding her of her headache.

"Piss off!" she told it.

It was so senseless. There could now be nobody remaining in Crackmore who desired to live there. Most of them would be attached to the ground staff of the airport or something similar, and lived where they did purely for financial interest. Anyone with any spark of humanity in them had fled from the area long ago.

She turned off by the old war memorial ("Faithful Unto Death" 1914–1918, 1939–1945) and headed towards her father's house. The road shimmered in its own heat, creating imaginary pools and quagmires into which she drove.

Round the last corner, she passed the burnt-out shell of the Standish mansion. Burdock grew along its drive, rusty with July, and eager green things had sprung up round what was left the structure. Sweet rocket flowered haphazardly. The shade under the high beeches behind was as dark as night. Ahead, lopping off the road, the airport fence. The fence put a terminator on everything—beyond was only the anticyclonic weather, breaking into slatey cumulus, which began to pile up the sky like out-of-hand elms, growing above low cloud and threatening a chance of thunder before the afternoon died.

The drive gates stood open. As the Triumph turned in, Anna saw that the drab green fence was closer to her father's house than she recalled. It was too long since she last visited Felix; her neglect of him was part of a greater neglect, of the wastage of everything.

On the other side of the fence, the road had been eradicated; machines had wiped it out of existence; on this side of the fence, nature was at work doing the same thing, throwing out an advance guard of wild grasses and buttercup, following up with nettles, dock, thistles, and brambles. Soon they would come sprawling their way along the road. It only needed a year or two, and they would be at the house.

Anna drew up before the front door, noting how the trees about the drive, beech and copper beech, had grown more ragged and encroached more since she was last here. She blew her nose before climbing out, not wishing her father to suspect she might have a cold developing.

The house had been solidly built just after the turn of the century, with grey slate roof and red brick, and a curious predilection for stone round the windows. It had never been fashionable or imposing, though perhaps aiming at both; nevertheless, even in its old neglected age, it manifested something of the rather flashy solidity of the epoch in which it had been designed and constructed.

Before entering, Anna let a certain dread provoke her into stepping across the weedy gravel to peer through the living room windows. Through the second window, she saw her father crouched in his swivel chair, looking fixedly at something beyond the range of her vision. She stared at him as at a stranger. Felix Macguire was still a powerful man, the lines of his face were still commanding, while the recession of his gums lent more emphasis than at any other stage in his life to a determined line of chin and jaw. His white hair, hanging forward over his brow, still contained something of the boisterousness she recalled in her childhood. All in all, he, like the house, had weathered· well, retaining the same flashy solidity of the Edwardian Age.

Feeling guilty for spying on him, she turned away, thinking in a depressed way that her father seemed scarcely changed in appearance from when she could first remember him in childhood; yet she herself no longer had youthful expectations of life, and was moving towards middle age. With her habitual quick shift of thought, she ironically pronounced herself resigned to her own listless company.

She tried the handle of the front door. It opened. Hinges squeaked as she entered the hall.

Despite the heat outside, the feeling in the house was one of cold and damp: a comfortlessness less physical than an attribute of the phantoms haunting it. But the lengths of coaxial cable running boldly over the carpet or snaking up the stairs, the doors—to garage, lavatory, coat cupboard, and living room—wedged open, all contributed to the discomfort—not to mention the slow stare of Camera Four, situated knee-high on its bracket on the corner of the coat cupboard, where it could survey front door, hall, passage, and stairs.

"Are you there, father? It's me, Anna."

She went down the passage and through the second door of the living room. He had risen from the console and stood awaiting her. She went over to him and kissed him.

"How are you? You're looking well! Why didn't you write or send me a few words on a tape? I've been worried. I'm sorry it's been so long since my last visit, but we've been terribly busy at the labs—trade's bad, and that always seems to mean more work, for me at least. I had to go up to Newcastle with one of the partners last weekend or I would have come over then. Did you get my card, by the way? I'm sure I've sent you that view of the Civic Hall before, but it seemed to be the only view they had at the tobacconist's . . ."

She paused and her father said, "It's good of you to bother to come at all, Anna. I'll get you a cup of coffee, or something, shall I?"

"No, no, I'll get it. That's what I'm here for, isn't it? And may I open a window or two? It's terribly stuffy in here—it is July, you know, and you need some warm air circulating. And why don't you keep the front door locked when you are alone in the house? Suppose someone broke in?"

"If the front door is unlocked, I can get out quicker if I need to, can't I?"

They stared at each other. Anna dropped her gaze first.

"You aren't exactly welcoming, are you, father?"

"I said it was good of you to come. I'm pleased to see you. But it's no good complaining about the way I live directly you get in the house."

"I'm sorry, father, really. I didn't mean to nag, of course. Just a motherly instinct—you know what women are!" She put on a smile and moved to embrace him, then clumsily cut off the gesture. "Father, you're alone far too much. I know what you think about me, but you don't make it easy—you've never made it easy. Even when I was a little girl and I used to run to you . . ."

"You are grown up now, Anna!"

"Oh God, don't rub it in! You took care of that! What does being grown up mean but being even more isolated than as a child? What made you so inhuman, father? You never really loved me, did you? Why do you still expect me to come all this way up here to visit you, and it's terribly difficult to get here, just to make fun of me?"

"I don't expect you to visit me, Anna. You have to come now and then just to reproach me. You know very well that what you say hurts. You have in some way failed to achieve a mature personality and so you blame me for that. Perhaps I am to blame. But what use is blame? Was it worth coming this far just to deliver it?"

"Nothing's of any use to you, is it?" she said sulkily. "I'll go and make coffee, if there's any in the house."

Her father went back to sit down before his monitor screens. He switched Camera Eight on to the big screen and sat looking at an image of the inner wall of the second bedroom which included part of a wardrobe and, hanging from the picture rail, an engraving of Sir Edward Poynter's "Faithful Unto Death," which had belonged to his mother.

In a minute, Anna poked her head round the door.

"Coffee's ready! Come and have it in the kitchen—it's a bit fresher in here."

He went through and took the cup she offered him. Anna had opened the door to the side-drive. Sunlight lay there in patches between trees.

"I'm pleased to see you have plenty of provisions in the house. At least you keep yourself fed properly. Prices of everything keep going up and up. I don't know where it will all end."

"I live very comfortably, Anna. I nourish myself, I exercise myself. I am entirely dedicated to my research and mean to keep myself as healthy as possible in order to pursue it. Did you manage to get that volume on convergence by Krost?"

"No, not yet. Foyle's had to order specially, and still it hasn't come through. Sorry. Everything takes so long. How's the research going?"

"Steadily."

"I know you aren't very keen to tell me about it, but you know I'm interested. Perhaps I could be of more help to you if you would tell me a bit more."

"My dear, I appreciate your interest, but I've told you before—the work has to be secret. I don't want it blabbed about and, in the sphere in which I'm working, you could not possibly be of any help."

"Ignoring the insulting suggestion that I should blab your secrets everywhere, couldn't I approach someone—"

"You know what I mean, you might tell one of your boy-friends casually—" He paused, knowing he had said the wrong thing, blinked, and said hastily, "You shall have, perhaps, a small demonstration of what I'm doing. But I must keep it all secret. I'm on the brink of something extraordinary, that I know . . . one of those discoveries—revelations—that can completely overturn the thinking of all men, as Galileo did when he turned his telescope to the sky. There were telescopes, there was sky. But *he* was the man who had the original thought, *he* was the man who looked in a new direction. I am doing that. To you—though you may be my daughter—I'm just an old eccentric, spending his days staring at television screens. Aren't I, admit it?! Well, that's much what they thought of Galileo . . . The name of Felix Macguire, my child . . . a few more years . . . I can't tell you . . ."

"Don't let your coffee get cold, father."

He turned his back to her and stared out of the door at the unkempt bushes.

"I understand, father. I mean, I understand your aspirations. Everyone has them. I know I have."

Her pathetic words, intended to contain a charge of reassurance through shared experience, died on her lips. In a more practical voice, she said, "All the same, it's not good for you to live here alone like this. I don't like it. It's a responsibility for me. I want you to come and live near me in Highgate where I can keep an eye on you . . . Or, if you won't do that, then I want a medical friend of mine to be allowed up here to see you. Robert Stokes-Wallis. He's a follower of Laing's. Perhaps you know his name."

She sniffed and blew her nose. Felix turned and watched her performance.

"I warn you, Anna, I want no interference with my routine. Tell your man to stay away. You think I'm cranky. Maybe I am. It's a cranky world. Whether I'm mad or not is really a question of no importance beside the magnitude of the questions I am confronting. Now, let's say no more on that subject."

"Drink your coffee," she said pettishly. "And what's this demonstration you want to give me?"

Felix picked up the mug and sipped. "Are you, in fact, particularly interested?"

Making an effort, she laid a hand on the arm of his sweater. "I'm sure that you understand that I really am interested, father, and always have been, when allowed to be. I am really quite an intelligent and loving creature to my friends. So of course I am keen to see your demonstration."

"Good, good. You need only say yes—speeches aren't necessary. Now, I don't want you to be disappointed by the demonstration, because there is a danger it may seem very flat to you, you understand? Let me explain something about it first."

He pulled a book off the top of the refrigerator.

"Milton's poems. 'Paradise Lost.' I read it sometimes when I'm not working. A marvellous poem, although it contains a view of reality as a theological drama to which we no longer subscribe. When Milton was in Italy, he visited Galileo Galilei, and something of the astronomer's involvement with the heavens has got into the poem. Galileo is the greater man, because the scientist must take precedence over the poet; but either must have a measure of the other for real greatness."

"Father, you forget that you read me most of Book IV of 'Paradise Lost' last time I came up here. It is not my favourite poem."

" 'What seest thou else in the dark backward and abysm of time?' Let me come to the point, which is not exactly Milton. We are talking about views of reality to which we no longer subscribe. The geocentric view of the universe prevailed for over a thousand years—needlessly, since a heliocentric view had been advanced before that. How can anything be correctly understood when such a great thing is misunderstood? It was not just a minor astronomical error—it was grounded in Man's erroneous view of his own importance in the universe.

"Nobody believes in the Ptolemaic geocentric view nowadays, and yet nevertheless thousands—millions of people have found a way of clinging to that ancient error by maintaining a belief in astrology: that the movements of remote suns can control a human destiny, or that, vice versa, human behavior can provoke eclipses or similar signs of heavenly displeasure. Clear views of reality are at a premium. Indeed, I've come to believe something always distorts our vision. Bacon comes very close to the same conclusions in his 'Novum Organum.'

"Take mankind's idea of its own nature. In the west, the view prevailed until the Nineteenth Century that we were God's creatures, especially made to act in some obscure drama of His making. Your grandmother believed in the tale of Adam and Eve, and in every word of Genesis. She preferred that version of reality to Darwin's. Darwin showed that we were different from the animals only in degree and not in kind. But the opposite view had prevailed practically unchallenged for centuries, and men still prefer to behave as if they were apart from Nature. Not only is the truth hard to come by—it's often refused when available."

"I see that but, surely, in this century we have had our noses rubbed in reality uncomfortably enough."

"I don't think so, Anna. I believe we have escaped again. Look at the way in which the so-called side-effects of technology are universally deplored. Everyone who pretends to any degree of civilization agrees to condemn nuclear warfare, the pollution of air, sea, and land, the sort of dreadful fate that has overtaken Crackmore, the hideous tide of automobiles which chokes our cities. Yet all these things are brought about by us. We have power over technological and legislative processes to end all such abuses tomorrow if we wished. Instead, we continue to stock-pile nuclear weapons, we go on making thousands of automobiles per day, we continue to destroy every accessible environment. Why? Why? Because we wish it. Because we *like* it that way, because we crave disaster. That is the truth—that we think we feel otherwise is yet another proof of how incapable mankind is of coping with reality."

"Oh, but to argue like that—that's silly, father! After all, growing numbers of people—"

"I know what you are going to say—"

"Oh, no, you don't—"

"I know what you are going to say. You are going to say that there are increasing numbers of people who are showing by action that they hate what technology is doing to us. Perhaps. I do not suggest all men feel the same. Indeed, part of my thesis is that man is divided. But by and large there is a mass wish for catastrophe, hidden under mass delusion. So a considerable amount of my time here is devoted to bringing reality under better control."

She shook her head. "Father, honestly, you just can't—"

He shut the door to the drive. "We must bring reality under control. The technology we turn against ourselves can be turned to fortify that weak link in our brains which always seeks to deceive us about our own natures! I'll show you how. You've had the lecture—now the demonstration. Go and sit in the other room at my chair and watch Number Five monitor screen."

Putting his hands on her shoulders, he guided her from the kitchen. He noticed how stiff and lifeless her body felt, and hurriedly removed his hands. In time to catch the expression on his face, Anna turned and said, "Father, I do want to be of help to you—desperately! It's awful how people in families get all tangled up with their relationships, but I do want to be more of a dau-"

"Demonstration first!" he said, briskly, pushing her forward. "Get in there and sit patiently watching Monitor Five. That's all you have to do."

Sighing, she went through into the living room. Most of its original furniture had been pushed back into one corner. An old sofa covered the unused fireplace. There were cushions, occasional tables, a magazine-rack, and an old box piled on top of the sofa. The room had been further reduced in meaning by the partition across it, with the television screen burning on it. Past the side of the partition, she could see through the other door of the room and out through the discomfort of the hall, the eye perforce following the intertwined snakes of black cable, into the garage, with its empty crates and wall of breeze-blocks.

She sat at the console, took a tissue out of her handbag, and blew her nose. The headache was there in full force, despite two aspirins she had swallowed with her coffee. The atmosphere was leaden.

On the large screen burned an image which she recognized as one of the bedrooms, although it was years since she had been upstairs. Despite herself, she was interested and, as she scrutinized the picture, tried to reason why she should be. She could see through an open door to a landing across which light and ill-defined shadows of bannisters lay, to a corner of wall; the continuation of landing had to be deduced from the chiaroscuro eclipsed by the bedroom doorpost. From this glimpse, Anna deduced she was seeing a view from the spare bedroom at the top of the stairs.

Inside the room, she could see the foot of a bed, part of a wardrobe, and a picture hanging against a patterned wallpaper. She leaned forward instinctively, interested to see if the bed were made up. It appeared not to be. She also stared at the picture on the wall. A man, perhaps a soldier, was holding a pike or a spear and gazing fearfully upwards at the entrance to a forbidding alley; behind him, something awful was going on; but she could make little of it.

All, on the surface, was dull and without any power to enchant; yet she felt herself enchanted.

The colours were of high quality, conveying an impression that they were true to reality but perhaps enhanced it slightly. For instance, the landing carpet: mauve: but did it actually present those tender lavender contrasts between shadowed and unshadowed strips? Or was it that the colours on the screen were true and one merely paid them a more attentive respect because they were images of the real thing? Was there an art about the reproduction that the reality lacked?

She noted belatedly that the sound was on, so that she was actually listening to this silent vista as well as watching it. And she noted something else: that the viewpoint was low, as if the camera was fixed just above the skirting. So one was forced into the viewpoint more of a child than an adult. That might explain why the shadows radiating from the wardrobe seemed both somewhat emphatic and somewhat menacing, as well as accounting for some of the fascination of the picture as a whole.

But was it a live picture or a still? Anna was convinced it was no still. Some quality about it suggested a second-by-second congruence with her own life. Yet how to be sure? Of course, a long enough vigil would reveal movement in the shadows, or a diminution in light towards evenings; but she found herself looking for a spider crossing her field of vision, perhaps a fly trapped in the room, circling vaguely under overhead lampshade. Nothing moved.

With an involuntary shiver, she thought, "That room's as lifeless as the top of Everest! It's not a real room any more—it's just a fossil!" Her attraction changed to revulsion and she looked down at the row of monitor screens to obey her father's directions.

Eight of the nine small screens were lit. All showed static views of rooms and, in the eighth, she saw duplicated—in miniature and in black-and-white—the view projected on the big screen. Its smallness gave it an even more hypnotic quality. It frightened her. As she averted her eyes, she caught sight of her father in the fifth screen, moving purposefully across it. Almost as soon as he was lost to sight on that screen, he was caught advancing in Number One screen, coming from a shadowy passage, and then he materialised in the room in person.

"Did you watch closely? What did you make of the demonstration?" he asked.

She stood up, vexed with herself.

"I was so fascinated with the view on the big screen . . . I was only just about to watch Number Five monitor."

Felix frowned and shook his head. "Such a simple thing I asked you to do . . ."

"Do the demonstration again, father. I will watch this time, honestly! I'm sorry!"

"No, no, it was just a small thing, as I warned you. To do it after this fuss would make it meaningless."

"Oh, no, that can't be so, surely. I wasn't making a fuss. I won't find it meaningless. You didn't give me enough time. You didn't give me a proper chance . . ." To her own dismay, she began to cry. Angrily, she turned her back on him, fumbling in her bag for a tissue.

"Always these over-heated personal nonsenses!" Felix shouted. "Isn't it enough that you should have been stupid without compounding it by bursting into tears? Dry your eyes, woman!—You're as bad as your mother!"

At that, she cried the louder.

When she turned round at length, he had left the room.

She stood there in a melancholy containment, with the unwinking monitors by her right hand. Should she leave, despite her headache, so much worse after the fit of weeping? Did he expect her to leave? And how much did his expectations influence whether she would actually leave or not?

In any case, it was past lunch time. She could either rustle up something from the kitchen, where she had found a surprisingly well-maintained range of food, or she could go down to the pub in Crackmore. She had meant to take him along to the pub, but his insufferable behaviour put a different aspect on things.

She glanced at the screens to see if she could catch sight of him. The view on Number Seven monitor was moving slowly; she looked and realized that the movement of the camera was automatic. The screen showed another bedroom, evidently her father's from its state of occupation. There was a cupboard, one door half-open to reveal suits within, and an untidy pile of clothes on a chair. She supposed the laundry man still called every week. The bed was unmade. The viewpoint was moving beyond it in a slow arc, taking in blank wall, an angle between walls complex with diffused shadow, then a window—seen obliquely, but revealing the tops of unkempt trees in the drive by the front gate—then the wall between windows, then the next window, rolling gently into view . . . No father there.

He had built neat switchboards; she realized that everything could be controlled from here. If she could set all the cameras tracking, then presumably she would detect him in one of the rooms. Tentatively, she pressed one of the piano-keys nearest to her.

His voice came out at her. "-st lot of tinned meat gave me diarrhea . . . My evolutionary discovery is greater than Charles Darwin's or his grandfather's . . . greater and far more world-shaking. Darwin revealed only part of the truth—"

She switched him off.

He was mad. No doubt of it. Madness suited him—there had always been a madness in the distance he had kept between himself and everyone else.

He was probably dangerous too. Men with monomania were generally violent when opposed. She'd better be careful. But she'd always been careful. And really—she told herself in the thick ticking room—she had hated him since childhood.

She saw him on Number Four screen. He must have rushed outside to avoid her crying; now he was entering the house, turning to close the door—my God, was locking it! Locking it! What did he mean to do?

Anna ran out of the nearer living room door and into the kitchen.

Panic momentarily overcame her. She ran across the kitchen and pulled open the door. Surely he was intending to trap her, or else why lock the front door? He had said he never locked it—What was that ghastly phrase?—"If I don't lock up, I can escape faster"? Nutty as a fruit cake!

She ran from the kitchen. The gravel outside had sprouted so many weeds, so much grass, that it hardly showed any more. She hurried through them, thinking she had better get to her car and clear off, or at least go and get a drink and then return, cautiously, and plead with him to let Stokes-Wallis examine him . . . As she turned the corner and came to the front of the house, her father emerged from the front door and—no, it was not a run—*hastened* to her car.

Anna stopped a few yards away.

"What are you playing at, father?"

"Are you going already, Anna?"

She went a little nearer.

"You aren't trying to stop me leaving, are you?"

"You are leaving, then, are you?" His hair almost concealed his eyes. She paused.

"It's best if I leave, father. I don't understand your work, you refuse to explain it to me, and I interrupt it in any case. It's not just a question of that, either, is it? I mean, there's the question of temperament, too, isn't there? We've never got on. It was your business—the way I look at it—to get on with me if you could, since I was your daughter, your only child, but, no, you never fucking well cared, did you? I was just an intrusion between you and mother. Okay, then I'll get out, and as far as I'm concerned you can sit and goggle at your empty screens till you fall dead. Now get out of my way!"

As she came forward, Felix stepped back from the car. He let his gaze drop so that his eyes were completely hidden by the overhanging lock of his hair. His arms hung by his side. In his stained grey trousers and his torn sweater, he looked helpless and negative.

Proud of her victory, Anna marched forward and grasped the door handle of the Triumph. As she pulled it open, he seized her fiercely from behind, locking his arms round her so that her elbows were pinned against her sides.

She yelled in fright. A passenger jet roared overhead, taking up and drowning the note of her cry while he spun her round and dragged her into the house.

Even in her fury and fear, she found time to curse herself for forgetting that mannerism of her father's. How often as a child had she seen him doing as he did then, suddenly turning deceptively limp and passive before springing on her like an enemy! She should not have been deceived!—But of course memory so often worked to obliterate the miseries of reality!

Once he had got her into the hall, he pulled her toward the side door into the garage. Anna recovered her wits and kicked backwards at his legs. He was immensely strong! Together, they tripped over the cables in the entrance and half-fell down the concrete step into the garage. As she broke from his grip, he caught her again and momentarily they were face to face.

"You're the enemy!" he said. "You're one of the non-humans!"

Above their heads were unpainted wood shelves, crudely fixed to the wall with brackets and loaded with boxes of spools of plastic-covered wire. Pinning his daughter to the wall, Felix reached up and dragged down one of the spools. The action tumbled a couple of boxes, and nails cascaded over their heads. Tugging savagely at her, Felix commenced to bind her round and round with wire, securing her ankles as well as her wrists.

He was just finishing when they heard a distant knocking.

Felix straightened. He pushed his hair from his eyes.

"That'll be the grocer. Don't make a sound, Anna, or I'll be forced— well, you know what I'll be forced to do!" He gave her a hard straight look which included no recognition of her as a human being.

As soon as he had got into the hall and was making for the kitchen, from which the knocking came, Anna struggled upright and hobbled towards the door. It was impossible to climb up the step into the hall with her ankles bound; she fell up it. Before she was on her feet again, her father was coming back. He had a letter in his hand, and was smiling.

"A Glasgow postmark—this will be from Professor Nicholson! The grocer kindly brings my mail along from the post office. He's a good fellow. He recognized your car; I told him I was having the pleasure of a visit from you. Now, my dear, we are going to get you upstairs. If you help yourself a bit, it won't be so painful."

"Father, what are you going to do with me? *Please* let me go! I'm not a little girl any more, to be punished when I disobey your orders."

He laughed. "No, you are far from being a little girl, Anna. Just how far, I intend to discover for myself."

She stared at him in shock, as if for the first time the helplessness of her position was made real to her. He read her expression and laughed again, a lot less pleasantly.

"Oh, no, my dear, I didn't mean what you think—whatever fantasies you entertain in the depths of your mind!"

"You don't know what I'm thinking!"

"I don't want to know what you're thinking! What a miserable generation yours was, obsessed by sex, yet totally unable to come to terms with your own sexuality. Your mother and I had a far better time than you or any of your friends will ever have!"

By dint of pushing and lifting, he got her upstairs and trundled her past the bathroom into the bedroom whose door stood open opposite the head of the stairs. She found herself in a bedroom at the back of the house, recognizing it indifferently as the room she had seen on the viewing screen.

"Now!" he said, looking round frowning.

He loosed some of the wire from her ankles, led her over to the bed, and tied her legs to the bedpost, so that she was forced to sit there. Then he disappeared. She heard him going downstairs. A minute later, he was back, a tenon saw in one hand. He knelt by the door and started to saw low down on the leading edge. When he had got six inches in, he stood and kicked vigorously at the bottom of the door. The wood splintered and a piece sagged outward. He kicked at it until it was loose.

The door would now shut, despite the cables trailing over the floor. Looking meaningfully at her once, he went out, and she heard him turning the key in the lock. She was properly imprisoned.

Impotently listening, she heard him march downstairs. Silence, then the sound of the Triumph engine starting up. What a fool she was to have left the key in the ignition—by no means for the first time! But he could always have taken the key from her bag; she had left it in the kitchen.

She heard the car engine fade almost immediately; so he had driven it round the side of the house, parking it beyond the kitchen door, where it would not be noticed from the road.

The grocer might see it when he called again—but how long ahead would that be? Evidently no postman called—the grocer had agreed to deliver her father's post. Perhaps no other tradesman came up this cul-de-sac; her father might well rely on the friendly grocer for all supplies. Of course, she had told Trevor and some of the fellows in the labs where she was going, but Trevor was not to be relied on, while the rest of them would not give her another thought until Monday, when she did not show up for work. She was on her own.

Well, that was nothing new. It was just that the situation was more extreme than usual.

Anna was already working to free her hands. It should be possible. She had already noticed that her father had left—carelessly or by design?—the saw on the floor by the door. It might come in useful.

The front door slammed.

Of course, he could watch her over the Omniviewer. She glared across the room at the dull lens of the camera, bracketed in the wall against the disused grate, a foot above floor-level. She would just have to hope that he was unable to watch all the time.

Her feet were less tightly tied than her wrists and arms. After working away carefully, she managed to slip one of her brogues off, and then to wriggle her stockinged foot from the coils. The other one came out easily, and she could walk round the room.

Still pulling at her wrists, she ran over to the window and looked out.

Clouds had piled up in the sky. The afternoon was torpid. She was looking over what had once been a vegetable garden. Impenetrable weeds grew there. They stopped at the high wire fence, drab green and stretching away into the distance. Beyond the fence lay the airport, flat and featureless. She could see no building from this window, only a distant plane, deserted on a runway.

The view was blank and alien. It offered her no courage.

Hooking her wrists over the catch of the window, she pulled and wriggled to such effect that in a minute her hands were free. As she rubbed her hands together, she listened for his footstep on the stair.

Just how dangerous was he? She could not estimate. That he was her father made it all more difficult to calculate, more bizarre. If he came up, would he not, this time—at last—put his arms round her and love and forgive her for all her shortcomings?

No, he bloody well wouldn't!

The door was locked, as expected.

Anna crossed to the single picture on the wall above the bed, a sepia reproduction mounted and set in a solid oak frame. As she pulled it down, she saw that it represented a Roman sentry in armor standing guard before a gateway leading into a luridly lit court in which people were dying and dead—flares of some kind were falling from the skies on to them. The picture was called "Faithful Unto Death." She swung it in front of the camera, propping it against a chair so that the view was obstructed. Then she opened the window and looked out.

Felix Macguire was standing among the weeds aiming a gun of some kind at her. A rifle, possibly. Aimed at her. Half-fainting, she sank back inside the room.

Leaning against the wall, she heard him shouting. She began listening to his words.

"I'd have fired if you'd tried to jump. I warn you, Anna! You may not fully understand the situation, but I do. The fact that you are my daughter makes no difference. You are not going to leave here, or not until I say you can. Professor Basil Nicholson is coming tomorrow, and I want him to look at you. Behave yourself and you'll come to no harm. If you don't behave yourself, I'll lock you in the landing cupboard without food. Forget you're my daughter—remember you're my captive. Now then— shut that window. Do you hear, shut the window?!"

She summoned enough presence of mind to look out and say, though without all the spirit she hoped for, "Try and realize what you are saying and doing, father! You are now formally renouncing me as your daughter, which is what you have wished to do all your life. You are also threatening to shoot me!"

He said angrily, "This is a French carbine, used against rioters. I'll fire if you don't get back. I mean every word." A few drops of rain began to fall.

"I'm sure you do! I don't doubt that. I'm sure you do! I'm sure you'd love to fire. But you should recognize what it means. You have now crossed the dividing line between sanity and madness. You are also committing a criminal act!"

"Get your head inside and close—" His words were drowned by the roar of an airliner coming in to land, but his threatening gestures were enough for her. Anna pulled her head back and wearily shut the window. She laid down on the bed and tried to think what she should do. Her stomach rumbled like thunder.

It was a problem to understand how matters between them had deteriorated so rapidly. Was it just because she had forgotten to watch his demonstration on the monitor, or because of some other fault of which she was unaware? And what had the demonstration been? Something minor, despite its build-up, that was clear: perhaps merely watching her father in the kitchen over the closed-circuit. Instead, she had been hooked into watching an empty room—this room. "Getting control of reality": that had been his phrase. Had he, her all-powerful and untouchable father, been rewarded for his years of isolation—whether unwished for or self-imposed—by some amazing insight into the physical conditions governing man? Had he really stumbled on an equivalent to Galileo's proof of the heliocentric system? It was not past the bounds of credibility—but nothing was past the bounds of credibility these days. And if he had so done, he would naturally be impatient (though *impatient* was scarcely the word) with any silly girl who failed to follow him closely when he attempted to explain.

She lay looking up at the ceiling. She could hear rain outside, and another slight sound. The camera was still working.

Warmth and comfort overcame her. Perhaps the aspirins were taking effect; her headache had gone. She began to recall summer days in their old house, before she had grown up, when her mother was alive, and she had lain as she was now lying on her bed, idly reading a book; the window was open to the summer breezes, and she could hear her parents down in the garden, exchanging an odd sentence now and again. Her mother was gardening, her father working on a monograph on lacunae in the theory of evolution which never got published. Evolutionary theory was always his hobby—a complete contrast from the pushing world of electronics into which his job took him. She had put her book down and gone over—yes, she had been barefoot—gone over to the window and looked out. He had waved to her and called something . . .

"Can you hear me, father? I didn't mean to miss your demonstration, whatever it was, if that is why you're punishing me. If possible, I'd like to understand and help. It could be that when watching the big screen I had a useful insight into what you meant about reality. A view over the screen is different in some undefined way to a view direct, isn't it?"

No answer. She lay looking up at the ceiling, listening. She had often listened like this before going to sleep as a child, wondering if someone would come up and visit her. The ceiling blurred; suggestions of warmth and other modes of being moved in; she slept.

Felix Macguire sat at the console, resting his elbow on the desk and rubbing his chin, as he peered at the big screen. It showed part of a scene at the Herculanean Gate of Pompeii in A.D. 79, with the inhabitants about to be destroyed; a soldier in close-up stood at his post, eyes raised fearfully towards the unknown.

The light values on the soldier's face changed almost unnoticeably as Felix ran back the tape and played over again the words his daughter had spoken.

". . . had a useful insight into what you meant by reality. A view over the screen is different in some undefined way to a view direct, isn't it?"

He ran it back again, listening mainly to the tone of her voice.

"I didn't mean to miss your demonstration, whatever it was, if that is why you are punishing me. If possible I'd like to understand and help. It could be that when watching the big screen I had a useful insight into—"

He clicked her off. Always that pleading and cajoling note in her voice which he recalled from her childhood. A jarring note. No wonder no man had ever married her.

Silence in her room. But it was not the usual silence he received from Number Two bedroom. The usual silence had a sort of thin and rather angular dazed quality unique to itself, resembling the surface of a Vermeer canvas, and with a similar sense almost of *planning* behind it; he thought of it as an intellectual silence and, of course, it differed from the silence in the other rooms. With Anna's occupancy, the silence took on an entirely different weight, a bunched and heavy mottled feeling which he disliked.

The sound levels were so good that he could detect when she was drifting towards sleep. It was her way of eluding reality; a little editing of tape would soon bring her back to her uncomfortable senses.

She roused, sat up suddenly, aware that her mouth had fallen open. Someone was whispering in the room. She had caught the sound of her own voice.

". . . a useful insight . . ."

Then her father's voice, indistinct, and then her own, perfectly clear:

"Can you hear me, father?" And his reply:

"Why didn't you watch what your mother and I were doing? You're old enough to learn the facts of life."

"I didn't mean to miss your demonstration, whatever it was, if that is why you're punishing me."

"What do you mean, 'whatever it was,' Anna? Come back into the bedroom and watch—we're just going to start again."

"If possible, I'd like to understand and help."

"That's better. Jump in with your mother. You'll soon learn."

She sat on the edge of the bed, flushing with shame.

"You're right round the bloody twist, father!" she said aloud. "For Christ's sake let me out of here and let me get home. I'll never bother you again—you can be sure of that!"

He came in the bedroom door, grinning in an uneasy way.

"Forget all that—just a bit of innocent fun! You see what can be done with reality! Now look, Anna, you present me with a bit of a problem. I'll have to keep you here overnight, so you'd better resign yourself to the fact. Basil Nicholson is coming tomorrow—his visit is very important to me, because for the first time I'm going to present my findings to an impartial outside observer. Nicholson and I have been in communication for months, and he's sufficiently impressed by what I've told him to come and look for himself. You could be useful in more than one way. So you'll have to stay here and behave. If all goes well, you can go home tomorrow afternoon. Okay?"

She just sat and stared at him. The whole business was too horrifying to be believed.

Felix picked up the framed engraving and hung it back on the wall. As he went towards the door, he picked up the saw. He smiled and waved it at her, a gesture part-friendly, part-menacing.

"Why don't you kill me, father? You know I can never forgive you—pointing a gun at your own daughter. I saw murder in your eyes, I did."

He paused with a hand on the door. "Never forgive? You can't say that. Never forgive? Never? Think what a long journey it is between birth and death . . . anything is possible on the way."

"Go to hell!"

"Think what a long journey you and I have come, Anna! Here we are together in this house; perhaps in one sense we have always been here. Perhaps it doesn't matter that we don't understand each other. Perhaps we hate each other, who knows? We make the journey together. It's like crossing a glacier—in moments of danger, all the various differences between us become unimportant and we are forced to help each other to survive. There's no way of making sense out of such testing journeys until we have the tools to understand what human life is about."

Anna fumbled in her pocket for a tissue. One nostril was blocked with incipient cold. "I don't want your philosophizing."

"But you must understand what I'm saying. Nobody lives out their life without being brought up against a sudden moment when they see themselves as in a screen or mirror and ask themselves, 'What am I doing here?' Once, it used to be a religious question. Then people started to interpret it more in socio-economic terms. Your generation tried to answer it in terms of individual escape, and a poor job they made of it. I'm trying to provide an evolutionary solution which will take care of all the other aspects."

He sounded so reasonable. She was baffled by his changes of mood, always had been.

"If you didn't want to have me here, you should have phoned and told me so. How can you ill-treat me so? I've never harmed you. Pointing that gun at me! I just want to go away—I don't know whether I can ever recover from what you've done to me."

"You keep saying that. Try and pull yourself together, Anna. We are father and daughter—nothing can ever come between us, not even if I had to kill you."

He had put his arm round her, but now she drew away, looking at him with a face of dread, seeing only a blankness in his eyes and a cruel estrangement round his mouth.

"I want to go now, father, if you don't mind. Back home. Please let me go. I've never done you any harm. Let me go and I'll never bother you again!"

He was as unmoving as stone.

"Never done me any harm? What child had not harmed its parents? Didn't you, every day of your life, come between your mother and me with your insatiable craving for attention? Didn't you drive her into an early grave with your perpetual demands? But for you, wouldn't she be here, on this very bed, with us now?"

"Your evolutionary theory, father—are you sure you ought to talk about it with Nicholson? Shouldn't you publish a paper on the idea first? Or write to *Nature,* or something?"

He was standing now and looking down on her. She had hunched herself up on the bed with her legs tucked under her.

"You're frightened, aren't you? Why should you be interested in my theories? As—"

The roar of a plane swamped his sentence. For a moment, the room was darkened as the machine passed low overhead. It seemed to distract Macguire's attention. He wandered over to the window.

"The sooner we get control of reality, the better. One of these days, they're not just going to fly over—they'll drop an H-bomb on me, right smack down the chimney, since they can see their warnings don't scare me off." He turned back to her. "I must prepare my notes for Nicholson's arrival tomorrow. You'd better come down and clear the place up. If there's time, I'll give you the demonstration I plan to give him and see how you like it. This time, you'd better attend."

"Oh, I will, I will, father."

He walked out of the room, still clutching the saw in his hand. She hesitated, then climbed off the bed and followed him downstairs.

"The front door's locked, by the way, Anna, and I have the key in my pocket."

"I wasn't thinking of going out."

"No? Well, it's raining, but just in case you were . . ."

He went into the living room, pushed past the partition, and sat down at his console as if nothing had happened. She went into the kitchen, leaned her elbows on the window sill, and buried her face in her hands.

After a while, the involuntary shaking in her limbs died away and she looked up. The house was absolutely silent. No, not absolutely. The camera made a faint registration of its presence. With very intent listening, she could hear slight movements from her father in the next room. She looked at her watch, decided to make a cup of tea, and started the soothingly traditional preliminaries of filling the kettle, switching it on, and getting down teapot and tea-caddy from the shelf.

"Like a dutiful daughter, you are making me a cup too." A loud-speaker.

"Of course, father."

How could she persuade him that she loved him? It was impossible, because she did not love him. She had failed to love him. Shouldn't love have sprung up in her spontaneously, however he behaved, the way spring flowers—the modest and incorrigible snowdrops—bud and blossom even in the teeth of chilly winds? The truth was that she understood so little about herself; perhaps she even hoped that he would carry out his direst threats.

When the tea was made, she put everything on a tray and carried it through to him. Felix smiled and motioned her to put it on a side-table.

As she did as he indicated, she saw the carbine. Her father had stood it in the corner behind him. It was ready for action, she thought—was he secretly planning to grab it up and shoot her?

"There are some chocolate biscuits in the cupboard over the sink, if you'd like to get them. You always enjoyed chocolate biscuits, Anna."

"I still do, as it happens." She fetched the biscuits.

He drank his tea absently, staring into the miniature screens, switching the view from one or another on to the larger screen, scrutinising his static universe. Finally he settled on a panorama of the dining room through Camera Six, with the table, loaded with electronic gear, to one side of the screen and most of it filled by wall and desolate fireplace. This cheerless scene held his attention for so long that his tea grew cold by his elbow.

Anna sat staring towards the carbine.

At last, he sighed and looked up at her.

"Beautiful, isn't it? Human environment with humans abstracted. Almost a new art form—and utterly neglected. But that's neither here nor there."

Silence.

"Father, would it annoy you to explain to me what you see in the screen?"

"I see everything. The history of the world in that one shot. The grate, designed to burn fossil trees trapped in the earth since they grew in the jungles of the Carboniferous Age. Look at its Art Nouveau motif on the black-lead canopy. All obsolete. A great age of mankind gone for ever. Fires will never burn there again, prehistoric energy never be released there. Now the only function of that fireplace is to form part of this picture. The function of the picture is to activate part of my brain. My brain has been activated by retinal designs, formed in this house, never viewed before. I view them every day. They have made me conscious of my own brain structure, which in turn has modified that structure, so that I have been able to fit together facts—facts available to anyone through evolutionary study—and make them into a new whole. A new whole, Anna. You'd never understand."

He paused and drank down his cold tea.

Keeping herself under control, Anna reflected on the virtue of sanity; it was not half as boring as madness. With sudden impatience, she said, "Spare me the reasoning, please. Give me the facts. What exactly *is* this theory you keep bragging about?"

He looked rather guiltily up at her. "You must let it all soak in gradually. It needs practice to understand."

"I'm sorry, father, I have a job to go back to. You may not think it important but it is important to me. If you will not show me straightforwardly, then I shall have to leave before it gets dark."

He digested that. "I hoped you'd stay and have a bite of supper with me." His mild manner suggested he had forgotten his earlier threats.

"Why should I, after the way you have treated me? Explain at once or I shall go."

He shrugged. "As you will. If you feel up to it."

Pushing his teacup out of the way, he fiddled with various switches, rose, and messed about behind the partition, before saying, "Right, then, watch this carefully."

She dragged her eyes from the weapon in the corner.

The big screen lit. Anna looked with interest, but there was nothing except yet another view of the interior of the house. This was Camera Three working, moving slowly, so that the viewpoint descended from the upper landing to the hall, to a slow-moving shot of the hall cupboard and the ever-open door through to the garage. In the small section of the garage revealed, the door into the workshop could be seen. Only the eternal gleaming black cables, running across the floor, gave any sense of life. Then she saw a shadow move in the workshop. A man came through into the garage. She gasped.

"It's all right. This is tapex you're watching."

The man emerged into the hall. It was Felix, rather blank-faced, hair slanting across forehead. Without pausing, he moved forward and along the corridor towards the kitchen.

Now the scene was a blank again, unpopulated. The camera eye travelled over it in a leisurely and dispirited fashion. A shadow moved in the depths of the picture and a man passed from workshop to garage. Anna instinctively leaned forward, expecting something—she did not know what: something to frighten her. The man came out of the garage into the hall. It was her father, somewhat blank-faced. Without pausing, he moved out of camera range in the direction of the kitchen.

"Keep watching," Felix ordered.

The screen still showed only the view of the hall, its shadows, and the angles and perspectives created by the doorways beyond—a pattern that, by constant wearying repetition, seemed at once to annihilate sense and to acquire an ominous significance of its own: just as the single note of a dripping tap, listened to long enough, becomes an elusive tune. When something stirred in the shadows beyond the furthest doorway, she was prepared for it, prepared for the man who stepped from workshop to garage and then, after a pause, from garage to hall. It was her father, wearing his old sweater. Without pausing, blank-faced, he walked towards the kitchen and was lost from view.

The hall was empty. In a brief while, the whole insignificant action was repeated as before. Then it was repeated again. And again. Each time, the same thing happened.

At last the screen went blank, just when Anna thought she would have to scream if it happened once more.

"What have you seen, Anna?"

"Oh—you know. You coming out of the garage a million times!"

"Live or on tape?"

"On tape, obviously. The first time round, I thought it was live—well, except that you were here beside me. What does all that prove?"

"If I'd have been hidden in the kitchen, you couldn't have told what you saw from live. Or any of the re-runs, if they had been shown first."

"I suppose not."

"How many times did you see me come into the hall?"

"I've lost count. Twelve? Eighteen?"

"Nine times. Do you imagine they were all re-runs of one occasion on which I came into the hall?"

"Obviously."

"It's not obvious. You're wrong. What you witnessed was me coming into the hall on three different occasions—three different days, in fact. Each was re-run three times. And you didn't spot the difference?"

"One time must have been very like another." She was weary of the nonsense of his solemnity. "You always looked just the same. The light always looked just the same. Obviously the house always looked just the same."

"Okay. You're talking about the scientific theory of convergence."

He pressed a key, ran the videotape until he was once more stepping from garage to hall; then he froze the action. Staring out at his image, he said, "Obviously, ways of getting from one room to another are always closely alike. Right? So close you mistook them for identical. But they aren't identical. I've tried to remove the difference between one day and the next in this environment, as nearly as I can. Yet I—the living!—am aware of the change between one day and the next, as you were not when witnessing that change on the screen.

"Animals that adapt to similar environments and pursue the same inclinations also tend to resemble each other. However alien the animals themselves may be from each other, there are only a limited number of ways of getting through a doorway or living in a desert or swimming in a sea. To fly, you have to have wings; there are animals which mimic birds in that respect, and they are examples of convergence."

He pressed a key in front of him, and a shot of the wall of the workshop came up, a grey view with nothing on which to fix attention except three blown-up photographs ranged one under the other on the wall. The photographs depicted three gigantic sea-going creatures, each remarkably similar to the next in its functional streamlined form. Felix left them in view for a while before speaking.

"This is part of the big game I have been hunting for forty years, you might say. You know what these creatures are?"

"Are they all sharks?" Anna asked.

A plane roared overhead. The house vibrated, the picture on the screen shimmered and split into a maze of lines and dots. When it reassembled and the noise died, Felix said, "The top one is a shark. The next one down is a porpoise. The bottom one is an ichthyosaur. They all look alike—prime examples of convergence; yet one is a cartilaginous fish, one a marine mammal, and the other an extinct marine reptile—inwardly, they are nothing alike."

She fidgeted a little. It was growing dark and she wanted to be away from the house and its insane pedant. The rain had ceased; all was still outside, with the stillness of dripping trees.

"That's hardly a discovery, father. It has been known for a long time."

His head drooped, his shoulders slumped. She feared that he was about to burst into one of his insane rages. When he looked up again, his face was distorted with anger, so that she hardly recognized him, as if he had undergone some uncharted Jekyll-Hyde transformation. Instinctively, she took a step back. But he spoke with a measure of calm.

"You do not believe in me, you stupid vegetable . . . Have the wit at least to hear me out when I try to explain everything in layman's language and by analogy. My discovery is that there are creatures as strange as fish and extinct reptiles that go about the world under the same forms as man!"

Anna's first terrified thought was that he was living proof of his own hypothesis. Was there not, in that mottled jowl, that prognathous face, those blazing eyes, something that argued against idiothermous origin and whispered of a reptile brain lurking like an egg inside that bony nest of skull?

He stood up and stood glaring into her face, so that they confronted each other only a few inches apart.

"Reptiles structurally similar to man," he said. "Forms almost identical, intentions entirely different. Why is our world being destroyed? Why are the seas being polluted, why are nuclear weapons proliferating towards a holocaust, why do human beings feel increasingly powerless? Because there is an enemy in our midst as different from us as moon is from sun—an enemy intent on wiping out human civilization and reverting to a Jurassic world it still carries in its mind. These enemies are old, Anna, far older than mankind, still carrying a heritage from the Mesozoic in which they were formed, still hoping to bring the Mesozoic back down about our ears!"

With a mingling rush of light and dark in the room, another plane roared overhead, making everything in the room shake, Anna included. Felix rolled his eyes up to the ceiling. "There they go! They are gradually assuming power, and power for destruction. Men develop the technology, reptile-men take over its results and use them for destructive ends!"

She clutched at her throat to help bring out her voice. "Father—it's a terrifying idea you have . . . but . . . but it's—isn't it just your fancy?" The clouded swollen look was still on his face.

"There is archaeological evidence. Nicholson knows. He has some of it. Evidence from the past is all too scarce. There's my quarrel with Darwinism—a fine picture of evolution has been built up on too little evidence. The layman believes that deceptively whole picture of dinosaurs dying out and mammals developing, and finally homo sapiens rising out of several extinct man-forms; but the layman fails to realize how the picture is in fact conjured up merely from a few shards of bone, a broken femur here, a scatter of yellowed teeth there . . . And the picture we now accept is wrong in several vital instances.

"You may know that there is no understanding of why all the species of the two dinosaur genera, the saurischia and the ornithischia, suddenly died out. Ha! The reason for that lack of understanding is that they did not die out. Both the saurischians and the ornithischians were capable of tremendous variety, adapting to all kinds of conditions, even achieving flight, covering the globe. Both produced creatures which walked on their hind legs like man. But the saurischians also produced a man-creature, evolving from the theropod line."

"Is there physical proof of the development of this creature?"

"There is no physical proof of the development of any dinosaur—for all we know to the contrary, the brontosaur and tyrannosaur may have popped *out* of existence overnight . . . But a few remains of a late development of reptile-man have been found. You have heard of Neanderthal Man, I presume?"

"Certainly. You aren't going to tell me that Neanderthal Man was a development from a dinosaur!"

"He evolved from the same original stock as the dinosaurs. He was probably always few in number, but he helped kill off the big dinosaurs. The popular folk idea that men were about when the dinosaurs lived is nothing less than the truth—perhaps it's a sort of folk memory."

"Can I put the light on? It's getting dark in here. But you say the line died out?"

"I didn't say that. The so-called Neanderthal is popularly said to have died out. There's no evidence, though. The Neanderthal reptile-men merged with humanity—mammal-humanity, and we have never been able to sort them out since."

She stood by the door, hand on the light-switch, again thinking of flight. When the overhead light came on, it made the images of the three marine creatures on the screen appear faint and spectral, more suited to move through air than water.

"Father, my headache has come back. May I go upstairs and lie down in my room to think about what you have told me?"

He moved a little nearer to her.

"Do you believe what I have told you? Do you understand? Are you capable of understanding?"

"How is it that modern medicine has not tracked down these reptile-men if they still exist, by blood-analysis or something?"

"It has. But it has misinterpreted the evidence. I won't go into the whole complex question of blood-grouping. Another problem is that rep-tile-men and human stock now inter-breed. The lines are confused. There is reason to think that venereal disease is the product of in-terbreeding—another intravenous way in which the two species seek to destroy each other. Do you want some aspirins?"

"I have some eau-de-cologne in my case in the car. May I go and get it?"

"You go upstairs. I'll get your case for you."

Hesitating, she looked at him. Not liking what she saw, she moved reluctantly and walked along the hall corridor, turned right, and went up the stairs under the eye of Camera Three, holding to the bannisters as she went. She paused again on the landing. Reptile-men! Then she went ahead into the bedroom, glanced hopelessly up at "Faithful Unto Death," sullen in the twilight, and lay down. She could have locked her-self in but what was the point? In his madness, her father would break the door down whenever he felt like it. Perhaps he would come up and kill her; perhaps he imagined she was of reptilian stock.

She played with that idea, imagining the strange and aberrant al-legiances it might give her with gloomy green unflowering plants, with damp stones, with immense shapes that moved only when prompted by the sun, and with languid spans of time which could find no true lodge-ment within the consciousness of man. The idea of being cold-blooded alone made her tremble where she lay, and clutch at the blankets for warmth.

There was a dull light in the room, gloomy, green, and unflowering. Another plane blundered over, shaking the house.

Downstairs, he heard and felt the plane go over. He raised his heavy eyes up towards its path, imagining it furry and coleopterous while the room vibrated, saying to it, "One day, you too will lie broken and stoney in a shattered layer of sandstone."

He stood before the big screen, Camera One trained on him, throwing his image over his body. Eyes, mouth, head, limbs, vibrated, became double and detached, then settled back as the noise died.

A memory came back to him from far away that he had said he would go and get Anna's case from her car.

Moving with lethargy, he crossed to the console and set Camera One moving until it was trained through the living room door to the dining room door. This was the nearest he could get to covering the back door; some day, he must install a tenth camera in the passage, so that the back door was surveyed. All he could see on the screen now was the ugly concatenation of angles formed by the two doors between them. He walked out into the passage and headed down it, to the door with two glass panels in its frame which he always kept locked. He unlocked it, opened it, went out.

To his right stretched the length of the back of the house. At right angles to it, another wall stood along the left, punctuated by scullery and pantry windows. An uneven path flanked this walk. He moved slowly along it. There had been flagstones of good York stone underfoot, but weeds and grass had covered them. Blank eyes of scullery and pantry surveyed him.

The light was leaden now. Time and twilight were congealed and fixed like a murdered eye. Like something viewed in a long mirror, he was embedded far in the past, together with gymnosperms, woodlice, the first ungainly amphibians and things still unidentified by the peeping gaze of man.

When he turned left round by the corner of the woodshed, Macguire was only a few feet away from the sterile green wire fence. He knew a lot of things about the color green; it, more than any color, was involved in the guilty story of downfall.

He turned left again, pushing aside overgrown branches of elder. They still flowered, individual florets looming up before his eyes like galaxies in some dim-lit and cluttered universe. Now he was stalking along the south-west side of the house. The weeds of high summer crushed and sprang under his footfall.

There was her car, low under the overhanging branches of trees. Every year, the beeches grew nearer and nearer to the house. Some of them already nuzzled their first tender branches against the brick.

He stood glaring through the windows at the seats within, awaiting people. It was shabby and vacant in there, another unwelcoming human environment, depopulated. On the back seat lay a small case. Macguire pulled open the rear door, grasped the handle of the case, and dragged it out. He stood with it where he was, his other hand touching the car, staring at his daughter. Anna had come round the front of the house; she held his carbine in an efficient way, and was pointing it at his stomach. He looked at her face and saw it too belonged with the lost gymnosperms, woodlice, and amphibians hidden long ago behind the pantry, engendering only extinction.

"You can go if you don't shoot me, Anna. I'm the only one with the theory complete, although there are people everywhere piecing it together. It's a matter of time . . . It's not a race. I mean, there's no excitement—it's too late now for man to beat the reptile-men; they've had too long and they are virtually in control. Look at the light under these trees—if you understand such things, the light alone will tell you we're defeated. So there's no point in shooting."

"I'm going to shoot." The words came from her mouth. He watched the diagram of it, thinking how easy it was to understand human speech once you had the basic knowledge of the working anatomy of jaw and thorax and the formation of phonemes in the larynx by careful control of air, and how those sounds were carried into the listening labyrinths of those present. His daughter had the science of the whole thing off perfectly.

"I could show you yards of tapex—proof. Proof of all I say. I'm the only one who has studied a human being long enough. I've seen myself, caught myself off guard. I have to regard myself as heteromorphic. The reptile moves in my veins, too."

"Move away from the car."

He said, feeling the stiff discomfort of fear contort his lips and teeth and tongue, "Anna, this isn't the time of day . . . Just when I'm getting control of reality . . . Look, you're alien too. It's strong in you. Believe me. That's why you're so hostile. You're more lizard than I. Let me go! I won't hurt you! Let me show you!"

The gun-point lowered slightly. A moth blundered through the space between their two ghastly faces and fell under the trees.

"What do you mean?"

"I got it on tapex. You can come in and see for yourself. Camera Number Eight. It's betrayed in certain movements. Unhuman movements. The gesture of the hand, the way a knee hinges, spinal tension, hip flexibility, a dozen details of facial expression. Oh, I've observed them all in myself. One hundred and thirty-one differences docketed. Throughout life, human beings are motivated to watch others and not themselves, right from early years when they begin to learn by imitation. I realized years ago I was not fully human. With age, you become less human, the antique lizard shows through more and more—after all, it's the basic stock. That's why old people turn against human pleasures. Now, in your case, you've never had much time for human pleasures—"

"Father—"

Afterwards, she wondered if he had begun to fall before she fired. The first shot curved the top half of his body forward. She fired again. This time he jerked backwards, still standing, so that she saw how long and dark and lined his throat was. His mouth opened a little. She had a thought that he was looking down his nose and laughing at her, totally unharmed. She fired a third bullet, but was already trembling so violently that it missed.

An airbus came sizzling over the property so low that she fired again in sheer panic. The bullet whistled into the leaves of the trees, and still her father stood there, rocking a little, hands like claws digging into his belly. Then he fell over backwards, legs straight. When he hit the ground, the force of the fall caused his arms to spring out sideways. He lay there among the mid-summer weeds in that attitude of unknowing, and never moved again. The beeches dripped on him, the erosions of his last July.

His hair was quite wet before Anna managed to move again.

She dropped the gun, then had the presence of mind to fumble it up again and toss it into the car. She picked up the little case and tossed that into the car. She stood over the body.

"Father?" she asked it.

It continued to make its gesture of unknowing.

Fighting her palsy, she climbed into the driving seat of the car. After several attempts, she got the motor going and managed to back away to the front of the house. She gave a last look into that deep grey-green past under the beeches where time had ceased, and drove toward the front gates.

As she passed through them, bumping on to the cul-de-sac road, she experienced a flash of memory. She thought of the electricity still burning, the camera still processing the spirit of the empty house, the big screen still registering daylight dying between an ugly angle of doors, the inhuman sequence of mounting time slithering into tapex.

But she did not pause, certainly did not turn back. Instead, she pressed her foot more firmly to the accelerator, flicked on the side-lights, hunched herself over the wheel to control her shaking, forged ahead towards the tangle of tiny roads between her and Ashmansford.

She stared ahead. The shaggy elms outside the car, blue with advancing night, were reflected momentarily in her eyeballs. Overhead, another plane roared, its landing lights blazing, coming in to roost.

All at One Point

ﾟ⸱ᷧᷠᷣ

ITALO CALVINO

Through the calculations begun by Edwin P. Hubble on the galaxies' velocity of recession, we can establish the moment when all the universe's matter was concentrated in a single point, before it began to expand in space.

Naturally, we were all there—*old Qfwfq said*—where else could we have been? Nobody knew then that there could be space. Or time either: what use did we have for time, packed in there like sardines?

I say "packed like sardines," using a literary image: in reality there wasn't even space to pack us into. Every point of each of us coincided with every point of each of the others in a single point, which was where we all were. In fact, we didn't even bother one another, except for personality differences, because when space doesn't exist, having somebody unpleasant like Mr. Pber^t Pber^d underfoot all the time is the most irritating thing.

How many of us were there? Oh, I was never able to figure that out, not even approximately. To make a count, we would have had to move apart, at least a little, and instead we all occupied that same point. Contrary to what you might think, it wasn't the sort of situation that encourages sociability; I know, for example, that in other periods neighbors called on one another; but there, because of the fact that we were all neighbors, nobody even said good morning or good evening to anybody else.

In the end each of us associated only with a limited number of acquaintances. The ones I remember most are Mrs. Ph(i)Nk$_0$, her friend

De XuaeauX, a family of immigrants by the name of Z'zu, and Mr. Pber^t Pber^d, whom I just mentioned. There was also a cleaning woman— "maintenance staff" she was called—only one, for the whole universe, since there was so little room. To tell the truth, she had nothing to do all day long, not even dusting—inside one point not even a grain of dust can enter—so she spent all her time gossiping and complaining.

Just with the people I've already named we would have been overcrowded; but you have to add all the stuff we had to keep piled up in there: all the material that was to serve afterwards to form the universe, now dismantled and concentrated in such a way that you weren't able to tell what was later to become part of astronomy (like the nebula of Andromeda) from what was assigned to geography (the Vosges, for example) or to chemistry (like certain beryllium isotopes). And on top of that, we were always bumping against the Z'zu family's household goods; camp beds, mattresses, baskets; these Z'zus, if you weren't careful, with the excuse that they were a large family, would begin to act if they were the only ones in the world: they even wanted to hang lines across our point to dry their washing.

But the others also had wronged the Z'zus, to begin with, by calling them "immigrants," on the pretext that, since the others had been there first, the Z'zus had come later. This was mere unfounded prejudice— that seems obvious to me—because neither before nor after existed, nor any place to immigrate from, but there were those who insisted that the concept of "immigrant" could be understood in the abstract, outside of space and time.

It was what you might call a narrow-minded attitude, our outlook at that time, very petty. The fault of the environment in which we had been reared. An attitude that, basically, has remained in all of us, mind you: it keeps cropping up even today, if two of us happen to meet—at the bus stop, in a movie house, at an international dentists' convention—and start reminiscing about the old days. We say hello—at times somebody recognizes me, at other times I recognize somebody—and we promptly start asking about this one and that one (even if each remembers only a few of those remembered by the others), and so we start in again on the old disputes, the slanders, the denigrations. Until somebody mentions Mrs. Ph(i)Nk$_o$—every conversation finally gets around to her—and then, all of a sudden, the pettiness is put aside, and we feel uplifted, filled with a blissful, generous emotion. Mrs. Ph(i)Nk$_o$, the only one that none of us has forgotten and that we all regret. Where has she ended up? I have long since stopped looking for her: Mrs. Ph(i)Nk$_o$, her bosom, her thighs, her orange dressing gown—we'll never meet her again, in this system of galaxies or in any other.

Let me make one thing clear: this theory that the universe, after having reached an extremity of rarefaction, will be condensed again has never convinced me. And yet many of us are counting only on that, continually making plans for the time when we'll all be back there again. Last month, I went into the bar here on the corner and whom did I see? Mr. Pber^t Pber^d. "What's new with you? How do you happen to be in this neighborhood?" I learned that he's the agent for a plastics firm, in Pavia. He's the same as ever, with his silver tooth, his loud suspenders. "When we go back there," he said to me, in a whisper, "the thing we have to make sure of is, this time, certain people remain out . . . You know who I mean: those Z'zus . . ."

I would have liked to answer him by saying that I've heard a number of people make the same remark, concluding: "You know who I mean . . . Mr. Pber^t Pber^d . . ."

To avoid the subject, I hastened to say: "What about Mrs. Ph(i)Nk$_0$? Do you think we'll find her back there again?"

"Ah, yes . . . She, by all means . . ." he said, turning purple.

For all of us the hope of returning to that point means, above all, the hope of being once more with Mrs. Ph(i)Nk$_0$. (This applies even to me, though I don't believe in it.) And in that bar, as always happens, we fell to talking about her, and were moved; even Mr. Pber^t Pber^d's unpleasantness faded, in the face of that memory.

Mrs. Ph(i)Nk$_0$'s great secret is that she never aroused any jealousy among us. Or any gossip, either. The fact that she went to bed with her friend, Mr. De XuaeauX, was well known. But in a point, if there's a bed, it takes up the whole point, so it isn't a question of *going* to bed, but of *being* there, because anybody in the point is also in the bed. Consequently, it was inevitable that she should be in bed also with each of us. If she had been another person, there's no telling all the things that would have been said about her. It was the cleaning woman who always started the slander, and the others didn't have to be coaxed to imitate her. On the subject of the Z'zu family—for a change!—the horrible things we had to hear: father, daughters, brothers, sisters, mother, aunts: nobody showed any hesitation even before the most sinister insinuation. But with her it was different: the happiness I derived from her was the joy of being concealed, punctiform, in her, and of protecting her, punctiform, in me; it was at the same time vicious contemplation (thanks to the promiscuity of the punctiform convergence of us all in her) and also chastity (given her punctiform impenetrability). In short: what more could I ask?

And all of this, which was true of me, was true also for each of the others. And for her: she contained and was contained with equal happiness, and she welcomed us and loved and inhabited all equally.

We got along so well all together, so well that something extraordinary was bound to happen. It was enough for her to say, at a certain moment: "Oh, if I only had some room, how I'd like to make some noodles for you boys!" And in that moment we all thought of the space that her round arms would occupy, moving backward and forward with the rolling pin over the dough, her bosom leaning over the great mound of flour and eggs which cluttered the wide board while her arms kneaded and kneaded, white and shiny with oil up to the elbows; we thought of the space that the flour would occupy, and the wheat for the flour, and the fields to raise the wheat, and the mountains from which the water would flow to irrigate the fields, and the grazing lands for the herds of calves that would give their meat for the sauce; of the space it would take for the Sun to arrive with its rays, to ripen the wheat; of the space for the Sun to condense from the clouds of stellar gases and burn; of the quantities of stars and galaxies and galactic masses in flight through space which would be needed to hold suspended every galaxy, every nebula, every sun, every planet, and at the same time we thought of it, this space was inevitably being formed, at the same time that Mrs. Ph(i)Nk$_0$ was uttering those words: ". . . ah, what noodles, boys!" the point that contained her and all of us was expanding in a halo of distance in light-years and light-centuries and billions of light-millennia, and we were being hurled to the four corners of the universe (Mr. Pber^t Pebr^d all the way to Pavia), and she, dissolved into I don't know what kind of energy-light-heat, she, Mrs. Ph(i)Nk$_0$, she who in the midst of our closed, petty world had been capable of a generous impulse, "Boys, the noodles I would make for you!," a true outburst of general love, initiating at the same moment the concept of space and, properly speaking, space itself, and time, and universal gravitation, and the gravitating universe, making possible billions and billions of suns, and of planets, and fields of wheat, and Mrs. Ph(i)Nk$_0$s, scattered through the continents of the planets, kneading with floury, oil-shiny, generous arms, and she lost at that very moment, and we, mourning her loss.

The Waiting Place

༄༅

SARAH ORNE JEWETT

It was a long time after this; an hour was very long in that coast town where nothing stole away the shortest minute. I had lost myself completely in work, when I heard footsteps outside. There was a steep footpath between the upper and the lower road, which I climbed to shorten the way, as the children had taught me, but I believed that Mrs. Todd would find it inaccessible, unless she had occasion to seek me in great haste. I wrote on, feeling like a besieged miser of time, while the footsteps came nearer, and the sheep-bell tinkled away in haste as if some one had shaken a stick in its wearer's face. Then I looked, and saw Captain Littlepage passing the nearest window; the next moment he tapped politely at the door.

"Come in, sir," I said, rising to meet him; and he entered, bowing with much courtesy. I stepped down from the desk and offered him a chair by the window, where he seated himself at once, being sadly spent by his climb. I returned to my fixed seat behind the teacher's desk, which gave him the lower place of a scholar.

"You ought to have the place of honor, Captain Littlepage," I said.

"A happy, rural seat of various views,"

he quoted, as he gazed out into the sunshine and up the long wooded shore. Then he glanced at me, and looked all about him as pleased as a child.

"My quotation was from Paradise Lost: the greatest of poems, I suppose

64

you know?" and I nodded. "There's nothing that ranks, to my mind, with Paradise Lost; it's all lofty, all lofty," he continued. "Shakespeare was a great poet; he copied life, but you have to put up with a great deal of low talk."

I now remembered that Mrs. Todd had told me one day that Captain Littlepage had overset his mind with too much reading; she had also made dark reference to his having "spells" of some unexplainable nature. I could not help wondering what errand had brought him out in search of me. There was something quite charming in his appearance: it was a face thin and delicate with refinement, but worn into appealing lines, as if he had suffered from loneliness and misapprehension. He looked, with his careful precision of dress, as if he were the object of cherishing care on the part of elderly unmarried sisters, but I knew Mari' Harris to be a very commonplace, inelegant person, who would have no such standards; it was plain that the captain was his own attentive valet. He sat looking at me expectantly. I could not help thinking that, with his queer head and length of thinness, he was made to hop along the road of life rather than to walk. The captain was very grave indeed, and I bade my inward spirit keep close to discretion.

"Poor Mrs. Begg has gone," I ventured to say. I still wore my Sunday gown by way of showing respect.

"She has gone," said the captain,—"very easy at the last, I was informed; she slipped away as if she were glad of the opportunity."

I thought of the Countess of Carberry and felt that history repeated itself.

"She was one of the old stock," continued Captain Littlepage, with touching sincerity. "She was very much looked up to in this town, and will be missed."

I wondered, as I looked at him, if he had sprung from a line of ministers; he had the refinement of look and air of command which are the heritage of the old ecclesiastical families of New England. But as Darwin says in his autobiography, "there is no such king as a sea-captain; he is greater even than a king or a schoolmaster!"

Captain Littlepage moved his chair out of the wake of the sunshine, and still sat looking at me. I began to be very eager to know upon what errand he had come.

"It may be found out some o' these days," he said earnestly. "We may know it all, the next step; where Mrs. Begg is now, for instance. Certainty, not conjecture, is what we all desire."

"I suppose we shall know it all someday," said I.

"We shall know it while yet below," insisted the captain, with a flush of impatience on his thin cheeks. "We have not looked for truth in the right direction. I know what I speak of; those who have laughed at me little know how much reason my ideas are based upon." He waved his hand toward the village below. "In that handful of houses they fancy that they comprehend the universe."

I smiled, and waited for him to go on.

"I am an old man, as you can see," he continued, "and I have been a shipmaster the greater part of my life,—forty-three years in all. You may not think it, but I am above eighty years of age."

He did not look so old, and I hastened to say so.

"You must have left the sea a good many years ago, then, Captain Littlepage?" I said.

"I should have been serviceable at least five or six years more," he answered. "My acquaintance with certain—my experience upon a certain occasion, I might say, gave rise to prejudice. I do not mind telling you that I chanced to learn of one of the greatest discoveries that man has ever made."

Now we were approaching dangerous ground, but a sudden sense of his sufferings at the hands of the ignorant came to my help and I asked to hear more with all the deference I really felt. A swallow flew into the schoolhouse at this moment as if a kingbird were after it, and beat itself against the walls for a minute, and escaped again to the open air; but Captain Littlepage took no notice whatever of the flurry.

"I had a valuable cargo of general merchandise from the London docks to Fort Churchill, a station of the old company on Hudson's Bay," said the captain earnestly. "We were delayed in lading, and baffled by head winds and a heavy tumbling sea all the way north-about and across. Then the fog kept us off the coast; and when I made port at last, it was too late to delay in those northern waters with such a vessel and such a crew as I had. They cared for nothing, and idled me into a fit of sickness; but my first mate was a good, excellent man, with no more idea of being frozen in there until spring than I had, so we made what speed we could to get clear of Hudson's Bay and off the coast. I owned an eighth of the vessel, and he owned a sixteenth of her. She was a full-rigged ship, called the Minerva, but she was getting old and leaky. I meant it should be my last v'y'ge in her, and so it proved. She had been an excellent vessel in her day. Of the cowards aboard her I can't say so much."

"Then you were wrecked?" I asked, as he made a long pause.

"I wa'n't caught astern o' the lighter by any fault of mine," said the captain gloomily. "We left Fort Churchill and run out into the Bay with a light pair o' heels; but I had been vexed to death with their red-tape rigging at the company's office, and chilled with stayin' on deck an' tryin' to hurry up things, and when we were well out o' sight o' land, headin' for Hudson's Straits, I had a bad turn o' some sort o' fever, and had to stay below. The days were getting short, and we made good runs, all well on board but me, and the crew done their work by dint of hard driving."

I began to find this unexpected narrative a little dull. Captain Littlepage spoke with a kind of slow correctness that lacked the longshore high flavor to which I had grown used; but I listened respectfully while he explained the winds having become contrary, and talked on in a dreary sort of way about his voyage, the bad weather, and the disadvantages he was under in the lightness of his ship, which bounced about like a chip in a bucket, and would not answer the rudder or properly respond to the most careful setting of sails.

"So there we were blowin' along anyways," he complained; but looking at me at this moment, and seeing that my thoughts were unkindly wandering, he ceased to speak.

"It was a hard life at sea in those days, I am sure," said I, with redoubled interest.

"It was a dog's life," said the poor old gentleman, quite reassured, "but it made men of those who followed it. I see a change for the worse even in our own town here; full of loafers now, small and poor as 't is, who once would have followed the sea, every lazy soul of 'em. There is no occupation so fit for just that class o' men who never get beyond the fo'cas'le. I view it, in addition, that a community narrows down and grows dreadful ignorant when it is shut up to its own affairs, and gets no knowledge of the outside world except from a cheap, unprincipled newspaper. In the old days, a good part o' the best men here knew a hundred ports and something of the way folks lived in them. They saw the world for themselves, and like's not their wives and children saw it with them. They may not have had the best of knowledge to carry with 'em sightseein', but they were some acquainted with foreign lands an' their laws, an' could see outside the battle for town clerk here in Dunnet; they got some sense o' proportion. Yes, they lived more dignified, and their houses were better within an' without. Shipping's a terrible loss to this part o' New England from a social point o' view, ma'am."

"I have thought of that myself," I returned, with my interest quite awakened. "It accounts for the change in a great many things,—the sad disappearance of sea-captains,—doesn't it?"

"A shipmaster was apt to get the habit of reading," said my companion, brightening still more, and taking on a most touching air of unreserve. "A captain is not expected to be familiar with his crew, and for company's sake in dull days and nights he turns to his book. Most of us old shipmasters came to know 'most everthing about something; one would take to readin' on farming topics, and some were great on medicine,—but Lord help their poor crews!—or some were all for history, and now and then there'd be one like me that gave his time to the poets. I was well acquainted with a shipmaster that was all for bees an' bee-keepin'; and if you met him in port and went aboard, he'd sit and talk a terrible while about their havin' so much information, and the money that could be made out of keepin' 'em. He was one of the smartest captains that ever sailed the seas, but they used to call the Newcastel, a great bark he commanded for many years, Tuttle's beehive. There was old Cap'n Jameson: he had notions of Solomon's Temple, and made a very handsome little model of the same, right from the Scripture measurements, same's other sailors make little ships and design new tricks of rigging and all that. No, there's nothing to take the place of shipping in a place like ours. These bicycles offend me dreadfully; they don't afford no real opportunities of experience such as a man gained on a voyage. No: when folks left home in the old days they left it to some purpose, and when they got home they stayed there and had some pride in it. There's no large-minded way of thinking now: the worst have got to be best and rule everything; we're all turned upside down and going back year by year."

"Oh, no, Captain Littlepage, I hope not," said I, trying to soothe his feelings.

There was a silence in the schoolhouse, but we could hear the noise of the water on a beach below. It sounded like the strange warning wave that gives notice of the turn of the tide. A late golden robin, with the most joyful and eager of voices, was singing close by in a thicket of wild roses.

"How did you manage with the rest of that rough voyage on the Minerva?" I asked.

"I shall be glad to explain to you," said Captain Littlepage, forgetting his grievances for the moment. "If I had a map at hand I could explain better. We were driven to and fro 'way up toward what we used to call Parry's Discoveries, and lost our bearings. It was thick and foggy, and at last I lost my ship; she drove on a rock, and we managed to get ashore on what I took to be a barren island, the few of us that were left alive. When she first struck, the sea was somewhat calmer than it had been, and most of the crew, against orders, manned the long-boat and put off in a hurry, and were never heard of more. Our own boat upset, but the carpenter kept himself and me above water, and we drifted in. I had no strength to call upon after my recent fever, and laid down to die; but he found the tracks of a man and dog the second day, and got along the shore to one of those far missionary stations that the Moravians support. They were very poor themselves, and in distress; 't was a useless place. There were but few Esquimaux left in that region. There we remained for some time, and I became acquainted with strange events."

The captain lifted his head and gave me a questioning glance. I could not help noticing that the dulled look in his eyes had gone, and there was instead a clear intentness that made them seem dark and piercing.

"There was a supply ship expected, and the pastor, an excellent Christian man, made no doubt that we should get passage in her. He was hoping that orders would come to break up the station; but everything was uncertain, and we got on the best we could for a while. We fished, and helped the people in other ways; there was no other way of paying our debts. I was taken to the pastor's house until I got better; but they were crowded, and I felt myself in the way, and made excuse to join with an old seaman, a Scotchman, who had built him a warm cabin, and had room in it for another. He was looked upon with regard, and had stood by the pastor in some troubles with the people. He had been on one of those English exploring parties that found one end of the road to the north pole, but never could find the other. We lived like dogs in a kennel, or so you'd thought if you had seen the hut from the outside; but the main thing was to keep warm; there were piles of birdskins to lie on, and he'd made him a good bunk, and there was another for me. 'T was dreadful dreary waitin' there; we begun to think the supply steamer was lost, and my poor ship broke up and strewed herself all along the shore. We got to watching on the headlands; my men and me knew the people were short of supplies and had to pinch themselves. It ought to read in the Bible, 'Man cannot live by fish alone,' if they'd told the truth of things; 'tain't bread that wears the worst on you! First part of the time, old Gaffett, that I lived with, seemed speechless, and I didn't know what to make of him, nor he of me, I dare say; but as we got acquainted, I found he'd been through more disasters than I had, and had troubles that wa'n't going to let him live a great while. It used to ease his mind to talk to an understanding person, so we used to sit and talk together all day, if it rained or blew so that we couldn't get out. I'd got a bad blow on the back of my head at the time we came ashore, and it pained me at times, and my strength was broken, anyway; I've never been so able since."

Captain Littlepage fell into a reverie.

"Then I had the good of my reading," he explained presently. "I had no books; the pastor spoke but little English, and all his books were foreign; but I used to say over all I could remember. The old poets little knew what comfort they could be to a man. I was well acquainted with the works of Milton, but up there it did seem to me as if Shakespeare was the king; he has his sea terms very accurate, and some beautiful passages were calming to the mind. I could say them over until I shed tears; there was nothing beautiful to me in that place but the stars above and those passages of verse.

"Gaffett was always brooding and brooding, and talking to himself; he was afraid he should never get away, and it preyed upon his mind. He thought when I got home I could interest the scientific men in his discovery: but they're all taken up with their own notions; some didn't even take pains to answer the letters I wrote. You observe that I said this crippled man Gaffett had been shipped on a voyage of discovery. I now tell you that the ship was lost on its return, and only Gaffett and two officers were saved off the Greenland coast, and he had knowledge later that those men never got back to England; the brig they shipped on was run down in the night. So no other living soul had the facts, and he gave them to me. There is a strange sort of a country 'way up north beyond the ice, and strange folks living in it. Gaffett believed it was the next world to this."

"What do you mean, Captain Littlepage?" I exclaimed. The old man was bending forward and whispering; he looked over his shoulder before he spoke the last sentence.

"To hear old Gaffett tell about it was something awful," he said, going on with his story quite steadily after the moment of excitement had passed. " 'T was first a tale of dogs and sledges, and cold and wind and snow. Then they begun to find the ice grow rotten; they had been frozen in, and got into a current flowing north, far up beyond Fox Channel, and they took to their boats when the ship got crushed, and this warm current took them out of sight of the ice, and into a great open sea; and they still followed it due north, just the very way they had planned to go. Then they struck a coast that wasn't laid down or charted, but the cliffs were such that no boat could land until they found a bay and struck across under sail to the other side where the shore looked lower; they were scant of provisions and out of water, but they got sight of something that looked like a great town. 'For God's sake, Gaffett!' said I, the first time he told me. 'You don't mean a town two degrees farther north than ships had ever been?' for he'd got their course marked on an old chart that he'd pieced out at the top; but he insisted upon it, and told it over and over again, to be sure I had it straight to carry to those who would be interested. There was no snow and ice, he said, after they had sailed some days with that warm current, which seemed to come right from under the ice that they'd been pinched up in and had been crossing on foot for weeks."

"But what about the town?" I asked. "Did they get to the town?"

"They did," said the captain, "and found inhabitants; 't was an awful condition of things. It appeared, as near as Gaffett could express it, like a place where there was neither living nor dead. They could see the place when they were approaching it by sea pretty near like any town, and thick with habitations; but all at once they lost sight of it altogether, and when they got close inshore they could see the shapes of folks, but they never could get near them,—all blowing gray figures that would pass along alone, or sometimes gathered in companies as if they were watching. The men were frightened at first, but the shapes never came near them,—it was as if they blew back; and at last they all got bold and went ashore, and found birds' eggs and sea fowl, like any wild northern spot where creatures were tame and folks had never been, and there was good water. Gaffett said that he and another man came near one o' the fog-shaped men that was going along slow with the look of a pack on his back, among the rocks, an' they chased him; but, Lord! he flitted away out o' sight like a leaf the wind takes with it, or a piece of cobweb. They would make as if they talked together, but there was no sound of voices, and 'they acted as if they didn't see us, but only felt us coming towards them,' says Gaffett one day, trying to tell the particulars. They couldn't see the town when they were ashore. One day the captain and the doctor were gone till night up across the high land where the town had seemed to be, and they came back at night beat out and white as ashes, and wrote and wrote all next day in their notebooks, and whispered together full of excitement, and they were sharp-spoken with the men when they offered to ask any questions.

"Then there came a day," said Captain Littlepage, leaning toward me with a strange look in his eyes, and whispering quickly. "The men all swore they wouldn't stay any longer; the man on watch early in the morning gave the alarm, and they all put off in the boat and got a little way out to sea. Those folks, or whatever they were, come about 'em like bats; all at once they raised incessant armies, and come as if to drive 'em back to sea. They stood thick at the edge o' the water like the ridges o' grim war; no thought o' flight, none of retreat. Sometimes a standing fight, then soaring on main wing tormented all the air. And when they'd got the boat out o' reach o' danger, Gaffett said they looked back, and there was the town again, standing up just as they'd seen it first, comin' on the coast. Say what you might, they all believed 't was a kind of waiting-place between this world an' the next."

The captain had sprung to his feet in his excitement, and made excited gestures, but he still whispered huskily.

"Sit down, sir," I said as quietly as I could, and he sank into his chair quite spent.

"Gaffett thought the officers were hurrying home to report and to fit out a new expedition when they were all lost. At the time, the men got orders not to talk over what they had seen," the old man explained presently in a more natural tone.

"Weren't they all starving, and wasn't it a mirage or something of that sort?" I ventured to ask. But he looked at me blankly.

"Gaffett had got so that his mind ran on nothing else," he went on. "The ship's surgeon let fall an opinion to the captain, one day, that 't was some o' the light and the magnetic currents that let them see those folks. 'T wa'n't a right-feeling part of the world, anyway; they had to battle with the compass to make it serve, an' everything seemed to go wrong. Gaffett had worked it out in his own mind that they was all common ghosts, but the conditions were unusual favorable for seeing them. He was always talking about the Ge'graphical Society, but he never took proper steps, as I view it now, and stayed right there at the mission. He was a good deal crippled, and thought they'd confine him in some jail of a hospital. He said he was waiting to find the right men to tell, somebody bound north. Once in a while they stopped there to leave a mail or something. He was set in his notions, and let two or three proper explorin' expeditions go by him because he didn't like their looks; but when I was there he had got restless, fearin' he might be taken away or something. He had all his directions written out straight as a string to give the right ones. I wanted him to trust 'em to me, so I might have something to show, but he wouldn't. I suppose he's dead now. I wrote to him, an' I done all I could. 'T will be a great exploit some o' these days."

I assented absent-mindedly, thinking more just then of my companion's alert, determined look and the seafaring, ready aspect that had come to his face; but at this moment there fell a sudden change, and the old, pathetic, scholarly look returned. Behind me hung a map of North America, and I saw, as I turned a little, that his eyes, were fixed upon the northernmost region and their careful recent outlines with a look of bewilderment.

Sketches among the Ruins of My Mind

༺࿇༻

PHILIP JOSÉ FARMER

1

June 1, 1980

It is now 11:00 P.M., and I am afraid to go to bed. I am not alone. The whole world is afraid of sleep.

This morning I got up at 6:30 A.M., as I do every Wednesday. While I shaved and showered, I considered the case of the state of Illinois against Joseph Lankers, accused of murder. It was beginning to stink as if it were a three-day-old fish. My star witness would undoubtedly be charged with perjury.

I dressed, went downstairs, and kissed Carole good morning. She poured me a cup of coffee and said, "The paper's late."

That put me in a bad temper. I need both coffee and the morning newspaper to get me started.

Twice during breakfast, I left the table to look outside. Neither paper nor newsboy had appeared.

At seven, Carole went upstairs to wake up Mike and Tom, aged ten and eight respectively. Saturdays and Sundays they rise early even though I'd like them to stay in bed so their horsing around won't wake me. School days they have to be dragged out.

The third time I looked out of the door, Joe Gale, the paperboy, was next door. My paper lay on the stoop.

I felt disorientated, as if I'd walked into the wrong courtroom or the judge had given my client, a shoplifter, a life sentence. I was out of phase

74

with the world. This couldn't be Sunday. So what was the Sunday issue, bright in its covering of the colored comic section, doing there? Today was Wednesday.

I stepped out to pick it up and saw old Mrs. Douglas, my neighbor to the left. She was looking at the front page of her paper as if she could not believe it.

The world rearranged itself into the correct lines of polarization. My thin panic dwindled into nothing. I thought, the *Star* has really goofed this time. That's what comes from depending so much on a computer to put it together. One little short circuit, and Wednesday's paper comes out in Sunday's format.

The *Star's* night shift must have decided to let it go through; it was too late for them to rectify the error.

I said, "Good morning, Mrs. Douglas! Tell me, what day is it?"

"The twenty-eighth of May," she said. "I think . . ."

I walked out into the yard and shouted after Joe. Reluctantly, he wheeled his bike around.

"What is this?" I said, shaking the paper at him. "Did the *Star* screw up?"

"I don't know, Mr. Franham," he said. "None of us knows, honest to God."

By "us" he must have meant the other boys he met in the morning at the paper drop.

"We all thought it was Wednesday. That's why I'm late. We couldn't understand what was happening, so we talked a long time and then Bill Ambers called the office. Gates, he's the circulation manager, was just as bongo as we was."

"Were," I said.

"What?" he said.

"We *were*, not *was*, just as bongo, whatever that means," I said.

"For God's sake, Mr. Franham, who cares!" he said.

"Some of us still do," I said. "All right, what did Gates say?"

"He was upset as hell," Joe said. "He said heads were gonna roll. The night staff had fallen asleep for a couple of hours, and some joker had diddled up the computers, or . . ."

"That's all it is?" I said. I felt relieved.

When I went inside, I got out the papers for the last four days from the cycler. I sat down on the sofa and scanned them.

I didn't remember reading them. I didn't remember the past four days at all!

Wednesday's headline was: MYSTERIOUS OBJECT ORBITS EARTH.

I did remember Tuesday's articles, which stated that the big round object was heading for a point between the Earth and the moon. It had been detected three weeks ago when it was passing through the so-called asteroid belt. It was at that time traveling approximately 57,000 kilometers per hour, relative to the sun. Then it had slowed down, had changed course several times, and it became obvious that, unless it changed course again, it was going to come near Earth.

By the time it was eleven million miles away, the radars had defined its size and shape, though not its material composition. It was perfectly spherical and exactly half a kilometer in diameter. It did not reflect much light. Since it had altered its path so often, it had to be artificial. Strange hands, or strange somethings, had built it.

I remembered the panic and the many wild articles in the papers and magazines and the TV specials made overnight to discuss its implications.

It had failed to make any response whatever to the radio and laser signals sent from Earth. Many scientists said that it probably contained no living passengers. It had to be of interstellar origin. The sentient beings of some planet circling some star had sent it out equipped with automatic equipment of some sort. No being could live long enough to travel between the stars. It would take over four years to get from the nearest star to Earth even if the object could travel at the speed of light, and that was impossible. Even one-sixteenth the speed of light seemed incredible because of the vast energy requirements. No, this thing had been launched with only electromechanical devices as passengers, had attained its top speed, turned off its power, and coasted until it came within the outer reaches of our solar system.

According to the experts, it must be unable to land on Earth because of its size and weight. It was probably just a surveying vessel, and after it had taken some photographs and made some radar/laser sweeps, it would proceed to wherever it was supposed to go, probably back to an orbit around its home planet.

2

Last Wednesday night, the president had told us that we had nothing to fear. And he'd tried to end on an optimistic note. At least, that's what Wednesday's paper said. The beings who had sent The Ball must be more advanced than we, and they must have many good things to give us. And we might be able to make beneficial contributions to them. Like what? I thought.

Some photographs of The Ball, taken from one of the manned orbiting laboratories, were on the second page. It looked just like a giant black billiard ball. One TV comic had suggested that the other side might bear a big white 8. I may have thought that this was funny last Wednesday, but I didn't think so now. It seemed highly probable to me that The Ball was connected with the four-days' loss of memory. How, I had no idea.

I turned on the 7:30 news channels, but they weren't much help except in telling us that the same thing had happened to everybody all over the world. Even those in the deepest diamond mines or submarines had been affected. The president was in conference, but he'd be making a statement over the networks sometime today. Meantime, it was known that no radiation of any sort had been detected emanating from The Ball. There was no evidence whatsoever that the object had caused the loss of memory. Or, as the jargon-crazy casters were already calling it, "mem-loss."

I'm a lawyer, and I like to think logically, not only about what has happened but what might happen. So I extrapolated on the basis of what little evidence, or data, there was.

On the first of June, a Sunday, we woke up with all memory of May 31 back through May 28 completely gone. We had thought that yesterday was the twenty-seventh and that this morning was that of the twenty-eighth.

If The Ball had caused this, why had it only taken four days of our memory? I didn't know. Nobody knew. But perhaps The Ball, its devices, that is, were limited in scope. Perhaps they couldn't strip off more than four days of memory at a time from everybody on Earth.

Postulate that this is the case. Then, what if the same thing happens tomorrow? We'll wake up tomorrow, June 2, with all memory of yesterday, June 1, and three more days of May, the twenty-seventh through the twenty-fifth, gone. Eight days in one solid stretch.

And if this ghastly thing should occur the following day, June 3, we'll lose another four days. All memory of June 2 will have disappeared. With it will go the memory of three more days, from May twenty-fourth through the twenty-second. Twelve days in all from June 2 backward!

And the next day? June 3 lost, too, along with May 21 through May 19. Sixteen days of a total blank. And the next day? And the next?

No, it's too hideous, and too fantastic, to think about.

While we were watching TV, Carole and the boys besieged me with questions. She was frantic. The boys seemed to be enjoying the mystery. They'd awakened expecting to go to school, and now they were having a holiday.

To all their questions, I said, "I don't know. Nobody knows." I wasn't going to frighten them with my extrapolations. Besides, I didn't believe them myself.

"You'd better call up your office and tell them you can't come in today," Carole said. "Surely Judge Payne'll call off the session today."

"Carole, it's Sunday, not Wednesday, remember?" I said.

She cried for a minute. After she'd wiped away the tears, she said, "That just it! I *don't* remember! My God, what's happening?"

The newscasters also reported that the White House was flooded with telegrams and phone calls demanding that rockets with H-bomb warheads be launched against The Ball. The specials, which came on after the news, were devoted to The Ball. These had various authorities, scientists, military men, ministers, and a few science-fiction authors. None of them radiated confidence, but they were all temperate in their approach to the problem. I suppose they had been picked for their level-headedness. The networks had screened out the hotheads and the crackpots. They didn't want to be generating any more hysteria.

But Anel Robertson, a fundamentalist faith healer with a powerful radio/TV station of his own, had already declared that The Ball was a judgment of God on a sinful planet. It was The Destroying Angel. I knew that because Mrs. Douglas, no fanatic but certainly a zealot, had phoned me and told me to dial him in. Robertson had been speaking for an hour, she said, and he was going to talk all day.

She sounded frightened, and yet, beneath the fear, was a note of joy. Obviously, she didn't think that she was going to be among the goats when the last days arrived. She'd be right in there with the whitest of the sheep. My curiosity finally overcame my repugnance for Robertson. I dialed the correct number but got nothing except a pattern. Later today, I found out his station had been shut down for some infraction of FCC regulations. At least, that was the explanation given on the news, but I suspected that the government regarded him as a hysteria monger.

At eleven, Carole reminded me that it was Sunday and that if we didn't hurry, we'd miss church.

The Forrest Hill Presbyterian has a good attendance, but its huge parking lot has always been adequate. This morning, we had to park two blocks up the street and walk to church. Every seat was filled. We had to stand in the anteroom near the front door. The crowd stank of fear. Their faces were pale and set; their eyes, big. The air conditioning labored unsuccessfully to carry away the heat and humidity of the packed and sweating bodies. The choir was loud but quavering; their "Rock of Ages" was crumbling.

Dr. Boynton would have prepared his sermon on Saturday afternoon, as he always did. But today he spoke impromptu. Perhaps, he said, this loss of memory *had* been caused by The Ball. Perhaps there were living beings in it who had taken four days away from us, not as a hostile move but merely to demonstrate their immense powers. There was no reason to anticipate that we would suffer another loss of memory. These beings merely wanted to show us that we were hopelessly inferior in science and that we could not launch a successful attack against them.

"What the hell's he doing?" I thought. "Is he trying to scare us to death?"

Boynton hastened then to say that beings with such powers, of such obvious advancement, would not, could not, be hostile. They would be on too high an ethical plane for such evil things as war, unless they were attacked, of course. They would regard us as beings who had not yet progressed to their level but had the potentiality, the God-given potentiality, to be brought up to a high level. He was sure that, when they made contact with us, they would tell us that all was for the best.

They would tell us that we must, like it or not, become true Christians. At least, we must all, Buddhists, Moslems and so forth, become Christian in spirit, whatever our religion or lack thereof. They would teach us how to live as brothers and sisters, how to be happy, how to truly love. Assuredly, God had sent The Ball, since nothing happened without His knowledge and consent. He had sent these beings, whoever they were, not as Destroying Angels but as Sharers of Peace, Love and Prosperity.

That last, with the big P, seemed to settle down most of the congregation. Boynton had not forgotten that most of his flock were of the big-business and professional classes. Nor had he forgotten that, inscribed on the arch about the church entrance was, THEY SHALL PROSPER WHO LOVE THEE.

3

We poured out into a bright warm June afternoon. I looked up into the sky but could see no Ball, of course. The news media had said that, despite its great distance from Earth, it was circling Earth every sixty-five minutes. It wasn't in a free fall orbit. It was applying continuous power to keep it on its path, although there were no detectable emanations of energy from it.

The memory loss had occurred all over the world between 1:00 A.M. and 2:00 A.M. Central Standard Time. Those who were not already asleep fell asleep for a minimum of an hour. This had, of course, caused hundreds of thousands of accidents. Planes not on automatic pilot had crashed, trains had collided or been derailed, ships had sunk, and more than two hundred thousand had been killed or seriously injured. At least a million vehicle drivers and passengers had been injured. The ambulance and hospital services had found it impossible to handle the situation. The fact that their personnel had been asleep for at least an hour and that it had taken them some time to recover from their confusion on awakening had aggravated the situation considerably. Many had died who might have lived if immediate service had been available.

There were many fires, too, the largest of which were still raging in Tokyo, Athens, Naples, Harlem, and Baltimore.

I thought. Would beings on a high ethical plane have put us to sleep knowing that so many people would be killed and badly hurt?

One curious item was about two rangers who had been thinning a herd of elephants in Kenya. While sleeping, they had been trampled to death. Whatever it is that's causing this, it's very specific. Only human beings are affected.

The optimism, which Boynton had given us in the church, melted in the sun. Many must have been thinking, as I was, that if Boynton's words were prophetic, we were helpless. Whatever the things in The Ball, whether living or mechanical, decided to do for us, or to us, we were no longer masters of our own fate. Some of them must have been thinking about what the technologically superior whites had done to various aboriginal cultures. All in the name of progress and God.

But this would be, must be, different. I thought. Boynton must be right. Surely such an advanced people would not be as we were. Even we are not what we were in the bad old days. We have learned.

But then an advanced technology does not necessarily accompany an advanced ethics.

"Or whatever," I murmured.

"What did you say, dear?" Carole said.

I said, "Nothing," and shook her hand off my arm. She had clung to it tightly all through the services, as if *I* were the rock of the ages. I walked over to Judge Payne, who's sixty years old but looked this morning as if he were eighty. The many broken veins on his face were red, but underneath them was a grayishness.

I said hello and then asked him if things would be normal tomorrow. He didn't seem to know what I was getting at, so I said, "The trial will start on time tomorrow?"

"Oh, yes, the trial," he said. "Of course, Mark."

He laughed whinnyingly and said, "Provided that we all haven't forgotten today when we wake up tomorrow."

That seemed incredible, and I told him so.

"It's not law school that makes good lawyers," he said. "It's experience. And experience tells us that the same damned thing, with some trifling variations, occurs over and over, day after day. So what makes you think this evil thing won't happen again? And if it does, how're you going to learn from it when you can't remember it?"

I had no logical argument, and he didn't want to talk any more. He grabbed his wife by the arm, and they waded through the crowd as if they thought they were going to step in a sinkhole and drown in a sea of bodies.

This evening, I decided to record on tape what's happened today. Now I lay me down to sleep, I pray the Lord my memory to keep, if I forget while I sleep . . .

Most of the rest of today, I've spent before the TV. Carole wasted hours trying to get through the lines to her friends for phone conversations. Three-fourths of the time, she got a busy signal. There were bulletins on the TV asking people not to use the phone except for emergencies, but she paid no attention to it until about eight o'clock. A TV bulletin, for the sixth time in an hour, asked that the lines be kept open. About twenty fires had broken out over the town, and the firemen couldn't be informed of them because of the tie-up. Calls to hospitals had been similarly blocked.

I told Carole to knock it off, and we quarreled. Our suppressed hysteria broke loose, and the boys retreated upstairs to their room behind a closed door. Eventually, Carole started crying and threw herself into my arms, and then I cried. We kissed and made up. The boys came down looking as if we had failed them, which we had. For them, it was no longer a fun-adventure from some science-fiction story.

Mike said, "Dad, could you help me go over my arithmetic lessons?"

I didn't feel like it, but I wanted to make it up to him for that savage scene. I said sure and then, when I saw what he had to do, I said, "But

all this? What's the matter with your teacher? I never saw so much . . ."
    I stopped. Of course, he had forgotten all he'd learned in the last three
days of school. He had to do his lessons all over again.
    This took us until eleven, though we might have gone faster if I hadn't
insisted on watching the news every half-hour for at least ten minutes. A
full thirty minutes were used listening to the president, who came on at
9:30. He had nothing to add to what the newsmen had said except that,
within thirty days, The Ball would be completely dealt with—one way or
another. If it didn't make some response to our signals within two days,
then we would send up a four-man expedition, which would explore The
Ball.
    If it can get inside, I thought.
    If, however, The Ball should commit any more hostile acts, then the
United States would immediately launch, in conjunction with other nations, rockets armed with H-bombs.
    Meanwhile, would we all join the president in an interdenomina-
tional prayer?
    We certainly would.
    At eleven, we put the kids to bed. Tom went to sleep before we were
out of the room. But about half an hour later, as I passed their door, I
heard a low voice from the TV. I didn't say anything to Mike, even if he
did have to go to school next day.
    At twelve, I made the first part of this tape.
    But here it is, one minute to one o'clock in the morning. If the same
thing happens tonight as happened yesterday, then the nightside hemi-
sphere will be affected first. People in the time zone which bisects the
South and North Atlantic oceans and covers the eastern half of Greenland, will fall asleep. Just in case it does happen again, all airplanes have
been grounded. Right now, the TV is showing the bridge and the salon
of the trans-Atlantic liner *Pax*. It's five o'clock there, but the salon is
crowded. The passengers are wearing party hats and confetti, and bal-
loons are floating everywhere. I don't know what they could be celebrat-
ing. The captain said a little while ago that the ship's on automatic, but
he doesn't expect a repetition of last night. The interviewer said that the
governments of the dayside nations have not been successful keeping people home. We've been getting shots from everywhere, the sirens are
wailing all over the world, but, except for the totalitarian nations, the
streets of the daytime world are filled with cars. The damned fools just
didn't believe it would happen again.

Back to the bridge and the salon of the ship. My God! They *are* falling asleep!

The announcers are repeating warnings. Everybody lie down so they won't get hurt by falling. Make sure all home appliances, which might cause fires, are turned off. And so on and so on.

I'm sitting in a chair with a tilted back. Carole is on the sofa.

Now I'm on the sofa. Carole just said she wanted to be holding on to me when this horrible thing comes.

The announcers are getting hysterical. In a few minutes, New York will be hit. The eastern half of South America is under. The central section is going under.

4

True date: June 2, 1980. Subjective date: May 25, 1980

My God! How many times have I said, "My God!" in the last two days?

I awoke on the sofa beside Carole and Mike. The clock indicated three in the morning. Chris Turner was on the TV. I didn't know what he was talking about. All I could understand was that he was trying to reassure his viewers that everything was all right and that everything would be explained shortly.

What was I doing on the sofa? I'd gone to bed about eleven the night of May 24, a Saturday. Carole and I had had a little quarrel because I'd spent all day working on the Lankers case, and she said that I'd promised to take her to see *Nova Express*. And so I had—if I finished work before eight, which I obviously had not done. So what were we doing on the sofa, where had Mike come from, and what did Turner mean by saying that today was June 2?

The tape recorder was on the table near me, but it didn't occur to me to turn it on.

I shook Carole awake, and we confusedly asked each other what had happened. Finally, Turner's insistent voice got our attention, and he explained the situation for about the fifth time so far. Later, he said that an alarm clock placed by his ear had awakened him at two-thirty.

Carole made some coffee, and we drank four cups apiece. We talked wildly, with occasional breaks to listen to Turner, before we became half-convinced that we had indeed lost all memory of the last eight days. Mike slept on through it, and finally I carried him up to his bed. His TV was still on. Nate Frobisher, Mike's favorite spieler, was talking hysterically. I turned him off and went back downstairs. I figured out later that Mike had gotten scared and come downstairs to sit with us.

Dawn found us rereading the papers from May 24 through June 1. It was like getting news from Mars. Carole took a tranquilizer to quiet herself down, but I preferred Wild Turkey. After she'd seen me down six ounces, Carole said I should lay off the bourbon. I wouldn't be fit to go to work. I told her that if she thought anybody'd be working today, she was out of her mind.

At seven, I went out to pick up the paper. It wasn't there. At a quarter to eight, Joe delivered it. I tried to talk to him, but he wouldn't stop. All he said, as he pedaled away, was, "It ain't Saturday!"

I went back in. The entire front page was devoted to The Ball and this morning's events up to four o'clock. Part of the paper had been set up before one o'clock. According to a notice at the bottom of the page, the staff had awakened about three. It took them an hour to straighten themselves out, and then they'd gotten together the latest news and made up the front page and some of section C. They'd have never made it when they did if it wasn't for the computer, which printed justified lines from voice input.

Despite what I'd said earlier, I decided to go to work. First, I had to straighten the boys out. At ten, they went off to school. It seemed to me that it was useless for them to do so. But they were eager to talk with their classmates about this situation. To tell the truth, I wanted to get down to the office and the courthouse for the same reason. I wanted to talk this over with my colleagues. Staying home all day with Carole seemed a waste of time. We just kept saying the same thing over and over again.

Carole didn't want me to leave. She was too frightened to stay home by herself. Both our parents are dead, but she does have a sister who lives in Hannah, a small town nearby. I told her it'd do her good to get out of the house. And I just had to get to the courthouse. I couldn't find out what was happening there because the phone lines were tied up.

When I went outside to get into my car, Carole ran down after me. Her long blonde hair was straggling; she had big bags under her eyes; she looked like a witch.

"Mark, Mark!" she said.

I took my finger off the starter button and said, "What is it?"

"I know you'll think I'm crazy, Mark," she said. "But I'm about to fall apart!"

"Who isn't?" I said.

"Mark," she said, "what if I go out to my sister's and then forget how to get back? What if I forget *you*?"

"This thing only happens at night," I said.

"So far!" she screamed. "So far!"

"Honey," I said, "I'll be home early. I promise. If you don't want to go, stay here. Go over and talk to Mrs. Knight. I see her looking out her window. She'll talk your leg off all day."

I didn't tell her to visit any of her close friends, because she didn't have any. Her best friend had died of cancer last year, and two others with whom she was familiar had moved away.

"If you do go to your sister's," I said, "make a note on a map reminding you where you live and stick it on top of the dashboard, where you can see it."

"You son of a bitch," she said. "It isn't funny!"

"I'm not being funny," I said. "I got a feeling . . ."

"What about?" she said.

"Well, we'll be making notes to ourselves soon. If this keeps up," I said.

I thought I was kidding then. Thinking about it later today I see that that is the only way to get orientated in the morning. Well, not the only way, but it'll have to be the way to get started when you wake up. Put a note where you can't overlook it, and it'll tell you to turn on a recording, which will, in turn, summarize the situation. Then you turn on the TV and get some more information.

I might as well have stayed home. Only half of the courthouse personnel showed up, and they were hopelessly inefficient. Judge Payne wasn't there and never will be. He'd had a fatal stroke at six that morning while listening to the TV. Walter Barbindale, my partner, said that the judge probably would have had a stroke sometime in the near future, anyway. But this situation must certainly have hastened it.

"The stock market's about hit bottom," he said. "One more day of this, and we'll have another worldwide depression. Nineteen twenty-nine won't hold a candle to it. And I can't even get through to my broker to tell him to sell everything."

"If everybody sells, then the market *will* crash," I said.

"Are you hanging onto your stocks?" he said.

"I've been too busy to even think about it," I said. "You might say I forgot."

"That isn't funny," he said.

"That's what my wife said," I answered. "But I'm not trying to be funny, though God knows I could use a good laugh. Well, what're we going to do about Lankers?"

"I went over some of the records," he said. "We haven't got a chance. I tell you, it was a shock finding out, for the second time, mind you, though I don't remember the first, that our star witness is in jail on a perjury charge."

Since all was chaos in the courthouse, it wasn't much use trying to find out who the judge would be for the new trial for Lankers. To tell the truth, I didn't much care. There were far more important things to worry about than the fate of an undoubtedly guilty murderer.

I went to Grover's Rover Bar, which is a block from the courthouse. As an aside, for my reference or for whoever might be listening to this someday, why am I telling myself things I know perfectly well, like the location of Grover's? Maybe it's because I think I might forget them someday.

Grover's, at least, I remembered well, as I should, since I'd been going there ever since it was built, five years ago. The air was thick with tobacco and pot smoke and the odors of pot, beer and booze. And noisy. Everybody was talking fast and loud, which is to be expected in a place filled with members of the legal profession. I bellied up to the bar and bought the D.A. a shot of Wild Turkey. We talked about what we'd done that morning, and then he told me he had to release two burglars that day. They'd been caught and jailed two days before. The arresting officers had, of course, filed their reports. But that wasn't going to be enough when the trial came up. Neither the burglars nor the victims and the officers remembered a thing about the case.

"Also," the D.A. said, "at two-ten this morning, the police got a call from the Black Shadow Tavern on Washington Street. They didn't get there until three-thirty because they were too disorientated to do anything for an hour or more. When they did get to the tavern, they found a dead man. He'd been beaten badly and then stabbed in the stomach. Nobody remembered anything, of course. But from what we could piece together, the dead man must've gotten into a drunken brawl with a person or persons unknown shortly before 1:00 A.M. Thirty people must've witnessed the murder. So we have a murderer or murderers walking the streets today who don't even remember the killing or anything leading up to it."

"They might know they're guilty if they'd been planning it for a long time," I said.

He grinned and said, "But he, or they, won't be telling anybody. No one except the corpse had blood on him nor did anybody have bruised knuckles. Two were arrested for carrying saps, but so what? They'll be out soon, and nobody, but nobody, can prove they used the saps. The knife was still half-sticking in the deceased's belly, and his efforts to pull it out destroyed any fingerprints."

5

We talked and drank a lot, and suddenly it was 6:00 P.M. I was in no condition to drive and had sense enough to know it. I tried calling Carole to come down and get me, but I couldn't get through. At 6:30 and 7:00, I tried again without success. I decided to take a taxi. But after another drink, I tried again and this time got through.

"Where've you been?" she said. "I called your office, but nobody answered. I was thinking about calling the police."

"As if they haven't got enough to do," I said. "When did *you* get home?"

"You're slurring," she said coldly.

I repeated the question.

"Two hours ago," she said.

"The lines were tied up," I said. "I tried."

"You knew how scared I was, and you didn't even care," she said.

"Can I help it if the D.A. insisted on conducting business at the Rover?" I said. "Besides, I was trying to forget."

"Forget what?" she said.

"Whatever it was I forgot," I said.

"You ass!" she screamed. "Take a taxi!"

The phone clicked off.

She didn't make a scene when I got home. She'd decided to play it cool because of the kids, I suppose. She was drinking gin and tonic when I entered, and she said, in a level voice, "*You*'ll have some coffee. And after a while you can listen to the tape you made yesterday. It's interesting, but spooky."

"What tape?" I said.

"Mike was fooling around with it," she said. "And he found out you'd recorded what happened yesterday."

"That kid!" I said. "He's always snooping around. I told him to leave my stuff alone. Can't a man have any privacy around here?"

"Well, don't say anything to him," she said. "He's upset as it is. Anyway, it's a good thing he did turn it on. Otherwise, you'd have forgotten all about it. I think you should make a daily record."

"So you think it'll happen again?" I said.

She burst into tears. After a moment, I put my arms around her. I felt like crying, too. But she pushed me away, saying, "You stink of rotten whiskey!"

"That's because it's mostly bar whiskey," I said. "I can't afford Wild Turkey at three dollars a shot."

I drank four cups of black coffee and munched on some shrimp dip. As an aside, I can't really afford that, either, since I only make forty-five thousand dollars a year.

When we went to bed, we went to bed. Afterward, Carole said, "I'm sorry, darling, but my heart wasn't really in it."

"That wasn't all," I said.

"You've got a dirty mind," she said. "What I meant was I couldn't stop thinking, even while we were doing it, that it wasn't any good doing it. We won't remember it tomorrow, I thought."

"How many do we really remember?" I said. "Sufficient unto the day is the, uh, good thereof."

"It's a good thing you didn't try to fulfill your childhood dream of becoming a preacher," she said. "You're a born shyster. You'd have made a lousy minister."

"Look," I said, "I remember the especially good ones. And I'll never forget our honeymoon. But we need sleep. We haven't had any to speak of for twenty-four hours. Let's hit the hay and forget everything until tomorrow. In which case . . ."

She stared at me and then said, "Poor dear, no wonder you're so belligerently flippant! It's a defense against fear!"

I slammed my fist into my palm and shouted, "I know! I know! For God's sake, how long is this going on?"

I went into the bathroom. The face in the mirror looked as if it were trying to flirt with me. The left eye wouldn't stop winking.

When I returned to the bedroom, Carole reminded me that I'd not made today's recording. I didn't want to do it because I was so tired. But the possibility of losing another day's memory spurred me. No, not another day, I thought. If this occurs tomorrow, I'll lose another four days. Tomorrow and the three preceding May 25. I'll wake up June 3 and think it's the morning of the twenty-second.

I'm making this downstairs in my study. I wouldn't want Carole to hear some of my comments.

Until tomorrow then. It's not tomorrow but yesterday that won't come.

I'll make a note to myself and stick it in a corner of the case which holds my glasses.

6

True date: June 3, 1980

I woke up thinking that today was my birthday, May 22. I rolled over, saw the piece of paper half-stuck from my glasses case, put on my glasses and read the note.

It didn't enlighten me. I didn't remember writing the note. And why should I go downstairs and turn on the recorder? But I did so.

As I listened to the machine, my heart thudded as if it were a judge's gavel. My voice kept fading in and out. Was I going to faint?

And so half of today was wasted trying to regain twelve days in my mind. I didn't go to the office, and the kids went to school late. And what about the kids in school on the dayside of Earth? If they sleep during their geometry class, say, then they have to go through that class again on the same day. And that shoves the schedule forward, or is it backward, for that day. And then there's the time workers will lose on their jobs. They have to make it up, which means they get out an hour later. Only it takes more than an hour to recover from the confusion and get orientated. What a mess it has been! What a mess it'll be if this keeps on!

At eleven, Carole and I were straightened out enough to go to the supermarket. It was Tuesday, but Carole wanted me to be with her, so I tried to phone in and tell my secretary I'd be absent. The lines were tied up, and I doubt that she was at work. So I said to hell with it.

Our supermarket usually opens at eight. Not today. We had to stand in a long line, which kept getting longer. The doors opened at twelve. The manager, clerks and boys had had just as much trouble as we did unconfusing themselves, of course. Some didn't show at all. And some of the trucks which were to bring fresh stores never appeared.

By the time Carole and I got inside, those ahead of us had cleaned out half the supplies. They had the same idea we had. Load up now so there wouldn't be any standing in line so many times. The fresh milk was all gone, and the powdered milk shelf had one box left. I started for it but some teen-ager beat me to it. I felt like hitting him, but I didn't, of course.

The prices for everything were being upped by a fourth even as we shopped. Some of the stuff was being marked upward once more while we stood in line at the checkout counter. From the time we entered the line until we pushed out three overflowing carts, four hours had passed.

While Carole put away the groceries, I drove to another supermarket. The line there was a block long; it would be emptied and closed up before I ever got to its doors.

The next two supermarkets and a corner grocery store were just as hopeless. And the three liquor stores I went to were no better. The fourth only had about thirty men in line, so I tried that. When I got inside, all the beer was gone, which didn't bother me any, but the only hard stuff left was a fifth of rotgut. I drank it when I went to college because I couldn't afford anything better. I put the terrible stuff and a half-gallon of cheap muscatel on the counter. Anything was better than nothing, even though the prices had been doubled.

I started to make out the check, but the clerk said, "Sorry, sir. Cash only."

"What?" I said.

"Haven't you heard, sir?" he said. "The banks were closed at 2:00 P.M. today."

"The banks are closed?" I said. I sounded stupid even to myself.

"Yes, sir," he said. "By the federal government. It's only temporary, sir, at least, that's what the TV said. They'll be reopened after the stock market mess is cleared up."

"But . . ." I said.

"It's destructed," he said.

"Destroyed," I said automatically. "You mean, it's another Black Friday?"

"It's Tuesday today," he said.

"You're too young to know the reference," I said. And too uneducated, too, I thought.

"The president is going to set up a rationing system," he said. "For The Interim. And price controls, too. Turner said so on TV an hour ago. The president is going to lay it all out at six tonight."

When I came home, I found Carole in front of the TV. She was pale and wide-eyed.

"There's going to be another depression!" she said. "Oh, Mark, what are we going to do?"

"I don't know," I said. "I'm not the president, you know." And I slumped down onto the sofa. I had lost my flippancy.

Neither of us, having been born in 1945, knew what a Depression, with a big capital D, was; that is, we hadn't experienced it personally. But we'd heard our parents, who were kids when it happened, talk about it. Carole's parents had gotten along, though they didn't live well, but my father used to tell me about days when he had nothing but stale bread and turnips to eat and was happy to get them.

The president's TV speech was mostly about the depression, which he claimed would be temporary. At the end of half an hour of optimistic talk, he revealed why he thought the situation wouldn't last. The federal government wasn't going to wait for the sentients in The Ball—if there were any there—to communicate with us. Obviously, The Ball was hostile. So the survey expedition had been canceled. Tomorrow, the USA, the USSR, France, West Germany, Israel, India, Japan and China would send up an armada of rockets tipped with H-bombs. The orbits and the order of battle were determined this morning by computers; one after the other, the missiles would zero in until The Ball was completely destroyed. It would be over-kill with a vengeance.

"That ought to bring up the stock market!" I said.

And so, after I've finished recording, to bed. Tomorrow, we'll follow our instructions on the notes, relisten to the tapes, reread certain sections of the newspapers and await the news on the TV. To hell with going to the courthouse; nobody's going to be there anyway.

Oh, yes. With all this confusion and excitement, everybody, myself included, forgot that today was my birthday. Wait a minute! It's *not* my birthday!

True date: June 5, 1980. Subjective date: May 16, 1980

I woke up mad at Carole because of our argument the previous day. Not that of June 4, of course, but our brawl on May 15. We'd been at a party given by the Burlingtons, where I met a beautiful young artist, Roberta Gardner. Carole thought I was paying too much attention to her because she looked like Myrna. Maybe I was. On the other hand, I really was interested in her paintings. It seemed to me that she had a genuine talent. When we got home, Carole tore into me, accused me of still being in love with Myrna. My protests did no good whatsoever. Finally, I told her we might as well get a divorce if she couldn't forgive and forget. She ran crying out of the room and slept on the sofa downstairs.

I don't remember what reconciled us, of course, but we must have worked it out, otherwise we wouldn't still be married.

Anyway, I woke up determined to see a divorce lawyer today. I was sick about what Mike and Tom would have to go through. But it would be better for them to be spared our terrible quarrels. I can remember my reactions when I was an adolescent and overheard my parents fighting. It was a relief, though a sad one, when they separated.

Thinking this, I reached for my glasses. And I found the note. And so another voyage into confusion, disbelief and horror.

Now that the panic has eased off somewhat, May 18 is back in the saddle—somewhat. Carole and I are, in a sense, still in that day, and things are a bit cool.

It's 1:00 P.M. now. We just watched the first rockets take off. Ten of them, one after the other.

It's 1:35 P.M. Via satellite, we watched the Japanese missiles.

We just heard that the Chinese and Russian rockets are being launched. When the other nations send theirs up, there will be thirty-seven in all.

No news at 12:30 A.M., June 5. In this case, no news must be bad news. But what could have happened? The newscasters won't say; they just talk around the subject.

7

True date: June 6, 1980. Subjective date: May 13, 1980

My records say that this morning was just like the other four. Hell.

One o'clock. The president, looking like a sad old man, though he's only forty-four, reported the catastrophe. All thirty-seven rockets were blown up by their own H-bombs about three thousand miles from The Ball. We saw some photographs of them taken from the orbiting labs. They weren't very impressive. No mushroom clouds, of course, and not even much light.

The Ball has weapons we can't hope to match. And if it can activate our H-bombs out in space, it should be able to do the same to those on Earth's surface. My god! It could wipe out all life if it wished to do so!

Near the end of the speech, the president did throw out a line of hope. With a weak smile—he was trying desperately to give us his big vote-winning one—he said that all was not lost by any means. A new plan, called Project Toro, was being drawn up even as he spoke.

Toro was Spanish for bull, I thought, but I didn't say so. Carole and the kids wouldn't have thought it funny, and I didn't think it was so funny myself. Anyway, I thought, maybe it's a Japanese word meaning *victory* or *destruction* or something like that.

Toro, as it turned out, was the name of a small irregularly shaped asteroid about 2.413 kilometers long and 1.609 kilometers wide. Its peculiar orbit had been calculated in 1972 by an L. Danielsson of the Swedish Royal Institute of Technology and a W. H. Ip of the University of California at San Diego. Toro, the president said, was bound into a resonant orbit with the Earth. Each time Toro came near the Earth—"near" was sometimes 12.6 million miles—it got exactly enough energy or "kick" from the Earth to push it on around so that it would come back for another near passage.

But the orbit was unstable, which meant that both Earth and Venus take turns controlling the asteroid. For a few centuries, Earth governs Toro; then Venus takes over. Earth has controled Toro since A.D. 1580. Venus will take over in 2200. Earth grabs it again in 2350; Venus gets it back in 2800.

I was wondering what all this stuff about this celestial Pingpong game was about. Then the president said that it was possible to land rockets on Toro. In fact, the plan called for many shuttles to land there carrying parts of huge rocket motors, which would be assembled on Toro.

When the motors were erected on massive and deep stands, power would be applied to nudge Toro out of its orbit. This would require many trips by many rockets with cargoes of fuel and spare parts for the motors. The motors would burn out a number of times. Eventually, though, the asteroid would be placed in an orbit that would end in a direct collision with The Ball. Toro's millions of tons of hard rock and nickel-steel would destroy The Ball utterly, would turn it into pure energy.

"Yes," I said aloud, "but what's to keep The Ball from just changing its orbit? Its sensors will detect the asteroid; it'll change course; Toro will go on by it, like a train on a track."

This was the next point of the president's speech. The failure of the attack had revealed at least one item of information, or, rather, verified it. The radiation of the H-bombs had blocked off, disrupted, all control and observation of the rockets by radar and laser. In their final approach, the rockets had gone in blind, as it were, unable to be regulated from Earth. But if the bombs did this to our sensors, they must be doing the same to The Ball's.

So, just before Toro's course is altered to send it into its final path, H-bombs will be set off all around The Ball. In effect, it will be enclosed in a sphere of radiation. It will have no sensor capabilities. Nor will The Ball *believe* that it will have to alter its orbit to dodge Toro. It will have calculated that Toro's orbit won't endanger it. After the radiation fills the space around it, it won't be able to *see* that Toro is being given a final series of nudges to push it into a collision course.

The project is going to require immense amounts of materials and manpower. The USA can't handle it alone; Toro is going to be a completly international job. What one nation can't provide, the other will.

The president ended with a few words about how Project Toro, plus the situation of memory loss, is going to bring about a radical revision of the economic setup. He's going to announce the outlines of the new structure—not just policy but structure—two days from now. It'll be designed, so he says, to restore prosperity and, not incidentally, rid society of many problems plaguing it since the industrial revolution.

"Yes, but how long will Project Toro take?" I said. "Oh, Lord, how long?"

Six years, the president said, as if he'd heard me. Perhaps longer.

Six years!

I didn't tell Carole what I could see coming. But she's no dummy. She could figure out some of the things that were bound to happen in six years, and none of them were good.

I never felt so hopeless in my life, and neither did she. But we do have each other, and so we clung tightly for a while. May 18 isn't forgotten, but it seems so unimportant. Mike and Tom cried, I suppose because they knew that this exhibition of love meant something terrible for all of us. Poor kids! They get upset by our hatreds and then become even more upset by our love.

When we realized what we were doing to them, we tried to be jolly. But we couldn't get them to smile.

True date: middle of 1981. Subjective date: middle of 1977

I'm writing this, since I couldn't get any new tapes today. The shortage is only temporary, I'm told. I could erase some of the old ones and use them, but it'd be like losing a vital part of myself. And God knows I've lost enough.

Old Mrs. Douglas next door is dead. Killed herself, according to my note on the calendar, April 2 of this year. I never would have thought she'd do it. She was such a strong fundamentalist, and these believe as strongly as the Roman Catholics that suicide is well-nigh unforgivable. I suspect that the double shock of her husband's death caused her to take her own life. April 2 of 1976 was the day he died. She had to be hospitalized because of shock and grief for two weeks after his death. Carole and I had her over to dinner a few times after she came home, and all she could talk about was her dead husband. So I presume that, as she trav-

eled backward to the day of his death, the grief became daily more unbearable. She couldn't face the arrival of the day he died.

Hers is not the only empty house on the block. Jack Bridger killed his
wife and his three kids and his mother-in-law and himself last month—
according to my records. Nobody knows why, but I suspect that he
couldn't stand seeing his three-year-old girl become no more than an
idiot. She'd retrogressed to the day of her birth and perhaps beyond.
She'd lost her language abilities and could no longer feed herself.
Strangely, she could still walk, and her intelligence potential was high.
She had the brain of a three-year-old, fully developed, but lacking all
postbirth experience. It would have been better if she hadn't been able to
walk. Confined to a cradle, she would at least not have had to be watched
every minute.

Little Ann's fate is going to be Tom's. He talks like a five-year-old now.
And Mike's fate . . . my fate . . . Carole's . . . God! We'll end up like
Ann! I can't stand thinking about it.

Poor Carole. She has the toughest job. I'm away part of the day, but
she had to take care of what are, in effect, a five-year-old and an eight-
year-old, getting younger every day. There is no relief for her, since
they're always home. All educational institutions, except for certain research laboratories, are closed.

The president says we're going to convert ninety percent of all indus-
tries to cybernation. In fact, anything that can be cybernated will be.
They have to be. Almost everything, from the mines to the loading
equipment to the railroads and trucks and the unloading equipment and
the arrangement and disperal of the final goods at central distribution
points.

Are six years enough to do this?

And who's going to pay for this? Never mind, he says. Money is on its
way out. The president is a goddamned radical. He's taking advantage of
this situation to put over his own ideas, which he sure as hell never
revealed during his campaign for election. Sometimes I wonder *who* put
The Ball up there. But that idea is sheer paranoia. At least, this gigantic
WPA project is giving work to those who are able to work. The rest are
on, or going to be on, a minimum guaranteed income, and I mean
minimum. But the president says that, in time, everybody will have all
he needs, and more, in the way of food, housing, schooling, clothing,
etc. *He* says! What if Project Toro doesn't work? And what if it does
work? Are we then going to return to the old economy? Of course not!

It'll be impossible to abandon everything we've worked on; the new establishment will see to that.

I tried to find out where Myrna lived. I'm making this record in my office, so Carole isn't going to get hold of it. I love her—Myrna, I mean—passionately. I hired her two weeks ago and fell headlong, burningly, in love with her. All this was in 1977, of course, but today, inside of *me*, *is* 1977.

Carole doesn't know about this, of course. According to the letters and notes from Myrna, which I should have destroyed but, thank God, never had the heart to do, Carole didn't find out about Myrna until two years later. At least, that's what this letter from Myrna says. She was away visiting her sister then and wrote to me in answer to my letter. A good thing, too, otherwise I wouldn't know what went on then.

My reason tells me to forget about Myrna. And so I will.

I've traveled backward in our affair, from our final bitter parting, to this state, when I was most in love with her. I know this because I've just reread the records of our relationship. It began deteriorating about six months before we split up, but I don't feel those emotions now, of course. And in two weeks I won't feel anything for her. If I don't refer to the records, I won't even know she ever existed.

This thought is intolerable. I have to find her, but I've had no success at all so far. In fourteen days, no, five, since every day ahead takes three more of the past, I'll have no drive to locate her. Because I won't know what I'm missing.

I don't hate Carole. I love her, but with a cool much-married love. Myrna makes me feel like a boy again. I burn exquisitely.

But where is Myrna?

True date: October 30, 1981

I ran into Brackwell Lee, the old mystery story writer, today. Like most writers who haven't gone to work for the government propaganda office, he's in a bad way financially. He's surviving on his GMI, but for him there are no more first editions of rare books, new sports cars, Western Reserve or young girls. I stood him three shots of the rotgut which is the only whiskey now served at Grover's and listened to the funny stories he told to pay me for the drinks. But I also had to listen to his tales of woe.

Nobody buys fiction or, in fact, any long works of any kind anymore. Even if you're a speed reader and go through a whole novel in one day, you have to start all over again the next time you pick it up. TV writing, except for the propaganda shows, is no alternative. The same old shows are shown every day and enjoyed just as much as yesterday or last year. According to my records, I've seen the hilarious pilot movie of the "Soap Opera Blues" series fifty times.

When old Lee talked about how he had been dropped by the young girls, he got obnoxiously weepy. I told him that that didn't say much for him or the girls either. But if he didn't want to be hurt, why didn't he erase those records that noted his rejections?

He didn't want to do that, though he could give me no logical reason why he shouldn't.

"Listen," I said with a sudden drunken inspiration, "why don't you erase the old records and make some new ones? How you laid this and that beautiful young thing. Describe your conquests in detail. You'll think you're the greatest Casanova that ever lived."

"But that wouldn't be true!" he said.

"You, a writer of lies, say that?" I said. "Anyway, you wouldn't know that they weren't the truth."

"Yeah," he said, "but if I get all charged up and come barreling down here to pick up some tail, I'll be rejected and so'll be right back where I was."

"Leave a stern note to yourself to listen to them only late at night, say, an hour before The Ball puts all to sleep. That way, you won't even get hurt."

George Palmer wandered in then. I asked him how things were doing.

"I'm up to here handling cases for kids who can't get drivers' licenses," he said. "It's true you can teach anybody how to drive in a day, but the lessons are forgotten the next day. Anyway, it's experience that makes a good driver, and . . . need I explain more? The kids have to have cars, so they drive them regardless. Hence, as you no doubt have forgotten, the traffic accidents and violations are going up and up."

"Is that right?" I said.

"Yeah. There aren't too many in the mornings, since most people don't go to work until noon. However, the new transit system should take care of that when we get it, sometime in 1984 or 5."

"What new transit system?" I said.

"It's been in the papers," he said. "I reread some of last week's this morning. The city of Los Angeles is equipped with a model system now, and it's working so well it's going to be extended throughout Los Angeles County. Eventually, every city of any size in the country'll have it. Nobody'll have to walk more than four blocks to get to a line. It'll cut air pollution by half and the traffic load by three-thirds. Of course, it'll be compulsory; you'll have to show cause to drive a car. And I hate to think about the mess *that's* going to be, the paperwork, the pile-up in the courts and so forth. But after the way the government handled the L. A. riot, the rest of the country should get in line."

"How will the rest of the country know how the government handled it unless they're told?" I said.

"They'll be told. Every day," he said.

"Eventually, there won't be enough time in the day for the news channels to tell us all we'll need to know," I said. "And even if there were enough time, we'd have to spend all day watching TV. So who's going to get the work done?"

"Each person will have to develop his own viewing specialty," he said. "They'll just have to watch the news that concerns them and ignore the rest."

"And how can they do that if they won't know what concerns them until they've run through everything?" I said. "Day after day."

"I'll buy a drink," he said. "Liquor's good for one thing. It makes you forget what you're afraid not to forget."

8

True date: late 1982. Subjective date: late 1974

She came into my office, and I knew at once that she was going to be more than just another client. I'd been suffering all day from the "mirror syndrome," but the sight of her stabilized me. I forgot the thirty-seven-year-old face my twenty-nine-year-old mind had seen in the bathroom that morning. She is a beautiful woman, only twenty-seven. I had trouble at first listening to her story; all I wanted to do was to look at her. I finally understood that she wanted me to get her husband out of jail on a murder rap. It seemed he'd been in since 1976 (real time). She wanted me to get the case reopened, to use the new plea of rehabilitation by retrogression.

I was supposed to know that, but I had to take a quick look through my resumé before I could tell her what chance she had. Under RBR was the definition of the term and a notation that a number of people had been released because of it. The main idea behind it is that criminals are not the same people they were before they became criminals, if they have lost all memory of the crime. They've traveled backward to goodness, you might say. Of course, RBR doesn't apply to hardened criminals or to someone who'd planned a crime a long time before it was actually committed.

I asked her why she would want to help a man who had killed his mistress in a fit of rage when he'd found her cheating on him?

"I love him," she said.

And I love you, I thought.

She gave me some documents from the big rec bag she carried. I looked through them and said, "But you divorced him in 1977?"

"Yes, he's really my ex-husband," she said. "But I think of him now as my husband."

No need to ask her why.

"I'll study the case," I said. "You make a note to see me tomorrow. Meantime, how about a drink at the Rover bar so we can discuss our strategy?"

That's how it all started—again.

It wasn't until a week later, when I was going over some old recs, that I discovered it was *again*. It made no difference. I love her. I also love Carole, rather, *a* Carole. The one who married me six years ago, that is, six years ago in my memory.

But there is the other Carole, the one existing today, the poor miserable wretch who can't get out of the house until I come home. And I can't come home until late evening because I can't get started to work until about twelve noon. It's true that I could come home earlier than I do if it weren't for Myrna. I try. No use. I have to see Myrna.

I tell myself I'm a bastard, which I am, because Carole and the children need me very much. Tom is ten and acts as if he's two. Mike is a four-year-old in a twelve-year-old body. I come home from Myrna to bedlam every day, according to my records, and every day must be like today.

That I feel both guilt and shame doesn't help. I become enraged; I try to suppress my anger, which is born out of my desperation and helplessness and guilt and shame. But it comes boiling out, and then bedlam becomes hell.

I tell myself that Carole and the kids need a tower of strength now. One who can be calm and reassuring and, above all, loving. One who can handle the thousand tedious and aggravating problems that infest every household in this world of diminishing memory. In short, a hero. Because the real heroes, and heroines, are those who deal heroically with the everyday cares of life, though God knows they've been multiplied enormously. It's not the guy who kills a dragon once in his lifetime and then retires that's a hero. It's the guy who kills cockroaches and rats every day, day after day, and doesn't rest on his laurels until he's an old man, if then.

What am I talking about? Maybe I could handle the problems if it weren't for this memory loss. I can't adjust because I can't ever get used to it. My whole being, body and mind, must get the same high-voltage jolt every morning.

The insurance companies have canceled all policies for anybody under twelve. The government's contemplated taking over these policies but has decided against it. It will, however, pay for the burials, since this service is necessary. I don't really think that many children are being "accidentally" killed because of the insurance money. Most fatalities are obviously just results of neglect or parents going berserk.

I'm getting away from Myrna, trying to, anyway, because I wish to forget my guilt. I love her, but if I didn't see her tomorrow, I'd forget her. But I *will* see her tomorrow. My notes will make sure of that. And each day is, for me, love at first sight. It's a wonderful feeling, and I wish it could go on forever.

If I just had the guts to destroy all reference to her tonight. But I won't. The thought of losing her makes me panic.

9

True date: middle of 1984. Subjective date: middle of 1968

I was surprised that I woke up so early.

Yesterday, Carole and I had been married at noon. We'd driven up to this classy motel near Lake Geneva. We'd spent most of our time in bed after we got there, naturally, though we did get up for dinner and champagne. We finally fell asleep about four in the morning. That was why I hadn't expected to wake up at dawn. I reached over to touch Carole, wondering if she would be too sleepy. But she wasn't there.

She's gone to the bathroom, I thought. I'll catch her on the way back.

Then I sat up, my heart beating as if it had suddenly discovered it was alive. The edges of the room got fuzzy, and then the fuzziness raced in toward me.

The dawn light was filtered by the blinds, but I had seen that the furniture was not familiar. I'd never been in this place before.

I sprang out of bed and did not, of course, notice the note sticking out of my glass case. Why should I? I didn't wear glasses then.

Bellowing, "Carole!" I ran down a long and utterly strange hall and past the bathroom door, which was open, and into the room at the other end of the hall. Inside it I stopped. This was a kids' bedroom: bunks, pennants, slogans, photographs of two young boys, posters and blowups of faces I'd never seen, except one of Laurel and Hardy, some science fiction and Tolkien and Tarzan books, some school texts, and a large flat piece of equipment hanging on the wall. I would not have known that it was a TV set if its controls had not made its purpose obvious.

The bunks had not been slept in. The first rays of the sun fell on thick dust on a table.

I ran back down the hall, looked into the bathroom again, though I knew no one was there, saw dirty towels, underwear and socks heaped in a corner, and ran back to my bedroom. The blinds did not let enough light in, so I looked for a light switch on the wall. There wasn't any, though there was a small round plate of brass where the switch should have been. I touched it, and the ceiling lights came on.

Carole's side of the bed had not been slept in.

The mirror over the bureau caught me, drew me and held me. Who was this haggard old man staring out from my twenty-three-year-old self? I had gray hair, big bags under my eyes, thickening and sagging features, and a long scar on my right cheek.

After a while, still dazed and trembling, I picked up a book from the bureau and looked at it. At this close distance, I could just barely make out the title, and, when I opened it, the print was a blur.

I put the book down, *Be Your Own Handyman Around Your House*, and proceeded to go through the house from attic to basement. Several times, I whimpered, "Carole! Carole!" Finding no one, I left the house and walked to the house next door and beat on its door. No one answered; no lights came on inside.

I ran to the next house and tried to wake up the people in it. But there weren't any.

A woman in a house across the street shouted at me. I ran to her, babbling. She was about fifty years old and also hysterical. A moment later, a man her age appeared behind her. Neither listened to me; they kept asking me questions, the same questions I was asking them. Then I saw a black and white police car of a model unknown to me come around the corner half a block away. I ran toward it, then stopped. The car was so silent that I knew even in my panic that it was electrically powered. The two cops wore strange uniforms, charcoal gray with white helmets topped by red panaches. Their aluminum badges were in the shape of a spread eagle.

I found out later that the police throughout the country had been federalized. These two were on the night shift and so had had enough time to get reorientated. Even so, one had such a case of the shakes that the other told him to get back into the car and take it easy for a while.

After he got us calmed down, he asked us why we hadn't listened to our tapes.

"What tapes?" we said.

"Where's your bedroom?" he said to the couple.

They led him to it, and he turned on a machine on the bedside table.

"Good morning," a voice said. I recognized it as the husband's. "Don't panic. Stay in bed and listen to me. Listen to everything I say."

The rest was a resumé, by no means short, of the main events since the first day of memory loss. It ended by directing the two to a notebook that would tell them personal things they needed to know, such as where their jobs were, how they could get to them, where their area central distributing stores were, how to use their I.D. cards and so on.

The policeman said, "You have the rec set to turn on at 6:30, but you woke up before then. Happens a lot."

I went back, reluctantly, to the house I'd fled. It was mine, but I felt as if I were a stranger. I ran off my own recs twice. Then I put my glasses on and started to put together my life. The daily rerun of "Narrative of an Old-Young Man Shipwrecked on the Shoals of Time."

I didn't go any place today. Why should I? I had no job. Who needs a lawyer who isn't through law school yet? I did have, I found out, an application in for a position on the police force. The police force was getting bigger and bigger but at the same time was having a large turnover. My recs said that I was to appear at the City Hall for an interview tomorrow.

If I feel tomorrow as I do today, and I will, I probably won't be able to make myself go to the interview. I'm too grief-stricken to do anything but sit and stare or, now and then, get up and pace back and forth, like a sick leopard in a cage made by Time. Even the tranquilizers haven't helped me much.

I have lost my bride the day after we were married. And I love Carole deeply. We were going to live a long happy life and have two children. We would raise them in a house filled with love.

But the recs say that the oldest boy escaped from the house and was killed by a car and Carole, in a fit of anguish and despair, killed the youngest boy and then herself.

They're buried in Springdale Cemetery.

I can't feel a retroactive grief for those strangers called Mike and Tom. But Carole, lovely laughing Carole, lives in my mind.

Oh, God, why don't I just erase all my recs? Then I'd not have to suffer remorse for all I've done or failed to do. I wouldn't know what a bastard I'd been.

Why don't I do it? Take the past and shed its heartbreaks and its guilts as a snake sheds its skin. Or as the legislature cancels old laws. Press a button, fill the wastebasket, and you're clean and easy again, innocent again. That's the logical thing to do; and I'm a lawyer, dedicated to logic. Why not? Why not?

But I can't. Maybe I like to suffer. I've liked to inflict suffering, and according to what I understand, those who like to inflict, unconsciously hope to be inflicted upon.

No, that can't be it. At least, not all of it. My main reason for hanging on to the recs is that I don't want to lose my identity. A major part of me, a unique person, is not in the neurons of my mind, where it belongs, but in an electromechanical device or in tracings of lead or ink on paper. The protein, the flesh for which I owe, can't hang on to *me*.

I'm becoming less and less, dwindling away, like the wicked witch on whom Dorothy poured water. I'll become a puddle, a wailing voice of hopeless despair, and then . . . nothing.

God, haven't I suffered enough! I said I owe for the flesh and I'm down in Your books. Why do I have to struggle each day against becoming a dumb brute, a thing without memory? Why not rid myself of the struggle? Press the button, fill the wastebasket, discharge my grief in a chaos of magnetic lines and pulped paper?

Sufficient unto the day is the evil thereof.

I didn't realize, Lord, what that really meant.

10

I will marry Carole in three days. No, I would have. No, I did.

I remember reading a collection of Krazy Kat comic strips when I was twenty-one. One was captioned: COMA REIGNS. Coconing County was in the doldrums, comatose. Nobody, Krazy Kat, Ignatz Mouse, Officer Pupp, nobody had the energy to do anything. Mouse was too lazy even to think about hurling his brickbat. Strange how that sticks in my mind. Strange to think that it won't be long before it becomes forever unstuck.

Coma reigns today over the world.

Except for Project Toro, the TV says. And that is behind schedule. But the Earth, Ignatz Mouse, will not allow itself to forget that it must hurl the brickbat, the asteroid. But where Ignatz expressed his love, in a queer perverted fashion, by banging Kat in the back of the head with his brick, the world is expressing its hatred, and its desperation, by throwing Toro at The Ball.

I did manage today to go downtown to my appointment. I did it only to keep from going mad with grief. I was late, but Chief Moberly seemed to expect that I would be. Almost everybody is, he said. One reason for my tardiness was that I got lost. This residential area was nothing in 1968 but a forest out past the edge of town. I don't have a car, and the house is in the middle of the area, which has many winding streets. I do have a map of the area, which I forgot about. I kept going eastward and finally came to a main thoroughfare. This was Route 98, over which I've traveled many times since I was a child. But the road itself, and the houses along it, were strange. The private airport which should have been across the road was gone, replaced by a number of large industrial buildings.

A big sign near a roofed bench told me to wait there for the RTS bus. One would be along every ten minutes, the sign stated.

I waited an hour. The bus, when it came, was not the fully automated vehicle promised by the sign. It held a sleepy-looking driver and ten nervous passengers. The driver didn't ask me for money, so I didn't offer any. I sat down and watched him with an occasional look out of the window. He didn't have a steering wheel. When he wanted the bus to slow down or stop he pushed a lever forward. To speed it up, he pulled back on the lever. The bus was apparently following a single aluminum rail in the middle of the right-hand lane. My recs told me later that the automatic pilot and door-opening equipment had never been delivered and probably wouldn't be for some years—if ever. The grand plan of cybernating everything possible had failed. There aren't enough people who can provide the know-how or the man-hours. In fact, everything is going to hell.

The police chief, Adam Moberly, is fifty years old and looks as if he's sixty-five. He talked to me for about fifteen minutes and then had me put through a short physical and intelligence test. Three hours after I had walked into the station, I was sworn in. He suggested that I room with two other officers, one of whom was a sixty-year-old veteran, in the hotel across the street from the station. If I had company, I'd get over the morning disorientation more quickly. Besides, the policemen who lived in the central area of the city got preferential treatment in many things, including the rationed supplies.

I refused to move. I couldn't claim that my house was a home to me, but I feel that it's a link to the past, I mean the future, no, I mean the past. Leaving it would be cutting out one more part of me.

True date: late.1984. Subjective date: early 1967

My mother died today. That is, as far as I'm concerned, she did. The days ahead of me are going to be full of anxiety and grief. She took a long time to die. She found out she had cancer two weeks after my father died. So I'll be voyaging backward in sorrow through my mother and then through my father, who was also sick for a long time.

Thank God I won't have to go through every day of that, though. Only a third of them. And these are the last words I'm going to record about their illnesses.

But how can I not record them unless I make a recording reminding me not to do so?

I found out from my recs how I'd gotten this big scar on my face. Myrna's ex-husband slashed me before I laid him out with a big ashtray. He was shipped off this time to a hospital for the criminally insane where he died a few months later in the fire that burned every prisoner in his building. I haven't the faintest idea what happened to Myrna after that. Apparently I decided not to record it.

I feel dead tired tonight, and, according to my recs, every night. It's no wonder, if every day is like today. Fires, murders, suicides, accidents and insane people. Babies up to fourteen years old abandoned. And a police department which is ninety percent composed, in effect, of raw rookies. The victims are taken to hospitals where the nurses are only half-trained, if that, and the doctors are mostly old geezers hauled out of retirement.

I'm going to bed soon even if it's only nine o'clock. I'm so exhausted that even Jayne Mansfield couldn't keep me awake. And I dread tomorrow. Besides the usual reasons for loathing it, I have one which I can hardly stand thinking about.

Tomorrow my memory will have slid past the day I met Carole. I won't remember her at all.

Why do I cry because I'll be relieved of a great sorrow?

11

True date: 1986. Subjective date: 1962

I'm nuts about Jean, and I'm way down because I can't find her. According to my recs, she went to Canada in 1965. Why? We surely didn't fall in and then out of love? Our love would never die. Her parents must've moved to Canada. And so here we both are in 1962, in effect. Halfway in 1962, anyway. Amphibians of time. Is she thinking about me now? Is she unable to think about me, about anything, because she's dead or crazy? Tomorrow I'll start the official wheels grinding. The Canadian government should be able to find her through the International Information Computer Network, according to the recs. Meanwhile, I burn, though with a low flame. I'm so goddamn tired.

Even Marilyn Monroe couldn't get a rise out of me tonight. But Jean. Yeah, Jean. I see her as seventeen years old, tall, slim but full-busted, with creamy white skin and a high forehead and huge blue eyes and glossy black hair and the most kissable lips ever. And broadcasting sex waves so thick you can see them, like heat waves. Wow!

And so tired old Wow goes to bed.

February 6, 1987

While I was watching TV to get orientated this morning, a news flash interrupted the program. The president of the United States had died of a heart attack a few minutes before.

"My God!" I said. "Old Eisenhower is dead!"

But the picture of the president certainly wasn't that of Eisenhower. And the name was one I never heard, of course.

I can't feel bad for a guy I never knew.

I got to thinking about him, though. Was he as confused every morning as I was? Imagine a guy waking up, thinking he's a senator in Washington and then he finds he's the president? At least, he knows something about running the country. But it's no wonder the old pump conked out. The TV says we've had five prexies, mostly real old guys, in the last seven years. One was shot; one dived out of the White House window onto his head; two had heart attacks; one went crazy and almost caused a war, as if we didn't have grief enough, for crying out loud.

Even after the orientation, I really didn't get it. I guess I'm too dumb for anything to percolate through my dome.

A policeman called and told me I'd better get my ass down to work. I said I didn't feel up to it, besides, why would I want to be a cop? He said that if I didn't show, I might go to jail. So I showed.

True date: late 1988. Subjective date: 1956
Here I am, eleven years old, going on ten.

In one way, that is. The other way, here I am forty-three and going on about sixty. At least, that's what my face looks like to me. Sixty.

This place is just like a prison except some of us get treated like trusties. According to the work chart, I leave through the big iron gates every day at twelve noon with a demolition crew. We tore down five partly burned houses today. The gang chief, old Rogers, says it's just WPA work, whatever that is. Anyway, one of the guys I work with kept looking more and more familiar. Suddenly, I felt like I was going to pass out. I put down my sledgehammer and walked over to him, and I said, "Aren't you Stinky Davis?"

He looked funny and then he said, "Jesus! You're Gabby! Gabby Franham!"

I didn't like his using the Lord's name in vain, but I guess he can be excused.

Nothing would've tasted good the way I felt, but the sandwiches we got for breakfast, lunch and supper tasted like they had a dash of oil in them. Engine oil, I mean. The head honcho, he's eighty if he's a day, says his recs tell him they're derived from petroleum. The oil is converted into a kind of protein and then flavoring and stuff is added. Oil-burgers, they call them.

Tonight, before lights-out, we watched the prez give a speech. He said that, within a month, Project Toro will be finished. One way or the other. And all this memory loss should stop. I can't quite get it even if I was briefed this morning. Men on the moon, unmanned ships on Venus and Mars, all since I was eleven years old. And The Black Ball, the thing from outer space. And now we're pushing asteroids around. Talk about your science fiction!

12

September 4, 1988
Today's the day.

Actually, the big collision'll be tomorrow, ten minutes before 1:00 A.M. . . . but I think of it as today. Toro, going 150,000 miles an hour, will run head-on into The Ball. Maybe.

Here I am again, Mark Franham, recording just in case The Ball does dodge out of the way and I have to depend on my recs. It's 7:00 P.M. and after that raunchy supper of oil-burgers, potato soup and canned carrots, fifty of us gathered around set No. 8. There's a couple of scientists talking now, discussing theories about just what The Ball is and why it's been taking our memories away from us. Old Doctor Charles Presley—any relation to Elvis?—thinks The Ball is some sort of unmanned survey ship. When it finds a planet inhabited by sentient life, sentient means intelligent, it takes specimens. Specimens of the mind, that is. It unpeels people's minds four days' worth at a time, because that's all it's capable of. But it can do it to billions of specimens. It's like it was reading our minds but destroying the mind at the same time. Presley said it was like some sort of Heisenberg principle of the mind. The Ball can't observe our memories closely without disturbing them.

This Ball, Presley says, takes our memories and stores them. And when it's through with us, sucked us dry, it'll take off for another planet circling some far-off star. Someday, it'll return to its home planet, and the scientists there will study the recordings of our minds.

The other scientist, Dr. Marbles—he's still got his, ha! ha!—asked why any species advanced enough to be able to do this could be so callous? Surely, the extees must know what great damage they're doing to us. Wouldn't they be too ethical for this?

Doc Presley says maybe they think of us as animals, they are so far above us. Doc Marbles says that could be. But it could also be that whoever built The Ball have different brains than we do. Their mind-reading ray, or whatever it is, when used on themselves doesn't disturb the memory patterns. But we're different. The extees don't know this, of course. Not now, anyway. When The Ball goes home, and the extees read our minds, they'll be shocked at what they've done to us. But it'll be too late then.

Presley and Marbles got into an argument about how the extees would be able to interpret their recordings. How could they translate our languages when they have no references—I mean, referents? How're they going to translate *chair* and *recs* and *rock and roll* and *yucky* and so on when they don't have anybody to tell them their meanings. Marbles said they wouldn't have just words; they'd have mental images to associate with the words. And so on. Some of the stuff they spouted I didn't understand at all.

I do know one thing, though, and I'm sure those bigdomes do, too. But they wouldn't be allowed to say it over TV because we'd be even more gloomy and hopeless-feeling. That is, what if right now the computers in The Ball are translating our languages, reading our minds, as they're recorded? Then they know all about Project Toro. They'll be ready for the asteroid, destroy it if they have the weapons to do it, or, if they haven't, they'll just move The Ball into a different orbit.

I'm not going to say anything to the other guys about this. Why make them feel worse?

It's ten o'clock now. According to regulations posted up all over the place, it's time to go to bed. But nobody is. Not tonight. You don't sleep when the End of the World may be coming up.

I wish my Mom and Dad were here. I cried this morning when I found they weren't in this dump, and I asked the chief where they were. He said they were working in a city nearby, but they'd be visiting me soon. I think he lied.

Stinky saw me crying, but he didn't say anything. Why should he? I'll bet he's shed a few when he thought nobody was looking, too.

Twelve o'clock. Midnight. Less than an hour to go. Then, the big smash! Or, I hate to think about it, the big flop. We won't be able to see it directly because the skies are cloudy over most of North America. But we've got a system worked out so we can see it on TV. If there's a gigantic flash when the Toro and The Ball collide, that is.

What if there isn't? Then we'll soon be just like those grown-up kids, some of them twenty years old, that they keep locked up in the big building in the northwest corner of this place. Saying nothing but Da Da or Ma Ma, drooling, filling their diapers. If they got diapers, because old Rogers says he heard, today, of course, they don't wear nothing. The nurses come in once a day and hose them and the place down. The nurses don't have time to change and wash diapers and give personal baths. They got enough to do just spoon-feeding them.

Three and a half more hours to go, and I'll be just like them. Unless, before then, I flip, and they put me in that building old Rogers calls the puzzle factory. They're all completely out of their skulls, he says, and even if memloss stops tonight, they won't change any.

Old Rogers says there's fifty million less people in the United States than there were in 1980, according to the recs. And a good thing, too, he says, because it's all we can do to feed what we got.

Come on, Toro! You're our last chance!

If Toro doesn't make it, I'll kill myself! I will! I'm not going to let myself become an idiot. Anyway, by the time I do become one, there won't be enough food to go around for those that do have their minds. I'll be starving to death. I'd rather get it over with now than go through that. God'll forgive me.

God, You know I want to be a minister of the gospel when I grow up and that I want to help people. I'll marry a good woman, and we'll have children that'll be brought up right. And we'll thank You every day for the good things of life and battle the bad things.

Love, that's what I got, Lord. Love for You and love for Your people. So don't make me hate You. Guide Toro right into The Ball, and get us started on the right path again.

I wish Mom and Dad were here.

Twelve-thirty. In twenty minutes, we'll know.

The TV says the H-bombs are still going off all around The Ball.

The TV says the people on the East Coast are falling asleep. The rays, or whatever The Ball uses, aren't being affected by the H-bomb radiation. But that doesn't mean that its sensors aren't. I pray to God that they are cut off.

Ten minutes to go. Toro's got twenty-five thousand miles to go. Our sensors can't tell whether or not The Ball's still on its original orbit. I hope it is; I hope it is! If it's changed its path, then we're through! Done! Finished! Wiped out!

Five minutes to go; twelve thousand five hundred miles to go.

I can see in my mind's eyes The Ball, almost half a mile in diameter, hurtling on its orbit, blind as a bat, I hope and pray, the bombs, the last of the five thousand bombs, flashing, and Toro, a mile and a half long, a mile wide, millions of tons of rock and nickel-steel, charging toward its destined spot.

If it *is* destined.

But space *is* big, and even the Ball and Toro are small compared to all that emptiness out there. What if the mathematics of the scientists is just a little off, or the rocket motors on Toro aren't working just like they're supposed to, and Toro just tears on by The Ball? It's got to meet The Ball at the exact time and place, it's just *got* to!

I wish the radars and lasers could see what's going on.

Maybe it's better they can't. If we knew that The Ball had changed course . . . but this way we still got hope.

If Toro misses, I'll kill myself, I swear it.

Two minutes to go. One hundred and twenty seconds. The big room is silent except for kids like me praying or talking quietly into our recs or praying and talking and sobbing.

The TV says the bombs have quit exploding. No more flashes until Toro hits The Ball—if it does. Oh, God, let it hit, let it hit!

The unmanned satellites are going to open their camera lenses at the exact second of impact and take a quick shot. The cameras are encased in lead, the shutters are lead, and the equipment is special, mostly mechanical, not electrical, almost like a human eyeball. If the cameras see the big flash, they'll send an electrical impulse through circuits, also encased in lead, to a mechanism that'll shoot a big thin-shelled ball out. This is crammed with flashpowder, the same stuff photographers use, and mixed with oxygen pellets so the powder will ignite. There's to be three of the biggest flashes you ever saw. Three. Three for Victory.

If Toro misses, then only one flashball'll be set off.

Oh, Lord, don't let it happen!

Planes with automatic pilots'll be cruising above the clouds, and their equipment will see the flashes and transmit them to the ground TV equipment.

One minute to go.

Come on, God!

Don't let it happen, please don't let it happen, that some place way out there, some thousands of years from now, some weird-looking character reads this and finds out to his horror what his people have done to us. Will he feel bad about it? Lot of good that'll do. You, out there, I hate you! God, how I hate you!

Our Father which art in Heaven, fifteen seconds, Hallowed be Thy name, ten seconds, Thy will be done, five seconds, Thy will be done, but if it's thumbs down, God, why? Why? What did I ever do to You?

The screen's blank! Oh, my God, the screen's blank! What happened? Transmission trouble? Or they're afraid to tell us the truth?

It's on! It's on!

YAAAAAAY!

13

July 4, A.D. 2002

I may erase this. If I have any sense, I will. If I had any sense, I wouldn't make it in the first place.

Independence Day, and we're still under an iron rule. But old Dick the Dictator insists that when there's no longer a need for strict control, the Constitution will be restored, and we'll be a democracy again. He's ninety-five years old and can't last much longer. The vice-president is only eighty, but he's as tough an octogenarian as ever lived. And he's even more of a totalitarian than Dick. And when have men ever voluntarily relinquished power?

I'm one of the elite, so I don't have it so bad. Just being fifty-seven years old makes me a candidate for that class. In addition, I have my Ph.D. in education and I'm a part-time minister. I don't know why I say part-time, since there aren't any full-time ministers outside of the executives of the North American Council of Churches. The People can't afford full-time divines. Everybody has to work at least ten hours a day. But I'm better off than many. I've been eating fresh beef and pork for three years now. I have a nice house I don't have to share with another family. The house isn't the one my recs say I once owned. The People took it over to pay for back taxes. It did me no good to protest that property taxes had been canceled during The Interim. That, say the People, ended when The Ball was destroyed.

But how could I pay taxes on it when I was only eleven years old, in effect?

I went out this afternoon, it being a holiday, with Leona to Springdale. We put flowers on her parents' and sisters' graves, none of whom she remembers, and on my parents' and Carole's and the children's graves, whom I know only through the recs. I prayed for the forgiveness of Carole and the boys.

Near Carole's grave was Stinky Davis's. Poor fellow, he went berserk the night The Ball was destroyed and had to be put in a padded cell. Still mad, he died five years later.

I sometimes wonder why I didn't go mad, too. The daily shocks and jars of memloss should have made everyone fall apart. But a certain number of us were very tough, tougher than we deserved. Even so, the day-to-day attack by alarm syndromes did its damage. I'm sure that years of life were cut off the hardiest of us. We're the shattered generation. And this is bad for the younger ones, who'll have no older people to lead them in the next ten years or so.

Or is it such a bad thing?

At least, those who were in their early twenties or younger when The Ball was smashed are coming along fine. Leona herself was twenty then. She became one of my students in high school. She's thirty-five physically but only fifteen in what the kids call "intage" or internal age. But since education goes faster for adults, and all those humanities courses have been eliminated, she graduated from high school last June. She still wants to be a doctor of medicine, and God knows we need M.D.'s. She'll be forty-two before she gets her degree. We're planning on having two children, the maximum allowed, and it's going to be tough raising them while she's in school. But God will see us through.

As we were leaving the cemetery, Margie Oleander, a very pretty girl of twenty-five, approached us. She asked me if she could speak privately to me. Leona didn't like that, but I told her that Margie probably wanted to talk to me about her grades in my geometry class.

Margie did talk somewhat about her troubles with her lessons. But then she began to ask some questions about the political system. Yes, I'd better erase this, and if it weren't for old habits, I'd not be doing this now.

After a few minutes, I became uneasy. She sounded as if she were trying to get me to show some resentment about the current situation.

Is she an agent provocateur or was she testing me for potential membership in the underground?

Whatever she was doing, she was in dangerous waters. So was I. I told her to ask her political philosophy teacher for answers. She said she'd read the textbook, which is provided by the government. I muttered something about, "Render unto Caesar's what is Caesar's," and walked away.

But she came after me and asked if I could talk to her in my office tomorrow. I hesitated and then said I would.

I wonder if I would have agreed if she weren't so beautiful?

When we got home, Leona made a scene. She accused me of chasing after the younger girls because she was too old to stimulate me. I told her that I was no senile King David, which she should be well aware of, and she said she's listened to my recs and she knew what kind of man I was. I told her I'd learned from my mistakes. I've gone over the recs of the missing years many times.

"Yes," she said, "you know about them intellectually. But you don't *feel* them!"

Which is true.

I'm outside now and looking up into the night. Up there, out there, loose atoms and molecules float around, cold and alone, debris of the memory records of The Ball, atoms and molecules of what were once incredibly complex patterns, the memories of thirty-two years of the lives of four and a half billion human beings. Forever lost, except in the mind of One.

Oh, Lord, I started all over again as an eleven-year-old. Don't let me make the same mistakes again.

You've given us tomorrow again, but we've very little past to guide us.

Tomorrow I'll be very cool and very professional with Margie. Not too much, of course, since there should be a certain warmth between teacher and pupil.

If only she did not remind me of . . . whom?

But that's impossible. I can remember nothing from The Interim. Absolutely nothing.

But what if there are different kinds of memory?

Elephant's Ear

ᑲᖱᖱᖲ

JOAN AIKEN

"The fleas," said Miss Printer, "are not so bad here as they were at Sreb."

"Maybe not," said Mr. Humphreys, "but they are a lot worse than they were at Prijepolje. Have you finished buying wine?"

"I have plenty of slivovitz and riesling. But I'd like a few dozen more proseks and some retsina if we go home through Greece. How are you getting on?"

"I've bought a lot of hors-d'œuvres and twenty tapestries."

"We could do with some silver jewellery."

"We shall never be home by Christmas at this rate," grumbled Mr. Humphreys, a thin, dark, and irascible young man.

Miss Printer raised her fine brows and gazed at him reproachfully with enormous grey eyes, clear as November lochs. They were her best feature. She had passed her first youth, though she was still in her second; indeed there was a quality about the famous London store of Rampadges which seemed to preserve its employees, flavour and body, like the best ginger. Miss Printer had been with the firm no more than twenty years, since she was seventeen, but already, thin, smooth-skinned, pale-haired, she was touched with agelessness.

"Haven't you any loyalty to the firm?" she suggested.

When they set sail together on their buying excursion she had been on the verge of falling in love with Mr. Humphreys. Now she was over the brink, helpless and hopeless, and finding it an uphill emotion in the face of their differences.

"Surely we've bought enough for the Christmas market?"

"Enough staples," she said, considering their list. "French plums, Swiss cuckoo clocks, Czech embroidery, German toys. Not enough novelties. I'd like to go down to Galicnik and buy some stonework."

"Stonework?"

"People like it for ornamental gardens. And I do wish we could get hold of an elephant or a kangaroo."

Mr. Humphreys had exhausted his capacity for expressing surprise. He just gaped at her and said at length rather feebly, "Surely it's not very probable in the Balkans?"

"Not very, but it's possible," said Miss Printer. "I have done so before. There are many travelling menageries in these parts. And since we are limited to Europe, the Balkans are our best bet."

"Why do you want elephants and kangaroos?"

"In Mr. Tybalt's day they always had an elephant at Rampadges for Christmas," she said wistfully. "Or a camel or a zebra."

"He's dead now."

"I know." No need to say more. Mr. Tybalt had been the nephew of the original Rampadge who started the magnificent store, and his ideas had been as lavish and imperial as those of his Victorian forebear.

The two travellers got back into their car, having finished their frugal picnic of prsut, borak, ratluk lokum, and Cvicek drunk from plastic beakers—although she was a discerning and intrepid buyer, Miss Printer did not believe in wasting the firm's money—and continued on their way, Mr. Humphreys driving.

They were bound for a small Montenegrin town called Grksik, where Miss Printer hoped to buy some pairs of the famous local slippers embroidered with gold thread and heavily jewelled, which should sell like hot cakes at Christmas.

The bleak, wild Balkan scenery rose about them in tarnished autumnal colours. It made Mr. Humphreys shiver, but Miss Printer surveyed it affectionately.

"I had such a nice picnic here in 1947," she said. Her tone of comfortable reminiscence somehow annoyed Mr. Humphreys and he trod incautiously on the accelerator. Their powerful hired car zipped round a sharp turn in the road, and became disastrously entangled with the rear section of a procession which had been concealed from them by a spur of the mountain.

"Zalvaro!"

"Molim, molim?"

"Oh dear."

"Au secours!"

"Oimoi!"

Shouts, bellows, brays, and polyglot exclamations volleyed from the ramshackle cornice of men, animals, and rudimentary vehicles which had toppled backwards over the bonnet of their car.

"Oh dear," said Miss Printer again, "you seem to have bumped into a circus."

By now it was nearly dark.

Miss Printer knew that in some European countries the adjective *Balkan* is used to describe something uncouth, wild, savage.

Balkan, she thought to herself with satisfaction, gazing at the crazy torchlit mass that seethed over and round the front portion of their sedate car. Goats formed a kind of fringe to it; there were bearded, tarbushed men with staves, like Old Testament illustrations; two apes, apparently chained together; and a zebra, neat and dainty as a fairytale convict. The whole scene gave Miss Printer a deep and inexplicable pleasure.

Mr. Humphreys was standing commandingly in the midst of it all trying to make some sense out of the business. Her heart ached with love at the sight of him. He was so tall and well-cut and impeccable, his head was such a good shape, the curl on the bowler that he wore even in the Balkans was exactly right. He looked what he was, a young English businessman who would make good.

The best of his kind in the world, thought Miss Printer sorrowfully. If he had been an article for sale in the market she would have bought him unhesitatingly for Rampadges, whatever his price. But he belonged to Rampadges already, and whatever his price, he was not for her; she knew that she filled him with alarm and a vague resentment.

He came angrily back to the car. "I can't get what they are saying," he said. "Can you make it out?"

Miss Printer uncoiled her slender length from the other front seat. She had fluent French, German, Italian, Turkish, and a smattering of Greek, Russian, and Spanish, but none of these proved effective in the present case, so she fell back on the Serbo-Croat phrase book.

"*Molin rezervirati jednu sobu sa dva kreveta i kupatilom*, Please reserve one double room with a bathroom," hardly seemed to meet the situation, but she tried, "*Dobro vece*, Good evening. *Ne razumen*, I do not understand. *Zao mi je*, I am sorry," and followed it up with, "*Mogu li imati racun, molim?* Can I have the bill, please?"

This produced a hush. The chorus sorted themselves out, and the goats were dragged offstage. A small boy led the zebra away into the dark, while the monkeys were tidied back into a sort of wicker perambulator.

"Racun," she repeated hopefully.

An enormous smiling man with moustaches like brackets shouldered his way into the flaring light and burst into a torrent of explanation which Mr. Humphreys listened to in bewildered non-comprehension.

Miss Printer attended, nodding. A boy squatting beside them held a torch, so that she looked like a small cream-coloured witch interviewing an affable devil. At length the man bowed, bringing down his arms in a sweeping gesture of acceptance. Some money changed hands.

The procession disentangled itself with almost magical speed and whirled off into the darkness.

"Well! You settled that very easily," said Mr. Humphreys with unwilling respect. "How much did you have to give him?"

"Oh, only about four and six." Miss Printer spoke absently. She was straining her eyes, searching for something in the engulfing dark. "There was a condition attached, you see. We have injured one of the men and the condition was that we take him and his animal to the nearest monastery."

"Injured a man?" said Mr. Humphreys, aghast.

"He fainted from fright so far as I could gather."

"And they just went off like that and left him? Where is he?"

"Somewhere around. The ringmaster, or whatever he was, said this man, Iskandar, was a weakling. He seemed rather glad to be rid of him. Yes, there he is." Her eye had caught a gleam of white and she moved away. When Mr. Humphreys caught up with her she was kneeling by the side of what at first appeared to be a bundle of rags.

"He's still in a faint," she said, "we'd better get him into the back of the car before he comes to."

"Most extraordinary," Mr. Humphreys muttered, helping her lift the little man, who was piteously thin and light, no more than skin and bone. "What language were you talking to the ring-master?"

"Turkish. But I think he said this man was a Russian."

Iskandar came to as they put him in and uttered a loud groan. At the same moment Mr. Humphreys felt himself suddenly plucked backwards into the air as if a space-ship had lowered a grapnel and removed him, dangling, from the earth. He had not even time to yell, could not believe in his predicament, but the gasp he gave as he left all his breath behind was enough to attract Miss Printer's attention.

"Oh, good gracious," she said, "what a coincidence. Though I suppose one might have expected it in the circumstances."

"Expected *what?*"

"An elephant. Just the same it does seem like a miracle." With a characteristically irrelevant flight she added, "Isn't there a ballet called Miracle in the Balkans?"

"In the *Gorbals*," snapped Mr. Humphreys, who was something of an expert on ballet. "If you speak any elephant language, will you tell it to put me down?"

Miss Printer did not speak elephant language, but she rummaged among the remnants of the picnic for pieces of turkish delight and with these persuaded the elephant to relinquish Mr. Humphreys, who climbed, fuming and rubbing himself, into the car.

"It's a very nice *little* elephant," Miss Printer said acquisitively. "I believe it's a female. I wonder how we can get it to the monastery. Do you suppose Iskandar would sell it?"

The night was cool and smelt of dew and rock, and the mountainside was totally silent. They might have been all alone on the southern slopes of Europe. The elephant evidently felt lonely, for it drew nearer to the car and let out a plaintive sound somewhere between a gurgle and a hoot. The sick man in the car stirred and muttered an unintelligible answer.

"What language is that?" said Mr. Humphreys uneasily.

"Russian. Where did I put that bottle of Cvicek?" She delved once more among the picnic debris and found the wine and a beaker.

"Probably the worst thing for him if he's suffering from shock," Mr. Humphreys pointed out gloomily. However, Iskandar came to sufficiently under the influence of the wine to direct them to the nearest monastery, and also to assure them that Chloe, the elephant, would follow peaceably behind the car if she might be allowed to put her trunk in at the window and feel her master sitting inside.

They started off slowly, Miss Printer a little disappointed as she had been hoping in her romantic heart for an elephant ride through the moonlit uplands.

The brothers at the monastery took in Iskandar and his elephant without demur, and, as it was now late, invited Miss Printer and Mr. Humphreys to stay for the night, giving them each a tiny guest-cell.

In the small hours Miss Printer was wakened by knocking.

"Who is it?" she called sleepily.

"The sick man is asking for you," one of the brothers whispered through the keyhole. She hastily flung on clothes and followed him to the Infirmary, a long bare stone room facing east over the windswept hillside. Already the dawn was beginning to show wild and green, like streaks of toothpaste in the sky.

The little man Iskandar, washed and snug, a tiny kernel in a large nut, lay peacefully in a white bed, with the sharp lines of his face filed keener by the sharp light.

"I am dying," he said matter-of-factly to Miss Printer as soon as she reached him. "You have a good face, so to you I entrust my elephant because she is a good elephant. She is a clever elephant too. She is over seventy years old and has seen the Czar of Russia when there was a czar. She has been left me by my father, who was a Russian landowner. After the revolution she was all that remained of his wealth. She and I escaped from Russia together and since then we have wandered many hundreds of miles."

He gasped between his words and one of the brothers offered a drink.

Miss Printer was crying a little.

"Don't be disturbed," said Iskandar with a touch of impatience. "I have been journeying to this place for many years. I am glad to get here. All I ask of you is that you take care of Chloe—take particular care of her ears, please—and that you arrange for her to see, once, my younger brother in London. She will carry my dying message to him. You can do this? I have his address here, on a bit of paper." He fumbled at his small bundle of possessions and handed her a grubby scrap on which was written, in beautiful Cyrillic characters, the name Joachim Boyanus, and a London address.

"Oh yes, I can easily do that."

"Good," he said, and glanced through the window. A sheepish-looking lay brother had Chloe outside, and at a command from her master she threaded her black snake-like trunk through the window. Iskandar caressed it almost absently and then passed it over to Miss Printer for mutual recognition and inspection.

"Now you must go," he said in a businesslike tone. "I am about to die."

Drawing closer about him the brothers began a deep-toned chant.

"Don't distress yourself, miss," said the kindly infirmarian, who spoke good German. "It is not your fault he dies. In his condition it is amazing that he lived so long."

"But I had said that I wanted an elephant," Miss Printer wept. "And then to be given one like *this* . . ."

"But you must think of Iskandar too," the monk pointed out benignly. "How fortunate for him to meet a trustworthy English lady to carry out his last wish." Much to Miss Printer's surprise he gave her a cup of tea.

She wandered out into the windy dawn to escape from the sound of chanting and to become acquainted with her new responsibility.

Mr. Humphreys was frankly appalled when he heard of the matter, and more so when he discovered that he and Miss Printer would have to ride on Chloe if they were ever to reach a port.

Their car, apparently suffering from delayed effects of the collision, completely refused to start, and the nearest mechanic was fifty miles off. At length Humphreys gave in. After the monks had celebrated Iskandar's funeral with every Orthodox rite, they piled their luggage on Chloe and rolled away southwards over the mountains.

"How you expect to get past customs and quarantine I've no idea," Mr. Humphreys said sourly, but Miss Printer was perfectly serene.

"We shall manage somehow," she said. "Chloe will take care of us." And indeed Chloe took care of them to such good effect that they crossed two frontiers without troubling the Customs, sailing past the posts like something impalpable between dusk and dawn while once, when they were ambushed by Albanian bandits as they picnicked, Chloe picked up her two riders and stowed them about her person like a boy scout tucking knife and matches into his pockets, and drifted away down a rocky hillside before the astonished brigands had their sights set for this unexpected safety device. That time Mr. Humphreys' bowler got left behind. It did not sweeten his attitude to Chloe.

In Athens, Miss Printer sent two cables, one to Joachim Boyanus, the other to her immediate superior at Rampadges:

DOCKING HULL NOON 19TH ON KATINA PAXINOU HAVE ELEPHANT TAPES-TRIES STONEWORK CUCKOO CLOCKS ETC.

It was not her fault that the Greek telegraphist, always a bit shaky on translating to the Roman alphabet, should have sent the cable as ELE-GANT TAPESTRIES STONE CUCKOO CLOCK WORKS. Nor could she have been expected to know, off in the wilds, as she and Mr. Humphreys had been for the last two months, that Rampadges had been the subject of a vast takeover bid and was now under new ownership.

Nor could she have foretold that the new managing director, Mr. Appelbee, had decided to come down to the docks for a personal inspection of the rare goods brought back for the Christmas market by the firm's most discerning buyer.

Chloe and Miss Printer had suffered on the voyage. The Greek ship was a tiny one and neither of them was a good sailor. Mr. Humphreys, chilly, correct, and unsympathetic, had visited them both impartially with basins of arrowroot.

Mr. Appelbee was in an irritable mood the day the ship docked. He was a small dyspeptic man who looked as if he had been scrubbed all over with a fine brush and the very best soap. He had found much to criticise already in Rampadges, and was now wishing he had stayed in bed. The morning was bleak, the dock filthy, Hull a bad and foggy dream. And then the cuckoo clocks had turned out, most disappointingly, not to be made of stone at all, and the tapestries not all that elegant.

It was the last straw when Miss Printer, pale and unhappy, made her appearance on the wharf followed by a small greenish elephant.

"What do you call *that?*" he snarled. "Have you been spending the firm's money on *that?* Well, I tell you frankly, you had better take the next boat back to where you've come from and get rid of it. There's no place for elephants in the new Rampadges—nor for damn fools who buy such damn-fool objects!"

Miss Printer looked round for Mr. Humphreys to give her moral support, but he had gone, walking elegantly off to chat to the manager of the Transport Department, and when she saw this craven betrayal the last shred of her love blew away in the chilly breeze.

She nerved herself.

"Mr. Appelbee," she said, "you may have got enough money to buy Rampadges, but you can't buy the loyalty of its employees. Loyalty has to be earned.

"I had intended to *give* Chloe to the firm, but I've changed my mind. Since she saved my life we've grown very close. Looking after her, taking the splinters out of her feet, and washing her ears, has taught me something. You can give affection to an elephant that you can't give to a firm, Mr. Appelbee. I'm going to keep Chloe for myself, and here is my resignation for you. I'm sure you will find Mr. Humphreys an excellent buyer when he has learned a few more languages."

And she turned away, taking Chloe's trunk under her arm, and walked briskly along the dock. A dark and bearded man in a city suit came up to her.

"Miss Printer?" he said. "I am Joachim Boyanus. I thank you for letting me meet Chloe once again."

Chloe was delighted to see him. She wreathed her trunk round his neck.

"I have taken good care of her," said Miss Printer, looking at him very directly with her clear grey eyes. Joachim turned back the flap of one huge leather ear and saw a great many pieces of slate-coloured sticking-plaster. Thoughtfully he pulled one loose and found under it a diamond as large as a hazel nut.

"Ah yes," he said. "The family diamonds. I wondered where Iskandar had hidden them all these years. It was kind of him to send them, and kind of you to bring them. But really, you know, I have done so comfortably in the City that I hardly need them. Would you accept them, Miss Printer?"

"I?" She was dumbfounded.

"You have just left your job," he pointed out. "Could you not use them? What is your dearest wish?"

"Oh," she said, starry-eyed, "to travel, of course. To travel with Chloe."

"Miss Printer," he said, "you are a woman after my own heart. For some time I have been intending to leave the City, whose moneymaking possibilities I have explored to the uttermost, and wander off to an older and more peaceable world. Could we not go together, you and I and Chloe?"

They looked at one another, liking what they saw.

And since nothing is very difficult if two people are mutually attracted, and have plenty of money and a well-disposed elephant, it is probable that they are travelling still.

Bodies

❦

JOYCE CAROL OATES

She met him in the cafeteria of the Art Museum, on a Thursday. His name was Draier, Drayer—she couldn't quite make it out. "Please call me Anthony," he said, leaning forward against the wrought-iron table, jarring it, and his attempt at intimacy was blocked by the formality of that name also. Pauline's friend, their mutual friend, hadn't figured much in her life for several years, and she wondered where his loneliness was leading him—he had been reluctant to introduce Anthony to her, she could see that. Her friend's name was Martin. He had something to do with an art gallery; his art galleries were always failing, disappearing, and returning again with new names. Pauline wondered if Anthony was an artist.

"I'm not an artist. I'm not anything," he said. He smiled a sad, quick smile. She was startled by his frankness, distrusting it. He had a striking face, though he had not shaved for several days, his eyes set clearly beneath the strong, clear line of his eyebrows. Beside him, Martin was silent. Students from Pauline's art class were carrying their trays past this table with serious faces; their faces, like the work they did, were intense and prematurely aged.

"Pauline does beautiful work," Martin said. He seemed to be talking to no one in particular. "But it's very difficult to talk about art, or about anything. I can't explain her work."

"Why should you explain it?" Pauline said. She stood to leave; she never took much time for lunch. The noise of the cafeteria annoyed her. Formally, with a smile, she put out her hand to Anthony. "It was very nice to meet you," she said.

He looked surprised. "Yes, very nice. . . ."

She was out of the restaurant before he caught up with her. Before turning, she heard footsteps and it flashed through her mind, incredibly, that this man was following her—then she turned to face him, and her expression was curious rather than alarmed. "I thought—I thought I'd walk with you. Are you going to look at the pictures?" he said.

Look at the pictures. "No," she said. "I have a class at two."

His face, in the mottled light of the broad, marble-floored hall, looked sullen. She had thought he was fairly young, in his mid-twenties; now she supposed he was at least ten years older. His hair was curly, black but tinged with gray, and it fell down around the unclean neck of his sweater lazily, making her think of one of the heads she herself had done a few years ago . . . in imitation of a Greek youth, the head of a sweetly smiling child. This man stared at her rudely. She could not bear to face him.

"I have to teach a class at two . . ." she said.

They walked awkwardly together. Not far away were the stairs to the first floor, and once upstairs she could escape . . . the side of her face tingled from his look, she thought it foolish and degrading, she wondered what he thought of her face . . . was he thinking anything about her face?

"Do you live around here?" he said.

"No. Out along the lake."

"Out there?" His tone was suspicious, as if she had been deceiving him until now. This was her own fault—though she wore her pale blond hair in a kind of crown, braided tightly, and though her face was cool, slow to awaken to interest, held always in a kind of suspension, she wore the standard casual clothes of girls who were artists or wanted to be, living alone, freely, sometimes recklessly, down here in the center of the city. She wore dark stockings, leather shoes that had been ruined by this winter's icy, salted sidewalks, a dark, rather shapeless skirt, and a white blouse that had once been an expensive blouse but now looked as old as Anthony's sweater and blue jeans, its cuffs rolled up to her elbows, its first button hanging by a thread. Her hands were not stubby, but there was nothing elegant about them—short, colorless fingernails, slightly knobby knuckles, small wrists. She was anxious to get back to work, her fingers actually itched to return to work, and this man was a pull on the edge of her consciousness, like something invisible but deadly blown into her eye.

"I have to leave," she said abruptly.

"You don't have a place down here? In town?"

"I have a studio. But I live at home with my mother."

She faced him and yet was not facing him; her eyes were moving coldly behind his head. He had no interest for her, not even as someone whose head she might copy; she had done a head like his once, she had no desire to repeat herself. She felt very nervous beneath his frank, blunt scrutiny, but her face showed nothing. Like the head of an Amazon on a stand near the stairs—a reproduction of an Etruscan work—she was vacuous, smooth-skinned, patient. From art she had learned patience, centuries of patience. The man, Anthony, was humming nervously under his breath, sensing her desire to get away and yet reluctant to let her get away.

"Do you come around here often?" he said.

"No."

"Why are you so . . . unfriendly?" He smiled at her, his face grown suddenly shabby and appealing, his eyes dark with wonder. *Tell the truth,* he was pleading. It occurred to her that he was insane. But she laughed, looking from the inhuman composed face of that Amazon to his face, hearing him say again, *Are you going to look at the pictures?*

"Come over here. Can I show you something?" he said. He took her arm with a sudden childish familiarity that annoyed her. In the noisy confusion of this part of the museum, at noon, she had to give herself up to anything that might happen; it was part of coming here at all. When she had begun teaching at the Art Institute across the street, years ago, she had brought her own lunch and eaten in her studio, she had thrown herself into her work and that had been, maybe, the best idea. Meeting people down here was a waste of time. The people she spent time with socially were friends of her mother's, most of them older than she, a careful, genteel network of people who could never harm her. Down here, the city was open. Anything could happen. This stranger, whose name was Anthony Drayer, whose rumpled clothes told her everything she needed to know about him, now took her by the arm and led her over to a reproduction of another Etruscan work she had been looking at for years with no more than mild interest.

"Did you ever see this?" Anthony said. He was very excited. The piece was a tomb monument, showing a young man lying on a cushion with a winged woman at his side. The man's hair was bound up tightly, in a kind of band; his face was very strong, composed. Pauline had the idea that Anthony saw himself in that face, though his own was soft, sketchy, as if done with a charcoal pencil, not shaped vividly in stone. His smile moved from being gentle to being loose, almost out of control. "Who are these people?" he said, glancing at her.

She saw that his fingers were twitching. Her eye was too intimate, too quick to take in shameful details—it was a fault in her. She could not help noticing that the skin around his thumbnails was raw from his digging at it. "I moved down here a few months ago and almost every day I come to the museum," Anthony said. He spoke in a rapid, low murmur, as if sensing her coldness but unable to stop his words. He picked at his thumbnail. "I like to look at the pictures but especially the statues. You do statues? That must be expensive, isn't it, to buy the stone and all that . . . ? I could never do anything like this, my hands are too shaky, my judgment isn't right, I can't stand still long enough, but I love to look at these things, it makes me happy to know that they exist. . . . Are those two in love? Is that why she's reaching out toward him?"

"No, they're not in love," Pauline said, wondering if her tone could rid her of this man forever. "The man is dead. The woman is an angel of death, or a demon of death. You see how her hand is broken off?—she was holding out to him a scroll with his fate written on it. This is a monument to adorn a tomb. It isn't about life, it's about death. They're both dead."

Anthony stared at the figures.

"But they look alive . . . their faces look alive. . . ."

"Do you see how their bodies are twisted around? The demon's body is organically impossible, it's out of shape from the waist down, and the man's body is almost as unnatural. . . . That's a typical Etruscan characteristic."

"Why?"

"I don't know why," she said, avoiding his melancholy stare. "The artists weren't interested in that part of the body, evidently their interest was in the head, the face, the torso. . . ."

"Why is that?"

He scratched at his own head, at the dusky, graying curls. She could smell about him an odor of something stale, sad—cigarette smoke, unwashed flesh, the gritty deposit of decades in some walk-up room. Her own odor was clean and impersonal. Her hands smelled whitely of the clay in which she worked. Anthony looked sideways at her. His look was pleading, intense, threatening . . . for the first time in years she was afraid of another person.

"I have to leave," she said.

"Can I see you again?"

She was already walking away. Her heart was pounding. He was calling after her—she nearly collided with an elderly man making his way slowly down the stairs—she had the excuse of apologizing to this man, helping him, saying something about the danger of such wide stairs. "And outside it ain't no better, all that goddamn ice," the old man said angrily, as if blaming her for that too.

She escaped from them both.

> It is a festival of some kind. Mules with muddy bellies and legs; a young man with a bare chest leading one of the mules. He is laughing. His head falls back with drunken laughter, as if loose on his shoulders. Another man is riding a mule, slipping off into the mud, laughing. Garlands of flowers are woven in the manes of these mules. What is happening? Women run by . . . their shouts are hilarious, drunken. I see what it is—someone is being pulled in a wagon. The wagon's railings are decorated with bruised white flowers, the man inside the wagon is speechless, his face dark with a look of terror, as if blood has settled heavily in his face and will never flow out again. Now a soldier appears on a black horse, the horse's belly is splashed with mud. The leather of his complicated saddle creaks. . . .

She woke suddenly. Her head pounded. The dream was still with her—the raucous laughter in the room with her, the whinnying of a horse. She looked around wildly, for a moment suspended of all personal existence, of thinking, not even afraid. The wagon's wheels made a creaking noise and so perhaps it was the wheels, not the soldier's gear, that was creaking. . . . Then the dream faded and she felt only a dull, aching fear. For a while she lay unthinking in bed and felt the cool, contented length of her body beneath the covers, not thinking.

Twenty-nine years old, she had a sense of being much older, of being ageless. So many years of patience, the shaping of clay and stone, the necessity for patience had aged her magically; she was content in her age. Her work was heads. She was interested only in the human head. Out in the street she could not help but stare at the heads of strangers, at their unique, mysterious, miraculous shapes; sometimes their heads were a threat to her, unnerving her. She couldn't explain. But most of the time she brought back to her work a sense of excitement, as if her blood, in flowing out at the instant of glimpsing some rare sight, had returned again to her heart exhilarated and blessed. She felt at times an almost uncontrollable excitement, and she would spend hours at her work, feverish, unaware of time.

She and her mother had breakfast together every morning. They ate in the dining room, enjoying its size, undiminished by its high ceiling. The house was very large, very old, a house meant to store collections—paintings, manuscripts, first editions, antiques. Her father, now dead, had collected things. The house had become a small museum, but polished and sprightly, ruled by her mother's bustling efficiency. A woman with a firm place in local society, her days filled with luncheons and committee meetings and her weekends given over to entertaining or being entertained, Pauline's mother was that kind of middle-aged, generous, busy woman who becomes impersonal around the middle of her life. She too collected things, antiques and jewels, and kept up what she thought to be an enthusiastic interest in "culture"; it was something to talk about with enthusiasm. "We're stopping at the auction after lunch," she told Pauline. She chattered at breakfast, her rich, rosy face ready for the day that would never disappoint her, being a complicated day filled with women like herself, the making out of checks, endless conversations. . . . "You look a little pale. Are you well? Did you sleep well?"

"I had a strange dream, but I slept well. I'm fine."

"I still think you should give up that job. . . . I wish the weather would change. April is almost here and everything is still frozen, it depresses me when winter lasts so long. . . ." she said vaguely. She wore a dark dress, she wore pearls and pearl earrings; a slightly heavy woman, yet with a curious grace, a girlish flutter at the wrists and ankles, which Pauline herself had never had. She was in the mold of her father: tall, lean, composed, with a patient, cool kind of grace, never hurried. Pauline had never been able to accept the memory of her father in the hospital after his stroke, suddenly an elderly man, trembling, with tiny broken veins in his face. . . .

RITES TO BE HELD FOR PROMINENT
FINANCIER, PHILANTHROPIST

"Are you sure you're well?" her mother said suddenly.

"Yes. Please."

They parted for the day. Pauline's mother approved of her "work," though she did not like her teaching down at the Art Institute; she feared the city. She did not exactly approve of Pauline's clothes and her tendency to wear the same outfit day after day, but her daughter had a profession, a career, she was an *artist*, unlike the daughters of her friends. Every few years the newspapers did stories on her when she won some new award or had a new show for the art page or the splashy women's page, the daughter of the late Francis Ressner, with large photographs that showed her standing beside one of her stark, white heads, her own head beautiful as a work of art. There was a certain stubbornness in both her and in her work. She had very light blond hair that fell past her shoulders, but she wore it braided around her head, giving her a stiff, studied look; she had worn it like that since the age of fifteen. Her cheekbones were a little prominent because her face was too thin, but she attended to her face with some of the respect for clarity and precision that she applied to her work—though she wore no make-up, she kept her eyebrows plucked to a delicate, arched thinness, and she saw that her face was smoothed by oils and creams, protected against the city's sooty wind. She was pleased to have a kind of beauty, pale and unemphatic; her father too had been a beautiful man. Her mother, florid and conversational, had been startlingly pretty until recent years, a perfumed and likable woman, but Pauline was another kind of woman altogether and pleased with herself. Sometimes, in the privacy of her studio, she sat on a stool before a mirror, her long legs stretched out before her, and contemplated herself as if contemplating a work of art. She could remain like this for an hour, without moving. It pleased her to be so complete; unlike other women, she did not want to turn into anyone else.

That morning, entering the Institute, she saw one of her girl students talking to the man she had met the day before, Anthony—they were standing just inside the door, and both looked around at her. She smiled and said hello, not waiting for any reply. Her heart had jumped absurdly at the sight of him and she had no desire to hear his voice . . . she was afraid he would hurry after her, take hold of her arm. . . . Safe in her class, she put on a shapeless, soiled smock. She directed eight students in their own work with clay. She was efficient with them, not friendly, not unfriendly, never called anything except *Miss Ressner*. She felt no interest in her students' lives, no jealousy for the girls with their engagement rings and wedding bands. The girl who had been talking with Anthony had long black hair and an annoying eagerness. She had a small, minimal talent, but she was one of those students who want to be told, at once, whether they will succeed or not, whether their talent is great enough to justify work, as if the future could be handed to them on a scroll, everything figured out by a superior mind, determined permanently. . . . And she felt no interest in the men, who were both older and younger than she; their pretensions, their sincerity, their private, feverish plans did not interest her.

After class the girl said to her, "Miss Ressner, that man was asking about you. Out there. Did you notice him?"

Pauline showed no curiosity. "I saw you talking to someone."

"He asked a lot of questions about you. . . . I know him a little, not well, he hangs around down here in the bars and places. . . ." Then, embarrassed, she said quickly, "But of course I didn't tell him anything."

Pauline felt tension rising in her. She dropped her paper cup into a wastebasket, conscious of spilling coffee in the basket, onto napkins . . . coarse paper napkins that soaked up the liquid at once. . . . It was ugly, a mess. She went out into the drafty corridor. The dream was still with her. . . . She was tempted suddenly to go over to the museum to see if anything there could explain it, surely it had an origin in something she had seen and forgotten. . . . *Why a procession of mules, why garlands of flowers, why a bare-chested victim in a wagon?*

Later that day she saw Anthony again. He was standing in front of a restaurant, doing nothing, as if waiting for her. . . . She had left her studio, restless, wanting to get away from students who dropped in to talk with her. She was too polite to discourage visits. Why did people waste her time talking to her? Why did they ask her vulgar, personal questions, about where she got her ideas, about whose work she admired most . . . ? Why did people talk to one another, drawn together mysteriously, fatally, helpless to break the spell? She had sensed, in certain men and in a few women, a strange attraction for her—something she had never understood or encouraged. Gentle, withdrawing, but withdrawing permanently, she backed out of people's lives, turning aside from offers of friendship, from urgency, intensity, the admiration of men who did not know her at all. She liked all these people well enough, she just did not want to be close to them. And now this Anthony, whom she would not have liked anyway, was hanging around her, a dragging tug at the corner of her eye, a threat. Her mother's first command would be to call the police, but Pauline, being more sensible, knew that was not necessary. It would have been a mistake to ignore him. She said, "Hello, how are you?" Her smile was guarded and narrow in the cold sunlight.

"Hello," he said. His voice sounded uneven, as if he was so surprised by her attention that he could not control it. "Where are you going? Would you like some coffee?"

"I don't have time," she said, side-stepping him. She felt her face shape itself into a polite smile of dismissal. Anthony smiled back at her, mistaking the smile . . . or was he pretending to mistake it? Was he really very arrogant? She felt again a sense of fear, a suffocating pounding of her heart.

He rubbed his hands together suddenly, warmly, as if pleased by her. Today he looked more robust; he had shaved, his black curls fell more neatly down onto his collar; he wore a short, sporty coat that was imitation camel's hair, only a little soiled; he wore leather boots, cracked and marred like her own shoes.

"I'd like to talk with you," he said. "It's very important."

"Not today—"

"But I won't hurt you. I only want to talk." He smiled a dazzling smile at her—he was about to move toward her, about to take her arm again. She jumped back, frightened. But he only said, "I want to talk about different kinds of living, I want to know you . . . how it is for you, your life, a woman who looks like you. . . . I spend my time watching things, or listening to things, music, in a bar or in somebody's apartment, listening to records. . . ."

"I have to leave," she said thinly, bowing her head. She could not look up at him.

"Yesterday, when I saw you, I thought . . . I thought that I would like to meet you. . . . Why does that offend you?"

She said nothing.

"I asked him, what's-his-name, to introduce us. He didn't want to. It was very important to me, something gave me a feeling about you, meeting you, I was very nervous . . . last night I couldn't sleep. . . ." She stared at his boots. Strong lines and faint lines, a pattern made by the salted ice in leather, ruining it. The pattern was interesting. One of her own shoes was coming apart. . . . What if friends of her mother's saw her standing here, on Second Avenue, talking to this man? His long, shabby curls, his striking face, the slouch of his shoulders and the urgent line of his leg, bent dancerlike from the hip, even the stupid cowboy boots, would upset and please them probably: looking like that, he must be an artist of some kind.

Stammering, embarrassed, she interrupted him, "I'm older than you think . . . I'm over thirty . . . I don't have time to talk to you, I don't go out with people, I'm not the way you think. . . ."

"How do you know what I think?" he said angrily.

His anger frightened her. She was silent. Why was she here quarreling with a man she didn't know? She never quarreled with anyone at all. She never quarreled.

"If you're so anxious to leave, leave," he said.

Released, she could not move. For a moment she had not even heard him.

"Don't run—I won't follow you!" he said angrily.

Back for her two-o'clock class, trying to control herself. She had another cup of coffee. Shaking inside. The coffee tasted bad. Everything down here was cheap, her students' talent was cheap, common, their faces had no interest for her, she could not use them in her work, why was she pretending to need a job? She should quit. Move her studio out. There were only two genuinely talented students in her class, both men, and she guessed from their nervousness and the frequency with which they cut class that they would never achieve anything, they would disintegrate . . . other talented students of hers had appeared and disappeared over the years, where did they all end up? And yet when former students did come back to visit, most of them art teachers in high school, she was unable to show more than a perfunctory interest in their careers; why did people surround her, clamor into her ears, what did they want from her? What secret?

"He's crazy," she thought.

During the next several days, aware of him at a distance out on the street, she sometimes felt terror, sometimes a kind of dizzy, abandoned excitement. It was necessary for her to be afraid; she knew the police should be notified, barriers raised, bars put into place; yet she wondered idly why she should be afraid, why . . . ? She could not believe that anything might happen to her. She was safe in her composure, her strength, she had been taking care of herself for years, and so why should she be afraid of that man, why could she even think about him . . . ?

Getting into her car one afternoon, late, she saw him at the edge of the faculty parking lot, watching her. She was tempted to raise her hand casually in a greeting. Would that dispel the danger or make it worse? She imagined him leaping over the low wire fence and galloping up to her. . . . She did not wave. She did not give any sign of seeing him. But when she drove by him she saw him take several quick steps, faltering steps, after the car, in the street . . . his action was ludicrous, sad, crazy. . . . She wondered if she herself had become a little crazy.

> Bodies in a field. The field is sandy, a wasteland, but great spiky weeds grow in it, needing no water. The end of winter, not yet spring. The bodies come to life: a man and a woman. The woman has long, ratty hair, the man's hair is mussed. It is confused with his face. Their bodies are twisted and their faces in shadow. They laugh loudly, waking, they embrace right on the sand, in the open field. . . . Near them is something dead. Is it a dog or a large rat? Let it be a large rat. Frozen hard from winter, not decayed. . . . In the presence of that thing the man and woman embrace violently, tearing at each other's skin, their laughter sharp and wild. . . . They make love right there in the open, among the spiky weeds and the dead rat, aware of nothing around them.

She woke with a headache again, unable to remember what had wakened her. A dream? It was still dark. Only six o'clock. She got out of bed, her body suddenly aching. She dragged herself to her closet, put on a warm robe, stood in a kind of perplexed slouch, wondering what to do next. . . . Her shoulders and thighs ached, her head ached. Her eyes in their sockets were raw and burning, as if someone had been sticking his thumbs in them. Nearby, on a handsome old table, was a head she had done recently, in white; the model had been an old man, but very clean, dignified. He had had a light fringe of hair, almost like frost, but she had dismissed that and the head was bald, an exacting skull. It interested her strangely. The head of an old man, a dignified shape of bone, interlocking bone. Ingenious work of art, the human skull. His forehead was solid, bony, broad. The nose was rather flat, but broad at the bridge; a strong nose. The eyes were stern, the eyebrows strong and clear, the mouth slightly surprised, but withdrawing from surprise. She had wanted

to convey a certain emotion—terror, really, but at the same time the re-
fusal to accept this terror, even to allow the surface of the skin to register
it. She ran her hand over the top of the head, over the face. Cold lead.
Cold skin. She pressed her cheek against the top of the head. A completed work.

In her bathroom the light was too strong. It was reflected from the
cream-colored porcelain of the skin. The house was old but the
bathrooms and kitchen had been remodeled at great expense; Pauline had
never liked the change. She had liked the old-fashioned fixtures with
their heavy, exaggerated handles, the mirror beginning to show lead beneath it—like the gray bones beneath a skull's skin, without shame—and
the old, creaky shower, the worn black and white tile. Now everything
was new and clean, as if in a motel. It had no history.

She peered at herself in the mirror. In a few weeks she would be thirty
years old, which seemed to her surprisingly young. Surely she had lived
more than three decades . . . ? Yet her face looked very young. It was
pale, untouched, soft and baffled from sleep, as if with a child's appre-
hension. What had she dreamed? She took a jar of night cream out of the
cabinet and smoothed it onto her face. It was necessary to lubricate her
skin, she had to take care of herself. It was a duty. One day, twenty years
ago, her father had told her bluntly that she was dirty—disheveled hair,
socks running down into her shoes. "I don't want you to look ugly," he
had said. It was a command she took seriously, because she had his face,
a striking, beautiful face, and that face brought with it a certain responsibility. There is a terrible weight in all kinds of beauty.

> Skin is an organ of the body. It consists of many
> layers of cells. No one could have invented it.
> Cells absorb moisture and lose moisture; they
> pulsate in their own secret rhythm, in their own
> private time. Invisible, elastic. Each human being
> has his own skin, unique to him. It is a mystery.
> Someday a dead woman will wear the skin that
> belonged to a living woman, and it is the same
> skin exactly. Then it decomposes. . . . The skin
> is the most impermeable barrier of the body. It
> is always thirsty. Its thirst is insatiable. Human
> thirsts are satisfied from time to time, but the
> thirst of the human skin is never satisfied so long
> as it lives.

She wandered aimlessly through the house. Downstairs, she looked out the window down the slope of their long front lawn, at car lights on the avenue, a distance away. Where were all those people going? It surprised her to see the cars out there, people driving all night, into the dawn, with secret, private destinations. . . . Something moved out on the lawn. She did not look at it. Then, feeling helpless, she looked at it . . . she saw nothing, only shadow . . . it was not possible that anything had been there.

If that man followed her home?

Years ago, a student in London, she had modeled for a class. They were sketching heads, torsos. The instructor had been a peculiar man— middle-aged, wheedling, argumentative, but enormously talented, a big man with hairy arms. He had always spilled coffee on the floor, knocked ashes everywhere. Pauline had sat there in the center of a circle, motionless. She had never been shy or self-conscious. Her face, protected by its film of impersonality, was invulnerable. . . . The instructor's name was Julius. She had sat on a stool, relaxed, and he had stood wrenching her into shape, turning her face one way, then another. "Remain like that. Don't complicate our lives," he had said. Somewhere on the other side of the silent, working students he had stood, smoking, staring at her. He had a large, ungainly, gracefully clumsy body. He never talked to anyone personally, he never bothered to look anyone in the eye. She loved him, with rushes of enthusiasm that did not last, imagining him kneeling before her, kissing her knees, in the pose of a certain decadent painting . . . and her staring down through mild, half-closed eyelids at him, uncomprehending. But nothing happened. One day she imagined he was about to embrace her—they were alone for some reason in the studio— she had an uncanny, terrifying moment when she was certain he was going to embrace her, pressing her face against his, his large hands wild in her hair. . . . But he only opened a drawer and some objects inside rattled around. She had gone out into the wet air relieved, ready to weep, feeling totally herself once more.

Since that time she had thought herself in love with two other men, one of them a painter who still lived in this city but whom she no longer bothered to see, another a lawyer, the son of a wealthy couple in her parents' set of friends. But nothing had happened. Nothing. She had approached them as if in a dance, she had noticed something in their faces, a certain intense yearning, and she had gracefully, shyly, permanently withdrawn, not even allowing the surface of her skin to register the excitement and dread she had felt. So it had ended. She was complete in herself, like the heads she made, and like them she felt her skin a perfect organ, covering her, a surface that was impregnable because it was so still and cold.

> Statue of Mars. Brandishing a spear, attacking.
> The muscular body is in contrast with the
> graceful pose, almost a dancer's pose. One hand
> holds the lance, the other probably holds a
> libation bowl. Lips are inlaid in copper and eyes
> in some colored material; helmet separate and
> attached. Gently modeled eyes, strange
> expression of mouth, almost a smile. Tension
> of body: elegance of face. Small, tight, careful
> curls descending around ear, down onto
> cheek.

> EMERGENCY NUMBERS:
> FIRE   POLICE   SHERIFF   DOCTOR
> STATE POLICE   COAST GUARD
> or Dial Operator in any emergency and say "I
> want to report a fire at————" or "I want a
> policeman at————"

She was walking with a friend of hers, another art instructor, down a street of bookstores and bars and restaurants, student hangouts. While the man talked, her eyes darted about frantically. It was still cold. She had forgotten her gloves. Her fingers ached with something more than cold, because it was not that cold. Her friend—a married man with four children, a safe man—was talking about something she couldn't concentrate on when Anthony appeared in a doorway ahead of them. He looked out of breath, as if he had just been running. Pauline had the strange idea that he had run around the block just to head them off. He was staring at them, but her friend noticed nothing, and as if this were a scene carefully rehearsed, everyone between them—students in sloppy overcoats, a Negro woman with her children—moved away, clearing the view. Pauline and her friend were going to pass Anthony by a few feet, pass right by him. There was nothing she could do. She stared at him, unable to look away, catching the full angry glare of his eyes, the tension in his head. Cords in his neck were prominent. His coat was open, his hands thrust in his pockets. He glared at her, his glare surrounding her as if the coldness were forming a halo, magically, about her body. The line of his jaw was very hard, his mouth was slightly open as if he were breathing with great difficulty. . . .

He jumped out at them, grabbing her arm. She tried to break loose. In silence he swung a knife, the blade suddenly bright and decorative, and slashed at his own throat. Pauline screamed. Her friend yanked her away, but not before Anthony's blood had splashed onto her. "What are you doing? What—what is this?" the man cried. Anthony, staggering, caught her around the hips, the thighs, as he fell heavily, and she had not the power to break herself loose from him; she stared down at the top of his head, paralyzed.

In a few minutes it was over.

He was taken away; it was over. Her friend answered the policeman's questions. An ambulance had come with its lights and siren but now it was gone. "It's all over. Don't think about it," her friend said, as if speaking to one of his own children. Pauline was not thinking about anything. She walked woodenly, looking down at her blood-splattered shoes. Her coat was smeared with blood in front. Her stockings might have been bloody also, but she could not see; she walked stiffly, not bending at the waist, her shoulders rigid.

"You'd think they would catch people like that before they do something violent," her friend said.

Teen-aged girls, passing them on the sidewalk, stared in amazement at Pauline.

MAN SLASHES OWN THROAT IN UNIVERSITY AREA

Anthony Drayer, 35, of no fixed address, slashed his own throat with a butcher knife this noon on Second Avenue. He is in critical condition at Metropolitan Hospital. No motive was given for the act.

TEMPERATURE HOVERS AT 32°; WEATHERMEN
PREDICT FAIR AND WARMER THIS WEEKEND

When she got home, she went right up to her bathroom, avoiding the maid. Safe. She tore off her coat, sobbing, she threw it onto the floor, and stared at her legs—blood still wet on her knees, on her legs, splattered onto her shoes. As if paralyzed, she stared down at her legs; she could not think what this meant. She kept seeing him in the doorway, his chest heaving, waiting, and she kept reliving the last moment when she knew unmistakably that she dare not pass near him, it could not be done; and yet she had said nothing to the man she was with, had kept on walking as if in a trance. Why? Why had she walked straight toward him?

She was shivering. In horror, she raised her skirt slowly. More blood on her stockings. On the inside of her thigh, smeared there. It was a puzzle to her, she could not think. Why was that man's blood on her, what had happened? Had he really stabbed himself with a knife? How could a man bring himself to draw a blade hard across his own throat, why wouldn't the muscles rebel at the last instant, freezing?

She took off her stockings and threw them away. In a ball, squeezed in her fist, they seemed harmless. Blood on her legs, thighs. She stared. What must she do next?

She took a bath. She scrubbed herself.

She fell onto her bed and slept heavily, as if drugged.

On the table are four heads in a white material,
a ceramic material. It shines, gleams cheaply,
light glares out of the eyes of the heads. . . .
The first head is my own, the face is my own.
A blank white face. The next face is my own,
but smaller, pinched. Shocked. The next head,
also white, is my own head again . . . my own
face . . . the lips drawn back in a look of
hunger or revulsion, the eyes narrowed. Can
that be my face, so ugly a face? The fourth head
is also mine. White, stark white. A band tight
around the head has emphasized a vein on my
temple, a small wormlike vein in white, standing
out. The eyes are stern and empty, like the eyes
in Greek statues, gazing inward, fulfilled. That
head is in a trance-like sleep, like the sleep of a
pregnant woman. I walk around and around the
table as if choosing. My hands are itching for
work of my own. I can feel the white clay
beneath my fingernails, but when I look down
it is not clay but blood, hardening in the cracks
of my hands.

Driving to the Institute, she was overcome by a sudden attack of nausea and had to pull her car over to the side. Now it was April. She sat for a while behind the wheel, too faint to get out, helpless. The nausea passed. Still she did not drive on for a while but remained there, sitting, listening intently to the workings of her body.

> The doctor stands above me. I am lying on an old-fashioned table, he is holding a large pair of tweezers, his glasses are rimmed by metal, he is bald, the formation of his forehead shines, bumps shine in the light, I am ready to scream but the straps that hold down my legs also hold back my screams. . . . This happened centuries ago. A slop pail is beneath the sink. The doctor holds up his tweezers to the light and blows at a curly dark hair that is stuck to them . . . the hair falls slowly, without weight. . . .

While teaching her class, she felt a sudden urgency to get out of the room. She went to the women's rest room. Safe. She stared at herself in the mirror, seeing a tired, pale, angry face. Dull splotches of the metal that backed the mirror showed through, giving her a leprous look. She recalled a mirror like this in a public rest room, herself a girl of thirteen, pale and scared and very ignorant. She had thought she was pregnant. At that time she had thought pregnancy could happen to any woman, like a disease. Like cancer, it could happen.

For weeks she had imagined herself pregnant. Her periods had been irregular and very painful. She struck at her stomach, weeping, she went without eating until she was faint. . . . One day, kneeling with her forehead pressed against her old bathtub, thinking for the five-thousandth time of the terrible secret she held within her, she had felt the first painful tinge of cramps and then a slight, reluctant flow of blood. . . . So she was not pregnant after all . . . ?

How did a woman get pregnant?

She lifted her skirt again to stare at the smooth white skin of her leg. Blank. Blood had been smeared there, but now it was clean; she showered every morning and took a hot bath every night, anxious to be clean and soothed and free of his blood.

The living cells of the blood, insatiably hungry
for more life, flow upward. They rise anxiously,
viciously upward . . . in test tubes they may be
observed defying the well-known law of gravity.
Also, blood splashed onto bread mould will devour
it and be nourished by it. Also, blood on foreign
skin or fur will harden into a scab and work its
way into the new flesh, draining life from it.
Also, blood several days old, dropped into tubes
containing female reproductive cells, will unite
with these cells and form new life.

At a dinner party one Saturday in April. Her escort was a bachelor, a
lawyer. She rose suddenly from the table, trembling, careful to pull back
her chair without catching it in the rug, her head bowed, demure, her
diamond earrings brushing coldly against her cheeks. Not all the candlelight of this room could warm those earrings or those cheeks. She hurried
to the bathroom, she clutched at her head, her face, she realized with a
stunning certainty that she was pregnant.

She was sick to her stomach, as if trying to vomit that foreign life out
of her.

On Monday, not wanting to worry her mother, she drove out though
she had no intention of teaching her class. She parked around the university and walked for hours. She was looking for him, for evidence of him.
Her breasts felt sore, her thighs and shoulders ached. She knew that she
could not be pregnant and yet she was certain she was pregnant. Her face
burned. After hours of walking, exhausted, she called a cab and went
back home, abandoning her car. She wept.

"I just found out about Drayer," Martin said, stammering. "They said
he cut himself and attacked a woman, and I knew it would be you, I
knew it. . . ." Pauline was silent, holding the telephone to her ear
without expression. "I knew something like that would happen! He was
very strange, he never appreciated what I did for him, he was forgetful,
like a child—he was always forgetting my name and he had no grati-
tude—he was like a criminal—I would never have introduced you but he
insisted upon it, he said he couldn't take his eyes off your face—I knew I

shouldn't have done it, please, do you forgive me? Pauline? Do you forgive me?"
    She hung up.

> A woman in a stiff brocade dress, wearing
> jewels. Evening. Candlelight. Her face is
> shadowed . . . is it my mother, my aunt? She
> opens the window, which is a door, and a large
> dog appears. It is a greyhound, elegant and
> spoiled and lean, with a comely head. The
> woman takes hold of the dog's head in both
> hands, staring into its eyes. The dog begins to
> shake its head . . . its teeth flash . . . foam
> appears on its mouth. . . . I turn away with a
> scream, slamming my hand flat on the keyboard
> of a piano: the notes crash and bring everything
> to a stop.

Her mother was packing the large suitcase with the blue silk lining. Weeping, her mother. Her back is shaking. A friend of her mother's talks patiently to Pauline, who lies hunched up in bed, rigid. "If you would try to relax. If you would let us dress you," the woman says. Her own son, at the age of seventeen, once tried to kill her: so she has had experience with this sort of thing. No doubt why Pauline's mother called upon her.

"You understand that you cannot be pregnant and that you are not pregnant," the doctor says. He shapes his words for her to read, as if she might be deaf. She feels the foreign life inside her, hard as stone.

Bleeding from the loins, she aches with cramps, coils of cramps. The blood seeps through the embryonic sack, not washing it free. How to get it free? She has a sudden vision, though she is not sleeping, of a tweezers catching hold of that bloodswollen little sack and dragging it free. . . .

Dr. Silverman, a friend of her father's, visits her in this expensive hospital. He talks to her kindly, lovingly, holding her stone fingers. He is a very cultured man who, having lost most of his own family in a Nazi death camp, is especially suited to talk to her, arguing her out of madness and death. No doubt why her mother called upon him.
    Her hair has been cut off short. She cannot hear him.

The nurse says sourly, "You'll get over it." She is lying in warm water, frightened by a terrible floating sensation, as if her organs are floating free inside her, buoyed up by the water. Only the embryo is hard, hard as stone, fixed stubbornly to her arteries. She tries to scream but cannot scream. Anyway, it is dangerous to open her mouth: they feed her that way, tearing open her mouth and inserting a tube.

> . . . He is an ancient Chinese, his face unclear.
> He stands fishing in a delicate stream, his heavy,
> coarse robe pulled up and tucked in his belt. He
> catches a fish and pulls it out of the water, pulls
> it off the hook with one jerk of his hand . . . he
> tosses the fish onto the bank where the other
> fish lay, bleeding at the mouth, unable to close
> their eyes. . . .

Her mother brings a box of candy. Cheeks haggard, spring coat not very festive. She is a widow, and now it is beginning to show. She sits by the bedside weeping, weeping. . . . "Do you hear me? Why don't you talk to me? Do you hate me unconsciously? Why do you hate me?" Her mother weeps, words are all she knows, she turns them over and over again in her mind. "That man . . . you know . . . the one who stabbed himself, well, it was in the paper that he finally killed himself, in the hospital where he was being kept. . . . Why don't you hear me, Pauline? I said that man did away with himself. He won't bother you any more, he can't bother you. Are you listening? Why aren't you listening?"
She lies listening.

> It is a monument in dark stone. A body is being
> cremated. Birds in the air, crows. It is finally
> spring and everything is loose. Children are
> running around the base of the monument, with
> no eye for it. What do children care about the
> monuments of the world! They throw flowers at
> one another. . . . Atop the monument is a
> statue, two figures. One is a youth with curly
> hair, a thick torso, protruding blank eyes. The
> set of his mouth shows him both angry and
> frightened. The other figure is an angel of death,
> a beautiful woman with outspread wings, though

her body is shaped unnaturally from the waist
down. She holds out her hand to the young man.

I am standing before him. He sinks to his knees
and embraces me, he presses his face against me.
Leaning over him, with lust and tenderness that
is violent, like pain, I clutch him to me, I feel the
tight muscles of his shoulders, I press my face
against the top of his head. . . .

We kneel together. We press our faces together,
our tears slick and warm. . . .

Running Down

⌣⌐⌐⌣

M. JOHN HARRISON

I knew Lyall, certainly, and I was in the Great Langdale Valley at the time: but I had no place in the events of that Autumn in the late 70s—no active place, that is; and I could no more have prevented them than the eroded heather of the rhacomitrium-heath can "prevent" the wind. More important, perhaps, I could not have foreseen, much less averted, Lyall's end. He may have been insane long before the nightmare of Jack's Rake, but that does not explain why the earth shook; he may have murdered the hapless woman who lived with him to further some fantastic metaphysical image he had of himself, but that relates in no way you or I could understand to what I saw on the summit of Pavey Ark in the early hours of a haunted morning, the *ascent* that has remained with me, waking or sleeping, ever since.

Lyall was never more than an acquaintance of mine even at Cambridge, where we shared a room and might have been described as "close"; in fact, there were times when we found it difficult to disguise our dislike for one another. Nevertheless, we clung together, embittered and hurt—neither of us could make any warm contact with our contemporaries. To be honest: no-one else would put up with us, so we put up with each other. It's common enough. Even now, Cambridge is all comfortable November mists, nostalgic ancient quadrangles, the conspiracy of the choir practicing at King's—pure, ecstatic, and a constant wound to the outsider. It was inevitable that Lyall and I press those wounds together to achieve some sort of sour blood-fraternity. I suppose that's hard to understand; but it must be a common enough human compulsion.

Lyall was tall and ectomorphic, with a manner already measured, academic, middle-aged. His face was long and equine, its watery eyes, pursed mouth and raw cheeks accusatory, as if he blamed the world outside for his own desperate awkwardness. He did: and affected a callow but remorseless cynicism to cover it. He was a brilliant student, but already comically accident-prone—constantly scratched and bruised, his clothes stained with oil and ink and food. His background (he had been brought up by two impoverished, determined maiden ladies in Bath) chafed the tender flesh of my own early experience under the bleak shadow of the southern end of the Pennines—the open-coffin funerals of a failing industrial town, a savage unemployment, black Methodism.

We must have made a strange pair in those endless Winter fogs: Lyall as thin as a stick, hopeless in the tweed jacket and college scarf his aunts insisted he wear, his inflamed nose always running, his wrists and ankles protruding dismally from the awful clothes; and myself, short of leg, barrel chested and heavily muscled about the shoulders and ridiculous long arms for the solitary climbing and fell-walking that had in adolescence become my passionate escape from the back-terraces of the North. In those days, before the Dru accident, I could do a hundred press-ups with a fifty-pound pack on my back. I was sullen, dark, aggressive, and so terrified of being nicknamed "Ape" by the fragile, intellectual young women of the modern languages faculty that no-one but Lyall ever had the miserable chance. God knows why we do these things to ourselves.

So: it was a temporary alliance. I had memories of Lyall's high, complaining voice, his ruthless wit and feral disappointment as we separated on the last day of the last term. He took a poor Honors, due to an unfortunate bicycle accident a week before Finals: but mine was poorer (although somewhat ameliorated by the offer of a junior instructorship I'd received from an Outward Bound school in Kenya). His handclasp was curt, mine cursory. We were both faintly relieved, I think.

We never sought each other out. I believe he tried several jobs in the provinces before becoming the junior personnel officer of a small manufacturing firm in London, which was where I met him again, quite by chance, some two or three years later.

A week off the boat from North Africa—and finding it almost as difficult to accept the dirty chill of late Autumn in the city as to accept bacon at a hundred pence a pound after Kenya's steak at twenty-five the kilo—I was wandering rather morosely about in the West End, wonder-

ing grimly if I could afford to go into a cinema and waste another evening, when I spotted him teetering at a kerb trying to hail a taxi. Two ignored him while I watched. He hadn't changed much: his ghastly college
scarf was now tucked into the neck of a thin raincoat, and he was carrying one of those wretched little plastic "executive" cases. The contemptuous grooves round his mouth had deepened.

"Oh, hallo Egerton," he said off-handedly, staring away from me
down the road. He looked drunk. One of his hands was inexpertly bandaged with a great wad of dirty white gauze. He fiddled with his case.
"Why on earth did *you* come back to this rat-hole? I'd have thought you
were better off out of it."

I felt like a deserter returning to some doomed ship only to find its captain still alive and brooding alone over the white water and foul ground:
but I was surprised to be remembered at all, and, when he finally captured his taxi, I agreed to go home with him.

It turned out that he'd been in another taxi when it became involved in
some minor fracas with a pedestrian, and had to get out. "I should have
been home bloody hours ago," he said sourly. That was all: and by the
time we reached his flat I was beginning to regret an impulse which had
basically been one of sympathy. There was an argument with the driver,
too, over a malfunctioning meter. It was always like that with Lyall. But
Holloway isn't Cambridge.

He had two poky, unwelcoming rooms at the top of a large furnished
house. The place had a sink, a filthy gas-stove and some carpets glazed
with ancient grease: it was littered with dirty crocks, empty milk bottles,
every kind of rubbish conceivable; everything in it seemed to be damaged
and old; it was indescribably cheerless.

When I declined the offer of a can of soup (partly because he was at
pains to let me see he had nothing else in the cupboard where he kept his
food, and partly out of horror at that mephitic stove) he shrugged ungra-
ciously, sat crosslegged on the floor among the old newspapers and political pamphlets—he seemed to have become interested in some popular
nationalist organization, to the extent anyway of scrawling "Rubbish!" or
"A reasonable assumption" in the margins of some of the stuff—and ate it
ravenously straight out of the pan. He was preoccupied by some slight
he'd received at work. "Bloody jumped-up filing clerks," he explained,
"every one of them. You'd better sit on the bed, Egerton. There's nothing else, so you needn't bother to look for it."

Later, he insisted on going out to an off-license and fetching back
some half-pint bottles of stout. This produced a parody of fellowship,

strung with gaunt silences. We really had nothing in common any more, especially since Lyall would mention Cambridge only in the cryptical, barbed asides of which he was so fond.

But he seemed determined; and I took it as a desperate attempt on his part to achieve some sort of contact, some sort of human feeling among all that cold squalor. His loneliness was apparent—in deference to it, I talked; and I was quite happy to fall in with his mood until I realized that he had adopted a most curious conversational procedure.

This consisted in first eliciting from me some reminiscence of my time in Africa, then blatantly ignoring me as I talked—flicking through the pages of a girlie magazine, picking up books only to toss them aside again, staring out of the uncurtained windows at the ominous pall of sodium light outside, even whistling or humming. He took to breaking in on my anecdotes to say, apropos of nothing, "I really ought to have that scarf cleaned," or, "What's that racket in the street? Damned lunatics"; and then when (perfectly relieved to escape from what had become an agonizing monologue) I made some answering remark about the London air or traffic, demanding:

"What? Oh, go on, go on, you mustn't pay me any attention."

I talked desperately. I found myself becoming more and more determined to overcome his scarcely-veiled sneers and capture his attention, inventing at one point an adventure on Mount Nyiru that I simply hadn't had—although it did happen to a fellow instructor of mine shortly after his arrival at the school.

It was an eerie experience. What satisfaction he could have had from it, I can't imagine.

"Fairly pleased with yourself then, are you?" he said suddenly. He went on to repeat it to himself, rocking to and fro. "Fairly pleased—" And he laughed.

In the end, I got up and made some excuse, a train, a matter of an hotel key: what else could I have done?

He leapt immediately to his feet, the most ludicrous expression of regret on his face. "Wait, Egerton!" he said. He glanced desperately round the room. "Look here," he said, "you can't go without finishing the last bottle, can you?" I shrugged. "I'll only chuck it out. I'll just—" He lurched about, kicking up drifts of rubbish. He hadn't taken that flimsy raincoat off all night. "I can't seem—"

"Let me." And I took the bottle away from him.

I bought my knife at Frank Davies' in Ambleside, more than twenty years ago. Among its extensible, obsessive gadgets is a thing like a claw,

for levering off the caps of bottles. I'd used it a thousand times before that
night; more. I latched it onto the cap with my right hand, holding the
neck of the bottle with my left. An odd thing happened. The cap resisted;
I pulled hard; the bottle broke in my hand, producing a murderous fork
of brown glass.

Beer welled up over a deep and painful gash between my thumb and
forefinger, pink and frothy. I stared at it. "Christ."

But if the accident was odd, Lyall's reaction was odder.

He groaned. Then he began to laugh. I sucked at the wound, staring
helplessly at him over my hand. He turned away, fell on his knees in
front of his bed and beat his hands on it. "Bugger off, Egerton!" he
croaked. His laughter turned suddenly into great heaving sobs. "Get out
of my sight!" I stood looking stupidly down at him for a moment, at the
thin shoulders crawling beneath that dirty raincoat, the miserable drift of
Guardians and girlie magazines and Patriotic Front literature: then
turned and stumbled down the stairs like a blind man.

It wasn't until I'd slammed the outside door that the full realization of
what had happened hit me. I sat down for a minute among the dented
bins and rotting planks of the concrete area, shivering in what I suppose
must have been shock. I remember trying to read what was daubed on
the door. Then an upstairs window was flung open, and I could hear him
again, half laughing, half sobbing. I got up and went down the street; he
leaned out of the window and shouted after me.

I was terrified that he might follow me, to some lighted, crowded tube
station, still laughing and shouting. He'd been expecting that accident all
evening; he'd been waiting all evening for it.

For a couple of weeks after that, a thin, surly ghost, he haunted me
through the city. I kept imagining him on escalators, staring bitterly
through the dirty glass at the breasts of the girls trapped in the advertise-
ment cases; a question mark made of cynical and lonely ectoplasm.

Why he chose to live in squalor; why he had shouted "You aren't the
first, Egerton, and you won't be the bloody last!" as I fled past the broken
milk machines and dreary frontages of his street; how he—or anyone—
could have predicted the incident of the last bottle: all questions I never
expected to have answered, since I intended to avoid him like the plague
if I ever caught sight of him again. I had four stitches put in my hand.

Then the Chamonix climbing-school post I had been waiting for came
free, and I forgot him in the subsequent rush of preparation.

He stayed forgotten during a decade which ended for me—along with a lot of other things—on a stiffish overhang some way up the Dru, in a wind I can still feel on sleepless nights, like a razor at the bone.

When I left Chamonix I could still walk (some can't after the amputation of a great toe), but I left counting only losses. The English were just then becoming unpopular on the Continent—but I returned to Britain more out of the lairing instinct of a hurt animal than as a response to some fairly good-humored jostling outside Snell's sports shop. I simply couldn't stand to be in the same country as the Alps.

At home, I took a job in the English department of a crowded comprehensive school in Wandsworth; hobbled round classrooms for a year or so, no more bored than the children who had to sit day after day in front of me; while on Saturday mornings I received, at the Hampstead hospital, treatment for the lingering effect of the frost-bite on my fingers and remaining toes.

I found quickly that walking returned to me something of what I'd lost to a bit of frayed webbing and a twelve-hour Alpine night. During the long vacations that are the sole reward of the indifferent teacher, I rediscovered the Pennines, the Grampians, Snowdonia—and found that while Capel Curig and Sergeant Man are no substitute for the Aiguille Verte group, I could at least recapture something of what I'd felt there in Cambridge days and before. I walked alone, despite the lesson of the Dru (which I am still paying for in a more literal way: French mountain rescue is efficient, but it can cost you twenty years of whatever sort of life you have left to you; up there, many people pray *not* to be taken off the mountain); and I discouraged that obsessive desire to converse which seems to afflict hikers.

It was on one of these holidays that I heard next from Lyall.

I was staying in the "Three Peaks" district north and west of Settle, and beginning to find its long impressionistic sweeps of moorland arduous and unrewarding. Lyall's letter caught up with me after a day spent stumping half-heartedly over Whernside in the kind of morose warm drizzle only Yorkshire can produce. I was sufficiently browned-off on returning, I recall, to ruin a perfectly good pair of Vibrams by leaving them too close to Mrs. Bailey's ravenous kitchen stove.

So the surge of sentiment which took hold of me when I recognized Lyall's miserly handwriting may be put down to this: I was soaked to the skin, and receptive.

The letter had been forwarded from Chamonix (which led me to

wonder if he'd been as drunk as he seemed on the night of the accident—
or as indifferent), and again from my digs in Wandsworth: a round trip of
absurd length for something which bore a Westmorland postmark. That
in itself was curious; but it was the contents that kept me some time from
my shepherd's pie.

It seemed that Lyall's maiden ladies had finally succumbed, within two
months of one another and despite all that Bath could do, to the inroads
of heart-disease; leaving him—"Almost as an afterthought," as he described it, "among two reams of sound advice—" a property in the Langdale Valley. He had nothing good to say of the place, but was "hard up"
and couldn't afford to sell it. He had "funked" his personnel officership
in London because the place had begun to "stink of appeasement"—an
apparently political comment I couldn't unravel, although by now, like
all of us, I knew a little more about the aims of the Patriotic Front. He
had married: this, I found almost incredible.

He suggested with a sort of contemptuous bonhomie that if I was "tired
of grubbing about on the Continental muck-heap," I might do an old
friend the favor of dropping by to see him.

There was something else there; he was his usual mixture of cold formality and old colloquialisms; "It's not much to ask" and "Please yourself
of course" were there; but underneath it all I sensed again the desperation
I had witnessed in that squalid flat twelve or thirteen years before—a horrified sense of his own condition, like a sick man with a mirror. And his
last sentence was in the form of an admission he had, I'm quite sure,
never in his life made before:

"Since you seem to like that sort of mucking about," he finished, "I
thought we might walk up some of those precious hills of yours together.
It's what I need to cheer me up."

That, tempered no doubt by a twin curiosity as to the nature of his inheritance and the temperament of his unnamed wife, decided me. I
packed my rucksack that night, and in the morning left Mrs. Bailey's
inestimable boarding house to its long contemplation of Ingleborough
Common. Why I was so quick to respond to him, I don't know; and if I'd
suspected one half of the events that were to follow my decision, I would
have been content with any amount of rain, moss and moorland.

Ingleborough Hill itself is a snare and a delusion, since a full third of
its imposing height is attained by way of an endless gentle slope bare of
interest and a punishment to the ankles: but that morning it thrust up
into the weather like a warning—three hundred million years of geologi-

cal time lost without trace in the unconformity between its base and its flat summit, from which the specter of the brigand Celt chuckles down at that of his bemused, drenched Roman foe.

The Ambleside bus was empty but for a few peaky, pinch-faced children in darned pullovers and cracked shoes. Their eyes were large and austere and dignified, but for all that they taunted the driver unmercifully until they spilled out to ravage the self-involved streets of Kendal, leaving him to remark, "It don't bother the kids, though, does it?" It didn't seem to bother him much, either. He was a city man, he went on to explain, and you had to admit that things were easier out here.

In the thirty or so miles that separate Ingleton from Ambleside, geomorphology takes hold of the landscape and gives it a cruel wrench; and the moorland—where a five-hour walk may mean, if you are lucky, a vertical gain of a few hundred feet—gives way to a mass of threatening peaks among which for his effort a man may rise two thousand feet in half a mile of forward travel. If I saw the crowding, the steepness, of those hills as Alpine, it may be that the memory dulls in proportion to the wound's ripening, no more.

The weather, too, is prone to startling mutation in that journey between Yorkshire and Westmorland, and I found the Langdales stuporous under a heat wave of a week's standing (it works, as often as not, the other way round). Ambleside was lifeless. Being too early for the valley bus, and tiring finally of Frank Davies' display window, I decided to walk to Lyall's "property."

Heat vibrated from the greenstone walls of the new cottages at Skelwith Bridge, and the Force was muted. A peculiar diffused light hung over the fellsides, browning the haunted fern; Elterwater and Chapel were quiet, deserted; the sky was like brass. I had some conversation with a hard-eyed pony in the paddock by the Co-Op forecourt when I stopped to drink a can of mineral water; but none with the proprietor, who was languid even among the cool of his breakfast cereals and string.

Outside Chapel I took to the shade of the trees and discovered a dead hare, the flies quite silent and enervated as they crawled over its face; a little further on, in the dark well of shadow at the base of the drystone, a motionless adder, eyeless and dried up. The valley had undergone some deterioration in the fifteen years since I had last seen it: shortly after I got my first sight of the Bowfell crags and Mickleden (the Rosset Gill path a trembling vertical scar in the haze), I came upon the rusting corpse of a motor car that had run off the difficult narrow road and into the beck.

Here and there, drystone scattered in similar incidents simply lay in the pasture, white clumps infested by nettles, like heaps of skulls; and when I came finally to the address Lyall had given me, I found the fellside below Raw Pike blackened up to the five-hundred-foot line by fire. I didn't know then what I began to suspect later; I saw it all in terms of the children on the Ambleside bus, the price of bacon in Wandsworth—symptomatic of another kind of disorder.

And none of it prepared me for Lyall's "property," a low shambling affair of local stone, facing directly onto the road; the main cottage having two rooms on each floor, and a couple of ancillary buildings leaning up against it as if they would prefer not to but had no choice.

It was amazingly dilapidated. Much of the glass at the front had been replaced by inaccurately cut oblongs of hardboard; something seemed to have been spilt out of one of the upper windows to dry as an unpleasant brown smear on the stone. The barn roofs sagged, and wanted slates; uncovered rafters are an agony and here crude patches of corrugated iron did little to mitigate it. One corner of the cottage had been battered repeatedly by confused motorists returning at night from the pubs of Ambleside to the National Trust camp site at the head of the valley; the same fire that had wasted the fern on the slope above had charred and cracked it; small stones and mortar made a litter of the road.

I untied the binder twine that fastened the gate and wandered round, knocking shyly on doors and calling out. The valley, bludgeoned into stillness by the sun, gave back lethargic echoes.

Road-walking tires my mutilated foot quite quickly. I keep a stick buckled to my pack where an ice axe would normally go, and try to have as little recourse to it as possible: the first two miles had forced it on me that day. I knocked down a few nettles with it, watched the sap evaporate. Two or three minute figures were working their way slowly down the Band, heat and light resonating ecstatically from the 2,900-foot contour behind them. I sat on an upturned water trough, blinking, and cursing Lyall for his absence.

I'd been there for perhaps a quarter of an hour, wondering if I could hear the valley bus, when he came out of the house, swirling dirty water round an enamel bowl.

"Good God!" he exclaimed sarcastically, and the stuff in the bowl slopped down the front of his trousers. "The famous Alpinist deigns to visit." He shot the water carelessly into the nettles. "Why the hell didn't you knock, Egerton? Shy?" I had the impression that he'd been watching me ever since I arrived. It wouldn't have been beyond him.

"You'd better come in," he said, staring off into the distance, "now you're here."

The intervening years had made him a parody of himself—lined and raw, all bone and raging, unconscious self-concern; he'd developed a stoop, a "dowager's hump," during his London days; a small burn on his neck seemed to be giving him trouble, and he kept his head at a constant slight angle to ease the inflammation caused by his collar. He remembered I was there, nodded at my stick. An old cruelty heliographed out like the light from the peaks.

"Your fine mountaineering cronies won't be so interested in you now, then? Not that I'd have thought that thing stopped you buying their beer."

It may have been true. I honestly hadn't thought of it until then. "I've learnt to live with it," I said, as lightly as I could.

He paused in the doorway—Lyall always walked ahead—and looked me up and down. "You don't know the half of it, Egerton," he said. "You never will." Then, sharply: "Are you coming in, or not?" The crags of Bowfell broadcast their heat across Mickleden, and the Pikes gave it back like a thin, high song of triumph.

What the outer dilapidation of the cottage led me to expect, I don't know: but it was nothing to what I found inside; and despite all that has happened since it still unnerves me to think of that place.

Plaster had fallen from the ceiling of the grim cubby-hole of a kitchen, and still lay on the cracked tile floor; an atrocious wallpaper meant to represent blond Swedish panelling, put up by the maiden ladies or one of their tenants in an attempt to modernize, bellied slackly off the walls. In the living room there was only plaster, and one wall had actually fissured enough to admit a thin, wandering line of sunlight—just as well, since the windows let in very little. Across this tenuous wafer of illumination, motes danced madly; and the place stank.

All the furniture was scarred and loose-jointed. Everywhere, objects: table-lamps, ashtrays and paltry little ornaments of greenstone: and nothing whole. Everything he owned had become grubby and tired and used in a way that only time uses things, so that it looked as if it had been broken thirty years before: a litter of last month's paperbacked thrillers, spilling with broken spines and dull covers and an atmosphere of the secondhand shop from the bookcases; gramophone records underfoot, scratched and warped and covered in bits of dried food from the dinnerplates, with their remains of week-old meals, scattered over the carpet.

It was as if some new shift of his personality, some radical escalation of his *morgue* and his bitterness, had coated everything about him with a grease of hopelessness and age. I was appalled; and he must have sensed it, because he grinned savagely and said:

"Don't twitch your nose like that, Egerton. Sit down, if you can find something that won't offend your lilywhite bum." But he must have regretted it almost immediately—making tea with an air of apology that was the nearest he ever came to the real thing, he admitted, "I don't know what I'm doing in this hole. I don't seem to be any better off than I was." He had got a job correcting publishers' proofs, but it gave him nothing, "Not even much of a living." While I drank my tea, he stared at the floor.

I got nothing but the weather from him for about half an hour. Then he said suddenly: "I haven't seen—what was his name?—*Oxlade*—lately. You remember him. The guitarist."

I was astonished. Probably the last time either of us had seen Oxlade was at Cambridge, just before he went down in the middle of his second year to sing with some sort of band; and then Lyall had loathed the man even more than the music, if that were possible.

I chuckled embarrassedly. All I could think of to say was, "No. I suppose not." This threw him into a temper.

"Christ, Egerton," he complained, "I'm doing my bit. You might join in. We've got little enough in common—"

"I'm sorry," I began, "I—"

"You've brought some bloody funny habits home with you, I must say." He was silent again for a moment, hunched forward in his seat looking at something between his feet. He raised his eyes and said quietly: "We're stuck with each other, Egerton. You need me again now. That's why you came crawling back here." This with a dreadful flatness of tone.

I looked for my rucksack. "There's a place where I can camp further up the valley," I told him stiffly; perhaps because I suspected he was correct.

We were both on our feet when a large vehicle drew up in the road outside, darkening the room further and filling it with a smell of dust and diesel oil; airbrakes hissed. It was the valley bus, and down from it stepped Lyall's wife. Lyall, tensed in the gloom, seemed to shrug a little—we both welcomed the interruption. "Look, Egerton—" he said.

He went to let her in.

She was a tall, haggard woman, ten or even fifteen years older than him and wearing a headscarf tied in a strangely dated fashion. Her legs were swollen, and one of them was bandaged below the knee. From under the headscarf escaped thin wisps of brownish hair, framing a quiet, passive face. They greeted one another disinterestedly; she nodded briefly at me, her lips a thin line, and went immediately into the kitchen, swaying a little as if suffering from the heat. She was carrying two huge shopping bags.

"You didn't tell me we'd run out of coffee," she called. When she returned, it was to throw a couple of paperbacks on the floor in front of him. "There weren't any papers," she said. "Only the local one." She went upstairs, and I didn't see her again that day. Lyall hadn't introduced her, and I don't think he ever told me her name.

I didn't want to stay, but he insisted. "Forget all that," he said. Later, he opened some cans into a saucepan. While we ate, I stuck to Cambridge, the safe topic, and was glad to see his customary sense of the ridiculous steadily replacing the earnestness with which he'd introduced the subject of Oxlade. Afterwards, "Let me do the washing up," I offered: and so cleared enough floor space to unroll my sleeping bag. Nobody had unpacked the shopping; I couldn't coax more than a trickle from the kitchen taps. Lyall looked cynically on.

After he'd gone to bed, I heard them arguing in tight suppressed voices. The sound carried all over the house—hypnotic but meaningless. The darkness was stuffy and electrical, and I hadn't got rid of the smell.

They were up and sparring covertly over some domestic lapse before I got out of my sleeping bag the following morning—the woman throwing things round the sink, Lyall prowling restlessly out into the garden and back again. If my presence had acted as a brake the night before, it was clearly losing its effect; by the time breakfast was ready, they were nagging openly at one another over the eggs. I would have been more embarrassed if the argument had not been over who was to unpack yesterday's shopping.

"I emptied the bloody Elsan yesterday," said Lyall defensively. "You do the shopping, not me."

"For God's sake who eats it?"

I drank some reconstituted orange juice and bent my head over my plate. The woman laughed a bit wildly and retreated into the kitchen. " 'For God's sake who *eats* it?' " mimicked Lyall, ignoring me. I heard her scraping something into the sink tidy. There was a sudden sharp intake of breath. A moment later she reappeared, holding up her left hand. Blood was trickling slowly down the wrist.

"I'm sorry," she said desperately. "I cut it on a tin-lid. I couldn't help it."

"Oh, *Christ!*" shouted Lyall. He smashed his fist down on the table, jumped to his feet and stalked out.

She looked bemusedly after him. "Where are you going?" she called.

The cut was a ragged lip running across the base of her thumb, shallow but unpleasant. Worried by the grey tinge to her sallow, ageing face, I made her sit down while I rummaged through the place looking for some sort of dressing. In the end I had to raid my pack for a bit of plaster. When I got back to her she was slumped head-down on the table, her thin bony shoulders trembling. I saw to her hand, wishing Lyall would come back. While I was doing it, she said:

"You wonder why I stay here, don't you?"

The palm of her hand was cross-hatched with other, older scars. I might have been tempted to chuckle at the thought of these two sour accident-prones, trapped together in their crumbling backwater and taking miserable revenges on one another, if I hadn't had recollections of my own—chilly images of London in late Autumn, the pall of sodium light outside Lyall's poky rooms, the last bottle of beer.

"Lyall's hard to live with," I temporized. I didn't want her confidences, any more than I wanted his. "At Cambridge—"

She took hold of my wrist and squeezed it with a queer fervor. "It's because he needs someone." I shrugged. She hung on. "I love him, you know," she said challengingly. I tried to free my wrist. "So do you," she pressed. "You could be anywhere but here, but you're his best friend—"

"Look," I said angrily, "you're making this very difficult. Do you want your hand bandaged or not?" And when she simply stared: "Lyall just invited me to stay here. We knew each other at Cambridge, that's all. Hasn't he told you that?"

She shook her head. "No." Color had come back into her face. "He needs help. I made him write to you. He thinks—" Her mouth thinned; she seemed to withdraw. "Let him tell you himself." She looked down at her hand. "Thank you," she said formally.

I spent the rest of the day sitting on the water trough, staring out across the valley at quite another range of hills and wondering who I'd meet if I went to one of the hotels for a drink. At about mid-day she came out of the house, squinting into the sunlight.

"I'm sorry about this morning," she said. I muttered something, and drew her attention to a hawk of some kind hanging in the updraught over Raw Pike. She glanced at it impatiently. "I don't know anything about birds. I was in social work." She made a vague motion that took in the whole valley, the hot inverted bowl of the sky. "Sometimes I blame this place, but it isn't that." She had come out to say something else, but I gave her no encouragement. Perhaps I should have done. "Do you want any lunch?" she said.

Lyall returned with the valley bus.

"I suppose she's been talking to you," he said. He avoided my eyes. A little bit disgusted by the whole thing, I walked up to the the New Dungeon Ghyll and spent the evening drinking beer. The place was full of tourists who'd been running up and down Mill Gill all day in tennis shoes, making the rest of us look like old men. When I got back, Lyall and his wife were in bed, the eternal dull complaint rising and falling soporifically through the cottage. I was half asleep when the woman suddenly shouted:

"I'm twenty-five years old! *Twenty-five years!* What's happening? What's happened to me?"

After that, I got up and paced around until dawn, thinking.

Heat pumped down the valley from the secret fastnesses of Flat Crags, from the dry fall at Hell Ghyll; up in the high gullies, the rock sang with it. Further down, the hanging Langdale oakwoods were sapless, submissive—heat had them by the throat. A sense of immanence filled the unlovely living room of the Lyall cottage, reeked on the stairs, fingered out from the bedroom like ectoplasm from a medium. Lyall took to staring for hours at the crack in the wall, hands clasped between his knees. His wife was quiet and tense. Her despairing cry in the dark still hung between them.

Into this strange stasis or prostration, like a low, insistent voice, a thousand small accidents introduced themselves: the insect bite, the hand slipping on the can-opener, a loss of balance on the stair—cuts, rashes, saucepans dropped, items lost or broken; a constant, ludicrous, nerve-wracking communication from the realm of random incidence. For half a day the kitchen taps refused to give water of any sort, then leaked a slow, rusty liquor even when turned off; four slates fell from the roof in an afternoon of motionless air; Lyall's wife suddenly became allergic to the sun, and walked about disfigured.

Lyall's response to these events was divided equally between irritation and apathy. He brooded. Several times he took me aside as if to broach some mutually embarrassing subject, and on each occasion failed. I couldn't help him: the raging contempt of his Cambridge days, applied with as much rigor to his own motives as to those of others, was by now a memory. Out in one of the barns, cutting a piece of zinc to mend the roof, he said, "Don't you ever regret your childhood, Egerton?" I didn't think I did; I didn't think childhood meant much after a certain age. I had to shout this over the screech of the hacksaw. He watched my lips for a while, like a botanist with an interesting but fairly common specimen, then stopped working.

"In Bath, you know," he said, brushing his lank hair off his face, "it was all so clear-cut. A sort of model of the future, with neat sharp edges: English, Classics, Cambridge; and after that, God knows what—the Foreign Service, if the old dears had a thought in their heads." He laughed bitterly. "I had to play the piano." He held up the hand with the dirty ball of bandage on the thumb. "With this." He looked disgusted for a moment, but when he turned away, his eyes were watering. "I was really rather good at it."

This picture of the young Lyall, shut in some faded Regency drawing-room with a piano (his limbs protruding amazed and raw from the tubular worsted shorts and red blazer his maiden ladies would doubtless have insisted upon), was ludicrous enough. He compounded it by yearning, "We never deserve the future, Egerton. They never tell us what it's going to be like."

When I tried to laugh him out of it, he went angrily off with, "You might show a bit of interest in someone else's problems. It'd take your mind off your precious bloody foot."

He came back to the house late, with a half-empty bottle of brandy. God knows what fells he had been staggering across, red-faced and watery-eyed, his shirt pulled open to the waist. His wife and I had been listening to Bach; when he entered the room, she glanced at me and went straight upstairs. Lyall cocked his head, laughed, kicked out at the radiogram. "All that bloody Lovelace we had, eh?" he said, making some equation I couldn't follow.

"I don't know what I am, Egerton," he went on, pulling a chair up close to mine. "You don't, either. We'll never know the half of it," he said companionably. "Eh?" He was bent on baring his soul (or so I imagined): yearning for the emotional storm I was equally determined to avoid—Cambridge, recrimination, the maudlin reaffirmation of our interdependence. "Have a bloody drink, Egerton," he demanded.

"I think you ought to have some coffee," I said. "I'll make you some." I went into the kitchen.

"You bloody prig," he said quietly.

When I went back, he had gone upstairs. I listened for a moment, but could hear nothing. In the end I drank the coffee myself and went to bed. That night was one of vast heat and discomfort: the rancid smell I had noticed on my first day in the cottage oozed from the furniture as if the heat were rendering from the stuffing of the cushions some foul grease no scrubbing brush could touch; my sleeping bag was sticky and intolerable, and no amount of force would move the windows; I lay for hours in an exhausted doze poisoned by nightmares and incoherent, half-conscious fantasies.

Groaning from upstairs disturbed that dreary reverie. A sleepy moan, the dull thump of feet on the bedroom floor; something fell over. There was a moment of perfect silence, then Lyall saying loudly, "Oh Christ, I'm *sorry* then." Somebody came stumbling down through the thick, stale darkness of the staircase. My watch had stopped.

"Egerton?" called Lyall, bumping about in the dark. "Egerton? Egerton?"

He sounded like a dead child discovering that eternity is some buzzing, langorous dream of Bath. I heard him cough once or twice into the sink; then the brandy bottle gurgled, fell onto the kitchen tiles and was smashed. "Oh God," whispered Lyall. "Do you ever have nightmares, Egerton? Real ones, where you might just as well be awake?" I felt him coming closer through that ancient velvet darkness. "All this is my fault, you know." He swallowed loudly. He tried to touch my shoulder.

"You could get another job," I suggested cautiously, moving away. "The proofreading doesn't seem to make you much."

"When we came here, this place was perfect. Now look at it." There was a pause, as he scratched irritably about for the light switch. He failed to find it. "It's a slum, *and I'm doing it.* What difference can a job make?"

"Look," I said, "I don't quite understand." I couldn't bear the confines of the sleeping bag any more, but out there in the dark I was as lost as Lyall. I perched on what I hoped was the arm of a chair. "You'd better tell me about it," I invited, since there seemed to be no alternative; and added, feeling disgusted with myself even as I did it, "Old chap." I needn't have worried. He hardly noticed.

"Everything I touch falls to pieces," he said. "It's been happening since I was a kid." Then, with a dull attempt at dignity—"It's held me back, of course: I'd have had a First if it hadn't been for that bloody bicycle; the last job went down the chute with the office duplicator; I can't even get on a bus without it smashing into something."

"Everybody feels like that at some time or another," I said. "In the Alps—"

"Bugger the Alps, Egerton!" he hissed. "Listen to me for once!"

His mind was a back drain, it was an attic with a trap full of dry, eviscerated mice. In it he'd store up every incident of his childhood—a nursery *faux pas*, a blocked lavatory bowl, a favorite animal run down in the street—making no distinction between the act and the accident, between the cup and the lip. With a kind of quiet hysteria in his voice, he detailed every anticlimax of his maturity—each imagined slight carefully catalogued, each spillage, each coin lost among the rubbish beneath a basement grid; every single inkblot gathered and sorted into a relentless, unselective system of culpability.

It was nonsensical and terrifying. Typists, tutors and maiden ladies, his victims and pursuers, haunted him through that attic; *I* haunted him, it seemed, for he ended with: "It was me that cut your hand in London, Egerton, not the bottle. I couldn't help it. Something flows out of me, and I can't control it any more—"

"Look at this place. Look at it!" And he began to sob.

A dim, cobwebby light was filtering through the remaining panes of glass, greying his face, his scrawny, hopeless body. I have a horror of confession; I was angry with him for burdening me, and at the same time full of an awful empty pity; what could I have said to him?—That I thought he was mad? Self-concern makes us all mad. All I could do then was pat his shoulder reassuringly.

"Look," I said, "it's getting light, Lyall. Let's both have a bit of sleep. We can work it out later. You've obviously got a bit depressed, that's all. You'll feel better now."

He stiffened. One moment he was blubbering helplessly, the next he had said quite clearly, "I might have known. You've had it easy all your life, you bloody pompous bastard—"

I got to my feet. I thought of Chamonix, and the razor of wind that shaves the Aiguilles. I should have kept my temper; instead, I simply felt relieved to have a reason for losing it. I waited for a moment before saying, "Nobody paid my way through Cambridge, Lyall." Then, deliberately, "For God's sake pull yourself together. You're not a child any more. And you never were a Jonah—just a bloody great bag of self-pity."

He was hitting me the moment I turned away. I fell over the chair, upset more by the things he was screaming than by his clumsy attempts to re-enact some schoolyard fight of twenty years before. "Christ, Lyall, don't be silly!" I shouted. I got the chair between us, but he roared and knocked it away. I made a grab for his windmilling arms; found myself backed into a corner. I got a knock on my cheek which stung my pride. "You little fucker," I said, and hit him in the stomach. He fell down, belching and coughing.

I pulled him back into the room and stood over him. His wife discovered us there in our underpants—too old to be scrabbling about on a greasy carpet, too white and ugly to be anything but foolish. "What's the matter?" she pleaded, befuddled with sleep and staring at my mutilated foot. Lyall said something filthy. "You'd better look after the baby," I told her viciously. And then that old terrible boyhood cry of triumph. "He shouldn't start things he can't finish."

I got dressed and packed my rucksack, Lyall sniffing and moaning throughout. As I left, the woman was kneeling over him, wiping his runny nose—but she was gazing up at me. "No!" I said. "No more. Not from me. He needs a bloody doctor—" Turning in the doorway: "Why did you have to lie to him about your age? Couldn't *you* get anybody, either?" I felt a little sick.

It might have ended there, I might have taken away the simplest and most comforting solution to the enigma of Lyall, if I hadn't decided that while (for the second, or, now I could admit it, the third time in my life) I never wanted to see him again, I didn't intend to let him ruin the week or so of holiday I had left to me. It was unthinkable to return to Wandsworth with only that sordid squabble to remember through the winter.

So instead of catching the bus back to Ambleside I moved up the valley to the National Trust site, put up my little Ultimate tent, and for a week at least had some recompense for my stay beneath Raw Pike; pottering about in the silent, stone-choked ghylls of Oxendale, where nobody ever seems to go; drowsing among the glacial moraines of Stake Pass, where dragonflies clatter mournfully through the brittle reed-stems and the path tumbles down its spur into the Langstrath like an invitation; watching the evening climbers on Gimmer, colored motes against the archaic face of the rock, infinitely slow-moving and precarious.

It was a peculiar time. The heat wave, rather than abating, merely consolidated its grip and moved into its third week, during which temperatures of a hundred degrees were recorded in Keswick. Dead sheep dotted the fells like *roches moutonées*, and in dry gullies gaped silently over bleached pebbles. A middle-aged couple on a coach-outing for the blind wandered somehow onto the screes at Wastwater, to be discovered on the

1,700-foot line by an astonished rescue team and brought down suffering
from heat prostration and amnesia. Mickleden Beck diminished to a
trickle—at the dam beneath Stickle Breast, exhausted birds littered the
old waterline, staring passively up at the quivering peaks.

The camp site was empty, and curiously lethargic. A handful of
climbers from Durham University had set up in one field, some boys as
an Outward Bound exercise in the other: but there were none of the great
blue-and-orange canvas palaces which normally spread their wings beneath Side Pike all summer long, none of the children who in a moment
of boredom trip over your guylines on their way to pee secretly in the
brook. After dark each night, a few of us clustered round the warden's
caravan to hear the ten o'clock national news, while heat-lightning
played round Pike o' Stickle then danced gleefully away across Martcrag
Moor. Under a fat moon, the valley was greenish and ingenuous, like an
ill-lit diorama.

Despite my anger—or perhaps because of it—I couldn't exorcise the
Lyalls, and their dreamlike embrace of inadvertency and pain continued
to fascinate me. I even broke an excursion to Blea Rigg and Codale to sit
on the fellside for half an hour and muse over the cottage, small and
precise in the valley; but from up there it was uncommunicative. One of
the barn roofs had sagged; there was fresh rubble in the road; the whole
place had an air of abandonment and stupefaction in the heat. Where
was Lyall?—Prowling hungrily through the Ambleside bookshops, hag-
gling sourly over the price of a papercover thriller now that he couldn't
get the *Times*?

And the woman—what elusive thoughts, what trancelike afternoons,
staring out into the sunlight and the nettles? Her calm was mysterious.
Lyall was destroying her, but she stayed; she was a liar—but there was
something dreadfully apt in her vision, her metaphor of entropy. If this
seems a detached, academic attitude to her essential misery, it was not
one I was able to hold for long. The heat wave mounted past bearing; the
valley lay smashed and submissive beneath it; and eight days after my
brawl with Lyall, on a night when events human and geological seemed
to reach almost consciously toward union, I was forced from the specula-
tive view.

Sleep was impossible. Later than usual, we gathered round the warden's radio. But for the vibrant greenish haze in the sky, it might have
been day. Sweat poured off us. Confused by the evil half-light and the

heat rolling out of Mickleden, a pair of wrens were piping miserably and intermittently from the undergrowth by the brook, where a thousand insects hung in the air over an inch of slow water.

With oil-tariff revelations compromising the minority government, public anger mounting over the French agricultural betrayal, and the constant specter of the Patriotic Front demanding proportional representation from the wings of an already shaky parliament, the political organism had begun to look like some fossil survivor of another age. That night, it seemed to wake up suddenly to its situation; it thrashed and bled in the malarial air of the twentieth century, and over the transistor we followed its final throes; the government fell, and something became extinct in Britain while we slapped our necks to kill midges.

After the announcement a group of the Durham students hung uneasily about in the wedge of yellow light issuing from the warden's door, speechless and shrugging. Later, they probed the bleeding gum cautiously, in undertones, while the warden's wife made tea and the radio mumbled unconvincingly into the night. They seemed reluctant to separate and cross the empty site to empty tents, alone.

It was one of them who, turning eventually to go, drew our attention to a curious noise in the night—a low, spasmodic bubbling, like some thick liquid simmering up out of a hole in the ground. We cocked our heads, laughed at him, and he deferred shyly to our judgement that it was only the brook on the stones beneath the little bridge. But shortly afterwards it came again, closer; and then a third time, not twenty yards away across the car-park.

"There's someone out there," he said wonderingly. He was a tall, wispy lad with a thin yellow beard and large feet, his face young and concerned and decent even in that peculiar beryline gloom. When we laughed at him again, he said gently, "I think I'll go and have a look, though." The gate creaked open, we heard his boots on the gravel. With an edgy grin, one of his friends explained to us, "Too much ale tonight." Silence.

Then, "Oh my God," he said in a surprised voice. "You'd better come and do something," he called, and gave himself up suddenly to a fit of choking and coughing. We found him sitting on the gravel with his head between his knees. He had vomited extensively. On the ground in front of him lay Lyall's wife.

"How did she walk?" he whispered, "Oh, how did she walk?" He wrapped his arms round his knees and rocked himself to and fro.

She was hideously burnt. Her clothes were inseparable from the charred flesh in which they had become embedded; one ruined eye glared sightlessly out of a massive swelling of the facial tissue; plasma leaked from the less damaged areas, and she stank of the oven. Whatever fear or determination had driven her from under the shadow of Raw Pike now kept her conscious, staring passively upwards from her good eye, her body quivering gently with shock.

"Egerton," she said, "Egerton, Egerton, Egerton—"

I knelt over her.

"—Egerton, Egerton—"

"Someone get that bloody Land Rover across here," said the warden thickly.

"What happened?" I said. She lay like a blackened log, staring up at the sky. She shuddered convulsively. "Where's Lyall?"

"—Egerton, Egerton, Egerton, Egerton—"

"I'm here."

But she was dead.

I staggered away to squirt up a thin, painful stream of bile. The warden followed me. "Did she know you?" he said. "Where did she come from? What's happened?" I wiped my mouth. How could I tell? She had come to get help from me, but not for herself. I hang on to that thought, even now. With some idea of protecting Lyall, at least until I could get to him, I said, "I've never seen her before in my life. Look, I've got to go. Excuse me."

I felt him staring after me. The Land Rover was maneuvering nervously round the car-park, but now they had nowhere to take her. The boy from Durham was asking himself, over and over again, "How did she *get* here?" He appealed to his friends, but they were shaken and grey-faced, and they didn't know what to say.

It was past midnight when I left the camp site. An almost constant flicker of heat-lightning lent a macabre formality to the lane, the hills and the drystone walls—like subjects in some steel engraving or high-contrast photograph, they were perfectly defined but quite unreal. At Middlefell Farm the lights were all out. Some sheep stared at me from a paddock, their sides heaving and their eyes unearthly.

I lurched along under that hot green sky for forty minutes, but it seemed longer. Like a fool, I kept looking for signs of the woman's blind, agonized flight; had she fallen here, and dragged herself a little way?— And there, had it seemed impossible to drive the quivering insensate hulk a yard further? I was brought up short, stupid and horrified, by every smear of melted tar on the road; yet I ignored the only real event of the journey.

I had stopped for a moment to put my back against a drystone and massage the cramped calf of my left leg. A curlew was fluting tentatively from the deep Gothic cleft of Dungeon Ghyll. I had been gazing vacantly down the valley for perhaps half a minute, trying to control my erratic breathing, when the sky over Ambleside seemed to *pulse* suddenly, as if some curious shift of energy states had taken place. Simultaneously, the road lurched beneath me.

I felt it distinctly: a brief, queasy swaying motion. And when I touched the wall behind me, a faint tremor was in it, a fading vibration. I was dazed through lack of proper sleep; I was obsessed—and knew it—by the grim odyssey of Lyall's wife: I put the tremor down to dizziness, and attributed that strange transitional flicker of the air to a flare of lightning somewhere over Troutbeck, a flash partially occluded by the mass of the fells between. But when I moved on, the peculiar hue of the sky was brighter; and although the event seemed to have no meaning at the time, it was to prove of central significance in the culminating nightmare.

The smoke was visible from quite a long way off, drifting filmy and exhausted up the fellside, clinging to the spongy ash and shrivelled bracken stems of that previous fire, to be trapped by an inversion about a hundred feet below Raw Pike and spread out in a thin cloudbank the color of watered milk.

Lyall's cottage was ruined. Both barns were down in a heap of lamp-blacked stone, here and there an unconsumed rafter or beam sticking up out of the mess; the roof of the main building had caved in, taking the upper floor with it, so that there remained only a shell full of smoking slates and white soft ash. It radiated an intense heat, and the odd glowing cinder raced erratically up from it on the updraughts, but the fire per se had burnt itself out long before.

The wreckage was curiously uncompact. An explosion, probably of the kitchen gas-cylinders, had flung rubble into the nettle patch; and for some reason most of the face of the building lay in the road.

There among a tangle of smashed window frames and furniture, motionless in contemplation of the wreck and looking infinitely lonely, stood the long, ungainly figure of Lyall. His tweed jacket had gone through at the elbows, his trousers were charred and filthy, and his shoes were falling to pieces, as if he'd been trampling about in the embers looking for something. I began to shout his name long before I reached him. He studied my limping, hasty progress down the road for a moment; then, as I got close, seemed to lose interest.

"Lyall!" I called. "Are you all right?"

I kicked my way through the rubbish and shook his shoulder. He watched a swirl of ash dance over the deep embers. Something popped and cracked comfortably down in that hot pit. When he faced me, his eyes, red and sore, glowed out of his stubbled, smoke-blackened face with another kind of heat. But his voice was quite inoffensive when he said, "Hello Egerton. I didn't get much stuff out, you see." Stacked neatly in the road a few yards off were twenty or thirty charred paperbacks. "She came to fetch you, then?"

He stared absently at the ruin. I had expected to find something more than a drowsy child, parching its skin in some reverie over the remains of a garden bonfire. I was sickened. "Lyall, you bloody moron!" I shouted: "She's *dead!*" He moved his shoulders slightly, stared on. I caught hold of his arm and shook him. He was relaxed, unresistant. "Did you send her away in that condition? Are you mad? She was burnt to pieces!" I might have been talking to myself. "What's been *happening* here?"

When he finally pulled up out of the dry trap of ashes, it was to shake his head slowly and say, "What? I don't know." He gaped, he blinked, he whispered, "She was getting so old. It was my fault—" He seemed about to explain something, but never did. That open-mouthed pain, that terrible passive acceptance of guilt, was probably the last glimpse I had of Lyall the human being. Had he, at some point during the dreadful events of that night, actually faced and recognized the corroding power of his self-concern? At the time I thought I understood it all—and standing uselessly amid all that rubble I needed to believe he had.

"I'm sorry," I said.

At this the most inhuman paroxysm of misery and loathing took hold of his swollen, grimy features. "Fuck you, Egerton!" he cried. He threw off my hand. For a second, I was physically afraid, and backed quickly away from him. He followed me, with, "What's it got to do with you? What's any of it got to do with you?" Then, quieter, "I can't seem to—"

The spasm passed. He looked down at his blistered hands as if seeing them for the first time. He laughed. His eyes flickered over me, cruel as heat-lightning. "Bugger off back home then Egerton, if you feel like that," he said. He put his hands in his trouser pockets and stirred the rubble with his toe. "*I* didn't break the bloody piano, and I'll tell the old bitch I didn't—" He whirled away and strode off rapidly across the scorched fellside, stopping only to pick up an armful of books and call: "I'm sick of all this filthy rubbish anyway."

Smoke wreathed round him. I saw him turn north and begin to climb.

With this absurd transition into the dimension of height began what must surely be the most extraordinary episode of the entire business. Lyall stalked away from me up the fell. Amazed, I shouted after him. When he ignored me, I could only follow: he may or may not have had suicidal intentions, but he was certainly mad; in either case, if only out of common humanity, I couldn't just stand there and watch him go.

It might have been better if I had.

He made straight for Raw Pike, and then, his torso seeming to drift legless above the pall of white smoke that hung beneath the outcrop, bore west to begin a traverse which took us into the deep and difficult gullies between Whitegill Crag and Mill Gill. Here, he seemed to become lost for a while, and I gained on him.

He blundered about those stony vegetation-choked clefts like a sick animal, trying to scale waterslides or scrape his way up the low but steep rock walls. His shoes had fallen off his feet, and he was leaving a damp, urgent trail. He ignored me if I called his name, but he was quite aware of my presence, and took a patent delight in picking at his emotional scabs, real or imagined, whenever I got close enough to hear him. His voice drifted eerily down the defiles. The piano seemed to preoccupy him.

"I never broke it," I heard him say, in a self-congratulatory tone, then: "Nowhere near it, Miss," mumbled as part of a dialogue in which he took both parts. She didn't believe him, of course, and he became progressively more sullen. Later, groping for a handhold three feet above his head, he burst out angrily, "You can tell him I *won't* be responsible for the bloody things. Staff loss isn't *my* problem." His hold turned out to be a clump of shallow-rooted heather, which came out when he put his weight on it. He laughed. "Go and lick her arse then—"

In this way, he visited almost every period of his life. He met his wife down by the Thames, in a filthy March wind; later, they whispered to one another at night in his Holloway flat. He conjured up mutual acquaintances from Cambridge, and set them posturing like the dowdy flamingoes they had undoubtedly been. And once my own voice startled me, echoing pompously over the fells as part of some student dispute which must have seemed excruciatingly important at the time, and which I still can't remember.

When he finally broke out on to the east bank of Mill Gill, he stared back at me for a moment as if reassuring himself that I was still there. He even nodded to me, with a sort of grim approval. Then he lurched unsteadily through the bracken to the ghyll itself and dropped his paperbacks into it one by one, looking over his shoulder each time to see if I was watching. He crouched there like a child, studying each bright jacket as it slipped beneath the surface of the water and was whirled away. His shoulders were moving, but I couldn't tell whether he was laughing or crying.

It was during the latter part of this unburdening that the earth began to shake again—and this time in earnest. I sensed rather than saw that energetic transition of the air. The whole sky pulsed, flickered with lightning, seemed to stabilize. Then, with an enormous rustling noise, the fell beneath my feet shifted and heaved, lifting into a long curved wave which raced away from me up the slopes to explode against the dark rock of Tarn Crag in a shower of small stones and uprooted bracken.

I tottered about, shouting, "Lyall! Lyall!" until a second, more powerful shock threw me off my feet and sent me rolling twenty or thirty feet down toward the road.

Mill Gill gaped. The last paperback vanished. A groan came up out of the earth. Abruptly, the air was full of loose soil and rock-chippings, mud and spray from the banks of the ghyll. Lyall stared up through it at the throbbing sky; spun round and set off up the path to Stickle Tarn at a terrific rate, his long legs pumping up and down. Rocks blundered and rumbled round him—he brandished his fist at the hills. "Lyall, for God's sake come back!" I begged, but my voice was sucked away into the filthy air, and all I could see of him was a dim untiring figure, splashing across the ghyll where Tarn Crag blocks the direct route.

I put my head down into the murk and scrambled upward. Black water vomited suddenly down the ghyll, full of dead sheep and matted vegetation. Through the spray of a new waterfall I had a glimpse of Lyall waving his arms about and croaking demented challenges at a landscape that changed even as he opened his mouth. Twice, I got quite close behind him; once, I grabbed his arm, but he only thrashed about and shouted "Bugger off home, Egerton!" over the booming of the water.

Five hundred feet of ascent opened up the gully and spread Stickle Tarn before us, the color of lead: fifty acres of sullen water simmering in its dammed-up glacial bowl. Up there on the 1,500-foot line, out of the confines of the gyll, it was quieter and the earth seemed less agitated. But the dam was cracked; a hot wind rumbled through the high passes and gusted across the cirque; and up out of the black screes on the far bank of the tarn there loomed like a threat the massive, seamed face of the Borrowdale Volcanics—

Pavey Ark lowered down at us, crawling with boulder slides and crowned with heat-lightning: the highest sheer drop in the Central Fells, four hundred and eighty million years old—impassive, unbending, orogenetic. A constant stream of material was pouring like fine dust from the bilberry terraces at its summit two thousand feet above sea level, crushed volcanic agglomerate whirling and smoking across the face; while, down by the water, larger rocks dislodged from the uneasy heights bounced a hundred feet into the air in explosions of scree.

Lyall stood stock-still, staring up at it.

Beside him, the dam creaked and flexed. A ton of water spilled over the parapet and roared away down Mill Gill. He paid it not the slightest attention, simply stood there, drenched and muddy, moving his head fractionally from side to side as he traced one by one the scars of that horrific cliff, like a man following a page of print with his index finger: Great Gully, unclimbable without equipment, Gwynne's Chimney, Little Gully, and, tumbling from the western pinnacle to the base of East Buttress, the long precipitous grooves and terraces of Jack's Rake.

He was looking for a way up.

"Lyall," I said, "haven't you come far enough?"

He shrugged. Without a word, he set off round the margin of the tarn.

I'm convinced that following him further would have done no good: he had been determined on this course perhaps as far back as Cambridge, certainly since his crisis of self-confidence in the cottage. Anyway, my foot had become unbearably painful: it was as much as I could do to catch up with him halfway round the tarn, and, by actually grabbing the tail of his jacket, force him to stop.

We struggled stupidly for a moment, tottering in and out of the warm shallows—the Ark towering above us like a repository of all uncommitted Ordovician time. Lyall disengaged himself and ran off a little way. He put his head on one side and regarded me warily, chest heaving.

Then he nodded to himself, returned, and, keeping well out of my reach, said quite amiably, "I'm going up, Egerton. It's too late to stop me, you know." Something detached itself from the cliff and fell into the tarn like a small bomb going off. He spun round, screaming and waving his fist. "Leave me alone! Fuck off!" He watched the water subside. He showed his teeth. "Listen, you bastard," he said quietly: "Why don't you just chuck yourself in *that?*" And he pointed to the torrent rumbling over the dam and down Mill Gill. "For all the help you've ever been to me, you might as well—"

He began to walk away. He stopped, tore at his hair, made an apologetic gesture in my direction. His face crumpled, and the Lyall I had beaten up in the living room of his own house looked out of it. "I can't seem to stop going up, Egerton," he whispered, "I can't seem to stop doing it—"

But when I stepped forward, he shook with laughter. "That got you going, you bloody oaf!" he gasped. And he stumbled off toward the screes.

It really would have done no good to go with him. Once or twice on the long walk back to the dam, I actually turned and began to follow him again. But it was useless by then, distance and the Ark had made of him a small mechanical toy. I called for him to wait, but he couldn't have heard me; in the end, I made my way up the northern slopes of Tarn Crag (I had to cross the dam to do it—I waited for a lull, but even so my feet were in six inches of fast water as I went over, and my skin crawled with every step) and from there watched his inevitable ascent.

He crabbed about at the base of the Great Gully for a while, presumably looking for a way up; when this proved impractical, he made a high easterly traverse of the screes and vanished into the shadow of East Buttress: to reappear ten minutes later, inching his way up Jack's Rake—an infinitely tiny, vulnerable mote against the face.

I didn't really imagine he would do it. God knows why I chose that moment to be "sensible" about him. I sat down and unlaced my boots, petulantly determined to see him through what was after all a rather childish adventure, and then say nothing about it when the cliff itself had sent him chastened away. There was so little excuse for this that it seems mad now, of course: the Ark was shaking and shifting, the very air about it groaned and rang with heat; St. Elmo's fire writhed along its great humped outline. How on earth I expected him to survive, I don't know.

He was invisible for minutes at a time even on the easy stretch up to the ashtree at the entrance of Rake End Chimney, inundated by that curtain of debris blowing across the sheer walls above him. He tried confusedly to scale the chimney; failed; trudged doggedly on up, the temperature rising as he went. A smell of dust and lightning filled the air. Negotiating the fifty-degree slope of the second pitch, he was forced to cling to the rock for nearly half an hour while tons of rubble thundered past him and into the tarn below. He should have been crushed; he must have been injured in some way, for it took him almost as long to complete fifteen yards of fairly simple scrambling along the Easy Terrace.

Perhaps I remembered too late that Lyall was a human being; but from that point on, I could no longer minimize the obsession that had driven him up there. When some internal rupture of the cliff flooded the channels above him and turned the Rake into a high-level drainage culvert, I could hear only that despairing mumble in the cottage at night, the voice of his wife; when he windmilled his arms against the rush of the water, regained his balance and crawled on up, insensate and determined, I bit my lip until it bled. Perhaps it's never too late.

In some peculiar way the Ark too seemed to respond to his efforts: two thousand feet up, spidering across the Great Gully and heading for the summit wall, he moved into quietude; the boulder slides diminished, the cliff stood heavy and passive, like a cow in heat. Down below, on Tarn Crag, the earth ceased to tremble. Stickle Tarn calmed, and lay like a vat of molten beryl, reflecting the vibrant, acid sky; there were no more shadows, and, when I took off my shirt to dip it in the Tarn Crag pool, I felt no movement of the air. Hundreds of small birds were rustling uncomfortably about in the heather; while up above the blind, blunt head of Harrison Stickle, one hawk wheeled in slow, magnificent circles.

Twenty minutes after his successful negotiation of the Great Gully intersection, Lyall crossed the summit wall. There I lost him for a short period. What he did there, I have no clue. Perhaps he simply wandered among the strange nodulate boulders and shallow rock pools of the region. But if any transition took place, if his sour and ludicrous metaphysic received its final unimaginable blessing, it must have come there, between summit wall and summit cairn, between the cup and the lip, while I fretted and stalked below.

All this aside: suddenly, the peaks about me flared and wavered ecstatically; and he was standing by the cairn—

He was almost invisible: but I can imagine him there, with his arms upraised, his raw wrists poking out of the sleeves of his tweed jacket: no more unengaging or desperate, no stranger than he had ever been among the evening mists of Cambridge or the broken milk machines of Holloway: except that, now, static electricity is playing over him like fire, and his mouth is open in a great disgusted shout that reaches me quite clearly through the still, haunted air—

For a moment, everything seemed to pause. The sky broadcast a heat triumphant—a long, high, crystalline song, taken up and echoed by summit after summit, from Wetherlam and the Coniston Old Man, from Scafell Pike and the unbearable resonant fastnesses of Glaramara, never fading. For a moment, Lyall stood transfigured, perched between his own madness and the madness of an old geography. Then, as his cry died away to leave the cry of the sky supreme, a series of huge cracks and ruptures spread out across the cliff face from beneath his feet; and, with a sound like the tearing of vast lace, the whole immense facade of Pavey Ark began to slide slowly into the tarn beneath.

Dust plumed half a mile into the air; on a mounting roar the cliff, like an old sick woman, fell to its knees in the cirque; the high bilberry terraces poised themselves for a long instant, then, lowering themselves gently down, evaporated into dust. Millions of tons of displaced water smashed the dam and went howling down Mill Gill, crashing from wall to wall; to spill—black and invincible, capped with a dirty grey spume—across the valley and break like a giant sea against the lower slopes of Oak Howe and Side Pike. Before the Ark had finished its weary slide, the valley road was no more, the New Hotel and Side House were rubbish on a long wave—and that pit of ashes, Lyall's house, was extinguished forever.

I watched the ruin without believing it. I remember saying something like, "For God's sake, Lyall—" Then I turned and ran for my life over the quaking crag, east toward the safety of Blea Rigg and the fell route to an Ambleside I was almost frightened to reach. As I went, an ordinary darkness was filtering across the sky; a cool wind sprang up; and there were rain clouds already racing in from the Irish Sea along a stormy front.

Even allowing for the new unreliability of the press, esoteric explanations of the Great Langdale earth movement—activity renewed among the Borrowdale Volcanics after nearly five hundred million years; the unplanned landing of some enormous Russian space probe—seem ridiculous to me. Beyond the discovery of that poor woman, there were no witnesses other than myself in the immediate area. Was *Lyall*, then, responsible for the destruction of Pavey Ark?

It seems incredible: and yet, in the face of his death, insignificant. He carried his own entropy around with him, which makes him seem monstrous, perhaps; I don't know. He believed in an executive misery, and that should be enough for any of us. It hardly matters to me now. Other events swept it away almost immediately.

As I stumbled through the dim, panicky streets of Ambleside in the aftermath of the earthquake, the Patriotic Front was issuing from dusty suburban drill halls and Boy Scout huts all over the country; and by noon England, seventy years too late, was taking her first hesitant but heady steps into this century of violence. Grouped about the warden's radio in the still, stupefied night, we could have guessed at something of the sort. I understand now why the Durham students were so affected: students have suffered more than most as the Front tightens its political grip.

In dreams, I blame Lyall for that, too; equate the death of reason with the collapse of Pavey Ark; and watch England crawl past me over and again in the guise of a burnt woman on her desperate journey to the head of a valley that turns out every time to be impassive and arid. But awake I am more reasonable, and I have a job at the new sports shop in Chamonix. It's no hardship to sell other climbers their perlon and pitons— although the younger ones will keep going up alone, against all advice. Like many of the more fortunate refugees I have been allowed to take a limited French nationality; I even have a second-class passport, but I doubt if I shall ever go back.

Walking about the town, I still hate to look up, in case the cruel and naked peaks surprise me from between the housetops: but the pain of that wound is at least explicable, whereas Lyall—

Everyone who ever met Lyall contributed in some small way to his death. It might have been averted perhaps, if, in some Cambridge mist of long ago, I had only come upon the right thing to say; and I behaved very badly toward him later: but it seems as futile to judge myself on that account as to be continually interpreting and reinterpreting the moment at which I was forced to realize that one man's raw and gaping self-concern had brought down a mountain.

And I prefer to picture Stickle Tarn not as it looked from the 1,600-foot contour during Lyall's final access of rage and despair, but as I remember it from my Cambridge days and before—a wide, cold pool in the shadow of an ancient and beautiful cliff, where on grey windy days a seabird you can never identify seems always to be trawling twenty feet above the water in search of something it probably can't even define to itself.

The Roaches

❧

THOMAS M. DISCH

Miss Marcia Kenwell had a perfect horror of cockroaches. It was an altogether different horror than the one which she felt, for instance, toward the color puce. Marcia Kenwell loathed the little things. She couldn't see one without wanting to scream. Her revulsion was so extreme that she could not bear to crush them under the soles of her shoes. No, that would be too awful. She would run, instead, for the spray can of Black Flag and inundate the little beast with poison until it ceased to move or got out of reach into one of the cracks where they all seemed to live. It was horrible, unspeakably horrible, to think of them nestling in the walls, under the linoleum, only waiting for the lights to be turned off, and then . . . No, it was best not to think about it.

Every week she looked through the *Times* hoping to find another apartment, but either the rents were prohibitive (this *was* Manhattan, and Marcia's wage was a mere $62.50 a week, gross) or the building was obviously infested. She could always tell: there would be husks of dead roaches scattered about in the dust beneath the sink, stuck to the greasy backside of the stove, lining the out-of-reach cupboard shelves like the rice on the church steps after a wedding. She left such rooms in a passion of disgust, unable even to think till she reached her own apartment, where the air would be thick with the wholesome odors of Black Flag, Roach-It, and the toxic pastes that were spread on slices of potato and hidden in a hundred cracks which only she and the roaches knew about.

At least, she thought, *I keep my apartment clean.* And truly, the linoleum under the sink, the backside and underside of the stove, and the

175

white contact paper lining her cupboards were immaculate. She could not understand how other people could let these matters get so entirely out-of-hand. *They must be Puerto Ricans,* she decided—and shivered again with horror, remembering that litter of empty husks, the filth and the disease.

Such extreme antipathy toward insects—toward one particular insect—may seem excessive, but Marcia Kenwell was not really exceptional in this. There are many women, bachelor women like Marcia chiefly, who share this feeling though one may hope, for sweet charity's sake, that they escape Marcia's peculiar fate.

Marcia's phobia was, as in most such cases, hereditary in origin. That is to say, she inherited it from her mother, who had a morbid fear of anything that crawled or skittered or lived in tiny holes. Mice, frogs, snakes, worms, bugs—all could send Mrs. Kenwell into hysterics, and it would indeed have been a wonder, if little Marcia had not taken after her. It was rather strange, though, that her fear had become so particular, and stranger still that it should particularly be cockroaches that captured her fancy, for Marcia had never seen a single cockroach, didn't know what they were. (The Kenwells were a Minnesota family, and Minnesota families simply don't have cockroaches.) In fact, the subject did not arise until Marcia was nineteen and setting out (armed with nothing but a high school diploma and pluck, for she was not, you see, a very attractive girl) to conquer New York.

On the day of her departure, her favorite and only surviving aunt came with her to the Greyhound Terminal (her parents being deceased) and gave her this parting advice: "Watch out for the roaches, Marcia darling. New York City is full of cockroaches." At that time (at almost any time really) Marcia hardly paid attention to her aunt, who had opposed the trip from the start and given a hundred or more reasons why Marcia had better not go, not till she was older at least.

Her aunt had been proven right on all counts: Marcia after five years and fifteen employment agency fees could find nothing in New York but dull jobs at mediocre wages; she had no more friends than when she lived on West 16th; and, except for its view (the Chock Full O'Nuts warehouse and a patch of sky), her present apartment on lower Thompson Street was not a great improvement on its predecessor.

The city was full of promises, but they had all been pledged to other people. The city Marcia knew was sinful, indifferent, dirty, and dangerous. Every day she read accounts of women attacked in subway stations, raped in the streets, knifed in their own beds. A hundred people looked on curiously all the while and offered no assistance. And on top of everything else there were the roaches!

There were roaches everywhere, but Marcia didn't see them until she'd been in New York a month. They came to her—or she to them—at Silversmith's on Nassau Street, a stationery shop where she had been working for three days. It was the first job she'd been able to find. Alone or helped by a pimply stockboy (in all fairness it must be noted that Marcia was not without an acne problem of her own), she wandered down rows of rasp-edged metal shelves in the musty basement, making an inventory of the sheaves and piles and boxes of bond paper, leatherette-bound diaries, pins and clips, and carbon paper. The basement was dirty and so dim that she needed a flashlight for the lowest shelves. In the obscurest corner, a faucet leaked perpetually into a gray sink: she had been resting near this sink, sipping a cup of tepid coffee (saturated, in the New York manner, with sugar and drowned in milk), thinking, probably, of how she could afford several things she simply couldn't afford, when she noticed the dark spots moving on the side of the sink. At first she thought they might be no more than motes floating in the jelly of her eyes, or the giddy dots that one sees after over-exertion on a hot day. But they persisted too long to be illusory, and Marcia drew nearer, feeling compelled to bear witness. *How do I know they are insects?* she thought.

How are we to explain the fact that what repels us most can be at times—at the same time—inordinately attractive? Why is the cobra poised to strike so beautiful? The fascination of the abomination is something that . . . Something which we would rather not account for. The subject borders on the obscene, and there is no need to deal with it here, except to note the breathless wonder with which Marcia observed these first roaches of hers. Her chair was drawn so close to the sink that she could see the mottling of their oval, unsegmented bodies, the quick scuttering of their thin legs, and the quicker flutter of their antennae. They moved randomly, proceeding nowhere, centered nowhere. They seemed greatly disturbed over nothing. *Perhaps*, Marcia thought, *my presence has a morbid effect on them?*

Only then did she become aware, aware fully, that these were the cockroaches of which she had been warned. Repulsion took hold; her flesh curdled on her bones. She screamed and fell back in her chair, almost upsetting a shelf of oddlots. Simultaneously the roaches disappeared over the edge of the sink and into the drain.

Mr. Silversmith, coming downstairs to inquire the source of Marcia's alarm, found her supine and unconscious. He sprinkled her face with tapwater, and she awoke with a shudder of nausea. She refused to explain why she had screamed and insisted that she must leave Mr. Silversmith's employ immediately. He, supposing that the pimply stockboy (who was his son) had made a pass at Marcia, paid her for the three days she had worked and let her go without regrets. From that moment on, cockroaches were to be a regular feature of Marcia's existence.

On Thompson Street Marcia was able to reach a sort of stalemate with the cockroaches. She settled into a comfortable routine of pastes and powders, scrubbing and waxing, prevention (she never had even a cup of coffee without washing and drying cup and coffeepot immediately afterward) and ruthless extermination. The only roaches who trespassed upon her two cozy rooms came up from the apartment below, and they did not stay long, you may be sure. Marcia would have complained to the landlady, except that it was the landlady's apartment and her roaches. She had been inside, for a glass of wine on Christmas Eve, and she had to admit that it wasn't exceptionally dirty. It was, in fact, more than commonly clean—but *that* was not enough in New York. If *everyone*, Marcia thought, *took as much care as I, there would soon be no cockroaches in New York City.*

Then (it was March and Marcia was halfway through her sixth year in the city) the Shchapalovs moved in next door. There were three of them— two men and a woman—and they were old, though exactly how old it was hard to say: they had been aged by more than time. Perhaps they weren't more than forty. The woman, for instance, though she still had brown hair, had a face wrinkly as a prune and was missing several teeth. She would stop Marcia in the hallway or on the street, grabbing hold of her coatsleeve, and talk to her—always a simple lament about the weather, which was too hot or too cold or too wet or too dry. Marcia never knew half of what the old woman was saying, she mumbled so. Then she'd totter off to the grocery with her bagful of empties.

The Shchapalovs, you see, drank. Marcia, who had a rather exaggerated idea of the cost of alcohol (the cheapest thing she could imagine was vodka), wondered where they got the money for all the drinking they did. She knew they didn't work, for on days when Marcia was home with the flu she could hear the three Shchapalovs through the thin wall between their kitchen and hers screaming at each other to exercise their adrenal glands. *They're on welfare*, Marcia decided. Or perhaps the man with only one eye was a veteran on pension.

She didn't so much mind the noise of their arguments (she was seldom home in the afternoon), but she couldn't stand their singing. Early in the evening they'd start in, singing along with the radio stations. Everything they listened to sounded like Guy Lombardo. Later, about eight o'clock they sang *a cappella*. Strange, soulless noises rose and fell like Civil Defense sirens; there were bellowings, bayings, and cries. Marcia had heard something like it once on a Folkways record of Czechoslovakian wedding chants. She was quite beside herself whenever the awful noise started up and had to leave the house till they were done. A complaint would do no good: the Shchapalovs had a right to sing at that hour.

Besides, one of the men was said to be related by marriage to the landlady. That's how they got the apartment, which had been used as a storage space until they'd moved in. Marcia couldn't understand how the three of them could fit into such a little space—just a room-and-a-half with a narrow window opening onto the air shaft. (Marcia had discovered that she could see their entire living space through a hole that had been broken through the wall when the plumbers had installed a sink for the Shchapalovs.)

But if their singing distressed her, *what* was she to do about the roaches? The Shchapalov woman, who was the sister of one man and married to the other—or else the men were brothers and she was the wife of one of them (sometimes, it seemed to Marcia, from the words that came through the walls, that she was married to neither of them—or to both), was a bad housekeeper, and the Shchapalov apartment was soon swarming with roaches. Since Marcia's sink and the Shchapalovs' were fed by the same pipes and emptied into a common drain, a steady overflow of roaches was disgorged into Marcia's immaculate kitchen. She could spray and lay out more poisoned potatoes; she could scrub and dust and stuff Kleenex tissues into holes where the pipes passed through the wall: it was all to no avail. The Shchapalov roaches could always lay another million eggs in the garbage bags rotting beneath the Shchapalov sink. In a few days they would be swarming through the pipes and cracks and into Marcia's cupboards. She would lay in bed and watch them (this was possible because Marcia kept a nightlight burning in each room) advancing across the floor and up the walls, trailing the Shchapalovs' filth and disease everywhere they went.

One such evening the roaches were especially bad, and Marcia was trying to muster the resolution to get out of her warm bed and attack them with Roach-It. She had left the windows open from the conviction that cockroaches do not like the cold, but she found that she liked it much less. When she swallowed, it hurt, and she knew she was coming down with a cold. And all because of *them!*

"*Oh go away!*" she begged. "*Go away! Go away! Get out of my apartment.*"

She addressed the roaches with the same desperate intensity with which she sometimes (though not often in recent years) addressed prayers to the Almighty. Once she had prayed all night long to get rid of her acne, but in the morning it was worse than ever. People in intolerable circumstances will pray to anything. Truly, there are no atheists in foxholes: the men there pray to the bombs that they may land somewhere else.

The only strange thing in Marcia's case is that her prayers were answered. The cockroaches fled from her apartment as quickly as their little legs could carry them—and in straight lines, too. Had they heard her? Had they understood?

Marcia could still see one cockroach coming down from the cupboard. "*Stop!*" she commanded. And it stopped.

At Marcia's spoken command, the cockroach would march up and down, to the left and to the right. Suspecting that her phobia had matured into madness, Marcia left her warm bed, turned on the light, and cautiously approached the roach, which remained motionless, as she had bidden it. "*Wiggle your antennas,*" she commanded. The cockroach wiggled its antennae.

She wondered if they would *all* obey her and found, within the next few days, that they all would. They would do anything she told them to. They would eat poison out of her hand. Well, not exactly out of her hand, but it amounted to the same thing. They were devoted to her. Slavishly.

It is the end, she thought, *of my roach problem.* But of course it was only the beginning.

Marcia did not question too closely the *reason* the roaches obeyed her. She had never much troubled herself with abstract problems. After expending so much time and attention on them, it seemed only natural that she should exercise a certain power over them. However she was wise enough never to speak of this power to anyone else—even to Miss Bismuth at the insurance office. Miss Bismuth read the horoscope magazines and claimed to be able to communicate with her mother, aged sixty-eight, telepathically. Her mother lived in Ohio. But what would Marcia have said: that *she* could communicate telepathically with cockroaches? Impossible.

Nor did Marcia use her power for any other purpose than keeping the cockroaches out of her own apartment. Whenever she saw one, she simply commanded it to go to the Shchapalov apartment and stay there. It was surprising then that there were always more roaches coming back through the pipes. Marcia assumed that they were younger generations. Cockroaches are known to breed fast. But it was easy enough to send them to the Shchapalovs.

"*Into their beds,*" she added as an afterthought. "*Go into their beds.*" Disgusting as it was, the idea gave her a queer thrill of pleasure.

The next morning, the Shchapalov woman, smelling a little worse than usual (Whatever was it, Marcia wondered, that they drank?), was waiting at the open door of her apartment. She wanted to speak to Marcia before she left for work. Her housedress was mired from an attempt at scrubbing the floor, and while she sat there talking, she tried to wring out the scrubwater.

"No idea!" she exclaimed. "You ain't got no idea how bad! 'S terrible!"

"What?" Marcia asked, knowing perfectly well what.

"The boogs! Oh, the boogs are just everywhere. Don't you have em, sweetheart? I don't know what to do. I try to keep a decent house, God knows—" She lifted her rheumy eyes to heaven, testifying. "—but I don't know what to do." She leaned forward, confidingly. "You won't believe this, sweetheart, but last night . . ." A cockroach began to climb out of the limp strands of hair straggling down into the woman's eyes. ". . . they got into bed with us! Would you believe it? There must have been a hundred of 'em. I said to Osip, I said—What's wrong, sweetheart?"

Marcia, speechless with horror, pointed at the roach, which had almost reached the bridge of the woman's nose. "Yech!" the woman agreed, smashing it and wiping her dirtied thumb on her dirtied dress. "Goddam boogs! I hate em, I swear to God. But what's a person gonna do? Now, what I wanted to ask, sweetheart, is do you have a problem with the boogs? Being as how you're right next door, I thought—" She smiled a confidential smile, as though to say this is just between us ladies. Marcia almost expected a roach to skitter out between her gapped teeth.

"No," she said. "No, I use Black Flag." She backed away from the doorway toward the safety of the stairwell. "Black Flag," she said again, louder. "Black Flag," she shouted from the foot of the stairs. Her knees trembled so, that she had to hold onto the metal banister for support.

At the insurance office that day, Marcia couldn't keep her mind on her work five minutes at a time. (Her work in the Actuarial Dividends department consisted of adding up long rows of two-digit numbers on a Burroughs adding machine and checking the similar additions of her co-workers for errors.) She kept thinking of the cockroaches in the tangled hair of the Shchapalov woman, of her bed teeming with roaches, and of other, less concrete horrors on the periphery of consciousness. The numbers swam and swarmed before her eyes, and twice she had to go to the Ladies' Room, but each time it was a false alarm. Nevertheless, lunchtime found her with no appetite. Instead of going down to the employee cafeteria she went out into the fresh April air and strolled along 23rd Street. Despite the spring, it all seemed to bespeak a sordidness, a festering corruption. The stones of the Flatiron Building oozed damp blackness; the gutters were heaped with soft decay; the smell of burning grease hung in the air outside the cheap restaurants like cigarette smoke in a close room.

The afternoon was worse. Her fingers would not touch the correct numbers on the machine unless she looked at them. One silly phrase kept running through her head: "Something must be done. Something must be done." She had quite forgotten that she had sent the roaches into the Shchapalovs' bed in the first place.

That night, instead of going home immediately, she went to a double feature on 42nd Street. She couldn't afford the better movies. Susan Hayward's little boy almost drowned in quicksand. That was the only thing she remembered afterward.

She did something then that she had never done before. She had a drink in a bar. She had two drinks. Nobody bothered her; nobody even looked in her direction. She took a taxi to Thompson Street (the subways weren't safe at that hour) and arrived at her door by eleven o'clock. She didn't have anything left for a tip. The taxi driver said he understood.

There was a light on under the Shchapalovs' door, and they were singing. It was eleven o'clock. "Something must be done," Marcia whispered to herself earnestly. "Something must be done."

Without turning on her own light, without even taking off her new spring jacket from Ohrbach's, Marcia got down on her knees and crawled under the sink. She tore out the Kleenexes she had stuffed into the cracks around the pipes.

There they were, the three of them, the Shchapalovs, drinking, the woman plumped on the lap of the one-eyed man, and the other man, in a dirty undershirt, stamping his foot on the floor to accompany the loud discords of their song. Horrible. They were drinking of course, she might have known it, and now the woman pressed her roachy mouth against the mouth of the one-eyed man—kiss, kiss. Horrible, horrible. Marcia's hands knotted into her mouse-colored hair, and she thought: *The filth, the disease!* Why, they hadn't learned a thing from last night!

Some time later (Marcia had lost track of time) the overhead light in the Shchapalovs' apartment was turned off. Marcia waited till they made no more noise. "Now," Marcia said, "all of you.

"All of you in this building, all of you that can hear me, gather around the bed, but wait a little while yet. Patience. All of you . . ." The words of her command fell apart into little fragments, which she told like the beads of a rosary—little brown ovoid wooden beads. ". . . gather round . . . wait a little while yet . . . all of you . . . patience . . . gather round . . ." Her hand stroked the cold water pipes rhythmically, and it seemed that she could hear them—gathering, scuttering up through the walls, coming out of the cupboards, the garbage bags—a host, an army, and she was their absolute queen.

"Now!" she said. "Mount them! Cover them! Devour them!"

There was no doubt that she could hear them now. She heard them quite palpably. Their sound was like grass in the wind, like the first stirrings of gravel dumped from a truck. Then there was the Shchapalov woman's scream, and curses from the men, such terrible curses that Marcia could hardly bear to listen.

A light went on, and Marcia could see them, the roaches, everywhere. Every surface, the walls, the floors, the shabby sticks of furniture, was mottly thick with *Blattelae Germanicae*. There was more than a single thickness.

The Shchapalov woman, standing up in her bed, screamed monotonously. Her pink rayon nightgown was speckled with brown-black dots. Her knobby fingers tried to brush bugs out of her hair, off her face. The man in the undershirt who a few minutes before had been stomping his feet to the music stomped now more urgently, one hand still holding onto the lightcord. Soon the floor was slimy with crushed roaches, and he slipped. The light went out. The woman's scream took on a rather choked quality, as though . . .

But Marcia wouldn't think of that. "Enough," she whispered. "No more. Stop."

She crawled away from the sink, across the room on to her bed, which tried, with a few tawdry cushions, to dissemble itself as a couch for the daytime. Her breathing came hard, and there was a curious constriction in her throat. She was sweating incontinently.

From the Shchapalovs' room came scuffling sounds, a door banged, running feet, and then a louder, muffled noise, perhaps a body falling downstairs. The landlady's voice: "What the hell do you think you're—" Other voices overriding hers. Incoherences, and footsteps returning up the stairs. Once more, the landlady: "There ain't no *boogs* here, for heaven's sake. The boogs is in your heads. You've got the d.t.'s, that's what. And it wouldn't be any wonder, if there were boogs. The place is filthy. Look at that crap on the floor. Filth! I've stood just about enough from you. Tomorrow you move out, hear? This *used* to be a decent building."

The Shchapalovs did not protest their eviction. Indeed, they did not wait for the morrow to leave. They quitted their apartment with only a suicase, a laundry bag, and an electric toaster. Marcia watched them go down the steps through her half-open door. *It's done*, she thought. *It's all over.*

With a sigh of almost sensual pleasure, she turned on the lamp beside the bed, then the other lamps. The room gleamed immaculately. Deciding to celebrate her victory, she went to the cupboard, where she kept a bottle of *crème de menthe*.

The cupboard was full of roaches.

She had not told them where to go, where *not* to go, when they left the Shchapalov apartment. It was her own fault.

The great silent mass of roaches regarded Marcia calmly, and it seemed to the distracted girl that she could read *their* thoughts, their thought rather, for they had but a single thought. She could read it as clearly as she could read the illuminated billboard for Chock Full O'Nuts outside her window. It was delicate music issuing from a thousand tiny pipes. It was an ancient music box open after centuries of silence: "We love you we love you we love you we love you."

Something strange happened inside Marcia then, something unprecedented: she responded.

"I love you too," she replied. "Oh, I love you. Come to me, all of you. Come to me. I love you. Come to me. I love you. Come to me."

From every corner of Manhattan, from the crumbling walls of Harlem, from restaurants on 56th Street, from warehouses along the river, from sewers and from orange peels moldering in garbage cans, the loving roaches came forth and began to crawl toward their mistress.

The Last Supper

c·ɔ⌐ɔ

RUSSELL FITZGERALD

Under "menus" the Larousse Gastronomique contains the following entry:

"Here, as a curiosity, is a menu whose originality, it is true, is due to exceptional circumstances. It is that of a meal which Marshal the Duc de Richelieu offered to all the princes and princesses and the members of their suites taken prisoner by him during the Hanoverian War. President Henault tells us how the menu for this memorable supper was drafted by the Duc de Richelieu himself. Its peculiarity lay in the fact that it was made up entirely of one kind of meat, namely beef, because, on that particular day, there was nothing in the Marshal's larder but a carcase of beef and a few root vegetables.

" 'My Lord,' said Rullières to the Marshal, somewhat anxiously observing that the Duc de Richelieu wished to offer supper to a large number of guests, 'there is nothing in the kitchens except a carcass of beef and a few roots . . .'

" 'Very good,' said the Marshal, 'that is more than is needed to provide the prettiest supper in the world.'

" 'But, my lord, it would be impossible . . .'

" 'Come, Rullières, calm yourself, and write out the menu I am about to dictate to you.'

"And the Marshal, seeing Rullières more and more alarmed, took the pen out of his hand and, seated in his secretary's place, wrote the following menu which, later, was brought into the collection of Monsieur de la Popelinière:

SUPPER MENU

Centerpiece: The large silver-gilt salver with the equestrian figure of the King, the statues of De Guesclin, Dunois, Bayard, Turenne. My silver-gilt plate with the arms embossed and enameled.

First Course: A tureen of garbure gratinée, made of beef consommé.

Four hors d'oeuvre: Palate of beef à la Saint-Mennehould; Little pâtés of chopped fillet of beef with chives; Kidneys with fried onions; Tripes à la poulette with lemon juice.

To follow the broth: Rump of beef garnished with root vegetables in gravy. (Trim these vegetables into grotesque shapes on account of the Germans.)

Six entrees: Oxtail with chestnut purée! Civet of tongue à la bourguignonne; Paupiettes of beef à la estoffade with pickled nasturtium buds; Fillet of beef braised with celery; Beef rissoles with hazelnut purée; Beef marrow on toast (ration bread will do).

Second course: Roast sirloin (baste it with melted bone marrow); Endive salad with ox-tongue; Beef à la mode with white jelly mixed with pistachio nuts; Cold beef gâteau with blood and Jurançon wine. (Don't make a mistake!)

Six final dishes: Glazed turnips with gravy of the roast; Beef bone marrow pie with breadcrumbs and candy sugar; Beef stock aspic with lemon rind and praline; Purée of artichoke hearts with gravy (beef) and almond milk; Fritters of beef brain steeped in Seville orange juice; Beef jelly with Alicante wine and Verdun mirabelles.

To follow, all that is left in the way of jams or preserves.

"And as a coda to this majestic menu (which we should like to regard as authentic and of its period, although in some respects it strikes us as somewhat odd!) the Marshal added:

" 'If by any unhappy chance, this meal turns out not to be very good, I shall withhold from the wages of Maret and Roquelere (his maître-d'hôtel and master-chef, no doubt) a fine of 100 pistols. Go, and entertain no more doubts!'

(signed:) Richelieu

"This menu, strange as its composition may seem, is perfectly orthodox. Structurally, it obeys all the rules which were in force at this period
concerning the organization of important meals."

Not then, such a curiosity as it at first appears. And structurally regular. These qualities at least, we can hope to attain. Alas, who would dare
aspire to that terrifying altitude above called "majestic." Who today
would lie in the teeth of truth and use such praise for the cuisine
bourgeoise, gussied up with crushed ice or flaming brandy, which passes
nowadays for elegance and is even styled "grand." Pfui! For our Love
Feast we can only offer the modest hope which that uncrowned prince,
Curnonsky, defines as good cooking, which is that things, "taste of what
they are."

Preparation of the Beloved—The Living Marinade

On the day before the third day before the day of your Agape you must
arrange to get your beloved dead drunk before dinner, it being important
that he does not eat. For this purpose only Brandy Alexanders will do.
The true recipe for which is:

Two shots of Creme de Cacao,
one of best Brandy
& only one teaspoon of heavy cream;
shake with ice and strain into
a chilled four ounce cocktail glass.

This drink has among its many fine properties a definite aphrodisiac
quality which may be easily enhanced by the subjects of conversation
chosen to accompany it. When he is giddy and no longer brushes your
most importune caresses away, he may complain of the richness of the
drinks, may even refuse another. Pay no attention, mix another with less
cream and more brandy but make sure it reaches his lips *streaming* with
arctic vapors.

When he has fallen into a corpse-like slumber, broken perhaps with
snores which you alone have trained yourself to find endearing, remove
his clothes and arrange him upon your bed. Arrange your lights, mirrors,
music. Arrange yourself. Proceed to enjoy him, his every nook and
cranny with your tongue alone. Soon you will see that though the drink
has rendered him helpless it has not diminished his usefulness by an

inch. Indulge yourself with all the abandon attached to last things. Imagine that he will remember all this with contempt, that even in his absence you will feel only his scorn, remember only his sneering face.
Imagine that tomorrow he will disappear. Exhaust yourself and him with
this your:

Rite of Eternal Farewell

When your window first whitens with the mystical significance of
dawn, rise and adore him. Study the colors at which the wan light hints
in the moisture of his chest or the oils at the turn of his nose. Admire the
virility which the hour brings to men of such fine health and sweet
youth. Watch it loll across his thigh but do not touch it. No, for that
season has passed and you must content yourself with the sight alone of
that jewel of light, pendent at the tip within the bezel of his foreskin, glittering with that promise which three days of labor and devotion will soon
bring to you more intimately than ever before.

Wake him. While he is still groggy lead him to the gilded *chaise percé*
(for which you have perhaps ransacked the entire length of Second Ave.).
The bonds will have been made ready the night before, when you will
also have replaced the enamelled tin bucket between its legs with a more
suitable silver tureen. Tie his wrists behind the caned back and his ankles, separately, to the back legs of this chair. Joke with him about fetishes
or photography or whatever is necessary to procure his docile acceptance
of your extraordinary conduct; then offer him a glass of chilled champagne. He will welcome it. His palate will be cleansed of deadmouse, his
eyes and uncomfortably his brain will also clear. He will begin to complain, perhaps to shout. If your residence is not lonely and safe from the
curious you will have to impose the first necessary cruelty: a tight gag.

Next, a small hypodermic needle becomes necessary. If that is impossible, visit a doctor on some pretense and, while his back is turned, steal
a packet of disposable needles. One of these points with a common
eyedropper will make an excellent substitute. If the large rubber nipple
from a child's pacifier is substituted for the dropper's meager bulb, so
much the better. (Should a leakage be noticed between the dropper and
the needle, this is easily remedied with a tiny strip of paper torn from a
paper match booklet, or, preferably, the end of a dollar bill.) This instrument is to be filled with brandy.

Make as many injections as you like, wherever it pleases you.

This finished, offer him more champagne and a tempting slice of authentic pound cake, provided he promises not to yell. A great deal of this pound cake will be necessary since it is, as it were, the pre-stuffing and indeed it may require so much that you would be wise to bake it yourself, as large purchases of such a luxury may not only arouse suspicions but prove too expensive. Hence the following recipe for Authentic Pound Cake:

Beat a dozen egg whites until they stand in stiff peaks. In another bowl stir the dozen yolks and a pound of melted butter into a pound of sifted flour. *Stir* in a pound of sugar and the egg whites. Pour into a large loaf pan, well buttered and floured. Bake in a moderate oven until a knife blade inserted in the center comes out clean. Cool in the pan.

Certain resemblances to the infamous ceremonies of St. John may by now have crossed your mind. Uncross it. No such horrors as that twisting-off of the living youth's head after he has been softened in a vat of honey and a diet of figs and oil, no such insults to the body of the beloved will be encountered here. And no such divinatory superstitions will insult his head. It is, let us be quite clear, the Ultimate Reality of Love with which we are concerned.

So this drink and this food will be his only nourishment during the triduum of marination. Nor may his body be washed, nor his bonds loosened, nor his brow dried, nor his tears heeded. His excretions, which will collect in the silver tureen, will be regularly disposed of, but its gilt interior must only be rinsed out with champagne.

The brandy injections must be repeated at least thrice daily, and you must press upon him as much of the cake and the wine as he can bear. Intoxication alone must keep him from injuring himself with any attempts at escape.

On the evening of the third day he will be weak. Therefore the cake may have to be intinctured with the wine and spooned into his mouth. At midnight examine the tureen. If there is nothing, wake him and spoon more cake and wine into him until he delivers. Then, promise that you will untie him if he will grant you one last wish; that he will drink another quart of Brandy Alexanders you have prepared for him. Have ready another quart container to catch the mixture when he regurgitates it back to you, changed into the perfect cocktail for your feast. Masturbate him into this container. Do *not* untie him. Gag him again, chill the cocktail, and go quickly to sleep thinking of the salt taste of his tears, for tomorrow you must face:

Some Unpleasantries—Dressing and Trussing

If you love him you will lavish great care on the sharpening of the knife. A twelve-inch French chopping knife is best. When it will shave the back of your arm without the slightest pressure it is ready. But before you use it you will finish the preparation of the soup.

Remove the tureen to your work table and mix its liquid with its solid contents by means of a wire whisk. When you are sure it is as smooth as possible, thin it by whisking in as much champagne as is necessary to produce a consistency like that of heavy cream. In the center of this golden liquid float several sprigs of fresh mint. Place the lid upon the tureen and dispose it proudly upon your serving table. No further attention is required, this is always served at room temperature, only do not lift the lid before serving.

Now the knife. Place the enamelled tin bucket beneath the chair. Kneeling behind him manipulate (for the last time!) the pendulous extremity of the beloved until it can only be pulled vertical with difficulty. With a rapid stroke of the blade cut through the pubic arch in the front and the anus in the back. It may be necessary to wait until a sufficient amount of bleeding has taken place so that weakened, he will not be able to wriggle enough to prevent your second cut from being as neat as the first. If so, hold the organs so that no tearing of the skin takes place at the incision. Have ready a basin to replace the bucket should it overflow while this tedious yet touching double genuflection of your devotion continues.

This most precious ornament (which in a turkey would be stood-in-for by a nubby tail sometimes called: The Pope's Nose) must be placed instantly in a small bath of cold milk. Do not let its sudden shrinkage dismay you. Gastronomic miracles will enable you to present it to yourself in all its pathetic arrogance.

When his fluids begin to run clear, transfer the meat to the bathtub. Secure the drain plug. With a silver table knife scrape the perspiration from all parts of the skin. (Death's Dew.) Using a bulb baster, draw up some of the sweat and any other fluids that collect at the drain stopper and, mixed with a teaspoon of brandy, reserve this in the refrigerator.

Contrary to the usual procedure it is now necessary to truss the body before it is dressed. Rigor mortis being, in this case, the enemy of art.

With the knife cut the tendons on the back and at either side of the knees, then that front skein just below the patella itself. This will make it possible to secure the knees up under the armpits while the ankle bonds are tied to the knots at the wrists. Next, cut off the toes of one foot and the fingers of one hand. Reserve these in a saucepan of water.

It is convenient now to remove any clothing you may be wearing. But all temptation to abuse the newly effeminated source of all your anguish must be resisted. From now on, from a culinary standpoint, the body must remain inviolate.

No sooner have I said that than I must make an immediate exception. Without delay rinse your hypodermic needle or its improvised substitute in champagne and force a full dropper of brandy into the center of each eye. The deterioration of these is so rapid and their inclusion in the final garnish so expressive, failure must not be risked.

Now then, you have equipped yourself with one of those small surgical spoons used in curettement or one of the small garden rakes which look like a giant's fork crushed in some giant's petty rage, or both, and a flashlight (which may be useful near the end).

If your bathroom is well ventilated and your tools sharp it should be possible to finish this task by noon. Remove the heart, lungs, kidneys and liver to a pail. See that these organs are unmarred. Refrigerate them. Wrap the discarded entrails in foil and pack into the freezing compartment.

Wash yourself off and take a light lunch of any of the cake which may be left and the last of the champagne. Nap or read for an hour, then dress for your shopping trip.

Before leaving add an onion stuck with two cloves, a small carrot, a bay leaf, and some parsley to the fingers and toes in the saucepan. Set it over the lowest possible flame. Remove the block of frozen offal from the freezer and take it out in an opaque garbage bag. Dispose of it in your usual way. Come alert now, while:

Shopping for the Garnish

This trip must be made quickly, for there is so much yet to be done. You are advised therefore to waste no time pitying the common citizens around you. Those aging ladies with their Diet Cola and TV dinners. Waste nothing so precious as scorn upon them; instead, study the produce you are about to buy and be certain that each is in every way not only worthy of the beloved but of the epicurean grandeur you are so rashly attempting to produce. The mushrooms, ten pounds of them, are they all the largest and whitest money can buy? Have you checked each box? The leeks; their leaves are still beaded with morning dew, the horror of crushed ice never having come near them. The black olives; almost the size of hen's eggs are they not? The artichokes; did their leaves actually squeak when you secretly squeezed them? And the watercress? Immaculate, of course.

Now quickly the two bottles of Chablis. No, no! Chateau Petrus (fool!) its ineffable odor of truffles thus compensating for their absence in this barbarous nation. Yes, yes, the Pomerol by all means, but what for the others? Romanee-Conti comes easily to mind; but the aroma, have we not so far successfully eliminated any of these bugs-and-bees smells? No! Back to the Médoc. Yes! Yes, of course, your choice seems to leap from the shelf: *Chateau Mouton-Rothschild*, and with the label designed by Dali. Or, the label by Cocteau? Both! Yes, yes, *too perfect* is the only justice. Now the Galliano, quickly, quickly, and just up the street those princes in peasant coats: Bosc pears.

You see, with my urging, that you have arrived just as the little saucepan has reduced its liquid by half. You salt it (a pinch) and proceed to sort and wash and admire your purchases. Throw them all into the salted bath around him. Is it not as though a willow-grown stream had pooled about him? (Turn him face up.) "There with fantastic garlands . . . of crow flowers, nettles, daisies, and long purples that liberal shepherds give a grosser name, but our cold maids do dead men's fingers call them: There" it is thus that a dedicated cook can gain inspiration from the simple contemplation of ingredients both perfect and appropriate. But now, it is time for:

The Ornamental Trussing and Final Infusion

Carry him from the tub. Place him in your huge ovenproof serving platter of teflon-coated steel. Then, with a coping saw remove the cap of his head, that is, above the hairline. It should produce a sort of zuccheto or, if one is of the Hebrew persuasion, a neat *yamulka* of hair-covered bone. Scrape out the brains and, wrapped in Saran, freeze them.

Push a large trussing needle with heavy twine through one ear, across the empty brain pan and out the other. Be sure the twine is long enough so that both ends may be tied to his wrist bonds. The purpose, obviously, is to make his head stand up. You will see though, that the weight of the head only draws his wrists up his back and then itself falls again, sadly askew. Remove a short fine sword or bayonet from your wall display. Place the fingerless hand beneath the perfect one (palms up) and pierce them both with this monstrous attelet. Push it on between the choice rondels of his buttocks and through both feet, these again arranged with the marred beneath the perfect.

Now, using the same heavier-weight strands you used to tie his ankles and wrists, make a pattern of tight bonds. A lattice, a stripe, or whatever imagination dictates and skill allows. If his skin is fair these need not be too tight. The roasting will leave a delightful pattern of gold upon the rich brown crust. If he is dark, or fortunately black, this decorative trussing must be made very tight. Then the skin will split so that when untied he will be beautifully marked with red on black incisions.

Now peel and crush forty cloves of garlic. Work them through a sieve into two cups of brandy and one teaspoon of soy sauce. Inject him as before. Carefully spoon out each eyeball and put them to soak with his genitals in the dish of cold milk. Cut out his tongue and put it to poach in the saucepan of stock from which you first remove the fingers, carrots, etc. Last force an empty Coca-Cola bottle as far into his throat as you can. This is to keep it open. Now you are ready for:

Other Dishes

Put the liver (raw) through the meat grinder, mix it with the remainder of the garlic and brandy, quite a bit of black pepper and some thyme with perhaps a pinch of sage. Add the yolk of one egg and enough bread crumbs to make a coherent loaf. Wrap it with bacon and place it in the head. Coat the edge of the skull with a simple flour-and-water paste, replace the lid and cover all the hair with this paste. Do this also to the eyebrows and mustache, if any. Does he need a shave? Quickly lather, shave and dry his distended cheeks. Also, plug the eye sockets with this paste.

Preheat your oven to 450°, rub him carefully with sesame oil, not forgetting his underside. Oil enough aluminum foil on one side to cover him loosely. Place the platter in the oven and turn your attention to his heart.

You are to cut from the face of this a valentine-style heart, remove the various membranes and divisions within, and rub the cavity with salt and pepper. With the two eggwhites from the liver pâté and two more whole eggs mix a half tablespoon of cornstarch and a full cup of coagulated blood which you have kept from the tin bucket. Stir in one tablespoon, not less, of Tabasco and stuff the heart with as much of this pudding as it will hold. Replace the valentine cover and, carefully sliding it by the blade of the sword, place it in the chest cavity.

Next remove the membrane from the kidneys. Slice off about a half cup of the meat and put it to soak in cold water and lemon juice. Discard the rest.

Now, of course, you are tired. But now also it is time to peek in the oven. Quickly baste your prize with a housepainter's brush with the rich drippings. Repeat this as often as you like thoughout the next hour. Then turn off the heat and leave it to cool in the closed oven. Is it rare? Yes!

Meanwhile, has the stock about the tongue reduced to a mere spoon of syrup? Remove it to a dish of thinly sliced lemons. Pour the syrup over it when it has cooled to room temperature. Chill it in the refrigerator.

Now remove the vegetables from the tub. Pick over the cress to be sure there are no yellow leaves, wrap it in foil and refrigerate it. Clean the leeks thoroughly, discarding the tough green ends and roots. Drop them in two quarts of boiling salted water. Cook uncovered until the root end is tender when pierced with a fork. Remove them with a leaking ladle to a bath of ice water. Do the same to the artichokes, leaving the leaves, however, untrimmed. Flute the mushrooms, trimming a fraction of an inch from their stems. Sauté them cap down so that their centers are rosy brown. Do not toss them about, the rims of their heads as well as their stems must remain ivory white.

Strain the boiling liquid. Reduce it to two cups. With a bulb baster remove all the cooking juices from the roasting platter. Add them to the butter in which the mushrooms were tinted. Stir in a heaping tablespoon of flour until it forms a smooth paste. Continue stirring it over a high fire until it ceases to foam. Remove half of the roux to a saucepan, but continue to stir the rest until it is a rich brown color. Remove it from the heat instantly and continue to stir as you add half of the vegetable stock (which is still hot). Return to the flame and stir just until the brown roux has begun to thicken. Add enough of the wine, one bottle of which you have opened, to make a slightly thick sauce. Stir in one full tablespoon of black pepper! Pour it into its service boat and keep warm at the back of the stove, or in some other way.

Heat the white roux in the saucepan and stir it together with its share of the vegetable liquor. Add a half pint of day-old cream and by boiling rapidly and stirring gently reduce it by less than a fourth. Dot the top with butter but let it cool. Sprinkle the top with fresh grated nutmeg, a little white pepper, and the little glass of sweat you collected from the scraping of the body in the bathtub.

Now rest.

Rest well, for as much time as is left before it is time to bathe and dress for this Passion, this Eucharistic Holocaust of Perfect Love.

The Last Rite

At seven o'clock your servant (hired for this night alone) wakes you by announcing that your bath is drawn. It is, of course, the same tub, but now blanketed with shimmering unscented bubbles of liquid Ivory soap. Soak in it. Do not move until the oven rouses you with the faint clang of its expanding metals. Wear nothing but your best dressing-gown, not even slippers. Seat yourself at table and, resting your feet upon a high cushion or low stool, watch the candlelight catch the droplets on the tall sides of your Purgative d'amor Cocktail. Sip it slowly while your man prepares Lung Straws Parmesan and Brain Fritters Vinaigrette. (So simple, so right.) They will arrive with your second cocktail. You will salt them lightly it is hoped, but heavily will also be understood. Your man smiles at your enjoyment and, at his nod, you rise and democratically assist his placement of the gorgeously garnished platter, sizzling from the oven, upon its waiting bed of crushed glass over cedar chips. He has followed your instruction about the hors d'oeuvre so perfectly, he will naturally have arranged the garnishes exactly as you diagrammed them to him during his interview.

Now he will serve the soup from its tureen; its ineffable aroma will mingle with that of your centerpiece as he deftly snips and withdraws its trussing strings. As you lower your head to sip your first spoon of soup you will see that the eyes have been perfectly replaced, that his mouth, wide open as so often you saw it in ribald laughter, has within it, upon its bed of crushed ice his Tongue Glittering in Aspic. The perfectly basted face is unmarred. The rapidly melting ice fills his mouth and your mind with memories of never-to-be-repeated autumn days when his sweet breath steamed in the apple crisp winds of an already leafless park.

A single spoon of the soup and it disappears. If it were not that your servant will return momentarily to remove the tiny plate where you have left the second slice of tongue, you would not bother to savour the tender, tart, pebbly tip you now nibble, you would at once relieve yourself and, no matter how hot their juices, bite from that laughing face those fiercely chapped lips, and so ruin the rest of your supper. But this servant understands. Invisibly the tiny, icy plate disappears and in its place an ancient ironstone soup plate presents in its pool of lemon butter an artichoke, its petals agape, its heart wrapped in white-of-leek and studded with kidney cut in the tiniest possible cubelets. The lemon butter fuses with the faint odor of urine. The leek, the olive, the artichoke heart, does it not yearn for the very wine which now falls clearly and coolly into your glass? Taste. Could it really be that this brash experiment has solved the problem of artichokes and wine? But enough, you will imagine next that you have solved the presentation of *coq au vin*. Taste each ingredient once, then finish another glass of wine. Another yet as you watch the preparation of the *Tendron Blanchette*.

The cream sauce is placed already bubbling on whichever side of the carcass is least attractive. There, unseen, your man removes the "false" or "Adam's ribs" to a very hot plate. On the surface of the sauce he dribbles flaming brandy from a small ladle. Immersing the ladle he stirs once and then spoons the hot spiked cream over the ribs and, placing a fluted mushroom beside it, serves it and retires. This morsel, gelatinous bones and all, requires solitude. Not only to hear its crunch in the mouth but to hear also through the salt of your tears, the heavy accelerated breathing which used to cause these tender things to cover themselves with big beads of sweat. Taste the mushroom. Finish the last drop of wine. Wipe your secret from your face. Watch the noiseless spilling of Chateau Mouton-Rothschild '53 into the invisible balloon of your glass; it is time for the grill.

Your man may make a show of this, either with a small Japanese charcoal grill or a very hot electric skillet sprinkled with coarse salt. The fillet has been removed with two spoons, and is just as deftly seared, sliced, and served with a single spoon of Poivrade Sauce. A single bite of this melting, crusted flesh and the wine springs to life on your tongue. Has a Médoc ever bloomed with such masculine tenderness not only on your palate but into the very crevasses of your mind? No. It *is*, relaxing thought, perfect.

Beside you a cut-glass bowl of ice appears, offering watercress. After the pepper sauce, its green tang is more like a memory of the mint of the soup. Now you are presented with a paper thin slice of the *Jambon au Saignant* on an oval plate of ruby red glass. A pinch of salt, a squeeze of the lemon left imbedded in the iced cress, and yet new mysteries emerge from the muddy mind of the grape. Is there here, now, at this solitary supper, not some silent presence forming?

Strange before you as if by magic, the little cushion of pâté displays the sullen radiance of an eye. Call now for the second bottle of Médoc. Surely only such a noble fluid should be used to drown the sort of pain that begins now to drip like gall from your heart. And of course, again, life imitating art, presents you also with a slice of that spiced savoury from the dark coffer of his heart. It is presented on the point of that heartless attulet by means of which it has been removed from the empty oven of his breast.

Finish the wine. All of it. No more is needed. The cheese must meet nothing but the soft sentimentality of the pear.

It arrives and again your man leaves you perfectly alone. Its slow poaching in heavy cream has expanded its tissues to full tumescence. The crisp heart of a carrot, inserted into the urethra and anchored in a dry canapé, has enabled it to exceed the usual presentation (*enbelle vue*) and appear as promised in all the arrogance suitable to its station and purpose; namely life's only indispensable ornament. The two large animelles, already shrinking slightly as they cool, cause the hairs on the restless scrotum to scatter their droplets of cream. A touch of your dessert spoon and the foreskin slides down. With its silver tip the tiny curds must be caught before they fall. Close your mouth on this minute serving. Close your eyes and breathe deeply. At the end of a minute add a sliver of cold pear. Do not speak. Let your man assist you from the table. He will pour the coffee and the liqueur, then, leave without a word.

Don't allow the salt of tears to interfere. Think on it. Has it not been indeed the ultimate reality of love with which we have been concerned?

MENU

Purgative d'amor Cocktails
  Brain Fritters Vinaigrette
  Lung Straws Parmesan
  Excretion Soup with Mint
  Tongue in Aspic
  Artichoke stuffed with Kidney

Chateau Petrus '61
  Tendron Blanchette with Fluted Mushroom

Chateau Mouton-Rothschild '53
  Grilled Fillet with Sauce Poivrade
  Iced Watercress
  Jambon au Saignant
  Pâté Trompe L'oeil and Savoury au Coeur

  Fromage Garçon Chaud and Bosc Pear

Galliano
  Coffee and Tabaceleros and Silence

Among the Dahlias

⌒⌒⌒⌒

WILLIAM SANSOM

The zoo was almost empty. It was a day in late September, dry and warm, quiet with sunshine. The school-holidays were over. And it was a Monday afternoon—most people had a week-end's enjoyment on their consciences and would forbear to appear until the Tuesday.

An exception to this was John Doole. He could be seen at about two o'clock making his way quietly past the owl-houses.

Doole is what may too easily be called an "ordinary" man, a man who has conformed in certain social appearances and comportments for a common good; but a man who is still alive with dreams, desires, whims, fancies, hates and loves—none particularly strong or frequent. The effect of a life of quiet conformity had been to keep such impulses precisely in their place as dreams or desires, writing them off as impracticable.

Doole would also have been called a phlegmatic man: at least, the opposite to a nervous type. When Doole compulsorily whistled to himself, or pulled up the brace of his trousers with his left hand while his right patted the back of his head, or took unnecessarily deep breaths while waiting for a train, so deep that he seemed to be saying Hum-Ha, Hum-ha with his mouth contorted into a most peculiar shape, or went through a dozen other such queer acrobatics during the course of his day—these gestures were never recognised as the symptoms of nervous unbalance, for too many other people did exactly the same, and Doole knew this too, he found nothing odd in such antics. In fact, he had just as many "nerves" as a Mayfair lady crammed with sleeping pills—only his manner of outlet was different: also, since he never recognised all this as neurotic, it was the more easy to control.

Doole was a man of forty, with a happy pink face and receding fair hair, a little paunch, and creased baby-fat round his wrists. He had three dimples, two in the cheeks and one on his chin, which gave him the happy, merry look—but his yellow eyebrows flew up at angles over pale lashed eyes, arching out like a shrimp's feelers, and this gave him a little the look of a startled horse, his eyeballs rolled and seemed to shoot out, while those dimples had the effect of stretching the lip over his teeth into an almost animal fixity. He wore a richly sober brown suit, a little rounded over his short figure; an eyeglass bounced on a black ribbon again his paunch; his tawny shoes were brilliantly shined. The paunch seemed to pull him forward, and he threw his arms back as he walked, fingers stretched taut, and his whole body rested back on a very straight, backward-pressed neck. It was easy to imagine him in a bathing costume: one knew he had thin, active legs.

He was in business, in fireplaces. But he would often take a walk in the afternoon between two and three. "Nobody comes back from lunch till three, you might as well not have a telephone," he often said. "I'm damned if I'm going to sit there like a stuffed dummy while they stuff the real man." He himself was principally a vegetarian, ate lightly and often alone. He loved animals. He often visited the zoo, though he shuddered a little at the hunks of raw meat dribbling from the vulture's beak and the red bones lying about the lion's cage.

Now he stood for a moment discussing a large white owl. The two appraised each other, Doole's eyes with their appearance of false anguish, the owl's with their false wisdom. The owl had its trousered legs placed neatly together. Unconsciously Doole moved his own into a similar position: at any moment the two might have clicked heels and bowed. "Just a flying puss," Doole said to himself, considering the owl's catface of night eyes and furry ears and feathered round cheeks. "Likes mice like puss, too," he thought with satisfaction, forgetting in the pleasure of this observation his vegetarian principles. It is satisfactory to come across a common coincidence in the flesh—and Doole expanded for a moment as he nodded, "How true!" As if to please him, the owl opened its beak and made, from a distance deep inside the vase of feathers, a thin mewing sound.

Doole smiled and passed on. All seemed very right with the world. Creatures were *really* so extraordinary, Particularly birds. And he paused again before a delicate blue creature which stood on one long brittle leg with its nut-like head cocked under a complicated hat of coloured feathers. This bird did not look at Doole. It stood and jerked its head backwards and forwards, like an urgent little lady in a spring hat practising the neck movements of an Indonesian dance. Doole took out his watch and checked the time. Nearly half-an-hour before he need think of the office. Delightful! And what a wholly delightful day, not a cloud in the golden blue sky! And so quiet—almost ominously quiet, he thought, imagining for a moment the uneasy peace of metropolitan parks deserted by plague or fear. The panic noon, he thought—well, the panic afternoon, then. Time for sunny ghosts. Extraordinary, too, how powerful the presence of vegetation grows when one is alone with it! Yet put a few people about the place—all that power would recede. Man is a gregarious creature, he repeated to himself, and is frightened to be alone—and how very charming these zinnias are! How bright, like a consortium of national flags, the dahlias!

Indeed these colourful flowers shone very brightly in that September light. Red, yellow, purple and white, the large flower-moons stared like blodges from a paint box, hard as the colours of stained-glass windows. The lateness of the year had dried what green there was about, leaves were shrunken but not yet turned, so that all flowers had a greater prominence, they stood out as they never could in the full green luxuriance of spring and summer. And the earth was dry and the gravel walk dusty. Nothing moved. The flowers stared. The sun bore steadily down. Such vivid, motionless colour gave a sense of magic to the path, it did not seem quite real.

Doole passed slowly along by the netted bird-runs, mildly thankful for the company of their cackling, piping inmates. Sometimes he stopped and read with interest a little white card describing the bird's astounding Latin name and its place of origin. Uganda, Brazil, New Zealand—and soon these places ceased to mean anything, life's variety proved too immense, anything might come from anywhere. A thick-trousered bird with a large pink lump on its head croaked at Doole, then swung its head back to bury its whole face in feathers, nibbling furiously with closed eyes. In the adjoining cage everything looked deserted, broken pods and old dried droppings lay scattered, the water bowl was almost dry—and then he spied a grey bird tucked up in a corner, lizard lids half-closed, sleeping or resting or simply tired of it all. Doole felt distress for this bird, it looked so lonely and grieved, he would far rather be croaked at. He passed on, and came to the peacocks: the flaming blue dazzled him and the little heads jerked so busily that he smiled again, and turned contentedly back to the path—when the smile was washed abruptly from his face. He stood frozen with terror in the warm sunshine.

The broad gravel path, walled in on the one side by dahlias, on the other by cages, stretched yellow with sunlight. A moment before it had been quite empty. Now, exactly in the centre and only some thirty feet away, stood a full-maned male lion.

It stared straight at Doole.

Doole stood absolutely still, as still as a man can possibly stand, but in that first short second, like an immensely efficient and complicated machine, his eyes and other senses flashed every detail of the surrounding scene into his consciousness—he knew instantly that on the right there were high wire cages, he estimated whether he could pull himself up by his fingers in the net, he felt the stub ends of his shoes pawing helplessly beneath; he saw the bright dahlia balls on the left, he saw behind them a high green hedge, probably privet, with underbush too thick to penetrate—it was a ten-foot hedge rising high against the sky, could one leap and plunge halfway through, like a clown through a circus hoop? And if so, who would follow? And behind the lion cutting across the path like a wall, a further hedge—it hardly mattered what was behind the lion, though it gave in fact a further sense of impasse. And behind himself? The path stretched back past all those cages by which he had strolled at such leisure such a very little time ago—the fractional thought of it started tears of pity in his eyes—and it was far, far to run to the little thatched hut that said *Bath Chairs for Hire*, he felt that if only he could get among those big old safe chairs with their blankets and pillows he would be safe. But he knew it was too far. Long before he got there those hammer-strong paws would be on him, his clothes torn and his own red meat staining the yellow gravel.

At the same time as his animal reflexes took all this in, some other instinct made him stand still, and as still as a rock, instead of running. Was this, too, an animal sense? Was he, Doole, in his brown suit, like an ostrich that imagines it has fooled its enemy by burying its head in the ground? Or was it rather an educated sense—how many times had he been told that savages and animals can smell fear, one must stand one's ground and face them? In any case, he did this—he stood his ground and stared straight into the large, deep eyes of the lion, and as he stared there came over him the awful sense: *This has happened, this is happening to ME.* He had felt it in nightmares, and as a child before going up for a beating—a dreadfully condemned sense, the sense of *no way out*, never, never and *now*. It was absolute. The present moment roared loud and intense as all time put together.

The lion, with its alerted head erect, looked very tall. Its mane—and he was so near he could see how coarse and strong the hair straggled—framed its big face hugely. There was something particularly horrible in so much hair making an oval frame. Heavy disgruntled jowls, as big as hams, hung down in folds of muscled flesh buff-grey against the yellow gravel. Its eyes were too big, and shaped in some sharp-cornered way like large convex glasses more than eyes—and from somewhere far back, as far away and deep as the beast's ancient wisdom, the two black pupils flickered at him from inside their lenses of golden-yellow liquid. The legs beneath had a coarse athletic bandiness: the whole creature was heavy and thick with muscle that thumped and rolled when it moved—as suddenly now it did, padding forward only one silent pace.

Doole's whole inside was wrenched loose—he felt himself panicked, he wanted to turn and run. But he held on. And a sense of the softness of his flesh overcame him, he felt small and defenceless as a child again.

The lion, large as it was, still had some of the look of a cat—though its heavy disgruntled mouth was downcurved, surly, predatory as any human face with a long upper lip. But the poise of the head had the peculiarly questioning consideration of cat—it smelled inwards with its eyes, there was the furry presence of a brain, or of a mass of instincts that thought slowly but however slowly always came to the same destined decision. Also, there was a cat's affronted look in its eyes. A long way behind, a knobbled tail swung slow and regular as a clock-pendulum.

Doole prayed: O God, please save me.

And then he thought: if only it could speak, if only like all these animals in books it could *speak*, then I could tell it how I'm me and how I must go on living, and about my house and my showroom just a few streets away over there, over the hedge, and out of the zoo, and all the thousand things that depend upon me and upon which I depend. I could say how I'm not just meat. I'm a person, a clubmember, a goldfish-feeder, a lover of flowers and detective-stories—and I'll promise to reduce that profit on fire-surrounds, I promise, from forty to thirty percent. I'd have to some day anyway, but I won't make excuses any more. . . .

His mind drummed through the terrible seconds. But above all two separate feelings predominated: one, an athletic, almost youthful alertness—as though he could make his body spring everywhere at once and at superlative speed; the other, an overpowering knowledge of guilt—and with it the canny hope that somehow he could bargain his way out, somehow expiate his wrong and avoid punishment. He had experienced this dual sensation before at moments in business when he had something to hide, and in some way hid the matter more securely by confes-

sing half of his culpability. But such agilities were now magnified enormously, this was life and death, and he would bargain his life away to
make sure of it, he would do anything and say anything . . . and much
the most urgent of his offerings was the promise never, never to do or
think wrong in any way ever again. . . .

And the sun bore down yellow and the flowers stared with their mad
colours and the lion stood motionless and hard as a top-heavy king—as
Doole thought of his cool shaded showroom with all the high-gloss fire-
stone slabs about, the graining and the marble flow, the toffee-streaming
arches, and never, never again would he feel dull among them . . .
never again. . . .

But it *was* never again, the ever was ever, at any minute now he would
be dead and how long would it take him to die, how slowly did they tear?

He suddenly screamed.

"No!" he screamed, "no, I can't bear it! I can't bear pain! I can't bear it
. . ." and he covered his face with his hands, so that he never saw the
long shudder that ran through the whole length of the lion's body, from
head to slowly swinging tail.

In the evening newspapers there were no more than a few lines about
the escape of a lion at the Zoological Gardens. Oddly—but perhaps
because no journalist was on the spot and the authorities wished to make
little of it—the story was never expanded to its proper dimension. The escape had resulted from a defection in the cage bolting, a chance in a
million, and more than a million, for it involved also a momentary blank
in a keeper's mind, and a piece of blown carton wedged in a socket—in
fact several freak occasions combining, including such as a lorry backfir-
ing that had reminded the keeper of a certain single gunshot in the whole
four years of the Kaiser's war—the kind of thing that is never properly
known and never can be explained, and certainly not in a newspaper.
However—the end of it was that the lion had to be shot. It was too precarious a situation for the use of nets or cages. The animal had to go.
And there the matter ended.

Doole's body was never found—for the lion in fact never sprang at
him. It did something which was probably, in a final evolution over the
years, worse for Doole; certainly worse for his peace of mind, which
would have been properly at peace had his body gone, but which was
now left forever afterwards to suffer from a shock peculiar to the occasion.
If we are not animals, if the human mind is superior to the simple

animal body, then it must be true to say that by not being killed, Doole finally suffered a greater ill.

For what happened was this—Doole opened very slowly the fingers that covered his eyes and saw through his tears and the little opening between his fingers, through the same opening through which in church during prayers he had once spied on the people near him, on the priest and the altar itself—he saw the lion slowly turn its head away! He saw it turn its head, in the worn weary way that cats turn from something dull and distasteful, as if the head itself had perceived something too heavy to bear, leaning itself to one side as if a perceptible palpable blow had been felt. And then the animal had turned and plodded off up the path and disappeared at the turn of the hedge.

Doole was left standing alone and unwanted. For a second he felt an unbearable sense of isolation. Alone, of all creatures in the world, he was undesirable.

The next moment he was running away as fast as his legs would carry him, for the lion might easily return, and secondly—a very bad second—the alarm must be given for the safety of others.

It was some days before his nerve was partly recovered. But he was never quite the same afterwards. He took to looking at himself for long periods in the mirror. He went to the dentist and had his teeth seen to. He became a regular visitor at a Turkish Bath house, with the vague intention of sweating himself out of himself. And even today, after dusk on summer evenings, his figure may sometimes be seen, in long white running shorts, plodding from shadow to lamplight and again into shadow, among the great tree-hung avenues to the north of Regent's Park, a man keeping fit—or a man running away from something? From himself?

Under the Garden

ᕗᔓᕬᔒ

GRAHAM GREENE

PART ONE

1

It was only when the doctor said to him, "Of course the fact that you don't smoke is in your favour," Wilditch realized what it was he had been trying to convey with such tact. Dr. Cave had lined up along one wall a series of X-ray photographs, the whorls of which reminded the patient of those pictures of the earth's surface taken from a great height that he had pored over at one period during the war, trying to detect the tiny grey seed of a launching ramp.

Dr. Cave had explained, "I want you clearly to understand my problem." It was very similar to an intelligence briefing of such "top secret" importance that only one officer could be entrusted with the information. Wilditch felt gratified that the choice had fallen on him, and he tried to express his interest and enthusiasm, leaning forward and examining more closely than ever the photographs of his own interior.

"Beginning at this end," Dr. Cave said, "let me see April, May, June, three months ago, the scar left by the pneumonia is quite obvious. You can see it here."

"Yes, sir," Wilditch said absent-mindedly. Dr. Cave gave him a puzzled look.

"Now if we leave out the intervening photographs for the moment and come straight to yesterday's, you will observe that this latest one is almost entirely clear, you can only just detect . . ."

"Good," Wilditch said. The doctor's finger moved over what might have been tumuli or traces of prehistoric agriculture.

"But not entirely, I'm afraid. If you look now along the whole series you will notice how very slow the progress has been. Really by this stage the photographs should have shown no trace."

"I'm sorry," Wilditch said. A sense of guilt had taken the place of gratification.

"If we had looked at the last plate in isolation I would have said there was no cause for alarm." The doctor tolled the last three words like a bell. Wilditch thought, Is he suggesting tuberculosis?

"It's only in relation to the others, the slowness . . . it suggests the possibility of an obstruction."

"Obstruction?"

"The chances are that it's nothing, nothing at all. Only I wouldn't be quite happy if I let you go without a deep examination. Not quite happy." Dr. Cave left the photographs and sat down behind his desk. The long pause seemed to Wilditch like an appeal to his friendship.

"Of course," he said, "if it would make you happy . . ."

It was then the doctor used those revealing words, "Of course the fact that you don't smoke is in your favour."

"Oh."

"I think we'll ask Sir Nigel Sampson to make the examination. In case there is something there, we couldn't have a better surgeon . . . for the operation."

Wilditch came down from Wimpole Street into Cavendish Square looking for a taxi. It was one of those summer days which he never remembered in childhood: grey and dripping. Taxis drew up outside the tall liver-coloured buildings partitioned by dentists and were immediately caught by the commissionaires for the victims released. Gusts of wind barely warmed by July drove the rain aslant across the blank eastern gaze of Epstein's virgin and dripped down the body of her fabulous son. "But it hurt," the child's voice said behind him. "You make a fuss about nothing," a mother—or a governess—replied.

2

This could not have been said of the examination Wilditch endured a week later, but he made no fuss at all, which perhaps aggravated his case in the eyes of the doctors who took his calm for lack of vitality. For the unprofessional to enter a hospital or to enter the services has very much the same effect; there is a sense of relief and indifference; one is placed quite helplessly on a conveyor-belt with no responsibility any more for anything. Wilditch felt himself protected by an organization, while the English summer dripped outside on the coupés of the parked cars. He had not felt such freedom since the war ended.

The examination was over—a bronchoscopy; and there remained a nightmare memory, which survived through the cloud of the anaesthetic, of a great truncheon forced down his throat into the chest and then slowly withdrawn; he woke next morning bruised and raw so that even the act of excretion was a pain. But that, the nurse told him, would pass in one day or two; now he could dress and go home. He was disappointed at the abruptness with which they were thrusting him off the belt into the world of choice again.

"Was everything satisfactory?" he asked, and saw from the nurse's expression that he had shown indecent curiosity.

"I couldn't say, I'm sure," the nurse said. "Sir Nigel will look in, in his own good time."

Wilditch was sitting on the end of the bed tying his tie when Sir Nigel Sampson entered. It was the first time Wilditch had been conscious of seeing him: before he had been a voice addressing him politely out of sight as the anaesthetic took over. It was the beginning of the week-end and Sir Nigel was dressed for the country in an old tweed jacket. He had tousled white hair and he looked at Wilditch with a far-away attention as though he were a float bobbing in midstream.

"Ah, feeling better," Sir Nigel said incontrovertibly.

"Perhaps."

"Not very agreeable," Sir Nigel said, "but you know we couldn't let you go, could we, without taking a look?"

"Did you see anything?"

Sir Nigel gave the impression of abruptly moving downstream to a quieter reach and casting his line again.

"Don't let me stop you dressing, my dear fellow." He looked vaguely around the room before choosing a strictly upright chair, then lowered himself on to it as though it were a tuffet which might "give." He began feeling in one of his large pockets—for a sandwich?

"Any news for me?"

"I expect Dr. Cave will be along in a few minutes. He was caught by a rather garrulous patient." He drew a large silver watch out of his pocket—for some reason it was tangled up in a piece of string. "Have to meet my wife at Liverpool Street. Are *you* married?"

"No."

"Oh well, one care the less. Children can be a great responsibility."

"I have a child—but she lives a long way off."

"A long way off? I see."

"We haven't seen much of each other."

"Doesn't care for England?"

"The colour-bar makes it difficult for her." He realized how childish he sounded directly he had spoken, as though he had been trying to draw attention to himself by a bizarre confession, without even the satisfaction of success.

"Ah yes," Sir Nigel said. "Any brothers or sisters? You, I mean."

"An elder brother. Why?"

"Oh well, I suppose it's all on the record," Sir Nigel said, rolling in his line. He got up and made for the door. Wilditch sat on the bed with the tie over his knee. The door opened and Sir Nigel said, "Ah, here's Dr. Cave. Must run along now. I was just telling Mr. Wilditch that I'll be seeing him again. You'll fix it, won't you?" and he was gone.

"Why should I see him again?" Wilditch asked and then, from Dr. Cave's embarrassment, he saw the stupidity of the question. "Oh yes, of course, you did find something?"

"It's really very lucky. If caught in time . . ."

"There's sometimes hope?"

"Oh, there's always hope."

So, after all, Wilditch thought, I am—if I so choose—on the conveyor-belt again.

Dr. Cave took an engagement-book out of his pocket and said briskly, "Sir Nigel has given me a few dates. The tenth is difficult for the clinic, but the fifteenth—Sir Nigel doesn't think we should delay longer than the fifteenth."

"Is he a great fisherman?"

"Fisherman? Sir Nigel? I have no idea." Dr. Cave looked aggrieved, as though he were being shown an incorrect chart. "Shall we say the fifteenth?"

"Perhaps I could tell you after the week-end. You see, I have not made up my mind to stay as long as that in England."

"I'm afraid I haven't properly conveyed to you that this is serious, really serious. Your only chance—I repeat your only chance," he spoke like a telegram, "is to have the obstruction removed in time."

"And then, I suppose, life can go on for a few more years."

"It's impossible to guarantee . . . but there have been complete cures."

"I don't want to appear dialectical," Wilditch said, "but I do have to decide, don't I, whether I want my particular kind of life prolonged."

"It's the only one we have," Dr. Cave said.

"I see you are not a religious man—oh, please don't misunderstand me, nor am I. I have no curiosity at all about the future."

3

The past was another matter. Wilditch remembered a leader in the Civil War who rode from an undecided battle mortally wounded. He revisited the house where he was born, the house in which he was married, greeted a few retainers who did not recognize his condition, seeing him only as a tired man upon a horse, and finally—but Wilditch could not recollect how the biography had ended: he saw only a figure of exhaustion slumped over the saddle, as he also took, like Sir Nigel Sampson, a train from Liverpool Street. At Colchester he changed onto the branch line to Winton, and suddenly summer began, the kind of summer he always remembered as one of the conditions of life at Winton. Days had become so much shorter since then. They no longer began at six in the morning before the world was awake.

Winton Hall had belonged, when Wilditch was a child, to his uncle, who had never married, and every summer he lent the house to Wilditch's mother. Winton Hall had been virtually Wilditch's, until school cut the period short, from late June to early September. In memory his mother and brother were shadowy background figures. They were less established even than the machine upon the platform of "the halt" from which he bought Fry's chocolates for a penny a bar: than the oak tree spreading over the green in front of the red-brick wall—under its shade as a child he had distributed apples to soldiers halted there in the hot August of 1914: the group of silver birches on the Winton lawn and the broken fountain, green with slime. In his memory he did not share the house with others: he owned it.

Nevertheless the house had been left to his brother not to him; he was far away when his uncle died and he had never returned since. His brother married, had children (for them the fountain had been mended), the paddock behind the vegetable garden and the orchard, where he used to ride the donkey, had been sold (so his brother had written to him) for building council-houses, but the hall and the garden which he had so scrupulously remembered nothing could change.

Why then go back now and see it in other hands? Was it that at the approach of death one must get rid of everything? If he had accumulated money he would now have been in the mood to distribute it. Perhaps the man who had ridden the horse around the countryside had not been saying goodbye, as his biographer imagined, to what he valued most: he had been ridding himself of illusions by seeing them again with clear and moribund eyes, so that he might be quite bankrupt when death came. He had the will to possess at that absolute moment nothing but his wound.

His brother, Wilditch knew, would be faintly surprised by this visit. He had become accustomed to the fact that Wilditch never came to Winton; they would meet at long intervals at his brother's club in London, for George was a widower by this time, living alone. He always talked to others of Wilditch as a man unhappy in the country, who needed a longer range and stranger people. It was lucky, he would indicate, that the house had been left to him, for Wilditch would probably have sold it in order to travel further. A restless man, never long in one place, no wife, no children, unless the rumours were true that in Africa . . . or it might have been in the East . . . Wilditch was well aware of how his brother spoke of him. His brother was the proud owner of the lawn, the goldfish-pond, the mended fountain, the laurel-path which they had known when they were children as the Dark Walk, the lake, the island . . . Wilditch looked out at the flat hard East Anglian countryside, the meagre hedges and the stubbly grass, which had always seemed to him barren from the salt of Danish blood. All these years his brother had been in occupation, and yet he had no idea of what might lie underneath the garden.

4

The chocolate-machine had gone from Winton Halt, and the halt had been promoted—during the years of nationalization—to a station; the chimneys of a cement-factory smoked along the horizon and council-houses now stood three deep along the line.

Wilditch's brother waited in a Humber at the exit. Some familiar smell of coal-dust and varnish had gone from the waiting-room and it was a mere boy who took his ticket instead of a stooped and greying porter. In childhood nearly all the world is older than oneself.

"Hullo, George," he said in remote greeting to the stranger at the wheel.

"How are things, William?" George asked as they ground on their way—it was part of his character as a countryman that he had never learnt how to drive a car well.

The long chalky slope of a small hill—the highest point before the Ural mountains he had once been told—led down to the village between the bristly hedges. On the left was an abandoned chalk-pit—it had been just as abandoned forty years ago, when he had climbed all over it looking for treasure, in the form of brown nuggets of iron pyrites which when broken showed an interior of starred silver.

"Do you remember hunting for treasure?"

"Treasure?" George said. "Oh, you mean that iron stuff."

Was it the long summer afternoons in the chalk-pit which had made him dream—or so vividly imagine—the discovery of a real treasure? If it was a dream it was the only dream he remembered from those years, or, if it was a story which he had elaborated at night in bed, it must have been the final effort of a poetic imagination that afterwards had been rigidly controlled. In the various services which had over the years taken him from one part of the world to another, imagination was usually a quality to be suppressed. One's job was to provide facts, to a company (import and export), a newspaper, a government department. Speculation was discouraged. Now the dreaming child was dying of the same disease as the man. He was so different from the child that it was odd to think the child would not outlive him and go on to quite a different destiny.

George said, "You'll notice some changes, William. When I had the new bathroom added, I found I had to disconnect the pipes from the fountain. Something to do with pressure. After all there are no children now to enjoy it."

"It never played in my time either."

"I had the tennis-lawn dug up during the war, and it hardly seemed worth while to put it back."

"I'd forgotten that there *was* a tennis-lawn."

"Don't you remember it, between the pond and goldfish-tank?"

"The pond? Oh, you mean the lake and the island."

"Not much of a lake. You could jump on to the island with a short run."

"I thought of it as much bigger."

But all measurements had changed. Only for a dwarf does the world remain the same size. Even the red-brick wall which separated the garden from the village was lower than he remembered—a mere five feet, but in order to look over it in those days he had always to scramble to the top of some old stumps covered deep with ivy and dusty spiders' webs. There was no sign of these when they drove in: everything was very tidy everywhere, and a handsome piece of ironmongery had taken the place of the swing-gate which they had ruined as children.

"You keep the place up very well," he said.

"I couldn't manage it without the market-garden. That enables me to put the gardener's wages down as a professional expense. I have a very good accountant."

He was put into his mother's room with a view of the lawn and the silver birches; George slept in what had been his uncle's. The little bedroom next door which had once been his was now converted into a tiled bathroom—only the prospect was unchanged. He could see the laurel bushes where the Dark Walk began, but they were smaller too. Had the dying horseman found as many changes?

Sitting that night over coffee and brandy, during the long family pauses, Wilditch wondered whether as a child he could possibly have been so secretive as never to have spoken of his dream, his game, whatever it was. In his memory the adventure had lasted for several days. At the end of it he had found his way home in the early morning when everyone was asleep: there had been a dog called Joe who bounded towards him and sent him sprawling in the heavy dew of the lawn. Surely there must have been some basis of fact on which the legend had been built. Perhaps he had run away, perhaps he had been out all night—on the island in the lake or hidden in the Dark Walk—and during those hours he had invented the whole story.

Wilditch took a second glass of brandy and asked tentatively, "Do you remember much of those summers when we were children here?" He was aware of something unconvincing in the question: the apparently harmless opening gambit of a wartime interrogation.

"I never cared for the place much in those days," George said surprisingly. "You were a secretive little bastard."

"Secretive?"

"And uncooperative. I had a great sense of duty towards you, but you never realized that. In a year or two you were going to follow me to school. I tried to teach you the rudiments of cricket. You weren't interested. God knows what you were interested in."

"Exploring?" Wilditch suggested, he thought with cunning.

"There wasn't much to explore in fourteen acres. You know, I had such plans for this place when it became mine. A swimming-pool where the tennis-lawn was—it's mainly potatoes now. I meant to drain the pond too—it breeds mosquitoes. Well, I've added two bathrooms and modernized the kitchen, and even that has cost me four acres of pasture. At the back of the house now you can hear the children caterwauling from the council-houses. It's all been a bit of a disappointment."

"At least I'm glad you haven't drained the lake."

"My dear chap, why go on calling it the lake? Have a look at it in the morning and you'll see the absurdity. The water's nowhere more than two feet deep." He added, "Oh well, the place won't outlive me. My children aren't interested, and the factories are beginning to come out this way. They'll get a reasonably good price for the land—I haven't much else to leave them." He put some more sugar in his coffee. "Unless, of course, you'd like to take it on when I am gone?"

"I haven't the money and anyway there's no cause to believe that I won't be dead first."

"Mother was against my accepting the inheritance," George said. "She never liked the place."

"I thought she loved her summers here." The great gap between their memories astonished him. They seemed to be talking about different places and different people.

"It was terribly inconvenient, and she was always in trouble with the gardener. You remember Ernest? She said she had to wring every vegetable out of him. (By the way he's still alive, though retired of course—you ought to look him up in the morning. It would please him. He still feels he owns the place.) And then, you know, she always thought it would have been better for us if we could have gone to the seaside. She had an idea that she was robbing us of a heritage—buckets and spades and sea-water-bathing. Poor mother, she couldn't afford to turn down Uncle Henry's hospitality. I think in her heart she blamed father for dying when he did without providing for holidays at the sea."

"Did you talk it over with her in those days?"

"Oh no, not then. Naturally she had to keep a front before the children. But when I inherited the place—you were in Africa—she warned Mary and me about the difficulties. She had very decided views, you know, about any mysteries, and that turned her against the garden. Too much shrubbery, she said. She wanted everything to be very clear. Early Fabian training, I daresay."

"It's odd. I don't seem to have known her very well."

"You had a passion for hide-and-seek. She never liked that. Mystery again. She thought it a bit morbid. There was a time when we couldn't find you. You were away for hours."

"Are you sure it was hours? Not a whole night?"

"I don't remember it at all myself. Mother told me." They drank their brandy for a while in silence. Then George said, "She asked Uncle Henry to have the Dark Walk cleared away. She thought it was unhealthy with all the spiders' webs, but he never did anything about it."

"I'm surprised *you* didn't."

"Oh, it was on my list, but other things had priority, and now it doesn't seem worth while to make more changes." He yawned and stretched. "I'm used to early bed. I hope you don't mind. Breakfast at 8.30?"

"Don't make any changes for me."

"There's just one thing I forgot to show you. The flush is tricky in your bathroom."

George led the way upstairs. He said, "The local plumber didn't do a very good job. Now, when you've pulled this knob, you'll find the flush never quite finishes. You have to do it a second time—sharply like this."

Wildich stood at the window looking out. Beyond the Dark Walk and the space where the lake must be, he could see the splinters of light given off by the council-houses; through one gap in the laurels there was even a street-light visible, and he could hear the faint sound of television-sets joining together different programmes like the discordant murmur of a mob.

He said, "That view would have pleased mother. A lot of the mystery gone."

"I rather like it this way myself," George said, "on a winter's evening. It's a kind of companionship. As one gets older one doesn't want to feel quite alone on a sinking ship. Not being a churchgoer myself . . ." he added, leaving the sentence lying like a torso on its side.

"At least we haven't shocked mother in that way, either of us."

"Sometimes I wish I'd pleased her, though, about the Dark Walk. And the pond—how she hated that pond too."

"Why?"

"Perhaps because you liked to hide on the island. Secrecy and mystery again. Wasn't there something you wrote about it once? A story?"

"Me? A story? Surely not."

"I don't remember the circumstances. I thought—in a school magazine? Yes, I'm sure of it now. She was very angry indeed and she wrote rude remarks in the margin with a blue pencil. I saw them somewhere once. Poor mother."

George led the way into the bedroom. He said, "I'm sorry there's no bedside light. It was smashed last week, and I haven't been into town since."

"It's all right. I don't read in bed."

"I've got some good detective-stories downstairs if you wanted one."

"Mysteries?"

"Oh, mother never minded those. They came under the heading of puzzles. Because there was always an answer."

Beside the bed was a small bookcase. He said, "I brought some of mother's books here when she died and put them in her room. Just the ones that she had liked and no bookseller would take." Wilditch made out a title, *My Apprenticeship* by Beatrice Webb. "Sentimental, I suppose, but I didn't want actually to *throw away* her favourite books. Good night." He repeated, "I'm sorry about the light."

"It really doesn't matter."

George lingered at the door. He said, "I'm glad to see you here, William. There were times when I thought you were avoiding the place."

"Why should I?"

"Well, you know how it is. I never go to Harrods now because I was there with Mary a few days before she died."

"Nobody has died here. Except Uncle Henry, I suppose."

"No, of course not. But why did you, suddenly, decide to come?"

"A whim," Wilditch said.

"I suppose you'll be going abroad again soon?"

"I suppose so."

"Well, good night." He closed the door.

Wilditch undressed, and then, because he felt sleep too far away, he sat down on the bed under the poor centre-light and looked along the rows of shabby books. He opened Mrs. Beatrice Webb at some account of a trade union congress and put it back. (The foundations of the future Welfare State were being truly and uninterestingly laid.) There were a number of Fabian pamphlets heavily scored with the blue pencil which George had remembered. In one place Mrs. Wilditch had detected an error of one decimal point in some statistics dealing with agricultural imports. What passionate concentration must have gone to that discovery. Perhaps because his own life was coming to an end, he thought how little of this, in the almost impossible event of a future, she would have carried with her. A fairy-story in such an event would be a more valuable asset than a Fabian graph, but his mother had not approved of fairy-stories. The only children's book on these shelves was a history of England. Against an enthusiastic account of the battle of Agincourt she had pencilled furiously,

> And what good came of it at last?
> Said little Peterkin.

The fact that his mother had quoted a poem was in itself remarkable.

The storm which he had left behind in London had travelled east in his wake and now overtook him in short gusts of wind and wet that slapped at the pane. He thought, for no reason, It will be a rough night on the island. He had been disappointed to discover from George that the origin of the dream which had travelled with him round the world was probably no more than a story invented for a school-magazine and forgotten again, and just as that thought occurred to him, he saw a bound volume called *The Warburian* on the shelf.

He took it out, wondering why his mother had preserved it, and found a page turned down. It was the account of a cricket-match against Lancing and Mrs. Wilditch had scored the margin: "Wilditch One did good work in deep field." Another turned-down leaf produced a passage under the heading Debating Society: "Wilditch One spoke succinctly to the motion." The motion was "That this House has no belief in the social policies of His Majesty's Government." So George in those days had been a Fabian too.

He opened the book at random this time and a letter fell out. It had a printed heading, Dean's House, Warbury, and it read, "Dear Mrs. Wilditch, I was sorry to receive your letter of the 3rd and to learn that you were displeased with the little fantasy published by your younger son in *The Warburian*. I think you take a rather extreme view of the tale which strikes me as quite a good imaginative exercise for a boy of thirteen. Obviously he has been influenced by the term's reading of *The Golden Age*—which after all, fanciful though it may be, was written by a governor of the Bank of England." (Mrs. Wilditch had made several blue exclamation marks in the margin—perhaps representing her view of the Bank.) "Last term's *Treasure Island* too may have contributed. It is always our intention at Warbury to foster the imagination—which I think you rather harshly denigrate when you write of 'silly fancies.' We have scrupulously kept our side of the bargain, knowing how strongly you feel, and the boy is not 'subjected,' as you put it, to any religious instruction at all. Quite frankly, Mrs. Wilditch, I cannot see any trace of religious feeling in this little fancy—I have read it through a second time before writing to you—indeed the treasure, I'm afraid, is only too material, and quite at the mercy of those 'who break in and steal.' "

Wilditch tried to find the place from which the letter had fallen, working back from the date of the letter. Eventually he found it: "The Treasure on the Island" by W.W.

Wilditch began to read.

5

"In the middle of the garden there was a great lake and in the middle of the lake an island with a wood. Not everybody knew about the lake, for to reach it you had to find your way down a long dark walk, and not many people's nerves were strong enough to reach the end. Tom knew that he was likely to be undisturbed in that frightening region, and so it was there that he constructed a raft out of old packing cases, and one drear wet day when he knew that everybody would be shut in the house, he dragged the raft to the lake and paddled it across to the island. As far as he knew he was the first to land there for centuries.

"It was all overgrown on the island, but from a map he had found in an ancient sea-chest in the attic he made his measurements, three paces north from the tall umbrella pine in the middle and then two paces to the right. There seemed to be nothing but scrub, but he had brought with him a pick and a spade and with the dint of almost superhuman exertions he uncovered an iron ring sunk in the grass. At first he thought it would be impossible to move, but by inserting the point of the pick and levering it he raised a kind of stone lid and there below, going into the darkness, was a long narrow passage.

"Tom had more than the usual share of courage, but even he would not have ventured further if it had not been for the parlous state of the family fortunes since his father had died. His elder brother wanted to go to Oxford but for lack of money he would probably have to sail before the mast, and the house itself, of which his mother was passionately fond, was mortgaged to the hilt to a man in the City called Sir Silas Dedham whose name did not belie his nature."

Wilditch nearly gave up reading. He could not reconcile this childish story with the dream which he remembered. Only the "drear wet night" seemed true as the bushes rustled and dripped and the birches swayed outside. A writer, so he had always understood, was supposed to order and enrich the experience which was the source of his story, but in that

case it was plain that the young Wilditch's talents had not been for literature. He read with growing irritation, wanting to exclaim again and again
to this thirteen-year-old ancestor of his, "But why did you leave that out?
Why did you alter this?"

"This passage opened out into a great cave stacked from floor to ceiling
with gold bars and chests overflowing with pieces of eight. There was a
jewelled crucifix"—Mrs. Wilditch has underlined the word in blue—"set
with precious stones which had once graced the chapel of a Spanish galleon
and on a marble table were goblets of precious metal."

But, as he remembered, it was an old kitchen-dresser, and there were
no pieces of eight, no crucifix, and as for the Spanish galleon . . .

"Tom thanked the kindly Providence which had led him first to the map
in the attic" (but there had been no map. Wilditch wanted to correct the
story, page by page, much as his mother had done with her blue pencil)
"and then to this rich treasure trove" (his mother had written in the
margin, referring to the kindly Providence, "No trace of religious feeling!!"). "He filled his pockets with the pieces of eight and taking one bar
under each arm, he made his way back along the passage. He intended to
keep his discovery secret and slowly day by day to transfer the treasures to
the cupboard in his room, thus surprising his mother at the end of the holidays with all this sudden wealth. He got safely home unseen by anyone
and that night in bed he counted over his new riches while outside it
rained and rained. Never had he heard such a storm. It was as though the
wicked spirit of his old pirate ancestor raged against him" (Mrs. Wilditch
had written, "Eternal punishment I suppose!") "and indeed the next day,
when he returned to the island in the lake, whole trees had been uprooted
and now lay across the entrance to the passage. Worse still there had been
a landslide, and now the cavern must lie hidden forever below the waters
of the lake. However," the young Wilditch had added briefly forty years
ago, "the treasure already recovered was sufficient to save the family home
and send his brother to Oxford."

Wilditch undressed and got into bed, then lay on his back listening to
the storm. What a trivial conventional day-dream W.W. had constructed—out of what? There had been no attic-room—probably no raft:
these were preliminaries which did not matter, but why had W.W. so fal-
sified the adventure itself? Where was the man with the beard? The old
squawking woman? Of course it had all been a dream, it could have been
nothing else but a dream, but a dream too was an experience, the images
of a dream had their own integrity, and he felt professional anger at this

false report just as his mother had felt at the mistake in the Fabian statistics.

All the same, while he lay there in his mother's bed and thought of her rigid interrogation of W.W.'s story, another theory of the falsifications came to him, perhaps a juster one. He remembered that agents parachuted into France during the bad years after 1940 had been made to memorize a cover-story which they could give, in case of torture, with enough truth in it to be checked. Perhaps forty years ago the pressure to tell had been almost as great on W.W., so that he had been forced to find relief in fantasy. Well, an agent dropped into occupied territory was always given a time-limit after capture. "Keep the interrogators at bay with silence or lies for just so long, and then you may tell all." The time-limit had surely been passed in his case a long time ago, his mother was beyond the possibility of hurt, and Wilditch for the first time deliberately indulged his passion to remember.

He got out of bed and, after finding some notepaper stamped, presumably for income-tax purposes, Winton Small Holdings Limited, in the drawer of the desk, he began to write an account of what he had found—or dreamed that he found—under the garden of Winton Hall. The summer night was nosing wetly around the window just as it had done fifty years ago, but, as he wrote, it began to turn grey and recede; the trees of the garden became visible, so that, when he looked up after some hours from his writing, he could see the shape of the broken fountain and what he supposed were the laurels in the Dark Walk, looking like old men humped against the weather.

PART TWO

1

Never mind how I came to the island in the lake, never mind whether in fact, as my brother says, it is a shallow pond with water only two feet deep (I suppose a raft can be launched on two feet of water, and certainly I must have always come to the lake by way of the Dark Walk, so that it is not at all unlikely that I built my raft there). Never mind what hour it was—I think it was evening, and I had hidden, as I remember it, in the Dark Walk because George had not got the courage to search for me there. The evening turned to rain, just as it's raining now, and George must have been summoned into the house for shelter. He would have told my mother that he couldn't find me and she must have called from the upstair windows, front and back—perhaps it was the occasion George spoke about tonight. I am not sure of these facts, they are plausible only, I can't yet *see* what I'm describing. But I know that I was not to find George and my mother again for many days . . . It cannot, whatever George says, have been less than three days and nights that I spent below the ground. Could he really have forgotten so inexplicable an experience?

And here I am already checking my story as though it were something which had really happened, for what possible relevance has George's memory to the events of a dream?

I dreamed that I crossed the lake, I dreamed . . . that is the only certain fact and I must cling to it, the fact that I dreamed. How my poor mother would grieve if she could know that, even for a moment, I had begun to think of these events as true . . . but, of course, if it were possible for her to know what I am thinking now, there would be no limit to the area of possibility. I dreamed then that I crossed the water (either by swimming—I could already swim at seven years old—or by wading if the lake is really as small as George makes out, or by paddling a raft) and scrambled up the slope of the island. I can remember grass, scrub, brushwood, and at last a wood. I would describe it as a forest if I had not already seen, in the height of the garden-wall, how age diminishes size. I don't remember the umbrella-pine which W.W. described—I suspect he stole the sentinel-tree from *Treasure Island,* but I do know that when I got into the wood I was completely hidden from the house and the trees were close enough together to protect me from the rain. Quite soon I was lost, and yet how could I have been lost if the lake were no bigger than a pond, and the island therefore not much larger than the top of a kitchen-table?

Again I find myself checking my memories as though they were facts. A dream does not take account of size. A puddle can contain a continent, and a clump of trees stretch in sleep to the world's edge. I dreamed, I *dreamed* that I was lost and that night began to fall. I was not frightened. It was as though even at seven I was accustomed to travel. All the rough journeys of the future were already in me then, like a muscle which had only to develop. I curled up among the roots of the trees and slept. When I woke I could still hear the pit-pat of the rain in the upper branches and the steady zing of an insect near by. All these noises come as clearly back to me now as the sound of the rain on the parked cars outside the clinic in Wimpole Street, the music of yesterday.

The moon had risen and I could see more easily around me. I was determined to explore further before the morning came, for then an expedition would certainly be sent in search of me. I knew, from the many books of exploration George had read to me, of the danger to a person lost of walking in circles until eventually he dies of thirst or hunger, so I cut a cross in the bark of the tree (I had brought a knife with me that contained several blades, a small saw and an instrument for removing pebbles from horses' hooves). For the sake of future reference I named the place where I had slept Camp Hope. I had no fear of hunger, for I had apples in both pockets, and as for thirst I had only to continue in a straight line and I would come eventually to the lake again where the water was sweet, or at worst a little brackish. I go into all these details, which W.W. unaccountably omitted, to test my memory. I had forgotten until now how far or how deeply it extended. Had W.W. forgotten or was he afraid to remember?

I had gone a little more than three hundred yards—I paced the distances and marked every hundred paces or so on a tree—it was the best I could do, without proper surveying instruments, for the map I already planned to draw—when I reached a great oak of apparently enormous age with roots that coiled away above the surface of the ground. (I was reminded of those roots once in Africa where they formed a kind of shrine for a fetish—a seated human figure made out of a gourd and palm fronds and unidentifiable vegetable matter gone rotten in the rains and a great penis of bamboo. Coming on it suddenly, I was frightened, or was it the memory that it brought back which scared me?) Under one of these roots the earth had been disturbed; somebody had shaken a mound of charred tobacco from a pipe and a sequin glistened like a snail in the moist moonlight. I struck a match to examine the ground closer and saw the imprint of a foot in a patch of loose earth—it was pointing at the tree from a few inches away and it was as solitary as the print Crusoe found on the sands of another island. It was as though a one-legged man had taken a leap out of the bushes straight at the tree.

Pirate ancestor! What nonsense W.W. had written, or had he converted the memory of that stark frightening footprint into some comforting thought of the kindly scoundrel, Long John Silver, and his wooden leg?

I stood astride the imprint and stared up the tree, half expecting to see a one-legged man perched like a vulture among the branches. I listened and there was no sound except last night's rain dripping from leaf to leaf. Then—I don't know why—I went down on my knees and peered among the roots. There was no iron ring, but one of the roots formed an arch

more than two feet high like the entrance to a cave. I put my head inside
and lit another match—I couldn't see the back of the cave.

It's difficult to remember that I was only seven years old. To the self we
remain always the same age. I was afraid at first to venture further, but so
would any grown man have been, any of the explorers I thought of as my
peers. My brother had been reading aloud to me a month before from a
book called *The Romance of Australian Exploration*—my own powers of
reading had not advanced quite as far as that, but my memory was green
and retentive and I carried in my head all kinds of new images and evoca-
tive words—aboriginal, sextant, Murumbidgee, Stony Desert, and the
points of the compass with their big capital letters E.S.E. and N.N.W.
had an excitement they have never quite lost. They were like the figure
on a watch which at last comes round to pointing the important hour. I
was comforted by the thought that Sturt had been sometimes daunted
and that Burke's bluster often hid his fear. Now, kneeling by the cave, I
remembered a cavern which George Grey, another hero of mine, had
entered and how suddenly he had come on the figure of a man ten feet
high painted on the wall, clothed from the chin down to the ankles in a
red garment. I don't know why, but I was more afraid of that painting
than I was of the aborigines who killed Burke, and the fact that the feet
and hands which protruded from the garment were said to be badly executed added to the terror. A foot which looked like a foot was only
human, but my imagination could play endlessly with the faults of the
painter—a club-foot, a claw-foot, the worm-like toes of a bird. Now I associated this strange footprint with the ill-executed painting, and I hesitated a long time before I got the courage to crawl into the cave under the
root. Before doing so, in reference to the footprint, I gave the spot the
name of Friday's Cave.

2

For some yards I could not even get upon my knees, the roof grated
my hair, and it was impossible for me in that position to strike another
match. I could only inch along like a worm, making an ideograph in the
dust. I didn't notice for a while in the darkness that I was crawling down
a long slope, but I could feel on either side of me roots rubbing my
shoulders like the banisters of a staircase. I was creeping through the
branches of an underground tree in a mole's world. Then the impedi-
ments were passed—I was out the other side; I banged my head again on
the earth-wall and found that I could rise to my knees. But I nearly

toppled down again, for I had not realized how steeply the ground sloped. I was more than a man's height below ground and, when I struck a match, I could see no finish to the long gradient going down. I cannot help feeling a little proud that I continued on my way, on my knees this time, though I suppose it is arguable whether one can really show courage in a dream.

I was halted again by a turn in the path, and this time I found I could rise to my feet after I had struck another match. The track had flattened out and ran horizontally. The air was stuffy with an odd disagreeable smell like cabbage cooking, and I wanted to go back. I remembered how miners carried canaries with them in cages to test the freshness of the air, and I wished I had thought of bringing our own canary with me which had accompanied us to Winton Hall—it would have been company too in that dark tunnel with its tiny song. There was something, I remembered, called coal-damp which caused explosions, and this passage was certainly damp enough. I must be nearly under the lake by this time, and I thought to myself that, if there was an explosion, the waters of the lake would pour in and drown me.

I blew out my match at the idea, but all the same I continued on my way in the hope that I might come on an exit a little easier than the long crawl back through the roots of the trees.

Suddenly ahead of me something whistled, only it was less like a whistle than a hiss: it was like the noise a kettle makes when it is on the boil. I thought of snakes and wondered whether some giant serpent had made its nest in the tunnel. There was something fatal to man called a Black Mamba . . . I stood stock-still and held my breath, while the whistling went on and on for a long while, before it whined out into nothing. I would have given anything then to have been safe back in bed in the room next to my mother's, with the electric-light switch close to my hand and the firm bed-end at my feet. There was a strange clanking sound and a duck-like quack. I couldn't bear the darkness any more and I lit another match, reckless of coal-damp. It shone on a pile of old newspapers and nothing else—it was strange to find I had not been the first person here. I called out "Hullo!" and my voice went on in diminishing echoes down the long passage. Nobody answered, and when I picked up one of the papers I saw it was no proof of a human presence. It was the *East Anglian Observer* for April 5th 1885—"with which is incorporated the *Colchester Guardian*." It's funny how even the date remains in my mind and the Victorian Gothic type of the titling. There was a faint fishy smell about it as though—oh, eons ago—it had been wrapped around a

bit of prehistoric cod. The match burnt my fingers and went out. Perhaps
I was the first to come here for all those years, but suppose whoever had
brought those papers were lying somewhere dead in the tunnel . . .

Then I had an idea. I made a torch of the paper in my hand, tucked
the others under my arm to serve me later, and with the stronger light advanced more boldly down the passage. After all wild beasts—so George
had read to me—and serpents too in all likelihood—were afraid of fire,
and my fear of an explosion had been driven out by the greater terror of
what I might find in the dark. But it was not a snake or a leopard or a
tiger or any other cavern-haunting animal that I saw when I turned the
second corner. Scrawled with the simplicity of ancient man upon the
left-hand wall of the passage—done with a sharp tool like a chisel—was
the outline of a gigantic fish. I held up my paper-torch higher and saw
the remains of lettering either half-obliterated or in a language I didn't
know.

$$\int' c \eta \quad {}^{\gamma c} \quad c \, \vdash_{\!\cdot\,/} {}^{\prime}$$

I was trying to make sense of the symbols when a hoarse voice out of
sight called, "Maria, Maria."

I stood very still and the newspaper burned down in my hand. "Is that
you, Maria?" the voice said. It sounded to me very angry. "What kind of
a trick are you playing? What's the clock say? Surely it's time for my
broth." And then I heard again that strange quacking sound which I had
heard before. There was a long whispering and after that silence.

3

I suppose I was relieved that there were human beings and not wild
beasts down the passage, but what kind of human beings could they be
except criminals hiding from justice or gypsies who are notorious for
stealing children? I was afraid to think what they might do to anyone who
discovered their secret. It was also possible, of course, that I had come on
the home of some aboriginal tribe . . . I stood there unable to make up
my mind whether to go on or turn back. It was not a problem which my
Australian peers could help me to solve, for they had sometimes found
the aboriginals friendly folk who gave them fish (I thought of the fish on
the wall) and sometimes enemies who attacked with spears. In any case—
whether these were criminals or gypsies or aboriginals—I had only a
pocket-knife for my defence. I think it showed the true spirit of an ex-

plorer that in spite of my fears I thought of the map I must one day draw if I survived and so named this spot Camp Indecision.

My indecision was solved for me. An old woman appeared suddenly and noiselessly around the corner of the passage. She wore an old blue dress which came down to her ankles covered with sequins, and her hair was grey and straggly and she was going bald on top. She was every bit as surprised as I was. She stood there gaping at me and then she opened her mouth and squawked. I learned later that she had no roof to her mouth and was probably saying, "Who are you?" but then I thought it was some foreign tongue she spoke—perhaps aboriginee—and I replied with an attempt at assurance, "I'm English."

The hoarse voice out of sight said, "Bring him along here, Maria."

The old woman took a step towards me, but I couldn't bear the thought of being touched by her hands, which were old and curved like a bird's and covered with the brown patches that Ernest, the gardener, had told me were "gravemarks"; her nails were very long and filled with dirt. Her dress was dirty too and I thought of the sequin I'd seen outside and imagined her scrabbling home through the roots of the tree. I backed up against the side of the passage and somehow squeezed around her. She quacked after me, but I went on. Round a second—or perhaps a third—corner I found myself in a great cave some eight feet high. On what I thought was a throne, but I later realized was an old lavatory-seat, sat a big old man with a white beard yellowing round the mouth from what I suppose now to have been nicotine. He had one good leg, but the right trouser was sewn up and looked stuffed like a bolster. I could see him quite well because an oil-lamp stood on a kitchen-table, beside a carving-knife and two cabbages, and his face came vividly back to me the other day when I was reading Darwin's description of a carrier-pigeon: "Greatly elongated eyelids, very large external orifices to the nostrils, and a wide gape of mouth."

He said, "And who would you be and what are you doing here and why are you burning my newspaper?"

The old woman came squawking around the corner and then stood still behind me, barring my retreat.

I said, "My name's William Wilditch, and I come from Winton Hall."

"And where's Winton Hall?" he asked, never stirring from his lavatory-seat.

"Up there," I said and pointed at the roof of the cave.

"That means precious little," he said. "Why, everything is up there, China and all America too and the Sandwich Islands."

"I suppose so," I said. There was a kind of reason in most of what he said, as I came to realize later.

"But down here there's only us. We are exclusive," he said, "Maria and me."

I was less frightened of him now. He spoke English. He was a fellow-countryman. I said, "If you'll tell me the way out I'll be going on my way."

"What's that you've got under your arm?" he asked me sharply. "More newspapers?"

"I found them in the passage . . ."

"Finding's not keeping here," he said, "whatever it may be up there in China. You'll soon discover that. Why, that's the last lot of papers Maria brought in. What would we have for reading if we let you go and pinch them?"

"I didn't mean . . ."

"Can you read?" he asked, not listening to my excuses.

"If the words aren't too long."

"Maria can read, but she can't see very well any more than I can, and she can't articulate much."

Maria went kwahk, kwahk behind me, like a bull-frog it seems to me now, and I jumped. If that was how she read I wondered how he could understand a single word. He said, "Try a piece."

"What do you mean?"

"Can't you understand plain English? You'll have to work for your supper down here."

"But it's not supper-time. It's still early in the morning," I said.

"What o'clock is it, Maria?"

"Kwahk," she said.

"Six. That's supper-time."

"But it's six in the morning, not the evening."

"How do you know? Where's the light? There aren't such things as mornings and evenings here."

"Then how do you ever wake up? " I asked. His beard shook as he laughed. "What a shrewd little shaver he is," he exclaimed. "Did you hear that, Maria? How do you ever wake up? he said. All the same you'll find that life here isn't all beer and skittles and who's your Uncle Joe. If you are clever, you'll learn and if you are not clever . . ." He brooded morosely. "We are deeper here than any grave was ever dug to bury secrets in. Under the earth or over the earth, it's there you'll find all that matters." He added angrily, "Why aren't you reading a piece as I told you to? If you are to stay with us, you've got to jump to it."

"I don't want to stay."

"You think you can just take a peek, is that it? and go away. You are wrong—but take all the peek you want and then get on with it."

I didn't like the way he spoke, but all the same I did as he suggested. There was an old chocolate-stained chest of drawers, a tall kitchen-cupboard, a screen covered with scraps and transfers, and a wooden crate which perhaps served Maria for a chair, and another larger one for a table. There was a cooking-stove with a kettle pushed to one side, steaming yet. That would have caused the whistle I had heard in the passage. I could see no sign of any bed, unless a heap of potato-sacks against the wall served that purpose. There were a lot of breadcrumbs on the earth-floor and a few bones had been swept into a corner as though awaiting interment.

"And now," he said, "show your young paces. I've yet to see whether you are worth your keep."

"But I don't want to be kept," I said. "I really don't. It's time I went home."

"Home's where a man lies down," he said, "and this is where you'll lie from now on. Now take the first page that comes and read to me. I want to hear the news."

"But the paper's nearly fifty years old," I said. "There's no news in it."

"News is news however old it is." I began to notice a way he had of talking in general statements like a lecturer or a prophet. He seemed to be less interested in conversation than in the recital of some articles of belief, odd crazy ones, perhaps, yet somehow I could never put my finger convincingly on an error. "A cat's a cat even when it's a dead cat. We get rid of it when it's smelly, but news never smells, however long it's dead. News keeps. and it comes round again when you least expect. Like thunder."

I opened the paper at random and read: "Garden fête at the Grange. The fête at the Grange, Long Wilson, in aid of Distressed Gentlewomen was opened by Lady (Isobel) Montgomery." I was a bit put out by the long words coming so quickly, but I acquitted myself with fair credit. He sat on the lavatory-seat with his head sunk a little, listening with attention. "The Vicar presided at the White Elephant Stall."

The old man said with satisfaction, "They are royal beasts."

"But these were not really elephants," I said.

"A stall is part of a stable, isn't it? What do you want a stable for if they aren't real? Go on. Was it a good fate or an evil fate?"

"It's not that kind of fate either," I said.

"There's no other kind," he said. "It's your fate to read to me. It's *her* fate to talk like a frog, and mine to listen because my eyesight's bad. This is an underground fate we suffer from here, and that was a garden fate— but it all comes to the same fate in the end." It was useless to argue with him and I read on: "Unfortunately the festivities were brought to an untimely close by a heavy rainstorm."

Maria gave a kwhak that sounded like a malicious laugh, and "You see," the old man said, as though what I had read proved somehow he was right, "that's fate for you."

"The evening's events had to be transferred indoors, including the Morris dancing and the Treasure Hunt."

"Treasure Hunt?" the old man asked sharply.

"That's what it says here."

"The impudence of it," he said. "The sheer impudence. Maria, did you hear that?"

She kwahked—this time, I thought, angrily.

"It's time for my broth," he said with deep gloom, as though he were saying, "It's time for my death."

"It happened a long time ago," I said trying to soothe him.

"Time," he exclaimed, "you can — time," using a word quite unfamiliar to me which I guessed—I don't know how—was one that I could not with safety use myself when I returned home. Maria had gone behind the screen—there must have been other cupboards there, for I heard her opening and shutting doors and clanking pots and pans.

I whispered to him quickly, "Is she your luba?"

"Sister, wife, mother, daughter," he said, "what difference does it make? Take your choice. She's a woman, isn't she?" He brooded there on the lavatory-seat like a king on a throne. "There are two sexes," he said. "Don't try to make more than two with definitions." The statement sank into my mind with the same heavy mathematical certainty with which later on at school I learned the rule of Euclid about the sides of an isosceles triangle. There was a long silence.

"I think I'd better be going," I said, shifting up and down. Maria came in. She carried a dish marked Fido filled with hot broth. Her husband, her brother, whatever he was, nursed it on his lap a long while before he drank it. He seemed to be lost in thought again, and I hesitated to disturb him. All the same, after a while, I tried again.

"They'll be expecting me at home."

"Home?"

"Yes."

"You couldn't have a better home than this," he said. "You'll see. In a bit of time—a year or two—you'll settle down well enough."

I tried my best to be polite. "It's very nice here, I'm sure, but . . ."

"It's no use your being restless. I didn't ask you to come, did I, but now you are here, you'll stay. Maria's a great hand with cabbage. You won't suffer any hardship."

"But I can't stay. My mother . . ."

"Forget your mother and your father too. If you need anything from up there Maria will fetch it down for you."

"But I can't stay here."

"Can't's not a word that you can use to the likes of me."

"But you haven't any right to keep me . . ."

"And what right had you to come busting in like a thief, getting Maria all disturbed when she was boiling my broth?"

"I couldn't stay here with you. It's not—sanitary." I don't know how I managed to get that word out. "I'd die . . ."

"There's no need to talk of dying down here. No one's ever died here, and you've no reason to believe that anyone ever will. We aren't dead, are we, and we've lived a long long time, Maria and me. You don't know how lucky you are. There's treasure here beyond all the riches of Asia. One day, if you don't go disturbing Maria, I'll show you. You know what a millionaire is?" I nodded. "They aren't one quarter as rich as Maria and me. And they die too, and where's their treasure then? Rockefeller's gone and Fred's gone and Columbus. I sit here and just read about dying—it's an entertainment that's all. You'll find in all those papers what they call an obituary—there's one about a Lady Caroline Winterbottom that made Maria laugh and me. It's summerbottoms we have here, I said, all the year round, sitting by the stove."

Maria kwahked in the background, and I began to cry more as a way of interrupting him than because I was really frightened.

It's extraordinary how vividly after all these years I can remember that man and the words he spoke. If they were to dig down now on the island below the roots of the tree, I would half expect to find him sitting there still on the old lavatory-seat which seemed to be detached from any pipes or drainage and serve no useful purpose, and yet, if he had really existed, he must have passed his century a long time ago. There was something of a monarch about him and something, as I said, of a prophet and something of the gardener my mother disliked and of a policeman in the next village; his expressions were often countrylike and coarse, but his ideas seemed to move on a deeper level, like roots speading below a layer of compost. I could sit here now in this room for hours remembering the things he said—I haven't made out the sense of them all yet: they are stored in my memory like a code uncracked which waits for a clue or an inspiration.

He said to me sharply, "We don't need salt here. There's too much as it is. You taste any bit of earth and you'll find it salt. We live in salt. We are pickled, you might say, in it. Look at Maria's hands, and you'll see the salt in the cracks."

I stopped crying at once and looked (my attention could always be caught by bits of irrelevant information), and true enough, there seemed to be grey-white seams running between her knuckles.

"You'll turn salty too in time," he said encouragingly and drank his broth with a good deal of noise.

I said, "But I really am going, Mr. . . ."

"You can call me Javitt," he said, "but only because it's not my real name. You don't believe I'd give you that, do you? And Maria's not Maria—it's just a sound she answers to, you understand me, like Jupiter."

"No."

"If you had a dog called Jupiter, you wouldn't believe he was really Jupiter, would you?'

"I've got a dog called Joe."

"The same applies," he said and drank his soup. Sometimes I think that in no conversation since have I found the interest I discovered in those inconsequent sentences of his to which I listened during the days (I don't know how many) that I spent below the garden. Because, of course, I didn't leave that day. Javitt had his way.

He might be said to have talked me into staying, though if I had proved obstinate I have no doubt at all that Maria would have blocked my retreat, and certainly I would not have fancied struggling to escape through the musty folds of her clothes. That was the strange balance—to and fro—of those days; half the time I was frightened as though I were caged in a nightmare and half the time I only wanted to laugh freely and happily at the strangeness of his speech and the novelty of his ideas. It was as if, for those hours or days, the only important things in life were two, laughter and fear. (Perhaps the same ambivalence was there when I first began to know a woman.) There are people whose laughter has always a sense of superiority, but it was Javitt who taught me that laughter is more often a sign of equality, of pleasure and not of malice. He sat there on his lavatory-seat and he said, "I shit dead stuff every day, do I? How wrong you are." (I was already laughing because that was a word I knew to be obscene and I had never heard it spoken before.) "Everything that comes out of me is alive, I tell you. It's squirming around there, germs and bacilli and the like, and it goes into the ground like a womb, and it comes out somewhere, I daresay, like my daughter did—I forgot I haven't told you about her."

"Is she here?" I said with a look at the curtain, wondering what monstrous woman would next emerge.

"Oh, no, she went upstairs a long time ago."

"Perhaps I could take her a message from you," I said cunningly.

He looked at me with contempt. "What kind of a message," he asked, "could the likes of you take to the likes of her?" he must have seen the motive behind my offer, for he reverted to the fact of my imprisonment. "I'm not unreasonable," he said, "I'm not one to make hailstorms in harvest time, but if you went back up there you'd talk about me and Maria and the treasure we've got, and people would come digging."

"I swear I'd say nothing" (and at least I have kept that promise, whatever others I have broken, through all the years).

"You talk in your sleep maybe. A boy's never alone. You've got a brother, I daresay, and soon you'll be going to school and hinting at things to make you seem important. There are plenty of ways of keeping an oath and breaking it in the same moment. Do you know what I'd do then? If they came searching? I'd go further in."

Maria khahk-kwahked her agreement where she listened from somewhere behind the curtains.

"What do you mean?"

"Give me a hand to get off this seat," he said. He pressed his hand down on my shoulder and it was like a mountain heaving. I looked at the lavatory-seat and I could see that it had been placed exactly to cover a hole which went down down down out of sight. "A moit of the treasure's down there already," he said, "but I wouldn't let the bastards enjoy what they could find here. There's a little matter of subsidence I've got fixed up so that they'd never see the light of day again."

"But what would you do below there for food?"

"We've got tins enough for another century or two," he said. "You'd be surprised at what Maria's stored away there. We don't use tins up here because there's always broth and cabbage and that's more healthy and keeps the scurvy off, but we've no more teeth to lose and our gums are fallen as it is, so if we had to fall back on tins we would. Why, there's hams and chickens and red salmons' eggs and butter and steak-and-kidney pies and caviar, venison too and marrow-bones, I'm forgetting the fish—cods' roe and sole in white wine, langouste legs, sardines, bloaters, and herrings in tomato-sauce, and all the fruits that ever grew, apples, pears, strawberries, figs, raspberries, plums and greengages and passion fruit, mangoes, grapefruit, loganberries and cherries, mulberries too and sweet things from Japan, not to speak of vegetables, Indian corn and taties, salsify and spinach and that thing they call endive, asparagus, peas and the hearts of bamboo, and I've left out our old friend the tomato." He lowered himself heavily back on to his seat above the great hole going down.

"You must have enough for two lifetimes," I said.

"There's means of getting more," he added darkly, so that I pictured other channels delved through the undersoil of the garden like the section of an ant's nest, and I remembered the sequin on the island and the single footprint.

Perhaps all this talk of food had reminded Maria of her duties because she came quacking out from behind her dusty curtain, carrying two bowls of broth, one medium size for me and one almost as small as an egg-cup for herself. I tried politely to take the small one, but she snatched it away from me.

"You don't have to bother about Maria," the old man said. "She's been eating food for more years than you've got weeks. She knows her appetite."

"What do you cook with?" I asked.

"Calor," he said.

That was an odd thing about this adventure or rather this dream: fantastic though it was, it kept coming back to ordinary life with simple facts like that. The man could never, if I really thought it out, have existed all those years below the earth, and yet the cooking, as I seem to remember it, was done on a cylinder of calor-gas.

The broth was quite tasty and I drank it to the end. When I had finished I fidgeted about on the wooden box they had given me for a seat— nature was demanding something for which I was too embarrassed to ask aid.

"What's the matter with you?" Javitt said. "Chair not comfortable?"

"Oh, it's very comfortable," I said.

"Perhaps you want to lie down and sleep?"

"No."

"I'll show you something which will give you dreams," he said. "A picture of my daughter."

"I want to do number one," I blurted out.

"Oh, is that all?" Javitt said. He called to Maria, who was still clattering around behind the curtain, "The boy wants to piss. Fetch him the golden po." Perhaps my eyes showed interest, for he added to me diminishingly, with the wave of a hand, "It's the least of my treasures."

All the same it was remarkable enough in my eyes, and I can remember it still, a veritable chamber-pot of gold. Even the young dauphin of France on that long road back from Varennes with his father had only a silver cup at his service. I would have been more embarrassed, doing what I called number one in front of the old man Javitt, if I had not been so impressed by the pot. It lent the everyday affair the importance of a ceremony, almost of a sacrament. I can remember the tinkle in the pot like far-away chimes as though a gold surface resounded differently from china or base metal.

Javitt reached behind him to a shelf stacked with old papers and picked one out. He said, "Now you look at that and tell me what you think."

It was a kind of magazine I'd never seen before—full of pictures which are now called cheese-cake. I have no earlier memory of a woman's unclothed body, or as nearly unclothed as made no difference to me then, in the skintight black costume. One whole page was given up to a Miss Ramsgate, shot from all angles. She was the favourite contestant for something called Miss England and might later go on, if she were successful, to compete for the title of Miss Europe, Miss World and after that Miss Universe. I stared at her as though I wanted to memorize her for ever. And that is exactly what I did.

"That's our daughter," Javitt said.

"And did she become . . ."

"She was launched," he said with pride and mystery, as though he were speaking of some moon-rocket which had at last after many disappointments risen from the pad and soared to outer space. I looked at the photograph, at the wise eyes and the inexplicable body, and I thought, with all the ignorance children have of age and generations, I never want to marry anybody but her. Maria put her hand through the curtains and quacked, and I thought, she would be my mother then, but not a hoot did I care. With that girl for my wife I could take anything, even school and growing up and life. And perhaps I could have taken them, if I had ever succeeded in finding her.

Again my thoughts are interrupted. For if I am remembering a vivid dream—and dreams do stay in all their detail far longer than we realize—how would I have known at that age about such absurdities as beauty-contests? A dream can only contain what one has experienced, or, if you have sufficient faith in Jung, what our ancestors have experienced. But calor-gas and the Ramsgate Beauty Queen? . . . They are not ancestral memories, nor the memories of a child of seven. Certainly my mother did not allow us to buy with our meagre pocket-money—sixpence a week?—such papers as that. And yet the image is there, caught once and for all, not only the expression of the eyes, but the expression of the body too, the particular tilt of the breasts, the shallow scoop of the navel like something carved in sand, the little trim buttocks—the dividing line swung between them close and regular like the single sweep of a pencil. Can a child of seven fall in love for life with a body? And there is a further mystery which did not occur to me then: how could a couple as old as Javitt and Maria have had a daughter so young in the period when such contests were the vogue?

"She's a beauty," Javitt said, "you'll never see her like where your folks live. Things grow differently underground, like a mole's coat. I ask you where there's softness softer than that?" I'm not sure whether he was referring to the skin of his daughter or the coat of the mole.

I sat on the golden po and looked at the photograph and listened to Javitt as I would have listened to my own father if I had possessed one. His sayings are fixed in my memory like the photograph. Gross some of them seem now, but they did not appear gross to me then when even the graffiti on walls were innocent. Except when he called me "boy" or "snapper" or something of the kind he seemed unaware of my age: it was not that he talked to me as an equal but as someone from miles away, looking down from his old lavatory-seat to my golden po, from so far away that he couldn't distinguish my age, or perhaps he was so old that anyone under a century or so seemed much alike to him. All that I write here was not said at that moment. There must have been many days or nights of conversation—you couldn't down there tell the difference—and now I dredge the sentences up, in no particular order, just as they come to mind, sitting at my mother's desk so many years later.

4

"You laugh at Maria and me. You think we look ugly. I tell you she could have been painted if she had chosen by some of the greatest—

there's one that painted women with three eyes—she'd have suited him. But she knew how to tunnel in the earth like me, when to appear and when not to appear. It's a long time now that we've been alone down here. It gets more dangerous all the time—if you can speak of time—on the upper floor. But don't think it hasn't happened before. But when I remember . . ." But what he remembered has gone from my head, except only his concluding phrase and a sense of desolation: "Looking round at all those palaces and towers, you'd have thought they'd been made like a child's castle of the desert-sand."

"In the beginning you had a name only the man or woman knew who pulled you out of your mother. Then there was a name for the tribe to call you by. That was of little account, but of more account all the same than the name you had with strangers; and there was a name used in the family—by your pa and ma if it's those terms you call them by nowadays. The only name without any power at all was the name you used to strangers. That's why I call myself Javitt to you, but the name the man who pulled me out knew—that was so secret I had to keep him as a friend for life, so that he wouldn't even tell me because of the responsibility it would bring—I might let it slip before a stranger. Up where you come from they've begun to forget the power of the name. I wouldn't be surprised if you only had the one name and what's the good of a name everyone knows? Do you suppose even I feel secure here with my treasure and all—because, you see, as it turned out, I got to know the first name of all. He told it me before he died, before I could stop him, with a hand over his mouth. I doubt if there's anyone in the world but me who knows his first name. It's an awful temptation to speak it out loud—introduce it casually into the conversation like you might say by Jove, by George, for Christ's sake. Or whisper it when I think no one's attentive.

"When I was born, time had a different pace to what it has now. Now you walk from one wall to another, and it takes you twenty steps—or twenty miles—who cares?—between the towns. But when I was young we took a leisurely way. Don't bother me with 'I must be gone now' or 'I've been away so long.' I can't talk to you in terms of time—your time and my time are different. Javitt isn't my usual name either even with strangers. It's one I thought up fresh for you, so that you'll have no power at all. I'll change it right away if you escape. I warn you that.

"You get a sense of what I mean when you make love with a girl. The time isn't measured by clocks. Time is fast or slow or it stops for a while altogether. One minute is different to every other minute. When you make love it's a pulse in a man's part which measures time and when you spill yourself there's no time at all. That's how time comes and goes, not by an alarm-clock made by a man with a magnifying glass in his eye. Haven't you ever heard them say, 'It's — time' up there?" and he used again the word which I guessed was forbidden like his name, perhaps because it had power too.

"I daresay you are wondering how Maria and me could make a beautiful girl like that one. That's an illusion people have about beauty. Beauty doesn't come from beauty. All that beauty can produce is prettiness. Have you never looked around upstairs and counted the beautiful women with their pretty daughters? Beauty diminishes all the time, it's the law of diminishing returns, and only when you get back to zero, to the real ugly base of things, there's a chance to start again free and independent. Painters who paint what they call ugly things know that. I can still see that little head with its cap of blonde hair coming out from between Maria's thighs and how she leapt out of Maria in a spasm (there wasn't any doctor down here or midwife to give her a name and rob her of power—and she's Miss Ramsgate to you and to the whole world upstairs). Ugliness and beauty; you see it in war too; when there's nothing left of a house but a couple of pillars against the sky, the beauty of it starts all over again like before the builder ruined it. Perhaps when Maria and I go up there next, there'll only be pillars left, sticking up around the flattened world like it was fucking time." (The word had become familiar to me by this time and no longer had the power to shock.)

"Do you know, boy, that when they make those maps of the universe you are looking at the map of something that looked like that six thousand million years ago? You can't be much more out of date than that, I'll swear. Why, if they've got picutres up there of us taken yesterday, they'll see the world all covered with ice—if their photos are a bit more up to date than ours, that is. Otherwise we won't be there at all, maybe, and it might just as well be a photo of the future. To catch a star while it's alive you have to be as nippy as if you were snatching at a racehorse as it goes by.

"You are a bit scared still of Maria and me because you've never seen anyone like us before. And you'd be scared to see our daughter too, there's no other like her in whatever country she is now, and what good would a scared man be to her? Do you know what a rogue-plant is? And do you know that white cats with blue eyes are deaf? People who keep nursery-gardens look around all the time at the seedlings and they throw away any oddities like weeds. They call them rogues. You won't find many white cats with blue eyes and that's the reason. But sometimes you find someone who wants things different, who's tired of all the plus signs and wants to find zero, and he starts breeding away with the differences. Maria and I are both rogues and we are born of generations of rogues. Do you think I lost this leg in an accident? I was born that way just like Maria with her squawk. Generations of us uglier and uglier, and suddenly out of Maria comes our daughter, who's Miss Ramsgate to you. I don't speak her name even when I'm asleep. We're unique like the Red Grouse. You ask anybody if they can tell you where the Red Grouse came from.

"You are still wondering why we are unique. It's because for generations we haven't been thrown away. Man kills or throws away what he doesn't want. Somebody once in Greece kept the wrong child and exposed the right one, and then one rogue at least was safe and it only needed another. Why, in Tierra del Fuego in starvation years they kill and eat their old women because the dogs are of more value. It's the hardest thing in the world for a rogue to survive. For hundreds of years now we've been living underground and we'll have the laugh of you yet, coming up above for keeps in a dead world. Except I'll bet you your golden po that Miss Ramsgate will be there somewhere—her beauty's rogue too. We have long lives, we—Javitts to you. We've kept our ugliness all those years and why shouldn't she keep her beauty? Like a cat does. A cat is as beautiful the last day as the first. And it keeps its spittle. Not like a dog.

"I can see your eye light up whenever I say Miss Ramsgate, and you still wonder how it comes Maria and I have a child like that in spite of all I'm telling you. Elephants go on breeding till they are ninety years old, don't they, and do you suppose a rogue like Javitt (which isn't my real name) can't go on longer than a beast so stupid it lets itself be harnessed and draw logs? There's another thing we have in common with elephants. No one sees us dead.

"We know the sex-taste of female birds better than we know the sex-taste of women. Only the most beautiful in the hen's eyes survives, so when you admire a peacock you know you have the same taste as a peahen. But women are more mysterious than birds. You've heard of beauty and the beast, haven't you? They have rogue-tastes. Just look at me and my leg. You won't find Miss Ramsgate by going round the world preening yourself like a peacock to attract a beautiful woman—she's our daughter and she has rogue-tastes too. She isn't for someone who wants a beautiful wife at his dinner-table to satisfy his vanity, and an understanding wife in bed who'll treat him just the same number of times as he was accustomed to at school—so many times a day or week. She went

away, our daughter did, with a want looking for a want—and not a want
you can measure in inches either or calculate in numbers by the week.
They say that in the northern countries people make love for their health,
so it won't be any good looking for her in the north. You might have to
go as far as Africa or China. And talking of China . . ."

5

Sometimes I think that I learned more from Javitt—this man who never
existed—than from all my schoolmasters. He talked to me while I sat
there on the po or lay upon the sacks as no one had ever done before or
has ever done since. I could not have expected my mother to take time
away from the Fabian pamphlets to say, "Men are like monkeys—they
don't have any season in love, and the monkeys aren't worried by this no-
tion of dying. They tell us from pulpits we're immortal and then they try
to frighten us with death. I'm more a monkey than a man. To the
monkeys death's an accident. The gorillas don't bury their dead with
hearses and crowns of flowers, thinking one day it's going to happen to
them and they better put on a show if they want one for themselves too.
If one of them dies, it's a special case, and so they can leave it in the
ditch. I feel like them. But I'm not a special case yet. I keep clear of
hackney-carriages and railway-trains, you won't find horses, wild dogs or
machinery down here. I love life and I survive. Up there they talk about
natural death, but it's natural death that's unnatural. If we lived for a
thousand years—and there's no reason we shouldn't—there'd always be a
smash, a bomb, tripping over your left foot—those are the natural deaths.
All we need to live is a bit of effort, but nature sows booby-traps in our
way.

"Do you believe those skulls monks have in their cells are set there for
contemplation? Not on your life. They don't believe in death any more
than I do. The skulls are there for the same reason you'll see a queen's
portrait in an embassy—they're just part of the official furniture. Do you
believe an ambassador ever looks at that face on the wall with a diamond
tiara and an empty smile?

"Be disloyal. It's your duty to the human race. The human race needs
to survive and it's the loyal man who dies first from anxiety or a bullet or
overwork. If you have to earn a living, boy, and the price they make you
pay is loyalty, be a double agent—and never let either of the two sides
know your real name. The same applies to women and God. They both
respect a man they don't own, and they'll go on raising the price they are

willing to offer. Didn't Christ say that very thing? Was the prodigal son loyal or the lost shilling or the strayed sheep? The obedient flock didn't give the shepherd any satisfaction or the loyal son interest his father.

"People are afraid of bringing May blossom into the house. They say it's unlucky. The real reason is it smells strong of sex and they are afraid of sex. Why aren't they afraid of fish then, you may rightly ask? Because when they smell fish they smell a holiday ahead and they feel safe from breeding for a short while."

I remember Javitt's words far more clearly than the passage of time; certainly I must have slept at least twice on the bed of sacks, but I cannot remember Javitt sleeping until the very end—perhaps he slept like a horse or a god, upright. And the broth—that came at regular intervals, so far as I could tell, though there was no sign anywhere of a clock, and once I think they opened for me a tin of sardines from their store (it had a very Victorian label on it of two bearded sailors and a seal, but the sardines tasted good).

I think Javitt was glad to have me there. Surely he could not have been talking quite so amply over the years to Maria who could only quack in response, and several times he made me read to him from one of the newspapers. The nearest to our time I ever found was a local account of the celebrations for the relief of Mafeking. ("Riots," Javitt said, "purge like a dose of salts.")

Once he told me to pick up the oil-lamp and we would go for a walk together, and I was able to see how agile he could be on his one leg. When he stood upright he looked like a rough carving from a tree-trunk where the sculptor had not bothered to separate the legs, or perhaps, as with the image on the cave, they were "badly executed." He put one hand on each wall and hopped gigantically in front of me, and when he paused to speak (like many old people he seemed unable to speak and move at the same time) he seemed to be propping up the whole passage with his arms as thick as pit-beams. At one point he paused to tell me that we were now directly under the lake. "How many tons of water lie up there?" he asked me—I had never thought of water in tons before that, only in gallons, but he had the exact figure ready, I can't remember it now. Further on, where the passage sloped upwards, he paused again and said, "Listen," and I heard a kind of rumbling that passed overhead and after that a rattling as little cakes of mud fell around us. "That's a motor-car," he said, as an explorer might have said, "That's an elephant."

I asked him whether perhaps there was a way out near there since we were so close to the surface, and he made his answer, even to that direct question, ambiguous and general like a proverb. "A wise man has only one door to his house," he said.

What a boring old man he would have been to an adult mind, but a child has a hunger to learn which makes him sometimes hang on the lips of the dullest schoolmaster. I thought I was learning about the world and the universe from Javitt, and still to this day I wonder how it was that a child could have invented these details, or have they accumulated year by year, like coral, in the sea of the unconscious around the original dream?

There were times when he was in a bad humour for no apparent reason, or at any rate for no adequate reason. An example: for all his freedom of speech and range of thought, I found there were tiny rules which had to be obeyed, else the thunder of his invective broke—the way I had to arrange the spoon in the empty broth-bowl, the method of folding a newspaper after it had been read, even the arrangement of my limbs on the bed of sacks.

"I'll cut you off," he cried once and I pictured him lopping off one of my legs to resemble him. "I'll starve you, I'll set you alight like a candle for a warning. Haven't I given you a kingdom here of all the treasures of the earth and all the fruits of it, tin by tin, where time can't get in to destroy you and there's no day or night, and you go and defy me with a spoon laid down longways in a saucer? You come of an ungrateful generation." His arms waved about and cast shadows like wolves on the wall behind the oil-lamp, while Maria sat squatting behind a cylinder of calorgas in an attitude of terror.

"I haven't even seen your wonderful treasure," I said with feeble defiance.

"Nor you won't," he said, "nor any lawbreaker like you. You lay last night on your back grunting like a small swine, but did I curse you as you deserved? Javitt's patient. He forgives and he forgives seventy times seven, but then you go and lay your spoon longways . . ." He gave a great sigh like a wave withdrawing. He said, "I forgive even that. There's no fool like an old fool and you will search a long way before you find anything as old as I am—even among the tortoises, the parrots and the elephants. One day I'll show you the treasure, but not now. I'm not in the right mood now. Let time pass. Let time heal."

I had found the way, however, on an earlier occasion to set him in a good humour and that was to talk to him about his daughter. It came quite easily to me, for I found myself to be passionately in love, as perhaps one can only be at an age when all one wants is to give and the thought of taking is very far removed. I asked him whether he was sad when she left him to go "upstairs" as he liked to put it.

"I knew it had to come," he said. "It was for that she was born. One day she'll be back and the three of us will be together for keeps."

"Perhaps I'll see her then," I said.

"You won't live to see that day," he said, as though it was I who was the old man, not he.

"Do you think she's married?" I asked anxiously.

"She isn't the kind to marry," he said. "Didn't I tell you she's a rogue like Maria and me? She has her roots down here. No one marries who has his roots down here."

"I thought Maria and you were married," I said anxiously.

He gave a sharp crunching laugh like a nut-cracker closing. "There's no marrying in the ground," he said. "Where would you find the witnesses? Marriage is public. Maria and me, we just grew into each other, that's all, and then she sprouted."

I sat silent for a long while, brooding on that vegetable picture. Then I said with all the firmness I could muster, "I'm going to find her when I get out of here."

"If you get out of here," he said, "you'd have to live a very long time and travel a very long way to find her."

"I'll do just that," I replied.

He looked at me with a trace of humour. "You'll have to take a look at Africa," he said, "and Asia—and then there's America, North and South, and Australia—you might leave out the Arctic and the other Pole—she was always a warm girl." And it occurs to me now when I think of the life I have led since, that I have been in most of those regions—except Australia where I have only twice touched down between planes.

"I will go to them all," I said, "and I'll find her." It was as though the purpose of life had suddenly come to me as it must have come often enough to some future explorer when he noticed on a map for the first time an empty space in the heart of a continent.

"You'll need a lot of money," Javitt jeered at me.

"I'll work my passage," I said, "before the mast." Perhaps it was a reflection of that intention which made the young author W.W. menace his elder brother with such a fate before preserving him for Oxford of all places. The mast was to be a career sacred to me—it was not for George.

"It'll take a long time," Javitt warned me.

"I'm young," I said.

I don't know why it is that when I think of this conversation with Javitt the doctor's voice comes back to me saying hopelessly, "There's always hope." There's hope perhaps, but there isn't so much time left now as there was then to fulfil a destiny.

That night, when I lay down on the sacks, I had the impression that Javitt had begun to take a favourable view of my case. I woke once in the night and saw him sitting there on what is popularly called a throne, watching me. He closed one eye in a wink and it was like a star going out.

Next morning after my bowl of broth, he suddenly spoke up. "Today," he said, "you are going to see my treasure."

6

It was a day heavy with the sense of something fateful coming nearer—I call it a day but for all I could have told down there it might have been a night. And I can only compare it in my later experience with those slow hours I have sometimes experienced before I have gone to meet a woman with whom for the first time the act of love is likely to come about. The fuse has been lit, and who can tell the extent of the explosion? A few cups broken or a house in ruins?

For hours Javitt made no further reference to the subject, but after the second cup of broth (or was it perhaps, on that occasion, the tin of sardines?) Maria disappeared behind the screen and when she reappeared she wore a hat. Once, years ago perhaps, it had been a grand hat, a hat for the races, a great black straw affair; now it was full of holes like a colander decorated with one drooping scarlet flower which had been stitched and re-stitched and stitched again. I wondered when I saw her dressed like that whether we were about to go "upstairs." But we made no move. Instead she put a kettle upon the stove, warmed a pot and dropped in two spoonfuls of tea. Then she and Javitt sat and watched the kettle like a couple of soothsayers bent over the steaming entrails of a kid, waiting for a revelation. The kettle gave a thin preliminary whine and Javitt nodded and the tea was made. He alone took a cup, sipping it slowly, with his eyes on me, as though he were considering and perhaps revising his decision.

On the edge of his cup, I remember, was a tea-leaf. He took it on his nail and placed it on the back of my hand. I knew very well what that meant. A hard stalk of tea indicated a man upon the way and the soft leaf a woman; this was a soft leaf. I began to strike it with the palm of my other hand counting as I did so, "One, two, three." It lay flat, adhering to my hand. "Four, five." It was on my fingers now and I said, triumphantly, "In five days," thinking of Javitt's daughter in the world above. Javitt shook his head. "You don't count time like that with us," he said. "That's five decades of years." I accepted his correction—he must know his own country best, and it's only now that I find myself calculating, if every day down there were ten years long, what age in our reckoning could Javitt have claimed?

I have no idea what he had learned from the ceremony of the tea, but at least he seemed satisfied. He rose on his one leg, and now that he had his arms stretched out to either wall, he reminded me of a gigantic crucifix, and the crucifix moved in great hops down the way we had taken the day before. Maria gave me a little push from behind and I followed. The oil lamp in Maria's hand cast long shadows ahead of us.

First we came under the lake and I remembered the tons of water hanging over us like a frozen falls, and after that we reached the spot where we had halted before, and again a car went rumbling past on the road above. But this time we continued our shuffling march. I calculated that now we had crossed the road which led to Winton Halt; we must be somewhere under the inn called The Three Keys, which was kept by our gardener's uncle, and after that we should have arrived below the Long Mead, a field with a small minnowy stream along its northern border owned by a farmer called Howell. I had not given up all idea of escape and I noted our route carefully and the distance we had gone. I had hoped for some side-passage which might indicate that there was another entrance to the tunnel, but there seemed to be none and I was disappointed to find that before we travelled below the inn we descended quite steeply, perhaps in order to avoid the cellars—indeed at one moment I heard a groaning and a turbulence as though the gardener's uncle were taking delivery of some new barrels of beer.

We must have gone nearly half a mile before the passage came to an end in a kind of egg-shaped hall. Facing us was a kitchen-dresser of unstained wood, very similar to the one in which my mother kept her stores of jam, sultanas, raisins and the like.

"Open up, Maria," Javitt said, and Maria shuffled by me, clanking a bunch of keys and quacking with excitement, while the lamp swung to and fro like a censer.

"She's heated up," Javitt said. "It's many days since she saw the treasure last." I do not know which kind of time he was referring to then, but judging from her excitement I think the days must really have represented decades—she had even forgotten which key fitted the lock and she tried them all and failed and tried again before the tumbler turned.

I was disappointed when I first saw the interior—I had expected gold bricks and a flow of Maria Theresa dollars spilling on the floor, and there were only a lot of shabby cardboard-boxes on the upper shelves and the lower shelves were empty. I think Javitt noted my disappointment and was stung by it. "I told you," he said, "the moit's down below for safety." But I wasn't to stay disappointed very long. He took down one of the biggest boxes off the top shelf and shook the contents on to the earth at my feet, as though defying me to belittle *that*.

And *that* was a sparkling mass of jewellery such as I had never seen before—I was going to say in all the colours of the rainbow, but the colours of stones have not that pale girlish simplicity. There were reds almost as deep as raw liver, stormy blues, greens like the underside of a wave, yellow sunset colours, greys like a shadow on snow, and stones without colour at all that sparkled brighter than all the rest. I say I'd seen nothing like it: it is the scepticism of middle-age which leads me now to compare that treasure-trove with the caskets overflowing with artificial jewellery which you sometimes see in the shop-windows of Italian tourist-resorts.

And there again I find myself adjusting a dream to the kind of criticism I ought to reserve for some agent's report on the import or export value of coloured glass. If this was a dream, these were real stones. Absolute reality belongs to dreams and not to life. The gold of dreams is not the diluted gold of even the best goldsmith, there are no diamonds in dreams made of paste—what seems is. "Who seems most kingly is the king."

I went down on my knees and bathed my hands in the treasure, and while I knelt there Javitt opened box after box and poured the contents upon the ground. There is no avarice in a child. I didn't concern myself with the value of this horde: it was simply a treasure, and a treasure is to be valued for its own sake and not for what it will buy. It was only years later, after a deal of literature and learning and knowledge at second hand, that W.W. wrote of the treasure as something with which he could save the family fortunes. I was nearer to the jackdaw in my dream, caring only for the glitter and the sparkle.

"It's nothing to what lies below out of sight," Javitt remarked with pride.

There were necklaces and bracelets, lockets and bangles, pins and rings and pendants and buttons. There were quantities of those little gold objects which girls like to hang on their bracelets: the Vendôme column and the Eiffel Tower and a Lion of St. Mark's, a champagne bottle and a tiny booklet with leaves of gold inscribed with the names of places important perhaps to a pair of lovers—Paris, Brighton, Rome, Assisi and Moreton-in-Marsh. There were gold coins too—some with the heads of Roman emperors and others of Victoria and George IV and Frederick Barbarossa. There were birds made out of precious stone with diamond-eyes, and buckles for shoes and belts, hairpins too with the rubies turned into roses, and vinaigrettes. There were toothpicks of gold, and swizzle-sticks, and little spoons to dig the wax out of your ears of gold too, and cigarette-holders studded with diamonds, and small boxes of gold for pastilles and snuff, horse-shoes for the ties of hunting men, and emerald-hounds for the lapels of hunting women: fishes were there too and little carrots of ruby for luck, diamond-stars which had perhaps decorated generals or statesmen, golden key-rings with emerald-initials, and sea-shells picked out with pearls, and a portrait of a dancing-girl in gold and enamel, with Haidee inscribed in what I suppose were rubies.

"Enough's enough," Javitt said, and I had to drag myself away, as it seemed to me, from all the riches of the world, its pursuits and enjoyments. Maria would have packed everything that lay there back into the cardboard-boxes, but Javitt said with his lordliest voice, "Let them lie," and back we went in silence the way we had come, in the same order, our shadows going ahead. It was.as if the sight of the treasure had exhausted me. I lay down on the sacks without waiting for my broth and fell at once asleep. In my dream within a dream somebody laughed and wept.

7

I have said that I can't remember how many days and nights I spent below the garden. The number of times I slept is really no guide, for I slept simply when I had the inclination or when Javitt commanded me to lie down, there being no light or darkness save what the oil-lamp determined, but I am almost sure it was after this sleep of exhaustion that I woke with the full intention somehow to reach home again. Up till now I had acquiesced in my captivity with little complaint; perhaps the meals of broth were palling on me, though I doubt if that was the reason, for I have fed for longer, with as little variety and less appetite, in Africa;

perhaps the sight of Javitt's treasure had been a climax which robbed my story of any further interest; perhaps, and I think this is the most likely reason, I wanted to begin my search for Miss Ramsgate.

Whatever the motive, I came awake determined from my deep sleep, as suddenly as I had fallen into it. The wick was burning low in the oil-lamp and I could hardly distinguish Javitt's features and Maria was out o. sight somewhere behind the curtain. To my astonishment Javitt's eye were closed—it had never occurred to me before that there were mo-ments when these two might sleep. Very quietly, with my eyes on Javitt, I slipped off my shoes—it was now or never. When I had got them off with less sound than a mouse makes, an idea came to me and I withdrew the laces—I can still hear the sharp ting of the metal tag ringing on the gold po beside my sacks. I thought I had been too clever by half, for Javitt stirred—but then he was still again and I slipped off my makeshift bed and crawled over to him where he sat on the lavatory-seat. I knew that, unfamiliar as I was with the tunnel, I could never outpace Javitt, but I was taken aback when I realized that it was impossible to bind together the ankles of a one-legged man.

But neither could a one-legged man travel without the help of his hands—the hands which lay now conveniently folded like a statue's on his lap. One of the things my brother had taught me was to make a slip-knot. I made one now with the laces joined and very gently, millimetre by millimetre, passed it over Javitt's hands and wrists, then pulled it tight.

I had expected him to wake with a howl of rage and even in my fear felt some of the pride Jack must have experienced at outwitting the giant. I was ready to flee at once, taking the lamp with me, but his very silence detained me. He only opened one eye, so that again I had the impression that he was winking at me. He tried to move his hands, felt the knot, and then acquiesced in their imprisonment. I expected him to call for Maria, but he did nothing of the kind, just watching me with his one open eye.

Suddenly I felt ashamed of myself. "I'm sorry," I said.

"Ha, ha," he said, "my prodigal, the strayed sheep, you're learning fast."

"I promise not to tell a soul."

"They wouldn't believe you if you did," he said.

"I'll be going now," I whispered with regeret, lingering there absurdly, as though with half of myself I would have been content to stay for always.

"You better," he said. "Maria might have different views from me." He tried his hands again. "You tie a good knot."

"I'm going to find your daughter," I said, "whatever you may think."

"Good luck to you then," Javitt said. "You'll have to travel a long way; you'll have to forget all your schoolmasters try to teach you; you must lie like a horse-trader and not be tied up with loyalties any more than you are here, and who knows? I doubt it, but you might, you just might."

I turned away to take the lamp, and then he spoke again. "Take your golden po as a souvenir," he said. "Tell them you found it in an old cupboard. You've got to have something when you start a search to give you substance."

"Thank you," I said, "I will. You've been very kind." I began—absurdly in view of his bound wrists—to hold out my hand like a departing guest; then I stooped to pick up the po just as Maria, woken perhaps by our voices, came through the curtain. She took the situation in as quick as a breath and squawked at me—what I don't know—and made a dive with her bird-like hand.

I had the start of her down the passage and the advantage of the light, and I was a few feet ahead when I reached Camp Indecision, but at that point, what with the wind of my passage and the failing wick, the lamp went out. I dropped it on the earth and groped on in the dark. I could hear the scratch and whimper of Maria's sequin dress, and my nerves leapt when her feet set the lamp rolling on my tracks. I don't remember much after that. Soon I was crawling upwards, making better speed on my knees than she could do in her skirt, and a little later I saw a grey light where the roots of the tree parted. When I came up into the open it was much the same early morning hour as the one when I had entered the cave. I could hear kwahk, kwahk, kwahk, come up from below the ground—I don't know if it was a curse or a menace or just a farewell, but for many nights afterwards I lay in bed afraid that the door would open and Maria would come in to fetch me, when the house was silent and asleep. Yet strangely enough I felt no fear of Javitt, then or later.

Perhaps—I can't remember—I dropped the gold po at the entrance of the tunnel as a propitiation to Maria; certainly I didn't have it with me when I rafted across the lake or when Joe, our dog, came leaping out of the house at me and sent me sprawling on my back in the dew of the lawn by the green broken fountain.

PART THREE

1

Wilditch stopped writing and looked up from the paper. The night had passed and with it the rain and the wet wind. Out of the window he could see thin rivers of blue sky winding between the banks of cloud, and the sun as it slanted in gleamed weakly on the cap of his pen. He read the last sentence which he had written and saw how again at the end of his account he had described his adventure as though it were one which had really happened and not something that he had dreamed during the course of a night's truancy or invented a few years later for the school-magazine. Somebody, early though it was, trundled a wheelbarrow down the gravel-path beyond the fountain. The sound, like the dream, belonged to childhood.

He went downstairs and unlocked the front door. There unchanged was the broken fountain and the path which led to the Dark Walk, and he was hardly surprised when he saw Ernest, his uncle's gardener, coming towards him behind the wheelbarrow. Ernest must have been a young man in the days of the dream and he was an old man now, but to a child a man in the twenties approaches middle-age and so he seemed much as Wilditch remembered him. There was something of Javitt about him, though he had a big moustache and not a beard—perhaps it was only a brooding and scrutinizing look and that air of authority and possession which had angered Mrs. Wilditch when she approached him for vegetables.

"Why, Ernest," Wilditch said, "I thought you had retired?"

Ernest put down the handle of the wheelbarrow and regarded Wilditch with reserve. "It's Master William, isn't it?"

"Yes. George said—"

"Master George was right in a way, but I have to lend a hand still. There's things in this garden others don't know about." Perhaps he *had* been the model for Javitt, for there was something in his way of speech that suggested the same ambiguity.

"Such as . . . ?"

"It's not everyone can grow asparagus in chalky soil," he said, making a general statement out of the particular in the same way Javitt had done. "You've been away a long time, Master William."

"I've travelled a lot."

"We heard one time you was in Africa and another time in Chinese parts. Do you like a black skin, Master William?"

"I suppose at one time or another I've been fond of a black skin."

"I wouldn't have thought they'd win a beauty prize," Ernest said.

"Do you know Ramsgate, Ernest?"

"A gardener travels far enough in a day's work," he said. The wheel-barrow was full of fallen leaves after the night's storm. "Are the Chinese as yellow as people say?"

"No."

There *was* a difference, Wilditch thought: Javitt never asked for infor-mation, he gave it: the weight of water, the age of the earth, the sexual habits of a monkey. "Are there many changes in the garden," he asked, "since I was here?"

"You'll have heard the pasture was sold?"

"Yes. I was thinking of taking a walk before breakfast—down the Dark Walk perhaps to the lake and the island."

"Ah."

"Did you ever hear any story of a tunnel under the lake?"

"There's no tunnel there. For what would there be a tunnel?"

"No reason that I know. I suppose it was something I dreamed."

"As a boy you was always fond of that island. Used to hide there from the missus."

"Do you remember a time when I ran away?"

"You was always running away. The missus used to tell me to go and find you. I'd say to her right out, straight as I'm talking to you, I've got enough to do digging the potatoes you are always asking for. I've never known a woman get through potatoes like she did. You'd have thought she ate them. She could have been living on potatoes and not on the fat of the land."

"Do you think I was treasure-hunting? Boys do."

"You was hunting for something. That's what I said to the folk round here when you were away in those savage parts—not even coming back here for your uncle's funeral. 'You take my word,' I said to them, 'he hasn't changed, he's off hunting for something, like he always did, though I doubt if he knows what he's after,' I said to them. 'The next we hear,' I said, 'he'll be standing on his head in Australia.' "

Wilditch remarked with regret, "Somehow I never looked there"; he was surprised that he had spoken aloud. "And The Three Keys, is it still in existence?"

"Oh, it's there all right, but the brewers bought it when my uncle die and it's not a free house any more."

"Did they alter it much?"

"You'd hardly know it was the same house with all the pipes and tubes They put in what they call pressure, so you can't get an honest bit of bee without a bubble in it. My uncle was content to go down to the cellar fo a barrel, but it's all machinery now."

"When they made all those changes you didn't hear any talk of a tun nel under the cellar?"

"Tunnel again. What's got you thinking of tunnels? The only tunnel know is the railway tunnel at Bugham and that's five miles off."

"Well, I'll be walking on, Ernest, or it will be breakfast time before I've seen the garden."

"And I suppose now you'll be off again to foreign parts. What's it to be this time? Australia?"

"It's too late for Australia now."

Ernest shook his brindled head at Wilditch with an air of sober disap-proval. "When I was born," he said, "time had a different pace to what it seems to have now," and, lifting the handle of the wheelbarrow, he was on his way towards the new iron gate before Wilditch had time to realize he had used almost the very words of Javitt. The world was the world he knew.

2

The Dark Walk was small and not very dark—perhaps the laurels had thinned with the passing of time, but the cobwebs were there as in his childhood to brush his face as he went by. At the end of the walk there was the wooden gate on to the green which had always in his day been locked—he had never known why that route out of the garden was forbid-den him, but he had discovered a way of opening the gate with the rim of a halfpenny. Now he could find no halfpennies in his pocket.

When he saw the lake he realized how right George had been. It was only a small pond, and a few feet from the margin there was an island the size of the room in which last night they had dined. There were a few bushes growing there, and even a few trees, one taller and larger than the others, but certainly it was neither the sentinel-pine of W.W.'s story nor the great oak of his memory. He took a few steps back from the margin of the pond and jumped.

He hadn't quite made the island, but the water in which he landed was only a few inches deep. Was any of the water deep enough to float a raft? He doubted it. He sloshed ashore, the water not even penetrating his shoes. So this little spot of earth had contained Camp Hope and Friday's Cave. He wished that he had the cynicism to laugh at the half-expectation which had brought him to the island.

The bushes came only to his waist and he easily pushed through them towards the largest tree. It was difficult to believe that even a small child could have been lost here. He was in the world that George saw every day, making his round of a not very remarkable garden. For perhaps a minute, as he pushed his way through the bushes, it seemed to him that his whole life had been wasted, much as a man who has been betrayed by a woman wipes out of his mind even the happy years with her. If it had not been for his dream of the tunnel and the bearded man and the hidden treasure, couldn't he have made a less restless life for himself, as George in fact had done, with marriage, children, a home? He tried to persuade himself that he was exaggerating the importance of a dream. His lot had probably been decided months before that when George was reading him *The Romance of Australian Exploration*. If a child's experience does really form his future life, surely he had been formed, not by Javitt, but by Grey and Burke. It was his pride that at least he had never taken his various professions seriously: he had been loyal to no one—not even to the girl in Africa (Javitt would have approved his disloyalty). Now he stood beside the ignoble tree that had no roots above the ground which could possibly have formed the entrance to a cave and he looked back at the house: it was so close that he could see George at the window of the bathroom lathering his face. Soon the bell would be going for breakfast and they would be sitting opposite each other exchanging the morning small talk. There was a good train back to London at 10:25. He supposed that it was the effect of his disease that he was so tired—not sleepy but achingly tired as though at the end of a long journey.

After he had pushed his way a few feet through the bushes he came on the blackened remains of an oak; it had been split by lightning probably and then sawed close to the ground for logs. It could easily have been the source of his dream. He tripped on the old roots hidden in the grass, and squatting down on the ground he laid his ear close to the earth. He had an absurd desire to hear from somewhere far below the kwahk, kwahk from a roofless mouth and the deep rumbling of Javitt's voice saying, "We are hairless, you and I," shaking his beard at him, "so's the hippopotamus and the elephant and the dugong—you wouldn't know, I suppose, what a dugong is. We survive the longest, the hairless ones."

But, of course, he could hear nothing except the emptiness you hear when a telephone rings in an empty house. Something tickled his ear, and he almost hoped to find a sequin which had survived the years under the grass, but it was only an ant staggering with a load towards its tunnel.

Wilditch got to his feet. As he levered himself upright, his hand was scraped by the sharp rim of some metal object in the earth. He kicked the object free and found it was an old tin chamber-pot. It had lost all colour in the ground except that inside the handle there adhered a few flakes of yellow paint.

3

How long he had been sitting there with the pot between his knees he could not tell; the house was out of sight: he was as small now as he had been then—he couldn't see over the tops of the bushes, and he was back in Javitt's time. He turned the pot over and over; it was certainly not a golden po, but that proved nothing either way; a child might have mistaken it for one when it was newly painted. Had he then really dropped this in his flight—which meant that somewhere underneath him now Javitt sat on his lavatory-seat and Maria quacked beside the calor-gas . . . ? There was no certainty; perhaps years ago, when the paint was fresh, he had discovered the pot, just as he had done this day, and founded a whole afternoon-legend around it. Then why had W.W. omitted it from his story?

Wilditch shook the loose earth out of the po, and it rang on a pebble just as it had rung against the tag of his shoelace fifty years ago. He had a sense that there was a decision he had to make all over again. Curiosity was growing inside him like the cancer. Across the pond the bell rang for breakfast and he thought, "Poor mother—she had reason to fear," turning the tin chamber-pot on his lap.

The Holland of the Mind

⌀⌀⌀⌀

PAMELA ZOLINE

The loss of six hours on the flight from New York to Amsterdam meant that night had rushed to meet them as they moved across and above the Atlantic. The water solid beneath them was a sheet of hammered metal, and the clouds, many-colored and substantial, provided the landscape, seemed the actual ocean. The closed, lighted capsule of the plane's interior, suspended in all that space, was just another of the tiny islands carved out of the ignorant universe; wrapped in the frailest of membranes against the darkness, like the hairy men around the first fires, wolves calling in the cold air, keeping to the edge of that circle of light.

Graham and Jessica sat, shifting the child occasionally from one lap to the other, her warm limbs loose, asleep. Americans amongst the other Americans filling the plane, the traditional journey away and back. Graham smoked steadily, plane nerves, he said, I can always see the skull beneath the stewardess's smile. They ate food out of the portioned containers, Rachel woke, two spoonfuls of mashed potato, refused the peas and lamb, and fell asleep again. They ate, drinking, feeling out what it meant, now that it was actual, to be leaving home and all the various complicated pieces of their lives, though how much they carried with them, how much and what kind of baggage could not yet be determined.

The bald man in front of Jess had shifted back his seat and was asleep, his mouth open, his naked, gleaming head almost in her lap. It was like a world, that head, continents of freckles on the sea of bright skin. Jess threatened to trace their journey in lipstick on the man's skull. Doris Day flickered through a movie on the multiple screens, still young in soft focus; a time lag produced by some quirk of the mechanism showed the same action taking place a few seconds later on each succeeding screen, making a whole small crowd of pasts and futures visible the length of the airplane. They yawned and slumped with the particular fatigue of sedentary travel, the woman behind them was talking of buying diamonds in Amsterdam, a Texas accent, there was a blurb on Dutch flowers in the chair's pocket; tiny salt and pepper containers, motors, the maps and air sickness bags and postcards of just such silver planes in just such cerulean spaces; all hanging, buzzing, through that great vault of sky.

The land began again beneath them, clumps of light, humps, puddles, and Europe spread out below like a map. The airport suddenly, a game board, they landed on the flat field amidst the red and green lamps. Fluorescent light poured through the airport building, down from the ceiling and up from the polished floors, filling the space through which they and the other travelers moved, stunned, like tired fish through bright water.

CITY ON THE WATER
Amsterdam has been called the "Venice of the North." It is laced by sixty canals, which are crossed by more than 550 bridges, and the city is a composite of ninety islands! The capital's center has grown around a series of concentric canals which were first dug more than 300 years ago and served as a principal means of transportation.

In the coach, moving towards the town, the difference of the place, the look of things, surrounded them. I don't like traveling by plane, Jess said. It's too fast and it out-runs my sense of displacement. I arrive places feeling slightly sick, the way you feel in a fast elevator, my ears popping, my mind blank.

The child pressed her face towards the glass, watching the city, and Graham, watching her, saw its reflection on her smooth skin, the colors gliding over that surface. Your nose is green, he said. We're here, he said.

the toilet   dĕ-wee-SEE   de W.C.
Where's the toilet? WAAR iz-de-wee-SEE? Waar is de W.C.?
It's (to the) right. hĕt-is-RECHTS. Het is rechts.
It's (to the) left. hĕt-is-LINKS. Het is links.
straight ahead. rechTUIT rechtuit
Go straight ahead. ghaa-rech-TUIT. Ga rechtuit.
It's here. hĕt-is-HIER. Het is hier.

Walking through the streets to the hotel, gray stone, the rough textured narrow passage ways, the canals repeated the clouded sky, reflecting light

and so supplying a luminous horizontal to the city. The meat-faced proprietor, polite, rented them two rooms on the top floor. Carrying, dragging their baggage they climbed the steep stairs, two small rooms and very
clean, suddenly, exhausted, they were asleep.

The ground plan of the innermost center of Amsterdam is still the same is it
was in the Middle Ages when the town first came into existence.

In the morning he woke first, Jess, buried in pillows and her massive
dark hair, holding stubbornly to sleep. The room in the daylight was
small, finely proportioned, bare. It took its shape from the necessity of
roof fitted on to wall, and the ceiling sloped down over the bed. A single
window gave a view of shingled roofs, streets with people going to work.
The air had a new taste, fresh, slightly bitter, the light a special quality: it
was, without doubt, a different place. She stirred in the bed and he said
to her, we're in Holland. Smiling, with her eyes still closed, Amsterdam,
she said, do you feel Dutch?

THE INFLECTED FORM IS USED WHEN THE ADJECTIVE PRECEDES THE NOUN
een grote tuin—a large garden
oude bomen—old trees
de rode daken—the red roofs
het warme continent—the warm continent

The plan was to spend some time in Holland and from there visit
Belgium and Italy, but the schedule was undertermined. They had even
talked of settling somewhere, not going back, at least not for a while.
Graham had some photographic work set up with several magazines, but
without particular deadlines. They would feel their way.
    After eight years of marriage, Graham found it difficult to look back
along the tube of weeks and months and recognise himself at the other
end; a tall, gawky young man from Oregon finding New York and New
Yorkers aggressive and exciting, trying to put together himself and the city
out of the hundreds of photographs he took, going slightly night-blind
from hours in the dark-room. He and Jess, Jessica Gebhardt, doing post-
graduate work in art history, had gone to the same party one Christmas
Eve and had awakened Christmas morning, the bells from the city's
churches sounding in their ears, in her apartment, hung over, Jess's red
dress a puddle of brilliance on the bare floor, the small Christmas tree,
which they had apparently taken to bed with them, odorous and prickly
under the sheets.

He was tall, very tall, naked he was awkward, thin, loose hinged, pale, slightly rounded, a shallow chest and a deep, knotted navel. It was a strangely anonymous body, unmarked by his particular life or character. His experiences seemed concentrated in his head and face, an off-sphere pumpkin, an underinflated balloon, a large, compact globe on a slender neck, webbed already with fine lines, blue eyes, a soft, opaque skin. He wore, at times, large round glasses with fine steel frames. The lenses looked like big, shallow bubbles set on his face. He had pale, blunt hands discolored by photographic chemicals and cigarettes; long, soft feet.

The ground plan of the innermost center

EXPOSURE
The exposure of a film or plate is the combined product of two things:
1. The *amount* of *light* which passes through the lens, and is controlled by the *aperture* used, together with
2. the *period* during which the light passes, known as the *exposure time.*

They spent the first days walking around the town, fucking, eating, visiting museums. Rachel was still of the age at which their presence, and that of a particular stuffed blue pig, were the main signs of continuity she required from the world. Late spring, and the town was already filling with tourists; American, English, German predominating. They all moved through the city, pointing, tasting, peering. Myself, said Graham, after one worthy but deadening guided tour, I always think of Amsterdam as the Venice of the North.

Graham's camera was a more complicated and precise machine eye than theirs, but he and Jess were joined with the other tourists in that peculiar state of pure observation. To tourists everything is a potential view, a possible object of holiday interest, everything is to be seen and reflected upon without participation. At whatever level, the cooing at a pair of wooden shoes or a Vermeer, aesthetics take over from the usual exigencies. The real Dutch who lived in the place were like a slightly different species, set apart by jobs, dishwashing, appendicitis.

In the strange city, the foreign country, amidst all the alienness, their bodies were the only familiar territory. The corporeal landscape, the topology of flesh, was their only point of reference.

The nights were long and dark and had the nature of journeys. In the small bed they slept wrapped close to each other, folded against each other and intertwined. Each was aware of the other's least movement, and they surfaced into consciousness several times during the night. In

the mornings, waking, it was as though they had not been separated into personal voyages of sleep, but had traveled together.
Rachel had been born on a rainy day in April; they were staying with Jess's family in St. Paul, and the baby had been two weeks early. Jess came in from the grocery store, her arms full of packages, tears and rain running down her face. She was one of the women who look most beautiful pregnant, the swell of her belly marking a tense, great curve into the air. The baby's hair, blonde at first, had later turned brown, and now she was as dark as *her* mother, *his* wife.

```
bread BROOT brood
water WAATĔR water
meat VLEES vlees
potatoes AARappelen aardappĕlĕn
coffee KOFFie koffie
milk MELK melk
beer BIER bier
Do you want coffee? wilt-uu-KOFFie-drinken? Wilt u koffie drinken?
How much is it? hoe-veel-IS-et? Hoeveel is het?
```

Dear Mother and Dad, We arrived in Amsterdam safe and well, and although Ray has a little cold now it's nothing serious and we're all fine. This city is splendid, small enough to comprehend, with a coherent, rhythmic structure based on concentric canals. How are you both? Will you be able to get away to the lake early this summer or are you, Dad, going to be teaching summer school again? Have you heard anything from Sally? I've written to her, but no word as yet. I hope Aunt Kate is better soon, have the doctors said what's the matter with her? Is it anything serious? The proprietor of the hotel has taken to Ray and keeps giving her chocolates every time we go out, so we wander around the city always with a smeary faced but happy little girl. There is an immense sense of community here after the facelessness of New York. The people are terrifically nice, clean, the bourgeois virtues uppermost and the marks of former greatness. History is lying around in great lumps everywhere. Graham and Ray join me is sending love. xxx Jess.

THE JEWISH BRIDE
For all its richness and splendor, the *matière* of painting is never an end in itself with Rembrandt, but a means of embodying his innermost thoughts. Such is the case with the *Jewish Bride* in the Rijksmuseum, Amsterdam. After countless attempts to explain this picture, its exact meaning remains a riddle. The magnificent, old-world garments worn by the couple are oriental in char-

acter. Isaac and Rebecca, Jacob and Rachel, Tobias and Sarah have all been suggested as the theme. Perhaps it is simply a double portrait. Yet the posing of the figures in their glittering garments of scarlet and gold against the dim background of an abandoned park, and the ritual gesture of the man, laying his hand on his wife's breast, seem to point to the fulfilment of a biblical destiny. The human element of such a portrait is so deep and universal in significance that living models, contemporaries of the artist, are turned into the timeless heroes of the Old Testament and symbolise eternal spiritual values.

They both smoked too many cigarettes, invited death? Jess's grandparents, the Illinois pair, had both died of cancer. Jess had long hair, dark, wavy, a trap for light. Her face, they recognised her in Titus, was strongly marked, seemed full of experience, and went straight from a near ugliness to an occasional beauty without ever passing through prettiness. She bitched at the weather.

What were the myths that they had learned, as children in America, about Holland? Hans Brinker and the silver skates, cheese, tulips, the boy with his finger in the dyke saving the town, windmills, wooden shoes.

REMBRANDT VAN RIJN
1606–1669 covers with his life the greater part of the period of true magnificence in Dutch painting, and within half a century of his birth falls the birth of almost every other Dutch painter of pre-eminence. His contemporaries and pupils form a galaxy of a brilliance hardly equalled in so short a space of time in any other age or place. Rembrandt Harmenszoon van Rijn was born at Leyden in the house of his father, a well-to-do miller of the lower middle class who encouraged his son's artistic bent by apprenticing him to a local "Italianist" painter, Jacob van Swanenburgh.
By 1631, he was in Amsterdam with an established reputation, and from 1632 dates his first masterpiece, the *Anatomical Lecture*, now at The Hague. In 1634 he married Saskia van Ulenborch, daughter of the burgomaster of Leeuwarden, and his fortune and happiness seemed secure. Of Saskia's four children, however, only Titus, the youngest, survived childhood; and Saskia herself died in 1642. Meanwhile Rembrandt was the leader of a flourishing and profitable school; in 1639 he bought and partly paid for the house in Jodenbreestraat which now contains a collection of his etchings, and the debt incurred was never fully paid off. Rembrandt's vogue as a fashionable portraitist seems to have begun to wane about 1642, the year of the so-called *Night Watch*, a masterpiece of free portraiture which sacrificed individual likeness to balance of composition and may on that account have given offence. At any rate, in July 1656, he was declared bankrupt and his effects, including the collection of art treasures he had amassed, were sold. However, with the loyal assistance of Titus and of the faithful Hendrickje Stoffels, his model and mistress and perhaps his second wife, Rembrandt continued painting with undiminished skill and ardor until his death in 1669.

Graham sat on the bed talking Rachel to sleep, the room half dark, his cigarette a single point of red. When I was six or seven I learned to swim. In Oregon? Yes. My father took me and my brothers and sister down to a swimming pool, a salt water pool near the ocean. They were older and could all swim already. The water was very warm and blue and for a while we all just played in the water, splashing, ducking each other. The little girl shifted in the bed, her eyes just open, her fine profile and shallow nose dusky against the pillow. Then my father took me down to the deeper end, he was a very big man, taller than I am now, and he showed me how to move my arms and legs. I was frightened, but he held on to me and then, when I understood the movements, he began to back away from me, a foot at a time, talking to me and telling me to swim to him. Every time I would almost reach him, he would move further away. I was scared, I think I was crying, but I swam, he moved away, I swam to get to him, until we reached the other side of the pool. The child was asleep now, her fingers curled, her mouth slightly open. Graham went on to finish the story, talking, softly, to himself. We all played some more before we went home, there was an inflated dragon that floated in the water, a beach ball, and, playing around, I discovered that, big as he was, in the salt water I could lift my father up and carry him around the shallow end of the pool. He pulled the blanket up over the child. We stopped in our wet suits and had ice cream cones on the way home.

". . . the Girl in a Turban in The Hague, could take its place beside a Bellini Madonna, the Petrus Christus portrait of a young woman in Berlin, and perhaps even Piero della Francesca. . . . And it comes as no surprise that in recent years an affinity has been repeatedly observed between the visual approach of Vermeer and that of Jan van Eyck: the lenslike vision, the luminous 'positive' color, the calm devoted attitude before still, silent objects—these are qualities common to both artists." Vitale Bloch, *All the paintings of Jan Vermeer.*

Amsterdam had them caught and they stayed on week after week, a little charmed by their own indulgent freedom. Getting to know some people they began to break through the almost complete wrapper of English with which English speaking visitors to Amsterdam are protected. Dutch fell against their ears plosive and slightly comic. Without the hate memories of German to reinforce its gutturals, and with the surprising double vowels, it seemed sometimes a kind of clown English. A new language unravels metaphors back to their first excitement and reacts back on one's own language so that one examines those natural stones.

They ate, walked. They had endless arguments about painting, talking and talking. Rembrandt, Vermeer. Somehow they set up these two painters in opposition to each other, Rembrandt and the subjective, the emotive, the lover. Vermeer the cool, the objective, the eye. Bad news from America. More riots, more public deaths. They read the newspaper with a thrill of guilt, a feeling that St. Louis burning was real, had a claim on them, that this fine city, the paintings, the parks, did not.

> spiegeling—reflection
> lenig—supple, pliant
> goochelkunst—juggling art, prestidigitation
> spietsen—spear (fish); pierce (man); impale (criminal)
> water—water
> sight, vision—gezicht, aanblik; vertoning; bezienswaardigheid, merkwaardigheid
> fish—vis
> storten—spill (milk); shed (tears, blood); shoot, dump (rubbish); pay in (money)
> sex—geslacht, sekse, kunne; seksualiteit; adj, seksueel
> helder—clear, bright, lucid, serene; clean.

Eating oranges in the room, they make love. Oh dearest darling fat, thin, lovely, love, oh kip, oh sweet wet vork. Breast, skin, kaas, oh lovely slippery love, wet, mouth, mond, vis, breathing hard in this room full of oranges and the smells of oranges, the seeds slide down the creases of your skin, the juices glaze your silver sides, oh my fish love, my vis, bubbles rise to the ceiling, burst and break against the light bulb as you move, puff, pant and sniff the air from the water.

Graham fell asleep, snoring, a weird musiking. Jess lit a cigarette, keyed up, unable to relax. A headache was beginning at the back of her neck, the love-making had, had again, a weird flavor, a taste of desperation. These rooms were too small, this city, she and Graham saw each other too much, were too much in each other's pockets. The feeling of panic, of lemmings to the sea. She could feel the marriage, that fragile edifice, buckling, breaking apart under his flailing hands.

Adjusting the light, she read, savoring the quiet, the absence of reaction and the need to react. A fly circled in the room, Graham grunting beside her in his sleep. Living with a person, cleaning ears, borrowing razors and occasionally sharing a toothbrush, not buying bananas to which he has an allergy. What fine curly hair full of various directions.

When, having embarked upon a certain course, do the alternatives cease to present themselves? What was this beside her in the bed?

The war paint designs used by the American Indian (illustrated). Their marriage had been a strange beast, with its own queer shape. She had thought that Europe might heal some of the fissures, but instead.

Jess's sister Sally, blue-eyed Sally. Three years younger, she had set up some kind of floating residence centering mainly on the East Coast of the States. Her parents still lived in St. Paul, the yellow house, her father teaching history at the night school. The two of them, her parents, stand side by side on some hill in her memory, mother's arm through father's, staring ahead and smiling like figures on a wedding cake. Having developed this conceit in talking about them to Graham it was so strong that, seeing them again before leaving for Europe, she found herself looking down at their feet to see whether traces of the icing, like snow, still clung to their shoes. Her mother translated Jess's and Sally's affairs, the comings and goings, connections, into the vocabulary of her own time; sweetheart, beau. In this language the dark fumblings and disasters became neat, romantic, very like her own nice world. There were, amongst the people she knew, divorces, car accidents, alcoholics, but these always seemed like aberrations, grave departures from the norm. Here, in these places, with these people, this generation, it was the basic coin, the declared form of things. The personal fallings, the difficult acts, breakings. Her mother, loving them, was now always sad and puzzled that these two daughters, so lovely as little girls, should have become such unhappy homeless creatures. That they were not, in their own terms, so lost she could not believe. She sent them letters and birthday presents, adored Ray, fussed over their health when they visited her home. She hoped, always, for more grandchildren and some magical suburb. They loved her, but could not explain.

The fly buzzed again, in thrall to the light, diving at her head. The Apache, Van Eyck, Manhattan, Vermeer. New Amsterdam. The Beatles. Lapis lazuli. Damn, have to piss again. Curious how the language of excretion varies from family to family, the private code. Piddle, wee, pee. Tinkle, in her childhood. Make water; wash your hands. With Ray they used Graham's word, piss, less coy than most.

A smell of baking bread from the bakery across the street. Outside the frequency of passing cars began gradually to increase, soon the milk trucks and the first shopkeepers would begin to unlock their various doors and engines, turn switches, push buttons, and like knives to a fallen beast, still warm, to cut away pieces of the failing dark. Jess flexed the muscles of her legs and feet, cramped by curling into Graham's sleeping form. If she did not get to sleep before the first real light and noise, she would not sleep at all. Pulling her legs cautiously away from him, then swinging them from the warm cave of sheets and blankets out into the chilly dark. Her feet are stiff, groping over the cold floor, in the hallway she punches the light button and then, the flood of brilliance painful after the small yellow illumination of the reading lamp, her pupils spasm, she goes shut-eyed the known way to the toilet, the light showing orange through her lids.

The surfaces are cold, and the rush of water sounds enormous in the quiet house. A sense of violating and anti-social noise, Jess creeps back. What she wants is a glass of water, her mouth already musty and sour with near sleep, but she fears that the noise of the faucets, more groaning of the plumbing, will finally wake Graham and the child sleeping in the next room. Instead she takes a handful of grapes, the spurt of sweet juice shocking her dry tongue, the gritty teeth. Turning out the light, the window's square of sky turns from black to cobalt.

TRANSLATE
These houses. That story. This garden. Those trees. I have read this book; it is much better than that one. I never smoke those cigars. This house has not been painted. Who is that man? This photograph is good, but those are very bad. These are our children, those people have no children. These books are mine. Do you know these people? Yes, of course, they are my neighbors. Those must be my pens. After that he stood up and went into the room. They looked at this for a long time.

The *View of Delft* is the purest square of pulsing light and air. Breath and absolute tonality. What is the nature of vision?

Amsterdam, the Venice of the North. They moved through the city. Even she, who had no sense of direction, began to learn her way around the streets. They argued, and Rachel grew fretful. Concentric canals.

A WALK ROUND AMSTERDAM
From the *station* (1) cross the bridge and go up the main street, Damrak, alongside the little harbor (2). Further on is the *Exchange* (3) built in 1903 (open 9–5; free admission to galleries). Continue along Damrak to Dam with the Royal Palace (4) originally built as the town hall in 1648 by Jacob van Campen (open summer 9–4, winter 9–3). Next to it stands the Nieuwe Kerk (4) begun in 1490 but frequently altered since.

In one section of the city prostitutes walked along the streets or sat looking out of large glass windows, tempting pedestrians with what seemed to
be the same psychology of plenty as that which filled the bakery and fruit
shop displays with pyramids of shining goods in juicy, lavish abundance.
Butter, chocolate, crystallised fruits, and these women. A big woman
smiled at them as they passed by her window, a pile of golden hair and
skin as sweet and fat as cream. Their open, vital presence in the city filled
the nostrils, gave to the whole place a smell of sex, a nervous excitation,
a flush of general body heat.

They ate herring from the stands in the street. They went every day
that week to the Rijksmuseum. What, she said, is the nature of vision?
Trying not to fight, to break the new bitter habit, they made resolutions,
broke them made more. Perversely enough, like separate animals, their
bodies were still mated, still sought each other out.

The surfaces of the paintings absorbed her, she returned to them again
and again, they were her richest food. At night he explored her body hoping to receive some of that nourishment at one remove. Her fingers
smelled of herring; later, her tongue, teeth, the soft cushions and hard
furniture of her mouth, of herring, raw fish, the pickled smell mixed with
the other smells.

Getting up to piss and rinse his mouth, to take the child to the toilet,
the strangeness of the plumbing fixtures, the odd, very shallow Dutch
toilet bowl, surprised him each morning. It was as though, during every
night, he forgot that he was not at home, in New York, and had to
relearn that fact at the beginning of each day. He would return to bed to
find Jess flung back into sleep again, deep under the blankets, growling at
intrusion. He would begin to rub her back, her sides, reach beneath her
to touch her round, soft belly and her breasts, loose in his hands, sweet-
tipped. A journey through her hair, the absolute abundance of the flowing waves outspringing from the brow, spreading over skin and sheets.
The fine hairs pencilled along her arms, rough, half shaved on the legs
and arm-pits, the warm, musty mound. The small arm hairs, forming his
horizon against the light, his chin resting on her belly, flamed and
moved like the leapings of light from an eclipsed sun. The very particular
shapes of flesh and textures of her skin, the odors rising from her, from
him, seemed to him at those times the constituents of the whole physical
world. The periodic table of desire and repletion.

The light in that city, that room, at that part of the morning, was particularly clear, not yellow but white and silver, filling the space with a
lucid intensity. No shadows and massing, just the clarity of surface and

color, and the quiet occupation of space by forms. In the movements, pressing, tonguings, vials of scent opened into the air. They would fall away from each other, grateful, tired, and sometimes sleep again.

DROWNING
Drowning is caused by complete immersion of the nose and mouth in water for a length of time which varies with the individual circumstances.

please—alstublieft
many thanks—dank U wel
good morning—goedemorgen
good night—goedenacht

Holland is one of the smallest countries in Europe, with its area of 13,514 square miles. Its greatest width is about 125 miles. 32% of the country is under plough, 36% pasturage, 7% forest, 9% heath and sand-dunes, 3% gardens and market gardens, and finally 13% built-up area.

Dear Mother, Jessica, Rachel and I are enjoying Amsterdam very much. We've had some rain, but it is pleasant even then. We visit the museums, of course, and I have been working on a photographic project on Water, water in all shapes and places. Mother, this may seem an odd request, but I should like you, when you write again, to answer several questions for me. (1) What was the name of the spaniel we had when I was about ten? (2) What was the name of that family that lived next door, the ones with red-headed children, when we lived on Dundee Road? (3) Did the large closet in Grandma's big upstairs bedroom *really* have a secret passage? I can remember, with awful clarity, a passage opening at the back of the closet, with stairs extending down the length of the house, but I *cannot* remember whether it was a dream. It may have been a dream, but the details are so fine. Please write and tell me the answers to these things as soon as you can—I'm just trying to get some things straight. Let me know how you are. Give my love to Linda and the others.

LAND UNDER WATER
The story of the Netherlands is one of the most remarkable chapters in all of mankind's history, involving a fierce struggle against nature which is still going on today, and is fascinating to witness.
    Centuries ago, most of the Netherlands was either permanently inundated, or periodically swept, by the sea. Yet men determined to live there neverthe-less. How? By reclaiming land from the sea itself.

Pre-historic men built huge mounds of earth in the sea, and then placed their homes and farms atop the mounds. Later they learned to wall off the sea by building dykes—first out of earth, centuries later out of stone, and today out of concrete and steel. The areas that were walled off were then drained of their water (originally, by windmill-driven pumps) to create reclaimed land— or *polders* as the Dutch call these once-below-the-sea areas. And the *polders* were then farmed and cultivated to create some of the most incredibly fertile and breath-taking scenery in the world today.

By building such *polders*, the Dutch reclaimed nearly half the land that today comprises the nation. "God created the earth," goes a famous epigram, "but the Dutch built the Netherlands."

The process is still going on. In the early 1930s the Dutch completed their famous nineteen-mile-long "Enclosure Dyke" (Afsluitdijk) which sealed off the stormy North Sea from the former Zuider Sea into a peaceful inland lake. Elsewhere, in the Western section of the country, the Dutch are presently building their gigantic "Delta Works"—a series of five new dykes that will seal off further large estuaries of the North Sea. And remember, too, that even after land in Holland is reclaimed, it must constantly be drained by canals and pumps—or else the water will rise again!

one een
two twee
three drie
four vier
five vijf
six zes
seven zeven
eight acht
nine negen
ten tien

Graham worked on a series of photographs of water, water in the Netherlands. The sea, the canals, the rivers, the whole country was knit by the presence of water, actual water, and the water which was no longer there but always threatened. The silver, shining, reflective surface. What, he took a picture of Rachel standing in a fountain ecstatic in a great fount of spray, is the nature of vision? Photographing Jess the light caught and recorded a magnificent aureole. Then sunlight on your hair! an extraordinary and beautiful luminescence. The phrase became a joke and a password.

TRANSLATE

The house was built a year ago. We were seen by his brother. The new ship has been sold. When will the letter be written? The boy was bitten by a dog. His name is Richard but he is called Dick. Have the horses and cows been rescued? I love you. The ship is not expected today. The raven was flattered by the fox. The books must be sent to my house. The country has always been governed well by its statesmen. He was trusted by his friends. The wheat has not been mown. I love you. The children were sent home. Were these vases sold? These glasses have not been washed. The bird was caught by a small boy. The girl was called by her father. The church had been built in the middle of the village. The roof of the house is on fire. I love you.

Saskia! No justice and early death. Such a beautiful Flora, the flowers in your hair, the oval face, slightly fat, the fine, bumpy nose and most stunning, endearing, dimple-forming, slight, up-curving smile.

The broad-brimmed hat of the Dresden portrait casts a shadow over Saskia's smiling face, so that her golden complexion, her strawberry-red lips and rosy cheeks lie partly in brightest light, partly in shadow dappled with surface reflections. Borne on a ray of light, this graceful image of a happy wife rises out of a fiery darkness.

As Rembrandt wrestled with the mighty task of the *Night Watch*, Saskia wrestled with death; on June 14, 1642, she died, aged barely thirty.

This must have come as a terrible shock to Rembrandt, for in the light of his art we can guess what Saskia meant to him, kindling and inspiring his imagination in all his work. Then, abruptly, after the abounding joy, the radiant delights of his life with Saskia, came darkness. While she lay dying, her features haunted his fervid imagination and pursued him into the thick of the soldiery peopling the *Night Watch*, conjuring up a world of strange imaginings in which we see her in the guise of a child, in a realm of fantasy where time has ceased to be.

The *Night Watch* and the dead Saskia. The life of Rembrandt. Bad news, bad news. All over Asia and Africa men are doing violence to each other, the Chinese are reported to be carrying out a genocide of the Tibetans, and in the West the grip on order is also precarious.

A letter at American Express. Aunt Kate is dead of cancer.

As though the devolution had its own momentum, they became more and more unhappy. With all the shaking glass, the sound of beams breaking loose, Graham became enormously hungry, a frantic hunger. He would eat huge meals, potatoes, bread, sausage, and then would rise, leave the restaurant, and peer into the window of the first food store they came to. The windows of candy stores and bakeries were stuffed full and bright as Christmas. Biscuits, cakes, cookies, glazed fruits, creams, huge crusty pies. The most splendid pastel candies, fudges, truffles.

Truffles were one of his favorites, the flakey powdered chocolate coat, the lump, and, breaking the faint tension of the surface, the cream which was itself a marvel of transience. It did not rest on the tongue but melted immediately into pure sweetness dripping down the throat.

Bitter Ballen	meat balls with mustard
Blinde Vinken	stuffed veal or beef rissoles with bread, milk, salt, nutmeg, egg, bacon, breadcrumbs, butter, margarine
Boerenkool met Worst	Smoked sausage and cabbage
Ertwensoep	Thick pea soup with smoked sausage, cubes of pork, pigs' feet, leek, celery
Hangop	A kind of gruel with milk
Paling	Smoked eel on toast
Rolpens met Rodekool	Minced beef and tripe topped with apple slices, served with red cabbage
Uitsmijter	Bread with a slice of cold meat topped with fried eggs. This is a popular "quick lunch"

Rachel became obsessed with mirrors; she would stand on a chair in front of the oval glass in their hotel room and stare at herself for long periods. Sometimes she would make faces, talk, but most often she would just sit and look.

With all the food Graham began, for the first time in his life, to grow fat. Layers of new flesh folded themselves around his bones; he slept for hours each day.

ARTIFICIAL RESPIRATION
Artificial respiration is used to make a person whose natural breathing has stopped start breathing again. It must be done deliberately and regularly for at least an hour, if the patient does not recover before then. Resuscitation as a result of artificial respiration may occur many hours after apparent death.

While artificial respiration is being applied, an assistant should loosen clothing at neck and waist of the patient, make sure that there is nothing in the mouth blocking the airway, get clothing or rugs to keep the patient warm, and massage the limbs from below upwards. This assistance must not interfere with the application of artificial respiration which is all-important.

One night, slightly drunk on beer, making love. She perceives her body, defined by its contact with his, as construct, architecture and earth. The old truisms sharpen their teeth. Body like a building, like a mountain, huge.

1. Lay the casualty face downwards with head turned to one side and arms stretched up beyond the head.

2. Make sure that the mouth and nose are not obstructed.

Haul out the analogies between the body and the landscape, the female earth. You down there, trying to get in, hey you. Help, help, knocking. Shifted to an exercise in communications. Pilot to tower, repeat, pilot to tower, request landing instructions. Instruments, radar. Nerves and switchboards. Shift to an art history lecture, images move through her head like slides projected on a screen, illuminated from behind. *Click.* An old Egyptian drawing, the sky as man, stars on his chest, legs and thighs, arching over the female earth. *Click.* Art Nouveau, the excited line which is its own purpose, vegetable energy and proliferation. *Click.* Persian miniatures, warped space, and pattern warring with form for ascendancy. *Click.* Bosch. *Click, click.* Rothko, Stella, the modern colorists. Colors. Oh. Colors.

3. Kneel to one side of the casualty's hips, facing his head.
4. Place your hands flat in the small of the back, over the lower ribs and just above top of the pelvic bone. Your thumbs should almost touch each other in the middle line, the fingers being over the loins.

Monumental sculpture. Two great pelvis pans pressed against each other. Picasso on the beach; a single eye in the center of the face, the warping of vision at close focus. *Click.* The body as earth, Henry Moore was right.

5. Sit on your heels, no weight being transmitted to the casualty, though your hands are maintained on his back.
6. Swing your body slowly forward from the knees keeping your arms straight and hands in place all the time, so that a steady pressure is transmitted by the weight of your body. Maintain this position for two seconds. This action presses the casualty's abdomen against the ground, forcing his abdominal contents up against the diaphragm, which is raised and expels some air out of the lungs—expiration.
7. Keeping your hands in position and arms straight, relax the pressure by swinging gently and steadily back on to your heels, counting three seconds before swinging forwards again. This allows air to enter the lungs—inspiration.

He looms over the horizon of her chest, drinking, great hills of breast. Lips, wet interior caves toothed and toothless, then the careful game with pace, form and time, equations of falling and acceleration, free fall, float, float, surface down from the air, up from the roiled water depths to the clear bubble of the middle space.

8. These swaying to-and-fro movements must be repeated regularly at a rate of twelve to fifteen a minute, and continue this, if necessary, by relays of helpers, until natural breathing begins. Even then, artificial respiration should be continued for another quarter of an hour. When apparent recovery has taken place, the casualty should be placed on his side in a warm bed, given a hot drink, and encouraged to sleep.

Now, the current off, the touches are neutral again. Peripheral parts, hair, the rim of an ear. Both have survived.

Jan van Eyck
Hieronymus Bosch
Pieter Brueghel the Elder
Frans Hals
Rembrandt van Rijn
Jan Vermeer
Vincent Van Gogh
Piet Mondrian

Wat is de Betekenis van het zien?

Leave me alone, shut up, just leave me alone.

She filled their hotel room with flowers. Finding the ageing flowers as beautiful as the fresh, she kept them for weeks, and the air smelled of the animal stink of the decaying blooms as well as the lighter odors of the new bouquets. He recognised some of the smells as cousin to those of their own flesh.

The colors of flowers as they decay grow hotter, pale yellows turn to bright yellows and golds, bright clear blues to redder blues and violets. (The hues in Cézanne's paintings undergo this same transformation, early to late.)

In the Netherlands in 1963 there were 44,597,000 chickens, 3,645,000 cattle, 2,423,000 pigs, 468,000 sheep, and 149,000 horses.

Bad news from America. Divorce, separation of friends. Death by drugs. Mistakes, wrong decisions, futile journeys, flawed plans.

FLOWER VIEWING
For flower-growing enthusiasts, or for tourists who simply appreciate the beauty of miles and miles of flowers, a visit to the flower-growing areas of the Netherlands is a must. At "tulip time," particularly April through mid-May, a

thirty-mile strip of land between Haarlem and The Hague is covered by a dazzling blanket of tulips, daffodils and hyacinths.

The most massive display of these floral wonders is found in a sixty-acre flower garden located near the town of Lisse, called Keukenhof, where there are greenhouses containing tens of thousands of tulips, vast areas of open-air gardens, a pavilion with photographic exhibitions of flowers, flower arrangement demonstrations, an information office, and all else a flower enthusiast could possibly desire.

Mirrors are water made abstract. They do not quench, nourish, flow. They simply reflect, reverse, reflect.

You're welcome. (nothing to thank) Neits te danken.
Excuse me. (take me not badly) Neem me niet kwalijk.
So long. ("until see") Tot ziens.
Do you understand what I say? Verstaat u wat ik zeg?

What are the sounds a drowning man makes?

Things were falling apart. One day, coming back to the hotel, he found Jess sitting in front of the mirror cutting at her hair with the sewing scissors. The dark pieces lay all around on the floor, and she had left only a short, curling cap, which made her head look suddenly very small, her neck very long.

Why do you do it? His face hung white and quivering in the mirror above her.

She was sweeping the clumps of hair into the waste-paper basket. It was too much trouble, I was tired of it.

But I *loved* your hair. He was shaking.

Graham, it's not important. It's *my* hair. Don't nag at me.

His bowels churned. It was such *lovely* hair.

Oh for God's sake can't you leave me alone? Her voice went shrill.

He saw it as the severing of another of their connections. When she went out of the room he bent, shaking, sick, he picked up one of the dark, separate pieces and stuffed it in his pocket to keep.

He was drowning in the multiplicity and lack of order in the world. Order is a lucky, rich, sexy, privileged, sought-after bird. She does not answer invitations to dinner.

Going to see the flowers in Holland had at first been rather a joke, like going to see the Eiffel Tower in Paris, or the Statue of Liberty in New

York. But having reached the gardens and finding themselves surrounded by the banks of glowing blossoms, the scent thick in the air, they became high with it, drunk, carried away.

What is it about flowers, he asked her, in bed, they had been fighting again, what is it about flowers which stuns and fascinates? Scent on a stalk, form on a stalk, color on a stalk. She lay propped up on pillows, her eyes still red and puffed with crying, the street light falling upon her face in spots, like the skin of a fawn. What makes a flower supremely beautiful, he continued, his voice taking on the juicy orotundity of his college debating team, is the fact that they are a paradigm of our own mortality. Their brief perfect lives are an example to us, a preparation for our own deaths. Bud, bloom, decay. These sights became for Graham so full of message, so supremely the case of the sensual wedded to the didactic, that he wondered why the other visitors to the gardens were not caught up in the grip of it along with him. They wandered casually through the massed fields of scent and color, seemingly indifferent to the enormity of the drama being played out there. Whenever he saw flowers now his eyes would sting, he was afraid he might break down and start weeping in the gardens or the parks some day, in front of all those people, in front of Jess.

Fug, fump, fook, fack, fub, fuck, feek.

Lovemaking in that sweet, stinking room. Things are falling apart. Alternations of light and dark, flashes of pattern, street light on the ceiling as they turn and swim through each other. Comes, and she, released, moves upwards to her goal, the progress is made in distinct steps, clear quantum jumps of sensation until the strings are finally tightened to their limit, vibration, spilling, breaking, overflowing. Limp, companionable grunts, thank you, ok, yes, I'm ok, great, wow. Off, on. Sense again of body as landscape, connections, movements those of the natural world, ebb and flow. Marks us with the sense of movement towards a goal, life as a journey, life as a cycle, goop, oof, great hard rod, lovely loose balls; playing with the doorway, finger in, out, in, the tremoring of a pianist's trill inside, jokes in the ears suspended miles away, finger in the dyke, good Dutch boy.

On that involved bed, the salty sheets and confusion of limbs in the stippled urban dark. In Ann Arbor the summers got so hot I wanted to strip off my skin and join the inanimate world, Jess, lying on her back, gesturing vaguely at the ceiling as she talks. In the partial, sporadic light her movements fall a bit behind her words like a movie out of synch.

Showers four times a day, she chants, gallons of ice cream. Completely unbidden, some childhood trigger not yet dismantled, juices squirt, Graham's mouth fills with spit. Chocolate, vanilla, strawberry, peach, butter pecan. Turning over on her stomach. There was a huge sign on the front of a bank, the time on one side and the temperature on the other. The sign would swivel slowly, all through the damned hot day; my mind too pulped with heat to think about anything else I used to fix on that sign. I used to wonder just how many calories the damned thing was adding to the atmosphere. Sweet entropy.

Good day! ghoeden-DACH Goeden dag!
Good morning! ghoeden-MORghen Goeden morgen!
Good evening! ghoeden-AAvent Goeden avond!
How HOE hoe
goes GHANN gaan
it Ghaa-ĕt gaat het
with you met-UU met u
How are you? hoe-GHAAT-ĕt-met-uu? Hoe gaat het met u?
Well, thank you GHOET DANK-uu Goed, dank u
And (with) you? en-met-UU? En met u?
Quite well HEEL GHOET heel goed.

Graham grew fatter, little pouches of flesh hung in his cheeks and there were rolls of soft, white meat around his waist. He bought food for the hotel room now, on top of the meals; jars of pickles, sausages, chocolate, loaves of bread, just in case we get hungry in the night, he said.

One morning at American Express, the place was always filled with caricatures of their countrymen, a letter arrived from Graham's sister. He put it in his shirt pocket first, then read it as they sat in the café. A thick envelope, there were snapshots, and the letter covered several pieces of that very thin airmail stationery. Jess could see through to the other side while he was reading, could see, backwards through the skin of the paper, the loopy ball-point script, exclamation points, underlinings. His face flickered as he read the letter, shuffled the photographs. Blond nephews and nieces arranged on the front steps of a large house, freckles, missing teeth, and another of the family group spread out on a beach by a very blue sea, the tanned forms dark against the brilliant sand. Dear Linda he wrote to his sister that evening. It was very good hearing from you. The kids look great. I envy, in a way, the solid life you and John seem to have made for yourselves. Amsterdam is very fine, very polished by history, but things are somewhat askew. Jess and I haven't been getting along too well, same old thing. I simply don't seem to be able to hold things together. There are too many things to balance, to keep in repair. (Don't tell Mother any of this, of course, it would just worry her.)

This is probably just the autumn getting to me, please don't you worry either. By the way, do you remember whether there was a secret passage in the big closet in Grandma's upstairs bedroom? I asked Mother, but she keeps forgetting to reply. Rachel is growing big and beautiful. Do you remember the autumn at home when we were kids, the giant molding heap of leaves in the back yard that we used to jump on? I find, curiously enough, that I am homesick, but for nothing that I can return to. It's like being homesick for the past.

DENSITY OF HOLLAND
Holland is the most densely populated country of Europe. With its 11,938,000 inhabitants living in an area of only 13,514 square miles, it has an average density of 884 people per square mile, compared with 783 per square mile in Belgium and 794 per square mile in England and Wales.

Since the population of Holland has more than doubled in the last fifty years it is not surprising that the Dutch authorities are much concerned with the problem of overpopulation. Though fresh areas are constantly being dyked in to provide new land for farms and villages, there is a steady stream of emigrants especially to Canada and Australia.

TRANSLATE
What are you doing? How many fish are there? The blue house is next to the red house. Please speak louder, I cannot hear you. Why are you crying? Can you speak Dutch? New York was once called New Amsterdam. What is the divorce rate in Holland? About three-quarters of the surface of the earth is covered with water. I cannot hear you. Please speak louder. What is wrong? Why are you crying? Why are you crying?

They were fighting again, sitting in a restaurant, almost yelling in that public place, although he hated such scenes and she was weary of them. Accusations, disappointments. She was angry, she was shaking, and she didn't want to hear the replies he gave because she knew it all, hadn't they been through all this a hundred times before, they knew their parts. They could have changed places, changed scripts, and the dialogue would have been the same.

There was nothing to say but they kept on. In the mirror across from them, on the wall of the restaurant, they saw themselves, dark stiffened figures, leaning close together, gesturing, lifting and cutting chunks of air with the edges of their hands. Things were falling apart.

Het zonlicht op je haar. Het zonlicht op je haar.

Springtime, especially April and May, is the most beautiful period in which the tourist has the opportunity to admire the Dutch bulb fields in full bloom. By then the large flat *polders* from Haarlem to Leyden and in the neighborhood of Alkmaar are a unique carpet of color from the roadside to the distant dunes, with mile after mile of waving tulips, hyacinths and daffodils.

At the house of some friends for dinner Rachel, climbing on a chair to reach a large, three-panelled mirror, fell, cut herself, and knocked over a bowl of four goldfish which lay, gasping, on the floor.

They were sitting on the bus which ran from their hotel to the museum, half dizzy from fucking through breakfast, no food, no coffee, too many cigarettes. On to the bus climbed a large, square Dutch mother with the number one pattern Dutch face; small straight nose, large, rounded eyes, round head, half-wide, even mouth. She had with her three children, of size increasing by regular intervals, and with faces exact copies of her own. So precise in fact was the rendering that it was as though no one else could have taken part in their making, no large Dutch husband full of beer braved those great pink thighs, she had seeded herself and given birth to these replicas.

Saskia, inflation, despair. Americans on a moral peninsula.

On January 15th, 1637, a bunch of tulips was worth 120 guilders, only a few weeks later 385 guilders, and on February 1st 400 guilders. For very rare examples as much as 10,000 guilders were offered, which in those days was equal to the value of 12 oxen, 24 pigs, 36 sheep, 6 bottles of wine, 12 barrels of beer, 6 casks of butter, 3,000 pounds of cheese, 3 silver beakers, 3 boats, and 20 tons of wheat.

Suddenly she saw that he had begun to save the bits and pieces they had accumulated on their journeys; pamphlets, guidebooks to places where he had lagged behind because his feet ached, matchbooks. Just to keep tabs, he said, stuffing the ticket stubs and the used Rittenkaart into a large manila envelope he had labelled with date and location. He dropped an ashtray he had been attempting to steal from a restaurant on the canal.

Why?

The waiter came with a broom.

Don't why me.

Why?

The new flesh beneath his chin quivered.

Don't you see it had a little map? It said just where we are. His eyes had moistened. He pointed at the glass, the waiter's back, the broken glass under the checkered tablecloths. Right here.

MADURODAM—NOT TO BE MISSED
Not to be missed is the miniature city of Madurodam, between Scheveningen
and The Hague (street car 29, bus 22). A visit to Madurodam is both instruc-
tive and amusing, for it contains a typical Dutch town in miniature—4% of
the normal size—with all the buildings, streets and squares as they are in
reality.

Rachel, cranky and out of sorts, tried to kick in the sides of one of the
buildings of the tiny town, Jess was too tired to care, and Graham disliked
it because, he said, it gave him an unwelcome glimpse into eternity.

There was an old friend, Richard, a friend of Jess's, living in Amsterdam. An academic, he had just got back from some months in Germany.
They had been to college together, had known each other, had, at one
time, almost been lovers, but the occasion had passed, other things inter-
vened, and a miss was as good as a mile in those things, in these times,
with these people. They had, in a casual way, kept track of each other,
through some friends in common, through a few long letters full of talk.
They had always loved talking to one another, it had been their big con-
nection, endless conversations of an indeterminate architecture.
Come and see us, he wrote Jess, I'm married to a Dutch girl and we're
going to have a baby, she, that is, come to dinner.
They brought flowers with them, red tulips. The apartment was large,
greenly lit with the reflected light from a canal. Richard greeted them, ef-
fusive, louder and more jocose than she remembered, hawk Jewish profile growing blurred. He was an historian with the university, was going
to live here forever, relished the city, loved the people. His wife, Anna?
Anneke, very quiet, blonde, small nose, breasts and belly swollen but not
yet fully extended, sixth, seventh month. They talked, had cocktails,
talked. Civilisation, sweet sauce, a precarious prize. A fragile, delicious,
delicate thing, a product of thousands of hands, always ready to tumble,
fall, headlong, splashing, finally, without a trace, into the sea.
The sky outside turned from gray to blue to a bruised black, and Anneke lit a cluster of fat candles on the small table, the tulips in a bowl in
the center, and began serving dinner. With the light coming only from
the one source, all the gestures magnified into shadows around the room.
The little area of warmth in the candles' pool of light was the energy center, the drama of plates and cups and moving hands and cold, bearded
beer was carried on in this nucleus, and from that hot center everything
graded off, fell away into the blue, deep corners of the room. Well, Richard was saying, it's as though Americans still believed (more ham) in the

perfectibility of humanity, and Europeans (please pass the bread; tomorrow we're going to visit Anne Frank's house) know that it's not possible. Thats what gives Americans this optimism and this terrible energy. They're just now learning (they?) that the story doesn't necessarily have a happy ending, Cinderella murders her sisters and sets fire to department stores, and the bears really do rape Goldilocks. The bubbles in the beer rose and burst themselves upon the surface of the air. Smells of cabbage and potato and hot sausage; a real Dutch meal. Richard stretched his mouth and puffed out the place where his belly would be in a few years. He patted Anneke's round bottom in a show of jocularity. The perfect burgher, this Jewish boy from Brooklyn and Harvard.

Jess was talking, her mouth full, her face glazed in the wavering glow. Light in some paintings is the equivalent, at least the analogue, of love. God's gaze on the world. Graham's face muscles began to ache with the effort of maintaining the creased smile. Richard and Jess were still at it, talking and talking, society, civilisation, the arts, war and revolution. Graham let himself sink into the silence from which Anneke watched the show. Her hair was very blonde, lighter in tone even than her skin, her ears slightly protruding, her face shiny. The mild Dutch face. She seemed several years younger than Richard and the rest of them. The talking and eating continued. The pregnant girl moved back and forth from the table to the kitchen, in and out of the light, blooming, unconcerned for the categories and fine distinctions being established. She moved slowly, weightily, pushing her full front before her. Watching her carrying the heavy, steaming dishes Graham, a little drunk, found himself flooded with a clear and sudden, irrelevant desire. He felt he could almost hear, through their common thick silence, the beating of the baby's heart, as though the instant love had created a stethoscope of spirit between him and the blind small creature in its waters.

Their mouths filled over and over with the eating and drinking. The level of their glasses and plates rose and fell until it seemed a function of nature, and flushed with food and beer and his new love Graham followed Anneke into the kitchen. He stood in the doorway watching her wash plates, cut bread with her deep, slow, underwater movements. Her cheeks red, her short nose red and shining, she filled the platters again. He moved towards her and bent to kiss her. Later, reviewing this, he was amazed at his gaucheness. The potatoes and beer and the stiff, quick pair waiting for them at the table, he would not have blamed her, this fat, fair love, if she had screamed and pushed him away amidst pieces of broken crockery. But her reaction was, wonderfully, not that. Simply, she accepted his embrace and stood, holding his head to her full breast, he standing stooped, pressed against the plate of cabbage which she still held in her other hand. The fragrant gray steam rose, enveloping them both.

Returning to the table Graham felt the tightness of the other two, trespass rank in the air, hell to pay. The reckoning would come later. For the moment, insulated from them, he was fed and full and they were only shadows on his eye. Fantasies in that pure, drunken moment in the kitchen, it had for Graham the taste of the annunciation paintings with the dove, Mary, and the seed sliding down the ray of light from God to Mary's *ear* (zap), that baby in the womb *his*, a miraculous infant.

Holland is not quite as big as Vermont but the dykes if placed in a straight line would reach from New York to beyond Chicago.

(De) dingen Vielen uiteen. Things were falling apart.

They would walk and walk through the city, gray skies, reflections, in the water everything was doubled. The city regarded itself, whole and multiplied, shimmering, in every piece of water, every shining surface.

Built entirely on huge piles driven through the marshy surface soil and intersected by countless canals, Amsterdam has inevitably been described as "the Venice of the North" though its canals differ from the Venetian in being almost invariably lined with quays.

They were it seemed to Jess like very early humans, prehistoric, cave dwellers, fumbling around with the beginnings of speech, clumsily attempting the shaping of tools, a small stirring in their muddled broths of brains. Hairy, cold, wet, scared, they groped their way through the peaty darkness, trying to reach each other, trying to read the marks scratched on the walls of the caves, but it was no use. There were not enough words, they were not fine enough, the ice age was coming and it was cold, there wasn't enough food, there wasn't enough fire, it was dark, they were lost.

In the next room the child cried.

The Zürich Doctor Konrad Gesner was the first to discover the tulip in the garden of the Fuggers in Augsburg in about 1555. The true home of the tulip, however, is not Augsburg, but much further east, in Armenia, the Crimea. In about 1560 the Austrian Ambassador at the court of Ibrahim Pascha brought a few tulips with him to Vienna and presented them to the botanist Carolus Clausius or Charles L'Ecluse. When the latter was appointed to the University of Lieden, his tulips came with him to the Netherlands to be ever afterwards associated with the name of that country.

bread   broad
doof   deaf
vies   dirty
waar   true
geel   yellow
dun   thin

It was his birthday, Thursday, and he must have a treat. He wanted to go to the Hilton Hotel for a celebration dinner. Come on, she said. You must be kidding, she said.

No, I really mean it. I want to go. His face was puffy and white. I want hamburgers and a milk shake and french fries and the whole deal. Just like him, he begged, just for a joke.

So they sat in the Drug Store Restaurant, the three of them, eating the American meal. Rachel was over-excited, her face bloody with ketchup. Graham had eaten three hamburger specials with all the trimmings, and Jess grew sick at the sight of the plates stacking into squat towers on the table.

He called the waitress over again. It's my birthday, he said. Do you have a cake?

Jesus, Graham, Jessica hissed.

The waitress brought a large cake, ornately iced, pink frosting roses on top and candles in plastic holders.

Jess stood up. I'm going home, she said. I've had enough.

Wait, wait just a minute. He was pleading. His forehead was wet, and there was grease on his mouth. Have some cake, please. It's my *birthday*. He bent to blow out the candles. Look, Ray, he said. I'm making a wish. I'm blowing out the candles.

Jess began putting on the child's coat. No more, she said. You can come back with us, or you can stay. We're going back to the hotel.

Not yet, he said. Just have one piece. It looks like very good cake. Rachel, bewildered, began to cry. Cake, she screamed, growing more excited, I want cake. People were staring at their table. Jess picked up the weeping child, and Graham grabbed her arm. Please, he said. Please. She tried to pull away. Rachel, suddenly, began to gag. She vomited, shuddering, covering Jess and the table.

In the ladies' room, cleaning up, Jess and the child cried and cried.

He grew fatter. None of his clothes fit any more. Gluttony is not a modern sin. His stomach distended, his face was wreathed with fat, he panted now, going up the stairs. They fought, were quiet, fought again. He brought her flowers, armfuls of flowers, they filled the vases, bowls, all the surfaces, and rotted sweetly in the room.

Remission and relapse. A cowboy movie was on in the center of town and they decided to go, on whim and something deeper, some obscure, pervasive homesickness that led them to a frantic consumption of American totem objects when they found them. Jess had bought some peanut butter and marshmallows in a shop and brought them home, they fell upon them, finished them all, and were sick through the night. Laughing, rueful, the ache persisted.

The cinema musty with generations of cigarettes and once gorgeous hangings of gilt and plum velvet (Van Eyck), they sit in the front row. Rachel, sitting between them, is rapt; her hands stuffed with melting chocolate which she forgets, in her abandon, to eat. Half full, an audience of devotees and the aimless on this Tuesday afternoon.

The newsreel is full of death. A bull in Spain, a group of anonymous, blurred soldiers in Vietnam, a black woman in a riot in Milwaukee. In that film, through some oddity of camera, her fall from the second story window to the street seemed endless. She falls and falls, the only movement on the screen, everyone else in the chiaroscuro scene frozen with inertia or surprise. Finally she lands, a small heap, strangely jointed, and the other figures, released, begin to move again, gesture, cry out. Fire, flood, war, disease. Bad news, bad news.

A man somewhere behind them coughs and spits, a boy, about ten, runs down the aisle and back. Then a fresh turning towards the great screen, a rustling, a hush, and the giant American West is spread before them, the mammoth pan of grass and the immense blue sky. Beyond the grass, in the weird hills glowing pink and purple in the coming sunset, the band of Indians wait. Big-nosed, feathered, striped with paint, they grunt to their spotted ponies, they wait to set upon the band of pioneers. A puff of smoke rises from a mesa towards the cloudless sky. The attack is about to begin.

The sub-titles give an odd extra dimension to this drama. Warhoop, smack, bang, thud, the attack. Only the horses are surprised. The air fills with bullets, with arrows and the sound of arrows. Indians, pioneers, horses are hit, quiver, fall to the grassy ground.

Blood and dust mingle, and the colors swim in Jess's eyes, the gum turns salt in her mouth. She cries for the pioneers adrift on the huge prairie, their wagons burning, their children screaming loudly in the flames; for the Indians who, victorious in this battle, she knows to be doomed; she cries for Graham and herself, and for the little band of believers huddled in the movie house, and for America, torn and awkward, rich and bewildered now, fumbling through history, the fat boy hated by his classmates.

The film ends and they stumble out into the streets of the foreign city, their pupils clench, their vision blurs. The lights and shops and herring stands, Wyoming is more real.

TRANSLATE
Who can sing this song? Who knows the answer to this question? Who has lived in this house? From whom did you hear the story? What have you painted your house with? What shall I talk about? Which man is your neighbor? What kind of cigarettes do you smoke?

The fighting went on and on, and it was about no reason in particular, it was about all the reasons, simply all the facts about them and the world, their lives, their birthdays, politics, the colors of hair, tooth-paste, painters; it was that the islands and the dykes, and the sanity and the civilisation were too hard to build, they could not build it, they had run out of stones and sand, there was not enough daylight, not enough words, they weren't strong enough, there was too much water.

They were so tired, they allowed each other no rest, and they couldn't leave each other alone, not even for a little while, just for a breath. Jess spoke of going, with Rachel, to Paris or Italy, just for a week or two, just for a break. But their unhappiness had paralysed them into a kind of puppet show, an absolute routine of sleep and anger, and she couldn't break it, couldn't get away.

He followed her through the streets one day, and kept asking her the questions they both knew, she wanted to be alone, just for a few minutes, but he followed her, into the café, down the street, through the park. They were standing on one of the small bridges over the canals. He pulled at her arm, her shoulder, and she tried to get away, people were looking at them, and she was crying. She tried to get away, and he kept holding on to her. Then she grabbed the camera from his other hand and while he yelled at her she threw it, threw it up and over the side and into the canal; it splashed in the dark green water, sank, circles spreading outwards, and he hit her, twice, over the ear and the side of the face. She tasted blood. She cried leave me alone, and ran down the street. He didn't follow her.

Hours later he found her, sitting in the American Express office, tears sliding down her face with no sound coming from her mouth, staring at all the Americans, fat and thin, who came and went in the rooms. He took her back to the hotel.

That night, Jess asleep in the hotel, he screwed one of the prostitutes who sat in the windows looking out at the streets. She was young, with long legs and gray eyes which, whenever he looked, were open. Afterwards he remembered mostly the calendar on her wall, a picture of a windmill standing against a very blue sky.

Could it be, he said to Jess one night, that where the water has been it still holds power? That this whole trip has been through water, under water, in that way?

They got a wire telling them to phone Graham's sister in Oregon. The two-languaged operators' voices and the strange mechanical syllables of sound seemed to Graham the tickings of a huge brain; such a black space extended from the receiver in his hand, pressed to his ear. The key hole at the other end of the space illuminated, his sister was on the line.

Her voice sounded very small and only just familiar.

Graham, she said. Graham, hello, I have some bad news. There was some interference on the line, a crackling like the sound for forest fires on a radio program.

What, what? he was shouting into the phone. Linda, I can't hear you. *Linda.* The operator's voice appeared, floating above the static, and then the line cleared.

It's *Mother,* he heard Linda's tiny yell from the other end of the cord, six thousand miles away. Mother. There's been a plane crash and Mother's dead.

Graham could hear that she was crying now, a strange grating noise that seemed to be some more of the machine's own mechanical conversation.

She was on her way to visit Gary in Ohio—some kind of freak storm over the Rockies. The line fizzed again, then healed itself. Everyone on the plane was killed.

When his sister hung up Graham held on a minute, listening to the links and synapses click themselves out. He hung up, and the silence roared in. The bottom dropped out of his bowels, and he barely made it to the toilet. In the great light of the men's room, in the spotty mirror, he looked like an old man.

There are 60 canals in Amsterdam.

When it came, it came quickly. Afterwards, looking back over the way they had travelled, they could see the signs which pointed and announced that *this* was coming, this and nothing else, but at the time it had not been so clear. The condition itself obscured their vision of it and left them unprepared, if one can ever be prepared for such a thing, all set, bags packed as it were, like getting ready to go to the hospital to have a baby, the new pink bed jacket, the kotex and the toothbrush.

All the bills came due at once, this in the sense of all the personal debts incurred, the most intimate transactions, the banks failed, the chickens came home to roost (this in the flat voice of the mid-western grandmother), the dykes, the dykes finally broke and the water came in and over, filling everything, covering everything.

Graham, surrounded by water, lay flat and quiet in that bed, in that room. People moved in the corner of his vision, forward and back, blurred white shapes, he could hear sounds come bubbling from them at him, but there was no sense to the sounds. Later they learned to wall off the sea by building dykes—first out of earth, centuries later out of stone, and today out of concrete and steel. The Dutch are presently building their gigantic "Delta Works"—a series of five new dykes that will seal off further large estuaries of the North Sea. And remember, too, that even after land in Holland is reclaimed, it must constantly be drained by canals and pumps—or else the water will rise again!

Creatures joined him in the fluid life, ugly fish with shining scales. With unclosing bulbous jeweled eyes and long transparent tails they swim around him, bumping into his flesh, chewing at his fingers and the bottoms of his feet. He could feel the snails creeping up his arms, leaving behind the trails of slime that are their histories. Other creatures, those convoluted in shells, and those made of clear, brilliant jellies, nestled in his crevices, his ears, beneath the sheets, between his legs. New Orleans was burning. Denver was burning. San Francisco was burning. Vietnam is bigger than Rhode Island but smaller than Texas. Van Eyck, the Chinese, salt water, the secret passage, the starving millions in India.

As Rembrandt wrestled with the mighty task of the *Night Watch* Saskia wrestled with death; on June 14, 1642, she died, aged barely thirty.

While she lay dying her features haunted his fervid imagination and pursued him into the thick of the soldiery peopling in *Night Watch*, conjuring up a world of strange imaginings in which we see her in the guise of a child, a realm of fantasy where time has ceased to be. Saskia! Saskia! Holland is the paradigm of civilisation, of the attempt to make civilisation; the island, bailing to keep above the sea, planted with flowers. They walked among the massed flowers. The sky was blue. De bloemen waren rood, geel, wit, roze, blauw, violet, and other colors, mixtures of colors. The scent, that compound scent, was indescribable. Het warme continent, de rode daken. To attempt to describe it would be foolish; it was like the smell of hair, of wet ground, het plekje tussen de borsten van een vrouw. Fish do not close their eyes. Little is known about the life of Vermeer. Translate: Do you expect your uncle today? De hond blafte en maakte de kinderen wakker. Waar is het toilet? What is the nature of vision? Het zonlicht op je haar. Food is good and plentiful in Holland, and need not be expensive. Saskia! De dijken, de bloemen, het water. De Koninklijke Familie gaat per fiets. Spreekt u Engels? Spreekt u Italiaans? Spreekt u Duits?

Another shape bent over him, the waves leaping up. He could remember that this was Jessica, and she was talking to him, but he was too tired. Make sure that the nose and mouth are not obstructed. Kneel to one side of the casualty's hips, facing his head. Artificial respiration is used to make a person whose natural breathing has stopped start breathing again. Saskia! These swaying to-and-fro movements must be repeated regularly at a rate of twelve to fifteen a minute (what are the sounds a drowning man makes?) and continue this until natural breathing begins. *Drowning* is caused by complete immersion of the *nose and mouth* in *water* for a length of time which varies with the individual circumstances. At "tulip time," particularly April through mid-May, a thirty-mile strip of land between Haarlem and The Hague is covered by a dazzling blanket of tulips, daffodils, and hyacinths. When *apparent recovery* has taken place, the *casualty* should be placed on his side in a warm bed, given a hot drink, and encouraged to sleep. Saskia!

The waves died down, and the water began, very slowly, to recede. Graham could feel its level with his fingers over the edge of the bed. He was asleep.

It was a long way back. Streets, and where they led, were impossible for a while. The fragile dominion he exercised over the bed was gradually extended to the boundaries of the room. In the faded blue pajamas he

would rise at noon and sit silent for moments on the edge of the bed, trying to extricate himself from the drugs. Then, later in the day, the slant
light yellow in the air, he would walk, carefully, holding his breakable
self, on short journeys around the room. From the bed to the desk, she
had put red and yellow flowers in a pot on the desk, from the desk to the
chair, a cup of coffee. Then he would move to the window, now the
shade was left up for part of the day, but the street and even the look of
the street still threatened, and he would move back to the bed, in a rush
except at such a slow pace, and fall back, his eyes shut, his face closed
and drawn.

Work not so hard as delicate, this gathering up and putting together of
parts. As the waters receded, they could inspect the damage done, the
carpets ruined, veneers curling, paint rotted away. The holes in solid
things. Jess had thoughts of the acrobats in circuses who built, with apparently ordinary apparatus, extravagant structures. The careful, precise
piling up of tables, chairs, bicycles, bottles, into a trembling tower, and
the final triumphant perching of the sequinned, sweating performer on
the top.

Slowly he began, with Jess and the child, to take short walks again, out
to the shops to buy milk, a newspaper. The first ventures seemed possible
only when they had a goal, to go out and bring something back. It was as
though without that he might be distracted, detoured, lost.

He had become, through this thing, very thin; the flesh he had put on
so quickly fell away as though it had been a costume, layers of cloth.
Now he was very thin and strangely hunched over. The doctor described
this bent state as common in cases of severe depression, and predicted
that with the return of health he would straighten. It was true. Jess
watched him unfold, slowly, like a calcium flower into the precarious,
upright, human state; head erect again on the fine bone stalk of spine.

Sometimes he wondered whether the answer lay in that lost six hours
between New York and Amsterdam. CITY ON THE WATER. Amsterdam has
been called the "Venice of the North." It is built on huge piles driven
through the marshy surface soil and intersected by countless *canals*.

The breakdown, they referred to it by name, his breakdown, "my"
breakdown, proprietorially, like old ladies talking of operations; became a
node to date by. Things had happened before or after the breakdown.
Going there and coming back. As he grew better, things took on some of
their old shape, the outward forms of eating, sleeping, seeing friends
began to be possible again without the conscious effort of holding things
together. But it was in the invisible area that permanent change had

taken place, the mind's dark library. Some of the things he had known, thought he knew, were gone, swept away with the floods or rotted away with water and mildew afterwards, and some new things were there. He understood now that the world, and his purchase on the world, were less protected and more vulnerable than he had thought. He knew of the way in which we build our islands out of the empty sea, how we fail, and how, with temporary dykes erected and windmills pumping out the brine, we inhabit our failures. He had discovered what we know and do not believe, that he was breakable, and that the dykes make only an uneasy peace with the water and that, in the end, the water is bigger and can wait longer for victory.

Jess was going back, Jess and the child, and he was to stay. They would see each other again, no final decision had been made, he would return sometime before too long or she would recross the water. But though these reassurances were made and given, he no longer had any sense of a sure future containing himself. It might happen, they might survive and meet and come together again, but he knew now the odds against any plan, against anything built staying built and he could admire the architecture but not invest.

TRANSLATE
How big those apples are! How we laughed! What nice apples these are! What a strange story! There is still some food in the kitchen. There are some old trees in the garden. Whose picutre is this? Whose are these flowers? How beautiful!

They said goodbye at the airport and he had, the whole time, the sense of a reel winding backwards. A last beer in the restaurant. Rachel was excited, wanted to see the airplanes, and they held her up to the window, her face against the glass. That morning, making love, Jess's face had tasted of salt. Now they were just polite, there seemed little to say, and she was extinguished, tired. The multi-language voices purled in their ears. He had the quick thought to take her, kiss, slap her, reach her again, but they talked, quietly, until it was time for her to go.

On the coach back from the airport, worn out, he fell asleep almost at once and dreamed a strange dream of the burning of New York; he dreamed that, over the ocean, Jess had leaped out, the child and the blue pig in her arms, and floated down; he dreamed of Holland and of moving through Holland, the *flowers*, the *water*.

Elephant with Wooden Leg

⌑⌑⌑

JOHN SLADEK

Note: Madmen are often unable to distinguish between dream, reality, and . . . between dream and reality. None of the incidents in Henry La Farge's narrative ever happened or could have happened. His "Orinoco Institute" bears no relation to the actual think tank of that name, his "Drew Blenheim" in no way resembles the famous futurologist, and his "United States of America" is not even a burlesque upon the real United States of Armorica.

I couldn't hear him.

"Can't hear you, Blenheim. The line must be bad."

"Or mad, Hank. I wonder what that would take?"

"What what?"

"What would it take to drive a telephone system out of its mind, eh? So that it wasn't just giving wrong numbers, but madly right ones. Let's see: Content-addressable computer memories to shift the conversations . . ."

I stopped listening. A bug was crawling up the window frame across the room. It moved like a cockroach, but I couldn't be sure.

"Look, Blenheim, I'm pretty busy today. Is there something on your mind?"

He ploughed right on. ". . . so if you're trying to reserve a seat on the plane to Seville, you'd get a seat at the opera instead. While the person who wants the opera seat is really making an appointment with a barber, whose customer is just then talking to the box-office of *Hair*, or maybe making a hairline reservation . . ."

"Blenheim, I'm talking to you."

"Yes?"

"What was it you called me up about?"

"Oh, this and that. I was wondering, for instance, whether parrots have internal clocks."

"What?" I still couldn't be sure whether the bug was a cockroach or not, but I saluted just in case.

"If so, maybe we could get them to act as speaking clocks."

He sounded crazier than ever. What trivial projects for one of the best brains in our century—no wonder he was on leave.

"Blenheim, I'm busy. Institute work must go on, you know."

"Yes. Tell you what, why don't you drop over this afternoon? I have something to talk over with you."

"Can't. I have a meeting all afternoon."

"Fine, fine. See you, then. Anytime around 4:43."

Madmen never listen.

Helmut Rasmussen came in just as Blenheim hung up. He seemed distressed. Not that his face showed it; ever since that bomb wrecked his office, Hel has been unable to move his face. Hysterical paralysis, Dr. Grobe had explained.

But Hel could signal whatever he felt by fiddling with the stuff in his shirt pocket. For anger, his red pencil came out (and sometimes underwent a savage sharpening), impatience made him work his slide rule, surprise made him glance into his pocket diary, and so on.

Just now he was clicking the button on his ballpoint pen with some agitation. For a moment he actually seemed about to take it out and draw worry lines on his forehead.

"What is it, Hel? The costing on Project Faith?" He spread the schedules on my desk and pointed to the snag: a discrepancy between the estimated cost of blasting apart and hauling away the Rocky Mountains, and the value of oil recovered in the process.

"I see. The trains, eh? Diesels seem to use most of the oil we get. How about steam locomotives, then?"

He clapped me on the shoulder and nodded.

"By the way, Hel, I won't be at the meeting today. Blenheim just called up. Wants to see me."

Hel indicated surprise.

"Look, I know he's a crackpot. You don't have to pocket-diary me, I know he's nuts. But he is also technically still the Director. Our boss. They haven't taken him off the payroll, just put him on sick leave. Besides, he used to have a lot of good ideas."

Hel took out a felt-tip pen and began to doodle with some sarcasm. The fact was, Blenheim had completely lost his grip during his last year at the Institute. Before the government forced him to take leave, he'd been spending half a million a year on developing, rumours said, glass pancakes. And who could forget his plan to arm police with chocolate revolvers?

"Sure he's had a bad time, but maybe he's better now," I said, without conviction.

Institute people never get better, Hel seemed to retort. They just kept on making bigger and better decisions, with more and more brilliance and finality, until they broke. Like glass pancakes giving out an ever purer ring, they exploded.

It was true. Like everyone else here, I was seeing Dr. Grobe, our resident psychiatrist, several times a week. Then there were cases beyond even the skill of Dr. Grobe: Joe Feeney, who interrupted his work (on the uses of holograms) one day to announce that he was a filing cabinet. Edna Bessler, who believed that she was being pursued by a synthetic *a priori* proposition. The lovely entomologist Pawlie Sutton, who disappeared. And George Hoad, whose rocket research terminated when he walked into the Gents one day and cut his throat. George spent the last few minutes of consciousness vainly trying to mop up the bloody floor with toilet paper . . .

Something was wrong with the personnel around this place, all right. And I suspected that our little six-legged masters knew more about this than they were saying.

Finally I mumbled, "I know it's useless, Hel. But I'd better find out what he wants."

You do what you think is best, Hel thought. He stalked out of my office then, examining the point on his red pencil.

The bug was a cockroach, *P. americana.* It sauntered across the wall until it reached the curly edge of a wall poster, then it flew about a foot to land on the nearest dark spot. This was Uncle Sam's right eye. Uncle Sam, with his accusing eyes and finger, was trying to recruit men for the Senate and House of Representatives. On this poster, he said, "The Senate Needs MEN." So far, the recruitment campaign was a failure.

Who could blame people for not wanting to go on the "firing line" in Washington? The casualty rate of Congressmen was 30 per cent annually, and climbing, in spite of every security measure we could think of.

Which reminded me of work. I scrubbed off the blackboard and started laying out a contingency tree for Project Pogo, a plan to make the whole cabinet—all one hundred and forty-three secretaries—completely mobile, hence, proof against revolution. So far the Security Secretary didn't care for the idea of "taking to our heels," but it was cheaper to keep the cabinet on the move than to guard them in Washington.

The cockroach, observing my industry, left by a wall ventilator, and I breathed easier. The contingency tree didn't look so interesting by now, and out the window I could see real trees.

The lawn rolled away down from the building to the river (not the Orinoco, despite our name). The far bank was blue-black with pines, and the three red maples on our lawn, this time of year, stood out like three separate, brilliant fireballs. For just the duration of a bluejay's flight from one to another, I could forget about the stale routine, the smell of chalk-dust.

I remembered a silly day three years ago, when I'd carved a heart on one of those trees, with Pawlie Sutton's initials and my own.

Now a security guard strolled his puma into view. They stopped under the nearest maple and he snapped the animal's lead. It was up the trunk in two bounds, and out of sight among the leaves. While that stupid-faced man in uniform looked up, the fireball shook and swayed above him. A few great leaves fell, bright as drops of blood.

Now what was *this* headache going to be about?

All the big problems were solved, or at least we knew how to solve them. The world was just about the way we wanted it, now, except we no longer seemed to want it that way. That's how Mr. Howell, the Secretary of Personal Relationships, had put it in his telecast. What was missing? God, I think he said. God had made it possible for us to dam the Amazon and move the Orinoco, to feed India and dig gold from the ocean floor and cure cancer. And now God—the way he said it made you feel that He, too, was in the Cabinet—God was going to help us get down and solve our personal, human problems. Man's inhumanity to man. The lack of communication. The hatred. God and Secretary Howell were going to get right down to some committee work on this. I think that was the telecast where Howell announced the introduction of deten-

tion camps for "malcontents." Just until we got our personal problems all
ironed out. I had drawn up the plans for these camps that summer. Then
George Hoad borrowed my pocket-knife one day and never gave it back.
Then the headaches started.

As I stepped outside, the stupid-faced guard was looking up the skirt of
another tree.

"Prrt, prrt," he said quietly, and the black puma dropped to earth beside him. There was something hanging out of its mouth that looked like
a bluejay's wing.

"Good girl. Good girl."

I hurried away to the helicopter.

Drew Blenheim's tumbledown mansion sits in the middle of withered
woods. For half a mile around, the trees are laced together with high-voltage fence. Visitors are blindfolded and brought in by helicopter. There
are also rumours of minefields and other security measures. At that time,
I put it all down to Blenheim's paranoia.

The engine shut down with the sound of a coin spinning to rest.
Hands helped me out and removed my blindfold. The first thing I saw,
hanging on a nearby stretch of fence, was a lump of bones and burnt fur
from some small animal. The guards and their submachine-guns escorted
me only as far as the door, for Blenheim evidently hated seeing signs of
the security he craved. The house looked dismal and decayed—the skull
of some dead Orinoco Institute?

A servant wearing burnt cork makeup and white gloves ushered me
through a dim hallway that smelled of hay and on into the library.

"I'll tell Mr. Blenheim you're here, sir. Perhaps you'd care to read one
of his monographs while you wait?"

I flicked through *The Garden of Regularity* (a slight tract recommending that older people preserve intestinal health by devouring their own
dentures) and opened an insanely boring book called *Can Bacteria Read?*
I was staring uncomprehendingly at one of its pages when a voice
said:

"Are you still here?" The plump old woman had evidently been sitting
in her deep chair when I came in. As she craned around at me, I saw she
had a black eye. Something was wrong with her hair, too. "I thought
you'd left by now—oh, it's *you.*"

"Madam, do I know you?"

She sat forward and put her face to the light. The black eye was tattooed, and the marcelled hair was really a cap of paper, covered with wavy ink lines. But it was Edna Bessler, terribly aged.

"You've changed, Edna."

"So would you, young man, if you'd been chased around a nuthouse for two years by a synthetic *a priori* proposition." She sniffed. "Well, thank heavens the revolution is set for tomorrow."

I laughed nervously. "Well, Edna, it certainly is good to see you. What are you doing here, anyway?"

"There are quite a few of the old gang here, Joe Feeney and—and others. This place has become a kind of repair depot for mad futurologists. Blenheim is very kind, but of course he's quite mad himself. Mad as a wet hen. As you see from his writing."

"*Can Bacteria Read?* I couldn't read it."

"Oh, he thinks that germs are, like people, amenable to suggestion. So, with the proper application of mass hypnosis among the microbe populations, we ought to be able to cure any illness with any quack remedy."

I nodded. "Hope he recovers soon. I'd like to see him back at the Institute, working on real projects again. Big stuff, like the old days. I'll never forget the old Drew Blenheim, the man who invented satellite dialling."

Satellite dialling came about when the malcontents were trying to jam government communications systems, cut lines and blow up exchanges. Blenheim's system virtually made each telephone a complete exchange in itself, dialling directly through a satellite. Voice signals were compressed and burped skywards in short bursts that evaded most jamming signals. It was an Orinoco Institute triumph over anarchy.

Edna chuckled. "Oh, he's working on real projects. I said he was mad, not useless. Now if you'll help me out of this chair, I must go fix an elephant."

I was sure I'd misheard this last. After she'd gone, I looked over a curious apparatus in the corner. Parts of it were recognizable—a clock inside a parrot cage, a gas laser, and a fringed shawl suspended like a flag from a walking-stick thrust into a watermelon—but their combination was baffling.

At 4:43 by the clock in the cage, the blackface servant took me to a gloomy great hall place, scattered with the shapes of easy chairs and sofas. A figure in a diving suit rose from the piano and waved me to a chair. Then it sat down again, flipping out its airhoses behind the bench.

For a few minutes I suffered through a fumbling version of some Mexican tune. But when Blenheim—no doubt it was he—stood up and started juggling oranges, I felt it was time to speak out.

"Look, I've interrupted my work to come here. Is this all you have to show me?"

One of the oranges vaulted high, out of sight in the gloom above; another hit me in the chest. The figure opened its face-plate and grinned. "Long time no see, Hank."

It was me.

"Rubber mask," Blenheim explained, plucking at it. "I couldn't resist trying it on you, life gets so tedious here. Ring for Rastus, will you? I want to shed this suit."

We made small talk while the servant helped him out of the heavy diving suit. Rather, Blenheim rattled on alone; I wasn't feeling well at all. The shock of seeing myself had reminded me of something I should remember, but couldn't.

". . . to build a heraldry vending machine. Put in a coin, punch out your name, and it prints a coat-of-arms. Should suit those malcontents, eh? All they probably really want is a coat-of-arms."

"They're just plain evil," I said. "When I think how they bombed poor Hel Rasmussen's office—"

"Oh, he did that himself. Didn't you know?"

"Suicide? So that explains the hysterical paralysis!"

My face looked exasperated, as Blenheim peeled it off. "Is that what Dr. Grobe told you? Paralyzed hell, the blast blew his face clean off. Poor Hel's present face is a solid plate of plastic, bolted on. He breathes through a hole in his shoulder and feeds himself at the armpit. If Grobe told you any different, he's just working on your morale."

From upstairs came a kind of machine-gun clatter. The minstrel servant glided in with a tray of drinks.

"Oh, Rastus. Tell the twins not to practice their tap-dancing just now, will you? Hank looks as if he has a headache."

"Yes sir. By the way, the three-legged elephant has arrived. I put it in the front hall. I'm afraid the prosthesis doesn't fit."

"I'll fix it. Just ask Jumbo to lean up against the wall for half an hour."

"Very good, sir."

After this, I decided to make my escape from this Bedlam.

"Doesn't anybody around here ever do anything straightforward or say anything in plain English?"

"We're trying to tell you something, Hank, but it isn't easy. For one thing, I'm not sure we can trust you."

"Trust me for what?"

His twisted face twisted out a smile. "If you don't know, then how can we trust you? But come with me to the conservatory and I'll show you something."

We went to a large room with dirty glass walls. To me it looked like nothing so much as a bombed-out workshop. Though there were bags of fertilizer on the floor, there wasn't a living plant in sight. Instead, the tables were littered with machinery and lab equipment: jumbles of retorts and coloured wires and nuts and bolts that made no sense.

"What do you see, Hank?"

"Madness and chaos. You might as well have pears in the light sockets and a banana on the telephone cradle, for all I can make of it."

He laughed. "That's better. We'll crazify you yet."

I pointed to a poster-covered cylinder standing in the corner. One of the posters had Uncle Sam, saying "I Need MEN for Congress."

"What's that Parisian advertising kiosk doing here?"

"Rastus built that for us, out of scrap alloys I had lying around. Like it?"

I shrugged. "The top's too pointed. It looks like—"

"Yes, go on."

"This is silly. All of you need a few sessions with Dr. Grobe," I said. "I'm leaving."

"I was afraid you'd say that. But it's you who need another session with Dr. Grobe, Hank."

"You think *I'm* crazy?"

"No, you're too damned sane."

"Well you sure as hell are nuts!" I shouted. "Why bother with all the security outside? Afraid someone will steal the idea of a minstrel show or the secret of a kiosk?"

He laughed again. "Hank, those guards aren't there to keep strangers out. *They're to keep us in.* You see, my house really and truly is a madhouse."

I stamped out a side door and ordered my helicopter.

"My head's killing me," I told the guard. "Take it easy with that blindfold."

"Oh, sorry, mac. Hey look, it's none of my business, but what did you do with that tree you brung with you?"

"Tree?" God, even the guards were catching it.

That evening I went to see Dr. Grobe.

"Another patient? I swear, I'm going to install a revolving door on this office. Sit down. Uh, Hank LaFarge, isn't it? Sit down, Hank. Let's see . . . oh, you're the guy who's afraid of cockroaches, right?"

"Not exactly afraid of them. In fact they remind me of someone I used to be fond of. Pawlie Sutton used to work with them. But my problem is, I know that cockroaches are the real bosses. We're just kidding ourselves with our puppet government, our Uncle Sham—"

He chuckled appreciatively.

"But what bugs me is, nobody will recognize this plain and simple truth, Doctor."

"Ah, ah. Remember last time, you agreed to call me by my first name."

"Sorry, uh, Oddpork." I couldn't imagine why anyone with that name wanted to be called by it, unless the doctor himself was trying to get used to it. He was an odd-pork of a man, too: plump and rumpy, with over-large hands that never stopped adjusting his already well-adjusted clothes. He always looked surprised at everything I said, even "hello." Every session, he made the same joke about the revolving door.

Still, repetitive jokes help build a family atmosphere, which was probably what he wanted. There was a certain comfort in this stale atmosphere of no surprises. Happy families are all alike, and their past is exactly like their future.

"Hank, I haven't asked you directly about your cockroach theory before, have I? Want to tell me about it?"

"I know it sounds crazy at first. For one thing, cockroaches aren't very smart, I know that. In some ways, they're stupider than ants. And their communication equipment isn't much, either. Touch and smell, mainly. They aren't naturally equipped for conquering the world."

Oddpork lit a cigar and leaned back, looking at the ceiling. "What do they do with the world when they get it?"

"That's another problem. After all, they don't *need* the world. All they need is food, water, a fair amount of darkness and some warmth. But there's the key, you see?

"I mean we humans have provided for all these needs for many centuries. Haphazardly, though. So it stands to reason that life would be better for them if we worked for them on a regular basis. But to get us to do that, they have to take over first."

He tried to blow a smoke ring, failed, and adjusted his tie. "Go on. How do they manage this takeover?"

"I'm not sure, but I think they have help. Maybe some smart tinkerer wanted to see what would happen if he gave them good long-distance vision. Maybe he was so pleased with the result that he then taught them to make semaphore signals with their feelers. The rest is history."

Dusting his lapel, Dr. Grobe said, "I don't quite follow. Semaphore signals?"

"One cockroach is stupid. But a few thousand of them in good communication could make up a fair brain. Our tinkerer probably hastened that along by intensive breeding and group learning problems, killing off the failures . . . it would take ten years at the outside."

"Really? And how long would the conquest of man take? How would the little insects fare against the armies of the world?"

"They never need to try. Armies are run by governments, and governments are run, for all practical purposes, by small panels of experts. Think tanks like the Orinoco Institute. And—this just occurred to me—for all practical purposes, you run the Institute."

For once, Dr. Grobe did not look surprised. "Oh, so I'm in on the plot, am I?"

"We're all so crazy, we really depend on you. You can ensure that we work for the good of the cockroaches, or else you can get rid of us—send us away, or encourage our suicides."

"Why should I do that?"

"Because you are afraid of them."

"Not at all." But his hand twitched, and a little cigar ash fell on his immaculate trousers. I felt my point was proved.

"Damn. I'll have to sponge that. Excuse me."

He stepped into his private washroom and closed the door. My feeling of triumph suddenly faded. Maybe I was finally cracking. What evidence did I really have?

On the other hand, Dr. Grobe was taking a long time in there. I stole over to the washroom door and listened.

". . . verge of suicide . . .," he murmured. ". . . yes . . . give up the idea, but . . . yes, that's just what I . . ."

I threw back the door on a traditional spy scene. In the half-darkness, Dr. G was hunched over the medicine cabinet, speaking into a microphone. He wore earphones.

"Hank, don't be a foo—"

I hit him, not hard, and he sat down on the edge of the tub. He looked resigned.

"So this is my imagined conspiracy, is it? Where do these wires lead?"

They led inside the medicine cabinet, to a tiny apparatus. A dozen brown ellipses had clustered around it, like a family around the TV.

"Let me explain," he said.

"Explanations are unnecessary, Doctor, I just want to get out of here, unless your six-legged friends can stop me."

"They might. So could I. I could order the guards to shoot you. I could have you put away with your crazy friends. I could even have you tried for murder, just now."

"Murder?" I followed his gaze back into the office. From under the desk, a pair of feet. "Who's that?"

"Hel Rasmussen. Poisoned himself a few minutes before you came in. Believe me, it wasn't pleasant, seeing the poor fellow holding a bottle of cynanide to his armpit. He left a note blaming you, in a way."

"Me!"

"You were the last straw. This afternoon, he saw you take an axe and deliberately cut down one of those beautiful maple trees in the yard. Destruction of beauty—it was too much for him."

Trees again. I went to the office window and looked out at the floodlit landscape. One of the maples was missing.

Dr. Grobe and I sat down again at our respective interview stations, while I thought this over. Blenheim and his mask came into it, I was sure of that. But why?

Dr. Grobe fished his lifeless cigar from the ashtray. "The point is, I can stop you from making any trouble for me. So you may as well hear me out." He scratched a match on the sole of Hel's shoe and relit the cigar.

"All right, Oddpork. You win. What happens now?"

"Nothing much. Nothing at all. If my profession has any meaning, it's to keep things from happening." He blew out the match. "I'm selling ordinary life. Happiness, as you must now see, lies in developing a pleasant, comfortable and productive routine—and then sticking to it. No unpleasant surprises. No shocks. Psychiatry has always aimed for that, and now it is within our grasp. The cockroach conspiracy hasn't taken over the world, but it has taken over the Institute—and it's our salvation.

"You see, Hank, our bargain isn't one-sided. We give them a little shelter, a few scraps of food. But they give us something far more important: real organization. *The life of pure routine.*"

I snorted. "Like hurrying after trains? Or wearing ourselves out on assembly-line work? Or maybe grinding our lives away in boring offices? Punching time-clocks and marching in formation?"

"None of the above, thank you. Cockroaches never hurry to anything but dinner. They wouldn't march in formation except for fun. They are free—yet they are part of a highly organized society. And this can be ours."

"If we're not all put in detention camps."

"Listen, those camps are only a stage. So what if a few million grumblers get sterilized and shut away for a year or two? Think of the *billions* of happy, decent citizens, enjoying a freedom they have earned. Someday, every man will live exactly as he pleases—and his pleasure will lie in serving his fellow men."

Put like that, it was persuasive. Another half-hour of this and I was all but convinced.

"Sleep on it, eh Hank? Let me know tomorrow what you think." His large hand on my shoulder guided me to the door.

"You may be right,' I said, smiling back at him. I meant it, too. Even though the last thing I saw, as the door closed, was a stream of glistening brown that came from under the washroom door and disappeared under the desk.

I sat up in my own office most of the night, staring out at the maple stump. There was no way out: Either I worked for *Periplaneta americana* and gradually turned into a kind of moral cockroach myself, or I was killed. And there were certain advantages to either choice.

I was about to turn on the video-recorder to leave a suicide note, when I noticed the cassette was already recorded. I ran it back and played it.

Blenheim came on, wearing my face and my usual suit.

"They think I'm you, Hank, dictating some notes. Right now you're really at my house, reading a dull book in the library. So dull, in fact, that it's guaranteed to put you into a light trance. When I'm safely back, Edna will come in and wake you.

"She's not as loony as she seems. The black eye is inked for her telescope, and the funny cap with lines on it, that looks like marcelled hair, that's a weathermap. I won't explain why she's doing astronomy—you'll understand in time.

"On the other hand, she's got a fixation that the stars are nothing but the shiny backs of cockroaches, treading around the heavenly spheres. It makes a kind of sense when you think of it: *Periplaneta* means around the

world, and America being the home of the Star-Spangled Banner.
"Speaking of national anthems, Mexico's is La Cucaracha—another
cockroach reference. They seem to be taking over this message!

"The gang and I have been thinking about bugs a lot lately. Of course
Pawlie has always thought about them, but the rest of us . . ." I missed
the next part. So Pawlie was at the madhouse? And they hadn't told me?

". . . when I started work on the famous glass pancakes. I discovered a
peculiar feature of glass discs, such as those found on clock faces.

"Say, you can do us a favour. I'm coming around at dawn with the
gang, to show you a gadget or two. We haven't got all the bugs out of
them yet, but—will you go into Dr. Grobe's office at dawn, and check
the time on his clock? But first, smash the glass on his window, will you?
Thanks. I'll compensate him for it later.

"Then go outside the building, but on no account stand between the
maple stump and the broken window. The best place to wait is on the
little bluff to the North, where you'll have a good view of the demonstration. We'll meet you there.

"Right now you see our ideas darkly, as through a pancake, I guess.
But soon you'll understand. You see, we're a kind of cockroach ourselves.
I mean, living on scraps of sanity. We have to speak in parables and work
in silly ways because *they* can't. *They* live in a comfortable kind of world
where elephants have their feet cut off to make umbrella stands. We have
to make good use of the three-legged elephants.

"Don't bother destroying this cassette. It won't mean a thing to any
right-living insect."

It didn't mean much to me, not yet. Cockroaches in the stars? Clocks?
There were questions I had to ask, at the rendezvous.

There was one question I'd already asked that needed an answer. Pawlie had been messing about in her lab, when I asked her to marry me.
Two years ago, was it? Or three?

"But you don't like cockroaches," she said.

"No, and I'll never ask a cockroach for its claw in marriage." I looked
over her shoulder into the glass case. "What's so interesting about these?"

"Well, for one thing, they're not laboratory animals. I caught them
myself in the basement here at the Institute. See? Those roundish ones
are the nymphs—sexless adolescents. Cute, aren't they?"

I had to admit they were. A little. "They look like the fat black exclamation points in comic strips," I observed.

"They're certainly healthy, all of them. I've never seen any like them. I—that's funny." She went and fetched a book, and looked from some illustration to the specimens under glass.

"What's funny?"

"Look, I'm going to be dissecting the rest of the afternoon. Meet you for dinner. Bye."

"You haven't answered my question, Pawlie."

"Bye."

That was the last I saw of her. Later, Dr. Grobe put it about that she'd been found, hopelessly insane. Still later, George Hoad cut his throat.

The floodlights went off, and I could see dawn greyness and mist. I took a can of beans and went for a stroll outside.

One of the guards nodded a wary greeting. They and their cats were always jumpiest at this time of day.

"Everything all right, officer?"

"Yeah. Call me crazy, but I think I just heard an elephant."

When he and his puma were out of sight, I heaved the can of beans through Dr. Grobe's lighted window.

"What the hell?" he shouted. I slipped back to my office, waited a few minutes, then went to see him.

A slender ray came through the broken window and struck the clock on the opposite wall. Grobe sat transfixed, staring at it with more surprise than ever. And no wonder, for the clock had become a parrot.

"Relax, Oddpork," I said. "It's only some funny kind of hologram in the clock face, worked by a laser from the lawn. You look like a comic villain, sitting there with that cigar stub in your face."

The cigar stub moved. Looking closer, I saw it was made up of the packed tails of a few cockroaches, trying to force themselves between his closed lips. More ran up from his spotless collar and joined them, and others made for his nostrils. One approached the queue at the mouth, found another stuck there, and had a nibble at its kicking hind leg.

"Get away! Get away!" I gave Grobe a shake to dislodge them, and his mouth fell open. A brown flood of kicking bodies tumbled out and down, over his well-cut lapels.

I had stopped shuddering by the time I joined the others on the bluff. Pawlie and Blenheim were missing. Edna stopped scanning the horizon with her brass telescope long enough to introduce me to the pretty twins,

Alice and Celia. They sat in the grass beside a tangled heap of revolvers, polishing their patent-leather tap shoes.

The ubiquitous Rastus was wiping off his burnt cork makeup. I asked him why.

"Don't need it anymore. Last night it was my camouflage. I was out in the woods, cutting a path through the electric fence. Quite a wide path, as you'll understand."

He continued removing the black until I recognized the late George Hoad.

"George! But you cut your throat, remember? Mopping up blood—"

"Hank, that was your blood. It was you cut your throat in the Gents, after Pawlie vanished. Remember?"

I did, giddily. "What happened to you, then?"

"Your suicide attempt helped me make up my mind; I quit the Institute next day. You were still in the hospital."

Still giddy, I turned to watch Joe Feeney operating the curious laser I'd seen in the library. Making parrots out of clocks.

"I understand now," I said. "But what's the watermelon for?"

"Cheap cooling device."

"And the 'flag'?" I indicated the shawl-stick arrangement.

"To rally round. I stuck it in the melon because they were using the umbrella stand for—"

"Look!" Edna cried. "The attack begins!" She handed me a second telescope.

All I saw below was the lone figure of Blenheim in his diving suit, shuffling slowly up from the river mist to face seven guards and two pumas. He seemed to be juggling croquet balls.

"Why don't we help him?" I shouted. "Don't just sit here shining shoes and idling."

The twins giggled. "We've already helped some," said Alice, nodding at the pile of weapons. "We made friends with the guards."

I got the point when those below pulled their guns on Blenheim. As each man drew, he looked at his gun and then threw it away.

"What a waste," Celia sighed. "Those guns are made from just about the best chocolate you can get."

Blenheim played his parlour trick on the nearest guard: one juggled ball flew high, the guard looked up, and a second ball clipped him on the upturned chin.

Now the puma guards went into action.

"I can't look," I said, my eye glued to the telescope. One of the animals stopped to sniff at a sticky revolver, but the other headed straight for his quarry. He leapt up, trying to fasten his claws into the stranger's big brass head.

Out of the river mist came a terrible cry, and then a terrible sight: a hobbling grey hulk that resolved into a charging elephant. Charging diagonally, so it looked even larger.

The pumas left the scene. One fled in our direction until Alice snatched up a pistol and fired it in the air. At that sound, the guards decided to look for jobs elsewhere. After all, as Pawlie said later, you couldn't expect a man to face a juggling diver *and* a mad elephant with a wooden leg, with nothing but a chocolate .38, not on *those* wages.

Pawlie was riding on the neck of the elephant. When he came to a wobbling stop I saw that one of Jumbo's forelegs was a section of tree with the bark still on it. And in the bark, a heart with PS + HL, carved years before.

I felt the triumph was all over—especially since Pawlie kept nodding her head yes at me—until George said:

"Come on, gang. Let's set it up."

Jumbo had been pulling a wooden sledge, bearing the Paris kiosk. Now he went off to break his fast on water and grass, while the rest of us set the thing upright. Even before we had fuelled it with whatever was in the fertilizer bags, I guessed that it was a rocket.

After some adjustments, the little door was let down, and a sweet, breakfast pancake odour came forth. Joe Feeney opened a flask of dark liquid and poured it in the entrance. The smell grew stronger.

"Maple sap," he explained. "From Jumbo's wooden leg. Mixed with honey. And there's oatmeal inside. A farewell breakfast."

I looked in the little door and saw the inside of the ship was made like a metal honeycomb, plenty of climbing room for our masters.

Pawlie came from the building with a few cockroaches in a jar, and let them taste our wares. Then, all at once, it was a sale opening at any big department store. We all stood back and let the great brown wave surge forward and break over the little rocket. Some of them, nymphs especially, scurried all the way up to the nose cone and back down again in their excitement. It all looked so jolly that I tried not to think about their previous meals.

Edna glanced at her watch. "Ten minutes more," she said. "Or they'll hit the sun."

I objected that we'd never get all of them loaded in ten minutes.

"No," said Pawlie, "but we'll get the best and strongest. The shrews can keep the rest in control."

Edna closed the door, and the twins did a vigorous tap-dance on the unfortunate stragglers. A few minutes later, a million members of the finest organization on earth were on their way to the stars.

"To join their little friends," said Edna.

Pawlie and I touched hands, as Blenheim opened his faceplate.

"I've been making this study," he said, "of spontaneous combustion in giraffes . . ."

The Wardrobe

c·୨ᏳᏛ

THOMAS MANN

It was cloudy, cool, and half-dark when the Berlin-Rome express drew in at a middle-sized station on its way. Albrecht van der Qualen, solitary traveller in a first-class compartment with lace covers over the plush upholstery, roused himself and sat up. He felt a flat taste in his mouth, and in his body the none-too-agreeable sensations produced when the train comes to a stop after a long journey and we are aware of the cessation of rhythmic motion and conscious of calls and signals from without. It is like coming to oneself out of drunkenness or lethargy. Our nerves, suddenly deprived of the supporting rhythm, feel bewildered and forlorn. And this the more if we have just roused out of the heavy sleep one falls into in a train.

Albrecht van der Qualen stretched a little, moved to the window, and let down the pane. He looked along the train. Men were busy at the mail van, unloading and loading parcels. The engine gave out a series of sounds, it snorted and rumbled a bit, standing still, but only as a horse stands still, lifting its hoof, twitching its ears, and awaiting impatiently the signal to go on. A tall, stout woman in a long raincoat, with a face expressive of nothing but worry, was dragging a hundred-pound suitcase along the train, propelling it before her with pushes from one knee. She was saying nothing, but looking heated and distressed. Her upper lip stuck out, with little beads of sweat upon it—altogether she was a pathetic figure. "You poor dear thing," van der Qualen thought. "If I could help you, soothe you, take you in—only for the sake of that upper lip. But each for himself, so things are arranged in life; and I stand here at this

303

moment perfectly carefree, looking at you as I might at a beetle that has fallen on its back."

It was half-dark in the station shed. Dawn or twilight—he did not know. He had slept, who could say whether for two, five, or twelve hours? He had sometimes slept for twenty-four, or even more, unbrokenly, an extraordinarily profound sleep. He wore a half-length dark-brown winter overcoat with a velvet collar. From his features it was hard to judge his age: one might actually hesitate between twenty-five and the end of the thirties. He had a yellowish skin, but his eyes were black like live coals and had deep shadows round them. These eyes boded nothing good. Several doctors, speaking frankly as man to man, had not given him many more months.—His dark hair was smoothly parted on one side.

In Berlin—although Berlin had not been the beginning of his journey—he had climbed into the train just as it was moving off—incidentally with his red leather hand-bag. He had gone to sleep and now at waking felt himself so completely absolved from time that a sense of refreshment streamed through him. He rejoiced in the knowledge that at the end of the thin gold chain he wore round his neck there was only a little medallion in his waistcoat pocket. He did not like to be aware of the hour or of the day of the week, and moreover he had no truck with the calendars. Some time ago he had lost the habit of knowing the day of the month or even the month of the year. Everything must be in the air—so he put it in his mind, and the phrase was comprehensive though rather vague. He was seldom or never disturbed in this programme, as he took pains to keep all upsetting knowledge at a distance from him. After all, was it not enough for him to know more or less what season it was? "It is more or less autumn," he thought, gazing out into the damp and gloomy train shed. "More I do not know. Do I even know where I am?"

His satisfaction at this thought amounted to a thrill of pleasure. No, he did not know where he was! Was he still in Germany? Beyond a doubt. In North Germany? That remained to be seen. While his eyes were still heavy with sleep the window of his compartment had glided past an illuminated sign; it probably had the name of the station on it, but not the picture of a single letter had been transmitted to his brain. In still dazed condition he had heard the conductor call the name two or three times, but not a syllable had he grasped. But out there in a twilight of which he knew not so much as whether it was morning or evening lay a strange place, an unknown town.—Albrecht van der Qualen took his felt hat out of the rack, seized his red leather hand-bag, the strap of which secured a

red and white silk and wool plaid into which was rolled an umbrella with
a silver crook—and although his ticket was labelled Florence, he left the
compartment and the train, walked along the shed, deposited his luggage
at the cloakroom, lighted a cigar, thrust his hands—he carried neither
stick nor umbrella—into his overcoat pockets, and left the station.

Outside in the damp, gloomy, and nearly empty square five or six
hackney coachmen were snapping their whips, and a man with braided
cap and long cloak in which he huddled shivering inquired politely:
"*Hotel zum braven Mann?*" Van der Qualen thanked him politely and
held on his way. The people whom he met had their coat-collars turned
up; he put his up too, nestled his chin into the velvet, smoked, and went
his way, not slowly and not too fast.

He passed along a low wall and an old gate with two massive towers; he
crossed a bridge with statues on the railings and saw the water rolling slow
and turbid below. A long wooden boat, ancient and crumbling, came by,
sculled by a man with a long pole in the stern. Van der Qualen stood for
a while leaning over the rail of the bridge. "Here," he said to himself, "is
a river; here is *the* river. It is nice to think that I call it that because I do
not know its name."—Then he went on.

He walked straight on for a little, on the pavement of a street which
was neither very narrow nor very broad; then he turned off to the left. It
was evening. The electric arc-lights came on, flickered, glowed, sput-
tered, and then illuminated the gloom. The shops were closing. "So we
may say that it is in every respect autumn," thought van der Qualen, proceeding along the wet black pavement. He wore no galoshes, but his
boots were very thick-soled, durable, and firm, and withal not lacking in
elegance.

He held to the left. Men moved past him, they hurried on their business or coming from it. "And I move with them," he thought, "and am
as alone and as strange as probably no man has ever been before. I have
no business and no goal. I have not even a stick to lean upon. More
remote, freer, more detached, no one can be, I owe nothing to anybody,
nobody owes anything to me. God has never held out His hand over me,
He knows me not at all. Honest unhappiness without charity is a good
thing; a man can say to himself: I owe God nothing."

He soon came to the edge of the town. Probably he had slanted across
it at about the middle. He found himself on a broad suburban street with
trees and villas, turned to his right, passed three or four cross-streets almost like village lanes, lighted only by lanterns, and came to a stop in a
somewhat wider one before a wooden door next to a commonplace house

painted a dingy yellow, which had nevertheless the striking feature of very convex and quite opaque plate-glass windows. But on the door was a sign: "In this house on the third floor there are rooms to let." "Ah!" he remarked; tossed away the end of his cigar, passed through the door along a boarding which formed the dividing line between two properties, and then turned left through the door of the house itself. A shabby grey runner ran across the entry. He covered it in two steps and began to mount the simple wooden stair.

The doors to the several apartments were very modest too; they had white glass panes with woven wire over them and on some of them were name-plates. The landings were lighted by oil lamps. On the third storey, the top one, for the attic came next, were entrances right and left, simple brown doors without name-plates. Van der Qualen pulled the brass bell in the middle. It rang, but there was no sign from within. He knocked left. No answer. He knocked right. He heard light steps within, very long, like strides, and the door opened.

A woman stood there, a lady, tall, lean, and old. She wore a cap with a large pale-lilac bow and an old-fashioned, faded black gown. She had a sunken birdlike face and on her brow there was an eruption, a sort of fungus growth. It was rather repulsive.

"Good evening," said van der Qualen. "The rooms?"

The old lady nodded; she nodded and smiled slowly, without a word, understandingly, and with her beautiful long white hand made a slow, languid, and elegant gesture towards the next, the left-hand door. Then she retired and appeared again with a key. "Look," he thought, standing behind her as she unlocked the door; "you are like some kind of banshee, a figure out of Hoffmann, madam." She took the oil lamp from its hook and ushered him in.

It was a small, low-ceiled room with a brown floor. Its walls were covered with straw-coloured matting. There was a window at the back in the right-hand wall, shrouded in long, thin white muslin folds. A white door also on the right led into the next room. This room was pathetically bare, with staring white walls, against which three straw chairs, painted pink, stood out like strawberries from whipped cream. A wardrobe, a washing-stand with a mirror. . . . The bed, a mammoth mahogany piece, stood free in the middle of the room.

"Have you any objections?" asked the old woman, and passed her lovely long, white hand lightly over the fungus growth on her forehead.—It was as though she had said that by accident because she could not think for the moment of a more ordinary phrase. For she added at once: "—so to speak?"

"No, I have no objections," said van der Qualen. "The rooms are rather cleverly furnished. I will take them. I'd like to have somebody fetch my luggage from the station, here is the ticket. You will be kind enough to make up the bed and give me some water. I'll take the house key now, and the key to the apartment. . . . I'd like a couple of towels. I'll wash up and go into the city for supper and come back later."

He drew a nickel case out of his pocket, took out some soap, and began to wash his face and hands, looking as he did so through the convex window-panes far down over the muddy, gas-lit suburban streets, over the arc-lights and the villas.—As he dried his hands he went over to the wardrobe. It was a square one, varnished brown, rather shaky, with a simple curved top. It stood in the centre of the right-hand wall exactly in the niche of a second white door, which of course led into the rooms to which the main and middle door on the landing gave access. "Here is something in the world that is well arranged," thought van der Qualen. "This wardrobe fits into the door niche as though it were made for it." He opened the wardrobe door. It was entirely empty, with several rows of hooks in the ceiling; but it proved to have no back, being closed behind by a piece of rough, common grey burlap, fastened by nails or tacks at the four corners.

Van der Qualen closed the wardrobe door, took his hat, turned up the collar of his coat once more, put out the candle, and set forth. As he went through the front room he thought to hear mingled with the sound of his own steps a sort of ringing in the other room: a soft, clear, metallic sound—but perhaps he was mistaken. As though a gold ring were to fall into a silver basin, he thought, as he locked the outer door. He went down the steps and out of the gate and took the way to the town.

In a busy street he entered a lighted restaurant and sat down at one of the front tables, turning his back to all the world. He ate a *soupe aux fines herbes* with croutons, a steak with a poached egg, a compote and wine, a small piece of green gorgonzola and half a pear. While he paid and put on his coat he took a few puffs from a Russian cigarette, then lighted a cigar and went out. He strolled for a while, found his homeward route into the suburb, and went leisurely back.

The house with the plate-glass windows lay quite dark and silent when van der Qualen opened the house door and mounted the dim stair. He lighted himself with matches as he went, and opened the left-hand brown door in the third storey. He laid hat and overcoat on the divan, lighted the lamp on the big writing-table, and found there his hand-bag as well as the plaid and umbrella. He unrolled the plaid and got a bottle of cognac, then a little glass and took a sip now and then as he sat in the armchair finishing his cigar. "How fortunate, after all," thought he, "that there is cognac in the world." Then he went into the bedroom, where he lighted the candle on the night-table, put out the light in the other room, and began to undress. Piece by piece he put down his good, unobtrusive grey suit on the red chair beside the bed; but then as he loosened his braces he remembered his hat and overcoat, which still lay on the couch. He fetched them into the bedroom and opened the wardrobe. . . . He took a step backwards and reached behind him to clutch one of the large dark-red mahogany balls which ornamented the bedposts. The room, with its four white walls, from which the three pink chairs stood out like strawberries from whipped cream, lay in the unstable light of the candle. But the wardrobe over there was open and it was not empty. Somebody was standing in it, a creature so lovely that Albrecht van der Qualen's heart stood still a moment and then in long, deep, quiet throbs resumed its beating. She was quite nude and one of her slender arms reached up to crook a forefinger round one of the hooks in the ceiling of the wardrobe. Long waves of brown hair rested on the childlike shoulders—they breathed that charm to which the only answer is a sob. The candlelight was mirrored in her narrow black eyes. Her mouth was a little large, but it had an expression as sweet as the lips of sleep when after long days of pain they kiss our brow. Her ankles nestled and her slender limbs clung to one another.

Albrecht van der Qualen rubbed one hand over his eyes and stared . . . and he saw that down in the right corner the sacking was loosened from the back of the wardrobe. "What—" said he . . . "won't you come in—or how should I put it—out? Have a little glass of cognac? Half a glass?" But he expected no answer to this and he got none. Her narrow, shining eyes, so very black that they seemed bottomless and inexpressive—they were directed upon him, but aimlessly and somewhat blurred, as though they did not see him.

"Shall I tell you a story?" she said suddenly in a low, husky voice.

"Tell me a story," he answered. He had sunk down in a sitting posture on the edge of the bed, his overcoat lay across his knees with his folded hands resting upon it. His mouth stood a little open, his eyes half-closed. But the blood pulsated warm and mildly through his body and there was a gentle singing in his ears. She had let herself down in the cupboard and embraced a drawn-up knee with her slender arms, while the other leg stretched out before her. Her little breasts were pressed together by her upper arm, and the light gleamed on the skin of her flexed knee. She talked . . . talked in a soft voice, while the candle-flame performed its noiseless dance.

Two walked on the heath and her head lay on his shoulder. There was a perfume from all growing things, but the evening mist already rose from the ground. So it began. And often it was in verse, rhyming in that incomparably sweet and flowing way that comes to us now and again in the half-slumber of fever. But it ended badly; a sad ending: the two holding each other indissolubly embraced, and while their lips rest on each other, one stabbing the other above the waist with a broad knife—and not without good cause. So it ended. And then she stood up with an infinitely sweet and modest gesture, lifted the grey sacking at the right-hand corner—and was no more there.

From now on he found her every evening in his wardrobe and listened to her stories—how many evenings? How many days, weeks, or months did he remain in this house and in this city? It would profit nobody to know. Who would care for a miserable statistic? And we are aware that Albrecht van der Qualen had been told by several physicians that he had but a few months to live. She told him stories. They were sad stories, without relief; but they rested like a sweet burden upon the heart and made it beat longer and more blissfully. Often he forgot himself.—His blood swelled up in him, he stretched out his hands to her, and she did not resist him. But then for several evenings he did not find her in the wardrobe, and when she came back she did not tell him anything for several evenings and then by degrees resumed, until he again forgot himself.

How long it lasted—who knows? Who even knows whether Albrecht van der Qualen actually awoke on that grey afternoon and went into the unknown city; whether he did not remain asleep in his first-class carriage and let the Berlin-Rome express bear him swiftly over the mountains? Would any of us care to take the responsibility of giving a definite answer? It is all uncertain. "Everything must be in the air. . . ."